THE WEST WIND OF LOVE

BY THE SAME AUTHOR

Novels and Romances

SINISTER STREET
SYLVIA SCARLETT
GUY AND PAULINE

CARNIVAL
FIGURE OF EIGHT
CORAL
THE VANITY GIRL
ROGUES AND VAGABONDS

THE ALTAR STEPS
THE PARSON'S PROGRESS
THE HEAVENLY LADDER

POOR RELATIONS
APRIL FOOLS
RICH RELATIVES
BUTTERCUPS AND DAISIES
WATER ON THE BRAIN

VESTAL FIRE
EXTRAORDINARY WOMEN

EXTREMES MEET
THE THREE COURIERS

OUR STREET
THE DARKENING GREEN

THE PASSIONATE ELOPEMENT
FAIRY GOLD
THE SEVEN AGES OF WOMAN
THE OLD MEN OF THE SEA
THE FOUR WINDS OF LOVE:
  THE EAST WIND
  THE SOUTH WIND

Plays

THE LOST CAUSE

History and Biography

GALLIPOLI MEMORIES
ATHENIAN MEMORIES
GREEK MEMORIES
AEGEAN MEMORIES

PRINCE CHARLIE
PRINCE CHARLIE AND HIS LADIES
CATHOLICISM AND SCOTLAND
MARATHON AND SALAMIS
PERICLES

Essays and Criticism

A MUSICAL CHAIR
UNCONSIDERED TRIFLES
REAPED AND BOUND
LITERATURE IN MY TIME

Children's Stories

SANTA CLAUS IN SUMMER
TOLD
MABEL IN QUEER STREET
THE UNPLEASANT VISITORS
THE CONCEITED DOLL
THE ENCHANTED BLANKET
THE DINING-ROOM BATTLE
THE ADVENTURES OF TWO CHAIRS
THE ENCHANTED ISLAND
THE NAUGHTYMOBILE
THE FAIRY IN THE WINDOW BOX
THE STAIRS THAT KEPT ON GOING DOWN

Verse

POEMS 1907
KENSINGTON RHYMES

THE WEST WIND OF LOVE

BEING BOOK THREE OF 'THE FOUR WINDS OF LOVE'

By

COMPTON MACKENZIE

LONDON

CHATTO & WINDUS

1940

PUBLISHED BY
Chatto & Windus
LONDON
*
The Macmillan Company
of Canada, Limited
TORONTO

TO

ROSAMUND LEHMANN

My dear Rosamund,

When on January 31*st*, 1935, *I noted that the first hundred pages of 'The Four Winds of Love' had been written, I made up my mind that when I should be writing of the years immediately after what was then still* the *War I would ask you to accept the dedication of 'The West Wind' in gratitude for your book 'Dusty Answer', which gave me the sharpest pleasure that any new novel gave me in those years. On January* 31*st*, 1940, *I write this dedicatory letter to keep that resolution and in keeping it to commemorate a friendship which has been precious to me.*

I had hoped to publish the third part of 'The Four Winds of Love' in a single volume under the title 'The West Wind of Love'; but the economic circumstances of war have made it impossible to publish a volume of well over a thousand pages at the price fixed upon as the maximum for a work of fiction. Hence, rather than spoil the design of the complete work by rejecting material planned for foundations already laid, it was decided to take advantage of the fact that the complete 'West Wind' fell naturally into two divisions by publishing it in two volumes with as short an interval between them as possible. I mention this because I do not want readers to suppose that the division has been made arbitrarily and that as it stands 'The West Wind of Love' does not make a coherent whole within the larger whole. I might have called this volume

'The South-West Wind' and its sequel 'The North-West Wind' if that larger whole were not 'The Four Winds of Love.' That being so, the continuation will be called 'West to North'.

I hope to finish 'The North Wind of Love' in time for publication early next year. That will bring 'The Four Winds of Love' to an end, and the complete work will cover a period of thirty-seven years.

There has been a much longer gap in publication than I had intended between 'The South Wind' and 'The West Wind', due to my having been compelled by anger to write 'The Windsor Tapestry' before continuing 'The Four Winds of Love'. On top of that I was able to secure the release of the ban on 'Greek Memories' and decided to finish off that broken series by writing 'Aegean Memories'. I am grateful now to that impulse of anger which diverted my pen, because this new war has enabled me to see the years immediately after the last war in all their tragic significance.

Writing to me at Gallipoli about 'Guy and Pauline', Henry James said, 'I assume that it is not now likely to appear before summer's end—by which time God knows what other monstrous chapters of history won't have been perpetrated!' I am in a similar mood to-day, close on a quarter of a century later, in writing about plans for future books. Yet I cannot pretend that the irruption of war has made me disinclined to write: the dreadful present has been brought so much nearer to those fateful years with which 'The West Wind of Love' and 'West to North' are occupied that they seem no farther away than the prologue of a play to its first act, and they are so much a part of this catastrophe that my mind is haunted by remorse for that misused past, which may have given my pen something that nostalgia for a happy and well-ordered past could never have given it.

I apologize for taking up so much of this letter with explanations; but, as I wrote to Eric Linklater in dedicating to him 'The East Wind of Love', '*I cannot help feeling that I am inviting fortune's mischief by setting out to build yet again a work in successive volumes*', *and if nothing worse happen to it than adjustments of the method of publication I shall count myself lucky.*

At any rate, I have been able to give myself the pleasure of inscribing to you one of those '*successive volumes*'.

Yours affectionately,

Compton Mackenzie

SUIDHEACHAN
ISLE OF BARRA
January 31st, 1940

The West Wind of Love

WHEN ATHENE LANGRIDGE LEFT JOHN OGILVIE IN the car and turned down into the narrow cobbled alley that led to the Villa Allegra, she was too much flustered by her failure to persuade him to accept her half of the cost of the hire from Naples to remember that it should have been her hospitable duty to invite him to dinner on this night of his return to Citrano, after an absence of over three years. It was not until she reached the door of the villa that she remembered. She paused in shocked indetermination between the aloes in the two great terra-cotta oil-jars on either side of the door. On an impulse to redeem her lapse she swung round and hurried back across the courtyard, but she was no sooner out in the alley than the surge of the west wind through the dishevelled vineyards beyond the ferny walls, and the boom of it in the gorges of the hills above, struck her with menace. She turned again, wondering suddenly if Arthur was all right. John Ogilvie's comfort on his first evening in the Torre Saracena was forgotten in anxiety about her small son. The door of the Villa Allegra closed behind Athene. The sound of the wind ceased. The dusk was excluded. In the square vestibule the light had been already switched on, but the entrance to Wacey's study yawned black.

"*Povero signore*," sighed her maid Assunta, who appeared at the head of the passage leading to the kitchen. "*Ah, signora, questa maledetta guerra!*"

This cursed war! That ejaculation was the melancholy refrain of all speech nowadays.

"Is Arthur all right?"

"*Sissignora, sta bene il piccolo*," Assunta exclaimed in

some surprise. To be sure, it was always the first question of the *signora* on returning home, but it was strange to ignore her sympathy over the departure of the *signore* for the cursed war. But they were strange, these foreigners, particularly the Americans and the English.

Athene hurried to the nursery. She found her son on the floor, babbling away in Italian over his wooden bricks to Maddalena, the grave young nursemaid. There was nothing the matter with Arthur. She checked a longing to hug him. That was typical of Athene's sensitive manners. She must not intrude with maternal demonstrativeness upon her son's absorption in his game.

The cuckoo-clock on the wall struck six. The child looked up from his bricks to scowl at the spoil-sport bird.

"*Zitto!*" he muttered—or in English, 'shut up!'

"Oh, don't look so fierce, darling," exclaimed his mother, in mock dismay. "You can play awhile yet before bed."

"*Sì, sto qui,*" Arthur declared firmly. He seemed disinclined to accept as a favour what he claimed as a right. The tone proclaimed his belief that he stayed here by his own will. At that moment the structure of bricks collapsed. Arthur grunted an Italian dissyllable.

The grave-eyed Maddalena held up her hands in shocked disapproval.

"*Che vergogna! Come sei cattivo, Arturo!*"

"Did he use a bad word?" asked her mistress, whose knowledge of Italian was narrowly domestic.

"*Una parola molto scostumata, signora,*" Maddalena affirmed. "Nobody would say such a word in this house."

"Darling, you must never say that word again," Athene enjoined solemnly, but without confidence, for she could not feel sure she should herself recognize the word if he did decide to use it again.

A quarter of an hour later Arthur surrendered equably enough to the suggestion of bed; and that business accomplished, Athene went to her own room to change her frock. She noticed that some of Wacey's things discarded from his luggage at the last moment were still lying about. She would put them away after dinner. Perhaps it was just as well she had not invited John Ogilvie this evening. Wacey was sure to have left his study in disorder, and the sooner it was tidied up the better. With the idea of being busy later she put on a silk negligé of lace and almond-green silk, and presently took her seat at the dinner-table. For the first time since they had parted at the station in Naples just before noon that morning she asked herself what Wacey was doing. It was not that she was sentimentally curious to know, but for so long now had she been accustomed to listen at dinner to Wacey's rambling account of his day that the sudden breach in habit seemed to require filling. He had not been sure whether the train for Paris was leaving to-night or to-morrow. So he might be spending to-night in Rome. In that case he would be sure to go to the Hôtel de Russie where they had stayed on so many visits to and transits through Rome during the seven and a half years of their married life. She had a vision of the golden-brown walls of the hotel in the March sun on their arrival in Rome before the birth of Arthur. When she first knew a baby was coming she had been anxious to go back to Atlanta, but Wacey had not wanted to give up the winter in the Engadine, where he was planning to lay the scene of a novel. Not yet written that novel, though Arthur was now six and a half. How richly coloured Rome had been after the whiteness of Switzerland, and the walls of the Hôtel de Russie had been preserved in her mind with all the intensity of that first glowing impression. And her room in the clinic, with the dark umbrella pine below and the campagna beyond the roofs and belfries of the city. Yet she had always gazed beyond that fair horizon to America. Never had she longed so ardently for her own home as during that fortnight before her son was born. Never had she asked herself so sharply what had induced her to yield to Wacey's soft persistency and marry him.

In abrupt repentance for turning back to such thoughts on this night when Wacey was on his way to the war, Athene looked across to where his empty chair was pushed into the table. Assunta sighed with the quick imaginative sympathy of the Italian maid.

"*Non c' è il signore*," she murmured as she placed a solitary cutlet before her mistress. "*Che guaio, questa maledetta guerra!*"

Athene tried to look suitably aware of what a woe indeed the cursed war was, and becomingly depressed by the absence of the *signore* from his chair. Without Arthur to worry about now, she could not have borne to chill Assunta's warm heart.

After dinner Athene sat for awhile over coffee reading a letter from her mother, which she had only had time to skim through rapidly yesterday before driving into Naples to speed Wacey warwards:

PEACHTREE STREET,
ATLANTA
October 7, 17.

My dearest Athene,

Your cable about Wacey's prospect of a staff position in France was a pleasure to receive. Indeed Fother was so glad about it that he suffered a two hours' visit from old Mr Langridge with better humour than I have ever known him do before. I do hope that when the war is over Wacey will have found regular work sufficiently attractive to give him an idea of fixing himself up in some permanent job. I went myself to see Mrs Langridge who was her usual sweet self and as such so very sweetly suggested I must be wishing I had three sons instead of three daughters in days like these. Never mind, I must bask in this reflected glory of a martial son-in-law.

I must say I do wish you were over here. We don't anticipate that the Germans will overrun Italy, but we do not like at all the notion of your being so far away in these disturbing days. However, there it is. Submarines make any question of your travelling out of the question. I am not going to bore you with tales of our warlike preparations at home, for I'm sure after three years of war in Europe you must be sick of belligerent enthusiasm, and no doubt dear Wacey has already planned quite enough battles to be won for your benefit.

The snapshots of Arthur Gilmer were a delight to us all. We are sure we see a likeness to his grandfather. 'That certainly is the obstinate Gilmer chin,' I told him. And grandfather was so tickled that he's put one of the snaps inside the lid of his watch, and Dr Haydon told me he was showing it around the club and sitting back in his chair and waiting to be congratulated on handing down the Gilmer chin to the rising generation. Yes, just sitting back as foolish as you like, waiting to be patted on the back by his fellow citizens. Poor old Father, he would have been prouder to own a son who was known as the biggest scapegrace in Georgia than to hear the praise of Lawton J. Gilmer's three Graces. 'Yes, they're lovely girls, honey, but . . .' how often has he said that to me and stopped short with a sigh. Never mind, if Arthur Gilmer Langridge keeps the Gilmer chin perhaps he'll forgive the Langridge contribution. Ellen has gone to New York for the winter with her baby girl, which like a good grandmother I tried to argue against, but she felt she ought to be with Walford, and of course she is right. Vera writes happily from New Orleans where Hugh is busy with his medical work, but she has promised to come home next month and let us have the baby as a Christmas gift.

Well, darling child, it's time this loquacious middle-aged woman stopped rambling on. I feel so happy for you over Wacey's expectation of a staff appointment. Our love to you and Wacey and Arthur Gilmer,

Your ever loving
Mother

As Athene laid down the letter from home she was overcome for a moment by an almost unbearable nostalgia for the spaciousness of her native land. New York, New Orleans . . . and Atlanta. All in one letter. It was four and a half years since she had been home. She sat back, dreaming. A gust of wind rattled the shutters. Wind from the west. For a moment Athene was tempted to open the window, fling wide the shutters, and breathe in this wind from the west. Then she thought of the way it would blow her hair about and she thrust the wild notion aside. And anyway she must go and put things straight in Wacey's study. But still she dallied. She read through her mother's letter again, smiling over the picture of old Mr Langridge spending two hours with her father to discuss the cable about Wacey's job. He would be as omniscient, of course, about the war as in his own opinion he had always been omniscient about everything. He would know exactly why the Germans were where they were and why the British were not where they were not. He could reckon the cost of the war per minute. He would handle the theory of munitions as he had handled the theory of store-keeping. And now that America was seized with the fever of war even her father was ready to endure his theorizing.

The nostalgia for home suddenly faded away. After three years and three months of war in Europe it would be unbearable to find it beginning all over again on the other side of the ocean. No, it was not for the Atlanta of to-day that she had been longing, but for the Atlanta of her childhood and youth. The three Graces! Lawton J. Gilmer's three Graces. Herself and Ellen and Vera all so fairly matched that none of them had been able to be jealous of another. That long ago June day when young Wacey Langridge had come back from his tour in Europe and never looked beyond herself. Naturally she had been excited. What girl of fourteen would not be excited when a travelled young man of twenty came home from seeing the beautiful women of the world and found the most beautiful for him was in his own city? And then over the next six years enough opposition to make it worth while to be married. No, that wasn't just. She *had* liked Wacey better than all the others, and except for Wacey's failure to become any of the things he had been so sure he would become it had been as happy a marriage as most people succeeded in achieving for themselves. Without Arthur . . . perhaps . . . but she was not without Arthur. . . . Athene looked up from her reverie. Was that Arthur calling to her? She went along the passage to the door of the nursery and listened. Fancy, nervous fancy. There was no sound.

She did not return to the sitting-room. She would keep her resolve to clear up in Wacey's study. It was not a favourite room of her own. It could remain tidy until he came back from the war.

Yet when she switched on the light to illuminate the deserted room she came for a while under the spell cast by the inanimate objects left behind. She had parted with Wacey on the platform of the Naples station without sorrow and jolted back down that long rackety street to the hotel without a thought except of her anxiety to be in the quiet of Citrano as soon as possible, though for the sake of economy she had made up her mind to return by the tram as far as Sorrento. And then in the lobby of the hotel she had seen a British naval officer and it had been John Ogilvie and he had kissed her. It had seemed so natural that he should kiss her. The world had still been at peace when they had last seen each other. And then they had driven back together in a car, for which when she saw him next she really must insist on paying her share. John had refused to talk about the war. He had told her he was surfeited with action. They had talked instead about that summer of 1914, before war came. 'I feel as if it was a summer holiday of childhood,' he had said. 'It's just as far away now.' And she had looked sidelong at him and noticed how much older he seemed. The mouth so tightly set, the smile faintly sardonic nowadays. 'What did you hate most?' she had asked. And staring away from her across the bay as the car bumped through Portici, 'Stupidity,' he had answered. 'And the power for harm war gives to the second- and third-rate mind, and the end it becomes in itself.' 'And what did you love most?' she had pressed. Had it been fancy, or had he winced before he replied, 'Two or three friends'? How dull of her it had been not to ask him to dinner to-night. Maria would have managed quite easily. And Wacey's room could have waited until the morning.

The pathetic spell cast by the relics of Wacey scattered about was broken. She could no longer be moved by the copy of a cheap edition of Matilda Serao's *Paese di Cuccagna* lying face downwards on the seat of his armchair, open at the page at which he had laid it aside. She picked it up and found a place for it on one of his bookshelves. No doubt he would buy himself another copy if he remembered he had not finished *Paese di Cuccagna*. That was the kind of extravagance he always scoffed at if it was pointed out to him—the kind of extravagance that somebody who relies on an allowance from a father does scoff at. Thirty-three, Wacey now. About the same age as John Ogilvie, who had tasted of success with two plays and lived through three years of war. And most of Wacey's attempts to express himself had been left half-finished like his reading of that Italian novel. Athene's gaze turned to the glass-fronted case above the bureau. Manuscripts and typescripts stuffed away, some promising well, but all unfinished. In one corner a neater and much smaller pile, with half a dozen magazines on top. The monument to his published work. 'Wacey, it's just self-indulgence!' 'It *would* be self-indulgence if I went on with work that didn't satisfy me.' At first she had argued with him, but for a long time now she had not bothered. She listened now to his enthusiasm about the book he was going to write, with as little heed as one pays to the narrative of another person's dream.

Athene opened the lid of the bureau and impatiently put aside pens, pencils, inkpot, the petrified lobster he used as a paperweight, the ivory paperknife cut from a small tusk, the blotter of old Spanish leather, and all the rest of Wacey's would-be professional equipment. There were some letters inside still unopened. Bills, by the shape of the envelopes. She frowned. Wacey had assured her that every bill in Naples was paid. But perhaps these were receipts, she thought not too hopefully, for one of Wacey's few efforts at being methodical was to spike his receipted bills, like trophies. She opened the envelopes one by one. Not yet paid, but nothing to bother about. The relief made her charitable. They must have come by yesterday's mail when she and Wacey were already in Naples, and Assunta would have put them in here. Only about five hundred liras altogether. Nothing unmanageable. She tore open the last envelope. It was a bill from the chemist in Rome with whom they dealt regularly, and it was accompanied by a note to say that the goods Mr Langridge had ordered were waiting for him to call for them.

The red rose faded from Athene's cheeks. She stood blanched, her brown eyes burning. Then shaking herself as if waking from a trance she looked at the date. No, it was not a mistake. The bill was dated the day before yesterday. So Wacey had forearmed himself. And done it so cleverly, as he thought. The damning evidence was to be outside any possibility of her discovering it. He had had to tell only one lie, and that was when he said he did not know if the train to Paris left Rome to-night or to-morrow night. Yet all his cleverness had gone for nothing because the chemist, innocent of the plan, had taken it for granted that the bill was to be sent as usual to Citrano like any other for the same goods . . . goods! What a word! Athene sat down at the bureau and dipping one of Wacey's own pens in his own ink she wrote:

> *This bill presumably ought not to have been sent to the Villa Allegra. I congratulate you on looking ahead, and on the prudence with which you stick to well tried 'goods'.*

'And I,' she told herself bitterly, 'shall get a letter from Rome two days hence to tell me that he has cared for no woman since he saw me first that day in the spring of 1904 standing under the magnolia-tree in our garden, as he has told me in every letter during those thirteen years.'

There were still relics of Wacey lying about the room, but now she could not bear to touch them. She would have seemed to herself in touching them to be surrendering to the physical intimacy she had always hated but until this moment had accepted as the price she must pay for her own wilfulness. Never again. She was released.

Back in the sitting-room Athene rang for Assunta, and in that nominatival Italian which Italian maids so miraculously manage to comprehend bade her fetch Maddalena and take the Signore's bed out of her room.

"*Ma dove lo metteremo, signora?*" Assunta asked in perplexed astonishment.

It was to be put in the Signore's own room.

"*Va bene, signora.*"

But it was clear from Assunta's expression that the removal was a shock to her conventional emotion. She had been supposing that until the *signore* returned she should sigh at intervals over that empty bed and draw a responsive sigh from the *signora* when she was not in one of those curious moods of frigidity to which foreigners were so unpredictably subject.

That night when Athene sat before her mirror brushing the deep brown hair that tumbled over her shoulders she brushed away thirteen years of her life. She caught sight of the mosquito-net looped back at the head of her own bed, and in fancy she beheld herself again as a bride. To sacrifice so much for that swiftly passing glory! Yet to others would it seem so much? Most women would say she was putting up with nothing. By their standards Wacey was the perfect husband: good-looking, good-tempered, popular, unlikely to fossilize prematurely, if anything too ready for experiments in living. He was always considerate, always unmistakably more interested in his wife than any other woman in the room, yet not so fondly as to make him ridiculous. If only after Arthur was born he had been content to abandon that persistent effort to persuade her into declaring that she loved him! She had refused to say as much years before they had been married. When she had yielded to his soft persistency it had been a capitulation to marriage, not to love. If only he had been as persistent with his writing as he had been with his passion for her, she would never have loved him, but at least she would have respected him. And now this intolerable affront! If she had discovered a letter from some other woman she would not have forgiven it, but at least she would have been spared the mortification of despising him. To be bored continually for years, and sometimes exasperated, by his eternal optimism, his everlasting expectation that the miracle would abruptly occur and that he would find his passion reciprocated, and now to be humiliated by this deliberate preparation for casual infidelity!

The brushing of her hair was like a relentless ritual, as with every downward sweep of the wrist she banished not merely the memory of what she had hated in their linked lives but all the pleasures which, superficial though they might be, had allowed her to cheat herself with the illusion enjoyed by the world that theirs was a happy marriage. She brushed away even the reproachful awareness which sometimes plucked at her mind that he was the father of her son. He deserved as much, because he had now proved that the demands he had made upon her complaisance were nothing better than the sensual urge of the male animal, and that all his eagerness to exact from her a response was nothing better than an added sensual gratification. No, she would not have forgiven him if she had discovered a letter from some woman which revealed that he had sought from her the love he could not win from his wife. She would have used the revelation to free herself, and then she would have forgiven him and wished him well. Now she hated him because he had made her pity for him ridiculous. She had believed that her inability to respond to his passion wounded him, and sometimes she had driven herself to try to respond. How often he had declared that his own passion was solely the expression of the love with which she had filled him since first he saw her as a girl of fourteen, and now it was proved to be one more expression of his own feeble self-indulgence.

Well, it was finished now. He could not come back to speak his excuses. He would have to write his lies, and she should be able to watch them shrivel in the fire. Oh, why, why was she confined in this war-ridden Europe? She could be on the ocean next week with Arthur but for this damnable war. No matter, she had lived for seven and a half years with Wacey in Europe. She could live without him for as long as the war lasted, and then she could go home and divorce him. She could go home and bring up her son to be a man.

Athene rose from the toilet-table. Her rippling brown hair was brushed. 'This exquisite solitude,' she thought, as with the luxurious deliberation of a cat she prepared herself for repose. She turned over to sleep tranquilly, lulled by the noisy wind.

The wind was much more noisy round that Torre Saracena which had been waiting for John to live in since he bought it in the summer before the war. In his library on the top floor it seemed to be buffeting all the four windows with equal violence. The room occupied the whole of the top floor except for the corner where a spiral staircase descended to the two bedrooms below. On the ground floor were the dining-room looking full south across the Tyrrhenian toward Africa, the kitchen with a view to the east across a sandy semilune to the port and the other horn of the small bay of Citrano, and, as befitted a *forestiere*, a bathroom which, supplied by a *cisterna*, would never be used except with a sense of guilt for the amount of water one was squandering.

Wacey must have taken much time and trouble to prepare the tower so well. In the library John had found a note from him to say he had thought it better to arrange the books on the shelves and leave their owner to rearrange them to his own taste and convenience. The cupboards had been well stocked with the help of Fofo, who had confounded all precedent in Citrano by calling personally just after John arrived to see if he had everything he needed. What was more Fofo had agreed with Wacey to let his third daughter Margarita, now twenty-two, a plump black-eyed girl waiting for the end of *questa maledetta guerra* to marry, look after John and his tower with the help of a younger daughter, Caterina, now fourteen. John was certainly in the hands of Don Alfonso Massa, but in what better Citrano hands could he be?

Here and there John noticed where he thought he could improve Wacey's arrangement of the furniture, but there would be little to alter. A pity Wacey had gone off to this damned war. And yet what did it matter? He was in no mood for the companionship of anybody. He was in his tower for three months, and that was all the companionship he needed.

In spite of the wind there was to John a wonderful peace in his library that night. The tower was beyond the radius of the unstable electric light of Citrano, and the lamp with its two legless birds of paradise painted on a shade of nankeen vellum glowed with that life which bulbs of electricity cannot give or get. The golden velvet curtains hung in steady folds across the four windows, except that occasionally the curtains over the west window would seem to breathe when a fierce gust struck the tower. The furniture, much of it lacquer, added to the peace with its patterns of motionless movement, with its pavilions and palanquins, with its bridges and serene anglers. The only adjunct of tranquil meditation missing was an open fireplace. The white porcelain stove was out of place, and the convex Dutch mirror above—which held the room in miniature—was ill-suited by it. However, the construction of chimneys had seemed too expensive and difficult in the mood of impermanence that war begets. And anyway chimneys always smoked in Citrano.

After dinner, served with many apologies from Margarita for its lack of substance and variety due to the difficulty of catering during *questa maledetta guerra*, John sat up in his library bewitched by the contemplation of the books and furniture that represented what he was before this cursed war. Nothing in this room except the white porcelain stove had been acquired since August 1914. There were books on those shelves he had not opened since he was at Oxford, books he had not opened since he was at school. His eye caught a small faded blue volume with a worn label, and he took it from the shelf. It opened at *Summer Dawn*:

Pray but one prayer for me 'twixt thy closed lips,
Think but one thought of me up in the stars.
The summer night waneth, the morning light slips,
Faint and grey 'twixt the leaves of the aspen, betwixt the cloud-bars,
That are patiently waiting there for the dawn:
Patient and colourless, though Heaven's gold
Waits to float through them along with the sun.
Far out in the meadows, above the young corn,
The heavy elms wait, and restless and cold
The uneasy wind rises; the roses are dun;
Through the long twilight they pray for the dawn,
Round the lone house in the midst of the corn.
Speak but one word to me over the corn,
Over the tender, bow'd locks of the corn.

So the volume still opened at *Summer Dawn*, still responded to a habit of seventeen years ago, when he, not much more than seventeen himself, used to wake before the earliest thrush and lie in bed thinking about Rose Medlicott, until he opened that blue volume of William Morris, not faded then.

The scent of those English dawns when he used to call to Rose across the sundering fields that lay between their homes came back sharply through the faint mustiness of the pages. And of that love-affair nothing remained except the way a book always opened at the same page.

These reflections were interrupted by the entrance of Margarita to say that Signor Noel had called. John's first impulse was to send word that he was working. He had no desire either to talk about his own life during the last three years or to hear about that of other people. When he had met Geoffrey Noel at Citrano in that summer before the war he had liked him much, but he might not like him now. And then there recurred to him the meeting with Athene Langridge and the pleasure of it expressed by the kiss of an old unspoilt friendship suddenly renewed. He bade Margarita show the signore up.

"I debated—m-m—for a long time—m-m—whether I would disturb you on your first night," Noel said, mumming and humming away with the embarrassment that accompanied his entrance into a room at any time and was now made so much more acute by the necessity of greeting somebody across a gulf of years. "Your gradus ad Parnassum!" he puffed, with a backward glance at the spiral staircase to help him over a couple of those self-conscious prances that would bring him nearer to the effort of shaking hands.

That fine classic face sunburnt and clean-shaven. The iron-grey hair whitened perceptibly since 1914. The same dancing, slightly effeminate walk. The short legs . . . the ground-bass of mumming and humming.

"How kind of you to look me up," said John, pushing forward a chair. "I met Athene Langridge in Naples. Do you remember that June evening in Cantone when we heard of the Sarajevo assassination? Three of us have met again. And I only just missed Wacey Langridge. Do you remember Julius Stern, and his wife? They made up the party. Julius has returned to his violin, and is touring the States giving concerts for warlike charities."

"That's a good phrase," Noel exclaimed in his breathless mumble. "It suggests rather a neat epigram. I still—m-m—essay the—m-m—lyre.' He gave a feminine wriggle, and dived quickly into the pockets of his tweed jacket for the pipe and pouch of masculinity. "Do you know the work of Pascoli? I've been having a shot at translating some of his poems. I think he's really good. Oh, and Pirandello!" he gulped. "I'd no idea he was so good. I've been reading him a lot lately. I do think he's the best living dramatist. So original."

"I used to think before the war he was good," said John. "But I won't commit myself to a judgment now until I read him again."

"I suppose Athene Langridge told you I'd lost Francesco?" Noel asked, hiding his embarrassment in the smoke of his pipe. "It was a terrible blow when he was called up for service at the beginning of 1916. However, I'm thankful to say he has a job some way behind the line. I send him what I can, but my wife —m-m—has behaved very oddly about money ever since the war started. You know I married her when she was literally almost starving?" Noel gasped with indignant emotion. "Yes, an American girl who had come to Italy to study music without a cent. And then a year after we were married she inherited a fortune—an immense fortune. I agreed to let her divorce me, and foolishly left it to her honour to make me an allowance. I should have had a proper settlement drawn up, but all that kind of thing is so sordid. The condition was that I should remain in Citrano, which of course I was perfectly willing to do. Even before the war the allowance had been gradually reduced and was paid irregularly, but since the war!" Poor Noel made a delicate gesture of despair. "My dear man, it has been simply frightful. She says the hospital she is running near Paris costs her so much. I have to write two or three letters every time reminding her that my allowance is overdue. I believe she enjoys the thought of humiliating me with the Citrano shopkeepers. I really don't know what I should have done without Fofo. Of course, he remembered Vanessa when she first came to Citrano. She was almost in rags in those days."

Noel stopped. He was gurgling with indignation, wriggling convulsively in the chair like a landed trout.

"Were you in love with her?" John asked.

"She had a certain—m-m-m—boyish charm, and I was sorry for her."

"That would have been unpardonable," John suggested.

"No, I don't think it's revenge. I think she gets a sort of sadistic pleasure out of humiliating me . . . one day I'll tell you the whole story."

John remembered that Noel had made this promise before the war. He would have been more interested to hear the story then. He was tired of stories now. Curiosity about human nature had been sated.

"You're looking thin, my dear man," his visitor observed.

"I've had a tiring time. However, I have leave for at least three months."

"You don't mean to say you're going back to the war?" Noel exclaimed. "Surely as an artist you've done all that could be expected of you?"

John smiled.

"The very Muses are doing war-work. Melpomene is a Waac. Thalia is a Wren. Calliope is in the V.A.D. Euterpe is sewing shirts for soldiers. Oh, the Muses, like all the women, are splendid."

"Dreadful," Noel exhaled fervidly, for by that strange paradox of the epicene mind he had a horror of female initiative.

"I was rather ill in the summer," John hurried on. He was afraid lest the conversation might move round again to Noel's matrimonial complexities. "And I'm not quite fit yet, but if I'm all right by the beginning of the New Year I shall certainly have to leave the Torre Saracena."

"Preposterous!" Noel ejaculated. "I thought it was preposterous when Wacey Langridge took this job at Saint Nazaire, and he is—m-m—just an amateur like myself. But you're different. You have a right to go back to your art now."

"Art?" echoed John.

"To play-writing."

"I'm suffering from such a surfeit of action that I wonder if I shall ever be able to write another play—or at any rate another play which will be recognized as such."

"Pirandello . . ." Noel began.

"I'm not going to seek inspiration from other dramatists," John interrupted. "At the moment, the notion of make-believe action is repulsive, but perhaps when I have assimilated the intensive experience of the last three years I may do something with it."

"You think an artist is at the mercy of experience? Surely the genuine creator is independent of it?"

"In a less sophisticated world he may have been. The variety of actual experience was so limited that one of the chief impulses to creative art must have been the extension of imaginative experience. It was a form of what nowadays we call escapism, but there was one profound difference between then and now. To the ancients escapism was a stimulant: to us it is a narcotic."

"What about books like *Wuthering Heights* or *Moby Dick*? Surely they were not produced by experience?"

"Not *Wuthering Heights* perhaps, but *Moby Dick*? Fantastic it may be, but surely you won't seriously suggest that Herman Melville could have written *Moby Dick* without his experience in a South Sea whaler when he was hardly out of his 'teens? If I were asked what I considered the most significant aspect of contemporary literature I should reply without hesitation that it was the almost complete dependency for all that is best in it upon the experience of early youth. With the steadily increasing predominance of industrialism in alliance with machinery man passes from youth to a stunted middle-age before he is thirty. But I grow didactic."

"No, no, elucidate—m-m—amplify," Noel urged.

"Take the Elizabethan age, for example," John continued. "The writers of that period were apparently capable of reacting to experience at forty with the gusto of a contemporary boy of fourteen. If we look back to our 'teens we look back to a world of heightened sensation in which vision was more intense, taste sharper, scent keener, touch finer. Not even a public-school or a board-school education could utterly deaden us, though the education we had was designed to make us docile slaves of the capitalist industrialism and finance which abetted by machinery were the prime cause of this infernal war. I call it infernal now, but when it started I welcomed it as a revivification. I supposed that it would provide me with an enlargement of experience beyond anything I had dreamed of as possible. I thought of Aeschylus at Marathon, of Sophocles at Samos. I forgot Aristophanes. In my fancy I was to emerge from war rich in wisdom, and if I died I was willing to welcome death because I should accept it as a boon granted by the gods to an artist who had already done what he could do. What was the reality? The war is not yet over. It may last another three or four years; but already I recognize that the action by which I expected to feed my creative imagination has been no more than a purposeless expenditure of energy. I understand now what Shakespeare meant by an idiot's tale full of sound and fury, signifying nothing. And mind you, Noel, I have had what people call 'a good war'. I have enjoyed the action itself, but I have discovered that action is its own fulfilment. It is as sterile mentally as a game of golf. Nothing that can be written about it or out of it is equal to action itself. For over three years now I have not considered the drama, because I was playing a part in a super-drama. I have been telling myself that as soon as I was off the scene I should hardly know where to begin, so much should I have to write about. Well, I'm off the scene now, and my imagination is a blank. It seems to me that no play I can write can be anything except an anticlimax to these three years of action. Nothing I invent can heighten the reality and nothing I report is communicable. Like all the rest of us Europeans, except perhaps the Russians, who really are not Europeans, I'm middle-aged, and therefore so much action has tired me out. Besides, I see already that it was all futile."

"You can hardly call it futile to help to defeat the Germans."

"We never had any desire to beat the Germans before the war began. We should never have set out to beat them if the Germans had not entered Belgium. True, we could not keep them from destroying it, but Belgium will rise again we tell ourselves, and we will not sheath the sword until it does, according to one of our eloquent statesmen. We went to war on behalf of plucky little Belgium, or at any rate the man in the street who turned into the man in the trenches did. Since then we have discovered a variety of abstract reasons for fighting. We are fighting for the rights of small nations, and as a proof of that we held up Irish Home Rule and provoked the Easter Rising. We are fighting to destroy not Germany but German Militarism, not Germans but Kaiserism and German Imperialism. A nation that starts fighting 'isms' is like Don Quixote tilting at windmills, an object of nobility to himself but to others either a knave or a fool. We are fighting to make the world safe for democracy.

America handed us that sublime anaesthetic. So then we are fighting for the bugs and lice of our city slums, for industrial slavery, for the tyranny of debt, for the development of the machine at the expense of the man, for bureaucrats, hireling politicians, profiteers, bankers and big business. Offer that democracy to Pericles, and ask him if he recognizes the word. And finally we are fighting for civilization, in order to do which we revert mentally to barbarism. If the Germans can only be defeated by Germanizing ourselves, who is the victor? Evil cannot be destroyed by evil."

"But unless we defeat the Germans, what security have we that they will not start all over again in another few years?"

"And when we have defeated them—a year hence, two years hence, three years hence, what are we going to do with them? The French would say, 'sterilize every male of a race which has been a curse to Europe for two thousand years.' The French point of view is intelligible, but not even a war like this can quite destroy man's moral sense, and such a solution is impossible. We shall compromise of course, and in the end we shall make a treaty of peace which will satisfy neither our allies, nor ourselves, nor our enemies. The world will be left unsafe for democracy, except perhaps in Russia by the way things are moving there, unsafe for small nations, and less civilized than when the war started. Of course we may have destroyed a few 'isms', but 'isms' are like green fly, prolific and parthenogenetic. There will always be plenty more to fight."

"You've come back to Citrano in a very discouraging mood," Noel mumbled. "I was hoping to hear some of your adventures. But you do think we *shall* win the war?"

"Now that the Americans have come in we must in time achieve at any rate a technical victory."

Geoffrey Noel leant back with a sigh of relief.

"My wife has suggested coming to Citrano when the war is over and discussing our affairs. And I must say I shall be very glad to get Francesco back. He's really an excellent boy, and I'm thankful to say that girl here he was inclined to run after has got married. Such a vixen, and a fearful slut."

The conversation turned to Citrano, and John was surprised to find himself amused by Noel's gossip.

When his visitor rose at midnight to go home, he thanked him for returning a sense of proportion to his mind. Noel's body was contorted with pleasure at the compliment as he protested his unworthiness of it.

"I'm serious," John assured him. "It was exactly what I needed. Mrs Heighington and the Contessa del Bufalò and all the rest of them are a pledge of permanence. Perhaps I shall set to work on a comedy after all. By the way, I thought Athene Langridge had developed a lot."

"Well, you know, my dear man, I have never somehow been able to get any further with her. Always charming to me. But I never progress. I think American women are always—m-m—rather like children playing at being grown up. Except my wife, of course. She is really a most remarkable woman. If only she had a greater sense of responsibility. She was two months behind with my money this time, and it does put me in such an impossible position. So you thought Mrs Langridge had developed?"

"I thought so, yes."

"Of course, after being away so long you would notice any difference. She'll miss poor Wacey very much."

"I expect she will."

John accompanied Geoffrey Noel to the door of the tower, and stood for a while watching his lantern go wavering up through the wind-blown rosemary. By the ragged moonshine he could see the young cypresses which Wacey Langridge had planted for him straining at the stakes to which they were tied.

The wind blew itself out before morning. At noon John was on the roof of the Torre Saracena drinking in the lustrous calm of a late autumn day over the Salernian Gulf. The sky was all a tender blue. The sea southward was outspread in a serenity of silver that was azured over to east and west out of the sun's direct and flashing eye, which lighted up woodland, gorge and precipice of the great limestone heights behind Citrano like an immense drop-curtain, so vividly indeed that the gashes in the forest made by the axes of prisoners-of-war could be seen without glasses. John cursed the need of war that drove men to destroy these primeval chestnuts and beeches and defile that immemorial sylvan peace. He looked ruefully down over the castellated parapet at the slim young cypresses on his own rocky promontory. They were a small guerdon to give back to earth in return for what was being robbed from it. Rosemary and lentisk grew sparsely round the base of the tower. Spurges were everywhere, tipped now with the flamy green of their new growth and turning autumn to spring. Higher up the slope the rosemary grew more boldly beside the zigzag path leading up toward the first alleys of Citrano, just below which a small boscage of myrtles, with here and there a twisted locust or wild olive, marked the boundary of the Torre Saracena's land.

The quicker way to reach the town was to cross the wide semilune of sandy beach and thence climb up one of the flights of steps cut down to the Marina. This was the way John took that morning to pay a call on Don Alfonso Massa, and thank him for the trouble he had taken to make his return to Citrano so comfortable.

In spite of there seeming little to account for, so empty was the café, Fofo himself was seated before an open ledger at his table in the darkest corner, as he had sat for the quarter of a century which had passed since he married the heiress of old Gargiulo and become at first the manager and now the proprietor of his wine-shop. He looked up when John came in, and rose to come forward and greet him, his sleek baby face plunged into furrows by a smile, his small jetty eyes bright as a lizard's.

"*Ah*, *questa maledetta guerra*, *signore mio!* When will she finish?"

John shrugged his shoulders. He had doffed his uniform, and in civilian tweeds he felt more resentful than ever against the war's prolongation.

"But I'm afraid we can't talk about peace now," he sighed, "after this tragic Caporetto business."

It was Fofo's turn to shrug his shoulders. With the amplitude of the gesture he expressed an opinion of his country's folly in May 1915. He himself had been for Giolitti and neutrality.

"If she does not finish soon we are rovined in Citrano."

He took John's arm and led him out into the Piazza. "Look to our hotel!"

The Hotel Excelsior and Imperial brooded like a *memento mori* above the white-domed roofs of the town. The building had been completed and furnished in the hope that it would provide a retreat from the war in a neutral country; but empty now except for a caretaker it was awaiting peace. The windows of its two hundred bedrooms de luxe stared blankly down at the deserted Piazza and the idle Marina.

The foreigners in Citrano had agreed that the Hotel Excelsior and Imperial would spoil the peculiar charm of the place and reduce it to the level of Capri, Sorrento, and Amalfi; but even they, once the garish sign of progress was built, would have preferred it to be full of guests.

"We must hope for peace in spring," said John, only too conscious of the optimistic platitude he was uttering.

"If we do notta to have peace next year Don Augusto, Don Rocco and myself are in rovins, how can you say?"

"In ruins," John corrected, quenching the flicker of a smile at the thought of that vast jelly Don Augusto Di Fiori in ruins.

"How has the Sirene been doing?" he asked. That was Don Augusto's own *albergo*.

"The same for him. The same for me. The same for the shop of Don Rocco. There is no business at all. Fifteena? Not so bad. We have no Germans, but we have some English peoples. Sixteena? It is bad. The English peoples are very few. *Ma diciassette!* Seventeena! We have nobody. Don Augusto has one old English woman who drinka the water from her beddaroom. How you say? The teef's glass. He has one *svedese*. Excuse to me that I speaka frank with you. This Swedeman is a . . ." Fofo pinched the lobe of his ear in the significant language of signs. "It is good. I say nothing when we have plenty peoples. But when it is one it makes a scandal because, *capisca*, *signore*, *i ragazzini si vogliono avvantaggiare*. *Ah*, *ecco!*"

Fofo pointed to a tall fair man strolling along the parapet of the terrace beyond the Piazza who was being followed by a chattering company of some two dozen youthful *citranitani*.

"It is rather conspicuous," John agreed. So deep did war dig its vile talons!

"And how are working Margarita and Caterina?" their father enquired, turning away from the spectacle of the voluptuous Swede and his shameless retinue to domestic virtue.

John expressed his gratitude for their services.

"Margarita will marry herself when the war will be finished. It is good she make a practice. I am very content she is in the Torre Saracena. So soon as Signor Langridge ask her for you I am very content."

"I wish I'd seen him before he went off," John said. Fofo drew in his chin to make the conventional Neapolitan grimace that expresses the futility of any phrase to voice an adequate comment.

"Why for he go?" he demanded of perverse human nature. "Here he is comfortable with a nice *signora* and a *bambino* and a *villa* for which he only pay two hundred fifty lire a month furnished and that is nothing when the exchange is so good for *americani*. But no, he must to go away and perhaps be killed. He is mad. *Ma, signore mio, tutto il mondo è uscito pazzo.* All of the world is mad."

They were by now inside the café again, its only occupants. On either side of the long shiny table which ran down the middle of the main portion the backs of the empty chairs had a skeleton look. And once this table was a congress of friendly nations, a babel of jovial talk.

"Have the Russians gone too?" John asked.

"One or two are still here, but nearly all are gone now to make the revolution. I think it is bad for us that revolution. I think Russia will not fight no more."

"In fact you're in a thoroughly gloomy mood, Fofo."

Again the chin was submerged in the circumfluent fat to suggest the inadequacy of words to express how gloomy that mood was.

At that moment Athene Langridge came into the café.

"Why, it's John. John, I'm just thoroughly mortificata to meet you this morning. I can't think what I was doing last night not to ask you to come around and have dinner at the Allegra. You must have thought me the most inhospitable uncouth female you met in your young life. I've been kicking myself ever since."

"Do not to pain yourself, *signora*," said Fofo, his eyes twinkling. "Signor Ogilvie has a very good girl for make him dinner."

"Oh, I know we can't compete with your Margarita, Fofo. But that doesn't let me out."

When she had made her purchases and was walking back with John toward the Villa Allegra, Athene added to her regrets about last night's failure of hospitality earnest entreaties that she should be allowed to pay her share of the car from Naples yesterday evening.

They had reached the head of one of the flights of steps that led down to the Marina, and John stopped abruptly.

"Look here, Athene," he protested, "if you say another word about dinner last night or the price of that car, I swear I won't come near you again for the rest of my leave. You've done all you could do for me by looking not a day older than when we said good-bye in June 1914. I love your orange jumper and I love your brown coat and skirt. . . ."

"These old things," she commented in quick disdain.

"They're young to me, but if you only knew how much old things mean to me nowadays you wouldn't despise them for that reason," he told her. "We shall have lost so much by the time this infernal war stops."

"Perhaps some things are better lost, John."

He looked at her in surprise. It was the first time he had ever heard her make a general statement.

"As for instance?" he asked.

"Well, one's ideas change, don't they?"

They had slowed down to take more cautiously a broken step, and pausing on the brink of it John turned to watch her. The trite remark suddenly acquired significance from Athene's own beauty of colour and form. Those deep brown eyes set at the slant that ancient Hellenic artists demanded from goddesses and mortal women alike, the sunburnt rose of those cheeks, and all the long-legged grace of her poised upon that step in the instant of trusting herself to one slim ankle made the mention of change absurd.

"I don't know about ideas," said John. "But in that moment you fixed yourself upon my mind in an attitude I shall never forget and which will be you in my mind's eye whenever I think about you."

They reached the sand and walked silently toward where the path to the Villa Allegra ascended from the shore between columns to the terrace above the garden.

"I didn't give you dinner last evening," she said at last. "But I'll give you lunch now. We'll eat it on the terrazza. It's quite warm enough."

So they sat out under the thatch of dried genista; and by the hum of a myriad insects on the air it might have been summer.

"I wonder if Wacey got a train from Rome last night," John speculated.

"No," she said quickly. "He'll leave for Paris to-night. He had one or two things he wanted to get in Rome."

After that lunch John called often at the Villa Allegra, and once or twice Athene came to the Torre Saracena. By the end of November he was inclined to agree with Geoffrey Noel that it was impossible to draw near even to the edge of an intimate friendship with Athene Langridge. Yet he was unwilling to admit that there was nothing in her which could form the foundation of such an intimate friendship. He felt that if at any moment he should venture to cut through the hedge of good manners by which she protected herself against contact with reality and try to establish the frankness of intercourse that is the only sustenance of friendship she would completely misunderstand his motive. Was Geoffrey Noel right? Was her beauty an empty shell? Looking back to his impression of Athene and Wacey together he could recall the way they had always treated one another with the politeness of two strangers. He had speculated then whether the marriage which appeared so happy was in essentials quite so happy as it seemed, but now he was beginning to wonder whether the fault did not lie with Athene's own self-consciousness, a self-consciousness so exaggerated that it left her no room to think about herself in the struggle of trying not to obtrude her own personality or personal desires on somebody else. He was aware of this even in her attitude towards her young son. It was not that she spoilt him; but the effort to assert her authority was obviously a torment to her, and her eagerness to win from six-year-old Arthur a rational appreciation of why he was not allowed to do this or why he was compelled to do that was pathetic in the sense of strain it conveyed. It was Athene's handling of her son which made John refuse to accept Noel's estimate of her character. That was not a revelation of emptiness.

Baffled by Athene's mental remoteness, John was tempted to test her capacity for sympathy by telling her the story of Zoe. He put that temptation aside, not only because it would have seemed a piece of emotional sacrilege, but also because he did not want to run the risk of reaching a final and unfavourable judgment of Athene. So much had been destroyed by the experience of the last three years that even the possibility of further destruction was abhorrent. He told himself he was being inconsistent to desire any change in Athene. That he should meet her again and find her unchanged except for a heightening of her beauty should have been the most welcome gift of this temporary escape from the war.

December was wearing away. John received a letter

from Captain Wade enquiring after his health and telling him not to come back until the beginning of March, when he hoped he would have a job for him after his own heart. John, who had been expecting to be summoned home by the middle of January at latest, took up three or four provisional outlines he had made for comedies, read them through with disgust, pitched them into the waste-paper basket, and determined to settle down seriously to express in drama his present mood. He must try somehow to get it out of his system. The maddening part of it was that the more he tried to tease his imagination for drama the more artificial any situation appeared against the background of the world. Then it occurred to him that the most dramatic situation would be a completely static condition against the restlessness of the contemporary world. And the longer he pondered over his idea the more successfully it eluded him.

"Ah, my imagination is tired," he exclaimed aloud in irritation. "Or is it the rustiness of disuse?"

He was pacing the roof of the tower in the benign sunshine of one of those true halcyon days about the winter solstice, and looking over the parapet he beheld winging out to sea a pair of kingfishers. On such a morning 3000 years ago a poet watching by some classic shore may have sung the fabled nesting of the halcyon on the calm midwinter waters. The kingfishers seemed bound for the Siren islets, those Galli of which Browning had sung to Fortù. John took a sudden resolution.

"Margarita," he called, "wrap me up some mortadella and cacciacavallo with bread and two bottles of wine, and tell Caterina to hurry across and fetch Andrea with his boat. I'm going out to the Galli."

"*Mamma mia!*" Margarita ejaculated. The implied criticism in the tone of her voice could hardly have been sharper if he had announced he was setting off with Andrea to the North Pole.

About three-quarters of an hour later, the time being eleven o'clock, Andrea, the ancient fisherman, had backed the stern of his boat against the flat rock at the end of the promontory which served the Torre Saracena as a quay. With Andrea was one of his grandsons, a young faun of twelve, preoccupied with the pastime of picking up a crablet with his lithe brown toes and dropping it again. His grandfather let out a reproachful yell to summon him to his senses and carry the *signorino's* package into the boat. Pino dropped the crablet and sprang over the thwarts to fetch the lunch and the wine.

As the boat glided out upon the glassy sea, above the creaking of the rowlocks the sound of bagpipes followed their progress. The *zampognari* had come down from the mountains to play their Christmas tunes.

When John had last landed on the Galli the aromatic herbage had been parching fast in the June sun. He and Julius and Leonora had spent a sun-steeped day among the fragments of broken mosaic which time had left here to commemorate the pavement of some old Roman who had built himself a summer villa on the largest of the three islets. This was covered now with tazetta narcissus whose white petals and yellow cups drenched the air with fragrance, growing so thick that the great bulbs pushed one another up out of the shallow soil. Reclining on a rug John ate his lunch and drank his wine. Down in the boat Andrea drowsed after his food. Pino, tired with leaping from rock to rock, lay slumberous among the flowers. There was no sign of the kingfishers whose seaward flight had tempted him to this islet.

The silence was profound. The piping of the *zampognari* was unheard beyond these stupendous limestone precipices of the peninsula. The water was too calm for even the faintest sigh to rise from the shore. No fly buzzed. A lizard lured from its crevice by this halcyon time sounded noisy, as it darted across the dry flaky tops of the narcissus bulbs.

A piece of the newspaper in which the lunch had been wrapped caught John's eye, and he began to read:

Mr Lloyd George declared that we must guarantee ourselves against a repetition of Germany's crime by destroying Kaiserism and militarism and by allowing the German people to enjoy democratization. The Russian Revolution might have postponed complete victory, but it had made victory more sure and of a better quality. He ended with these words: "My appeal is this: that we should continue to fight for the great goal of international right and international justice, so that never again can brute force sit on the throne of justice, nor barbaric strength wield the sceptre of right. . . ."

Dealing with the German Peace Offensive, Mr Asquith said that peace was the supreme interest of mankind, but subject to the all-important condition that it did not defeat the purpose for which the free democratic nations entered upon the war—freedom and justice and the destruction of the Kaiserism which made freedom and justice an impossibility while it prevailed. Belgium and Serbia must be restored. We should not be helping the advent of peace if we were to give the impression that there was any faltering in our determination to carry the burden which we had taken up with a clear conscience to rid Europe of militarism. . . .

Mr Bonar Law declared that people who talked about peace now had no conception of the real issue which was being fought out. The German peace offer was too vague. What in effect it said was that Germany, having achieved her object by the devastation and destruction of Serbia and her brutal violation of Belgium, was ready to make peace. That was not enough. We could not sheath the sword until we had absolute security that the same danger which had ruined this generation might not ruin our children. A patched-up peace would spell disaster. Nothing but a real and abiding peace could justify the suffering and sacrifice caused by the war. He wondered if Mr Ramsay MacDonald and his friends, who were so anxious that His Majesty's Government should state clearly the terms on which they were prepared to treat for peace with Germany, realized the harm they were doing to the cause of peace. His Majesty's Government had repeatedly stated the object of this war. It was to destroy

Kaiserism and militarism. We had no quarrel with the German people. When Kaiserism and militarism were destroyed it would be time to talk about a peace founded upon liberty and justice for all, on a peace which would make any repetition of a war like this impossible. . . .

John sighed. How serviceable an act to humanity if one after another the members of the war cabinet could be brought to these islets and kept here for eight hours of this halcyon weather to meditate in solitude upon peace! They never escaped from one another, as it was, and like schoolboys each of them was afraid to be thought different from his companions. The danger of letting this war change from a war for definite objects into a war for abstractions was that when the war was over the abstractions would disappear in a hitherto undeclared set of definite objects, and that the exhaustion of the victors would expect to renew its strength from the more complete exhaustion of the vanquished. That the Allies would win was certain. Whether an ultimately overwhelming victory was the best thing for the future peace of Europe was less certain. Could the Germans be obliterated no doubt it would be an advantage to the rest of the world. But they could not be obliterated, and that being the case they must be civilized. The process of civilizing them must involve a recognition of the grievances which had always made them such a pestilential nuisance. And the fact that they used such intolerable means to remedy their grievances did not give their opponents the right to deny the existence of any cause for grievances. Undoubtedly the best result of the war from a material point of view would be a close alliance between England, Germany and the United States—for these three nations, yes, but it might be hellish for the rest of the world to find itself dominated by a self-righteous and omnipotent commercial combine. And then there was Russia. The war might last long enough to bring about all over the rest of Europe what had happened in Russia, or Russia might produce a Napoleon. He must write to Emil. He had not heard from him for months. In Stockholm he must have better facilities than anywhere else for knowing what was really happening in Russia.

Well, one thing seemed certain, and that was that for the rest of his life true peace would never return to mankind. It would take a hundred years to recover from this convulsion.

"And just across there," he murmured, "three and a half years ago to-day we heard the news of the Archduke's assassination."

He stared pensively across the pale blue water to where the horn of Minerva's cape hid the far horizon of the west.

"Another world began to vanish that day, and soon there will be as little left of it as of the world of Imperial Rome."

He scooped up a handful of broken mosaic and let the fragments trickle through his fingers. It was time to row back. The chill of the afternoon was already perceptible upon this sweet-scented air, and there were the kingfishers again, winged with blue fire as they flew landward away from the sun.

The Torre Saracena was heavy with the perfume of narcissus that evening when John sat down to dinner, and later mingled with it was the sharp fragrance of mandarin oranges. How grandly the Italians had held their ground, he thought as he read his *Mattino*, sipping a potent glass of Cento Erbe, the bottle gleaming like a great tourmaline in the lamplight.

Suddenly there was a loud knocking on the door of the tower. John went to open it himself, for Margarita and Caterina were hastily washing up in the kitchen before going home, and in any case would have been too timorous to go to the door. They had been so much frightened by an owl two nights ago that their fifteen-year-old brother Pasquale had now been commandeered to escort them up the dangerous path through the rosemary and myrtles which ran nearly a quarter of a lonely mile before the comparative safety of the first cobbled alley was achieved. Pasquale, not relishing this quarter of a mile in the dark by himself, arrived before dusk and spent his time strumming on a mandoline until his sisters were ready.

John found outside seventeen-year-old Carlo, another member of Fofo's family.

"*Buona sera, signorino. Ecco il signore!*" he announced triumphantly.

"Begod, Judge, it *is* you!"

"Fitz! Have you escaped from Dartmoor?" John asked in amazement.

"Escaped from Dartmoor? We were all sent back to Ireland last summer. I couldn't wire you from Rome because I'm not there as Edward Fitzgerald, but let me come in and I'll tell you all about it."

John gazed at his old friend in the light.

"Why, Fitz, you're going grey."

"Begod, it's a wonder my hair isn't snow white."

"But where's your baggage?" John asked.

"I left it up at the inn. I didn't know what I was going to find. Give me a drink, though."

John poured out a glass of Cento Erbe. Fitz swallowed it at a gulp, and looked at his host with respect.

"That's the second real kick I've had out of this country. The other was when I was received by the Holy Father. What is this green liquid? Up the Republic!"

What impressed John about his old friend was that in

spite of obvious signs of physical and mental strain he had lost completely the savage bitterness which used to be always latent and liable to assert itself in his most hilarious moods. It was a spiritually happy man who sat on the other side of the white porcelain stove in the library, at the top of the Torre Saracena.

"I suppose it's because you have already gathered some of the fruits of action," he said. "All I've done for the last three years seems about as much use as the energy a fly wastes flying round and round a chandelier."

"Ah, Judge, there's a hell of a lot more to be done yet. I hope they don't keep me too long in Rome. I don't believe I was ever meant to be a diplomat. And, damn it, the reason they sent me at all was so insulting. My English accent!"

"It's not conspicuous," John assured him.

"It's conspicuous in the Kingdom of Kerry. Begod when I started practising at Tinoran they wouldn't believe I was a doctor. They thought I was a shooting tenant. But when they saw the kind of cartridges I brought from London they knew I was a shooting permanency. Yet, at the end, I missed the real fighting."

"You weren't in Dublin?"

"No, I was in the Kerry Brigade, and Eoin MacNeill called off any movement of the Volunteers on Easter Sunday. Luckily I was one of those who were detailed by Austin Stack to help with the landing of the arms from the German ship. So I played my part in that poor bloody muddle, and was condemned to death. However, I got off with penal servitude for twenty years."

"I know," said John. "I was in Salonica at the time. I thought you would probably be in Dublin, and expected all the time to hear you'd been killed. I wrote to you."

"I never had your letter."

"It was seized by the military authorities. I wrote to your mother too."

"I know. She showed it to me. The Censor left in a few words."

John told Fitz about his interview with Colonel Skinner over the letter to him.

"What really upset the military authorities was that I said you could rely on the taurine stupidity of Sir John Maxwell to win round the mass of Irish opinion to support your aspirations."

"You were right, Judge. And he was disappointed. He had a grave dug in the yard at Arbour Hill to hold a hundred dead, but they never let the poor old b—— fill it. It was the Bishop of Limerick who handed it to him when he demanded he should throw out of their parishes some of the priests in his diocese who had sympathized with the insurgents. I've got a copy of his letter to the Press with me. I had it translated into Italian and sent round to influential quarters in Rome. Listen to this."

He took a cutting from his pocket-book and read:

> You took care that no plea for mercy should interpose on behalf of the poor young fellows who surrendered to you in Dublin. The first intimation which we got of their fate was the announcement that they had been shot in cold blood. Personally I regard your action with horror, and I believe that it has outraged the conscience of the country.

"It's not often a Bishop speaks out like that," said John.

"You're right, Judge. There's too many of them tie the lappets of their mitres round their eyes when it comes to looking for trouble. Nevertheless, in spite of what Dr O'Dwyer thought of him, we owe a lot to Maxwell. He proved to Ireland that the British were the same as ever. Just Prussians who'd let their hair grow and parted it neatly on the side."

"I wish you wouldn't say British when you mean English," John exclaimed irritably.

"Oh, to hell with that, Judge. The worst things the

English have done have been done by Scots. What's Maxwell himself? Yes, yes, there's the decayed remains of an Irish colony in the West Highlands, but they've been good Britons for a century and a half. And what about Lloyd George? He's a Welshman, isn't he? And who's more British? He's the boy that's going to slip partition over on us if he can."

"All right. We won't start this old argument again. Tell me more about your own adventures," John asked.

"Well, we were handcuffed in pairs and sent over to English jails. I was taken to Dartmoor. That was built to hold the American prisoners of the Revolution. It's a great old monument to what the English think about those who prefer to rule themselves. There were about sixty of us there and we elected De Valera to be our commandant. Judge, that's a great man, and if he doesn't make the British, beg pardon, Judge, the English—make the English hop for it before he's finished with them, I'll settle down and become the President of the local Unionist Association. I'll tell you the kind of man he is. After we'd been in Dartmoor for about a month we were all lined up for inspection one morning staring in silence at the jailers lined up opposite, and down the iron stairs of that damned Central Hall came a body of new prisoners. The first of them was Eoin MacNeill. He's a big man, MacNeill. He had the guts to call off the Rising when he was Chief of Staff of the Volunteers because he believed it would cause the deaths of young men without any gratitude from the country as a whole. And begod, he was right, for if Maxwell and the British Government hadn't started shooting the men that surrendered to them the very way ungentlemanly Germans might have shot gallant little Belgians, the country would have been grateful. I tell you when they were driving back from the Fairyhouse Races that Easter Monday the people of Dublin were spitting and cursing for the way the rebels had upset their country. Where was I? Yes, well, when Eoin MacNeill came down those iron stairs that morning there were a lot of the boys felt bitter about MacNeill, and Dev must have known what it would mean if we split up amongst ourselves. So what did he do? He stepped out of the line and turned right about to face us as if he was one of the bloody jailers himself. 'Irish Volunteers!' he shouted, 'Attention! Eyes left!' And all of us obeyed as if we were on the parade ground, and gave Eoin MacNeill the salute. Now that was mutiny, Judge, and Dev could have been given the cat for that. Two jailers jumped for him, and marched him off to the separate cells. Luckily the Prison Governor had more sense than Maxwell, and Dev wasn't punished. But what a man, eh?"

"The man who won the East Clare election?"

"He'll win more than East Clare, Judge. Well, we played up Dartmoor while we were there, and all over the country the political prisoners were playing up the English jails. In the end they decided to concentrate all the so-called convicts in one prison—Lewes. We at Dartmoor went there handcuffed to a chain, though it's fair to admit we wouldn't give our word not to try to escape on the journey. We made it hot for Lewes jail. Last May under Dev's leadership we struck from working at convicts' labour and demanded to be treated as prisoners of war. When we were confined to our cells we broke the furniture. We even broke some of the partitions. Then they tried separating us again. Some were sent to Portland, some to Parkhurst, some to Maidstone. I was sent to Parkhurst, and we nearly broke the heart of Parkhurst. Dev was at Maidstone. At last, in the middle of June, we were told we were to be released next day and sent home, for by this time it was necessary for the British to do something about American opinion. Well, I suppose we expected we'd have some kind of a welcome from Ireland, but we didn't expect the welcome we were given."

For a moment Fitz hesitated.

"Damn it, Judge," he suddenly exclaimed with emotion. "I needn't try to pretend to you that it didn't mean everything, that welcome. They'd been waiting for us all night on the quays. Nobody in Dublin did a stroke of work that day, and they drove us in cars through the cheering crowds. There wasn't a hill in Ireland without a bonfire, and music in every village. We went away from a people that thought we were a pack of young fools who'd spoilt things for Johnnie Redmond and we came back to find a nation risen from the dead bodies of those who offered themselves as a sacrifice of blood."

Fitzgerald crossed himself, his pale blue eyes burning into the future. John felt his throat tighten. The silence in that room was holy.

"Don't look so solemn, Judge dear," Fitz said. "Who'd have thought that night you sat on the kerb in Claverton Street as drunk as an owl and told me you were the Inchcape Rock that I'd find you one day seventeen years later sitting up in a tower like the good old Abbot of Aberbrothock himself, and Ireland in sight of freedom at last?"

"But how did you find yourself in Italy, Fitz? You haven't told me that yet."

"It was thought advisable to present some aspects of our case in Rome, and they picked me for the job. I wouldn't care to call myself the official emissary of the Irish Republic, because, you'll understand, they're a cautious lot in Rome. Ah, I'm just taking soundings. Put it that way. A good deal will depend on whether the British Government try to force conscription on Ireland. If they do, let 'em see what they get. I'm going back after Christmas."

"Didn't you have any difficulty about your passport?"

"None at all. I got my passport in London. A respectable medical man who had business with a patient in Italy. It's an advantage to have had a public-school education when you're dealing with English officials. About the only advantage, I might add. Parnell missed the public-school, but he was at Cambridge. He could speak the language. And it's a bump for a sober Englishman when what he'd like to think was a poor bloody provincial Irishman can tell him in his own language that if the British Empire broke up to-morrow all that would remain of it in a hundred years' time would be a faint perplexity why it lasted so long."

"I wouldn't go as far as that," said John, with a smile.

"What will it leave?" the Irishman challenged.

"A sense of responsibility. Yes, I daresay often misplaced, but always growing. A fundamental decency. A capacity for forgiveness. . . ."

"It would need that," Fitz broke in, "with such a burden of crime upon its shoulders."

"Toleration. . . ."

"Only since it has grown fatter and lazier," Fitz broke in again.

"Would you prefer a Teutonic Empire?" John asked.

"I don't want any damned empires at all. I want small nations and small states. Why should Ireland's natural development have been throttled for seven hundred years because England found it convenient for her own safety and her own trade? Why should we have had a lot of blasted Scots planted in Ulster to act as policemen for England? There'd be a fine song if a horde of Protestant Germans were planted in Belgium at the end of this war. The British are quick enough to shout about the freedom of small nations when it serves the balance of power in Europe. But they don't love small nations for themselves. They only love them when they're a hindrance to other big nations."

"What worries me about the independence of Ireland is whether it won't come too late," John said.

"It'll come soon enough," Fitz prophesied.

"Yes, but whether, however soon it come, it won't have come too late," John insisted. "The way the world has moved through the nineteenth century and is moving faster than ever now I doubt if it's any longer possible for a small nation to be anything except a second-rate imitation of a great one. It'll depend on what happens after this infernal war. My dread at present is that it will have speeded up material progress. Obviously flying will go ahead. And wireless. And I suppose motoring. And America by coming in like this is bound to come out of the war the richest of all. And that means Americanization. Or else the war will go on so long that the Russian Revolution will spread, which may be a good thing, though I can't say I like the sound of these people called Bolsheviks."

"Ireland can stand aside from all that if she is free from British domination. We are not an industrial nation. We can still preserve a sane decent life for the individual."

"Yes, if the individual desires it," John agreed. "But I wonder if the individual's personality hasn't already been too much sapped by the all-round tendency toward living not as his own integral self, but as one of a lot of other individuals. I noticed that tendency leaping ahead in America before the war, and it's certain that after this infernal war Europe will go the way of America, not America the way of Europe. Comfort and amusement, that is what man craves to assuage the boredom of modern work caused by machinery, and to which he has now had added the boredom of modern war."

"I tell you Ireland is not an industrial country."

"I hope I'm wrong, Fitz. I can't tell you how much I hope I am wrong."

"Remember one of the things we shall do is to revive the Irish language. We're out to restore Gaelic culture. I don't think you need worry about Ireland's future, Judge. We'll keep ourselves to ourselves when we're free. But anyway what is the use of talking about what we will do when we are not yet free to do it? Freedom first. That's worth dying for, no matter what it leads to. And don't forget, the jibe at Irishmen has always been that they can't help quarrelling among themselves. If we started talking too much now about what we'll do with our freedom we'd lose our present unity of purpose and with it the freedom we're seeking. But that's enough of shop for to-night. I came down here to see you, Judge, not to talk about myself, or for that matter about Ireland. This is the worst kind of a busman's holiday."

The eloquent mouth was widened yet further than its normal width in a grin. The light-blue eyes glittered merrily. The thin peaked nose lost its fierceness.

"I wish I had a bottle of Johnny Jameson," John exclaimed.

"Don't be wishing anything of the kind. This green cordial was brewed by the fairies. I must smuggle a bottle back with me." He poured himself out another glass of Cento Erbe.

"When the war's over you must invite me to Caragh," John told him.

"You've not met Nora yet."

"No, I'm looking forward to that, and to seeing your mother again."

"Poor soul, it's she that won't forget 1916."

"No, nor many another woman in Europe," John added. He could not help it. Much as he loved Fitz and Emil, there were moments when he had to remind them that the Irish and the Jews did not share the monopoly of the world's suffering. He was remembering the starving refugees in Chios and Mytilene, and the women in Australia whose sons had died twelve thousand miles away, and old Medlicott flinging Ralph's posthumous D.S.O. through the stained-glass coat of arms in the red drawing-room at Medlicott Hall.

"You haven't asked me yet, Judge, how I found out you were down in Citrano here," said Fitz, divining John's faint resentment but not resenting it himself because he could never forget that there had once been a time when John was the only creature alive who would listen to his political dreams as if they were matter of fact plans for spending to-morrow afternoon. "It was through a pleasant Yank I met in Paris at the theatre. I saw that Gabrielle Derozier was playing and found myself next to this pleasant Yank. We got into conversation and I mentioned that I'd seen her in a play of yours some years ago, and he turned out to be a friend of yours—Wacey Langridge."

"His wife's here now."

"I know. She's a beauty, isn't she?"

"Did Wacey tell you that?"

"He gave me that impression. Augh, he was a nice simple soul. I liked the way he bragged about his wife. Now, don't spoil it by telling me she's not a beauty."

"She is," said John, after a moment's hesitation. He was uncomfortably conscious of a kind of disloyalty to Athene in admitting as much, for he knew how much she would dislike the notion of Wacey's talking about her like that to a stranger. He hoped when he introduced Fitz to Athene that he would not tell her what Wacey had said. She would be shy enough without that, and he did not want to hear Fitz criticize her self-consciousness.

"Well, I trust I shall have a chance to meet this charmer," Fitz was saying.

"Of course, of course. We'll go to tea at the Villa Allegra to-morrow."

"Then I'll sleep on that prospect, Judge. God, it's

good to see you again. I used to think about you in jail and wonder if you'd be dead when I came out of it."

"In a way I *am* dead at the moment."

"What the hell do you mean by that?"

"Oh, just war-weariness. I'm beginning to wonder if it will have been all worth while when peace comes."

They went to tea at the Villa Allegra next day. Athene was wearing a vivid green jumper which Fitz hailed as a pretty compliment.

"Why, I hadn't thought I had so much instinctive tact," she declared.

"Don't flatter yourself, Fitz. She was just as likely to be wearing an equally bright orange affair," John mocked.

"And that's enough from you, John," Athene laughed. "War doesn't give us poor females a chance to buy new clothes. So you met my husband in Paris, Mr Fitzgerald?"

"We met at the theatre where Gabrielle Derozier was acting."

"Gabrielle Derozier? Why, you brought her to lunch at the Allegra, John."

"Not one of my most successful introductions," he said, with a smile. "Poor Gabrielle was feeling the effects of a scirocco. That'll soon be five years ago."

"Your husband told me she was an old friend of you both," said Fitz.

John noticed that Athene's eyebrows rose a trifle as she murmured something about the ease with which Wacey made friends.

"Ah now, don't be saying that, Mrs Langridge, or I shall think you're having a cut at me."

"No, please, Mr Fitzgerald, you mustn't think that. I'd be heartbroken if you thought that."

"And I'd be heartbroken too," said Fitz, "after hearing so much about you from your husband."

"Wacey talked about me, did he?" Athene asked.

"Of course he talked about you," John put in quickly. "You know he always talks about you. So should I if I were Wacey."

"Would you, John? I wonder if you would."

Although the tone in which this was said accorded with the prevailing mood of light-hearted chaff, he had an uneasy sense of an emotion behind it nigh to anger.

"Of course I should, Athene," he insisted.

"Oh, well, we know that men always rally to the support of one another," she declared. "Mr Fitzgerald will be telling me in a moment that he and Wacey did not take two lovely ladies out to supper."

"And we did not, Mrs Langridge," Fitz assured her earnestly.

Was it then no more than the anxious jealousy of the commonplace wife? Fitz evidently thought so by the warmth with which he was now beginning to elaborate the theme of Wacey's preoccupation with the woman he had left behind.

"I give you my word, Mrs Langridge," he wound up, "that your husband and I spent the rest of the night till two in the morning bragging to each other about our wives over a bottle of whisky."

Luckily for John's embarrassment Arthur was escorted into the room at that moment by Maddalena. In a state of obviously high spiritual exaltation he announced in Italian that he had met the large dog belonging to the Contessa, that he had stroked it, and that it had licked his face. St George returning home after slaying the Dragon might have been in a similar mood of satisfied audacity.

"Darling, I didn't quite understand," said Athene, whose Italian loitered far behind her young son's.

"*Tu non capisci mai, mamma,*" Arthur muttered reproachfully.

"Would you be kind and tell mamma in English?"

"*No,*" Arthur replied stoutly. "*Io non voglio parlare inglese.*"

"That's the boy!" Fitz declared with enthusiasm. "I hope to God my own Padraig will hold fast to Irish like that. It's myself that will be the proud father when I can't understand a word of what he's saying to me."

"You never told me you had a son, Fitz," John exclaimed in surprise.

"Born three months after I went to jail, and a future President of the Irish Republic."

Athene looked bewildered, but before she meant to understand what Fitz was talking about she meant to hear the details of her son's adventure.

"He met the Contessa's big dog, stroked it, and had his face licked," John explained.

"Maddalena!" Athene protested.

Maddalena disclaimed her own responsibility. The encounter had taken place in a narrow street and she had been afraid to drag Arthur away for fear of his being devoured by *quella brutta bestia.*

"Much wiser to let him face up to the animal," John said.

"But, John, I think it's disgusting. Being licked all over his face by that brute."

"What kind of a fearful dog is this?" Fitz asked.

"It's a big white Maremma sheepdog," said John, "which belongs to an American woman married to a shrivelled little Calabrian count. Legend says she has trained it to fetch him in its mouth when he's wanted, as a collie is trained to fetch its master's slippers."

"*È un cane molto grande,*" announced Arthur, who had listened with sturdy complacency to John's account of the dog, for in spite of his refusal to speak English he understood it perfectly.

"Well, I think it's absurd for Contessa del Bufalò to let that great brute of hers wander around the way it does. Now, listen, darling," Athene went on, turning to her son. "I don't want you to stroke any more big dogs."

"*Va bene*," Arthur agreed, with what might have seemed an exquisite filial docility if above the lips that gave the promise two eyes had not been fixed intently upon a dish of cakes.

"Very well, you can take one," his mother told him.

There was no hesitation about the one he wanted. It was the largest in the dish. With it in his grasp Arthur retired with Maddalena to the nursery, uttering eloquent encomiums in Italian upon his booty.

"You must have thought me very rude, Mr Fitzgerald," said Athene. "You were telling me about your boy, and all I did was to pay attention to Arthur."

"Serve him right," John said. "It was the first time he's mentioned this heir."

"Augh, when the happy father is in jail on these occasions, the rejoicings are curtailed."

"In jail?" Athene repeated. "In prison?"

John hurriedly explained why Fitz had been in prison. Nevertheless she was obviously still perplexed.

"It's like one of Wacey's ideas for a book he's going to write," she said at last; and John knew that this was her measure for the fantastic and improbable.

Later, when he and Fitz were back in the tower, Fitz remarked:

"Curious! That pleasant Yank gave me quite another notion of what his wife would be like. But I might have guessed that anybody with so soft a voice would have dug up something hard to keep the home fires burning."

"You think she's hard?"

"Hard? She'd make adamant feel like a rubber hot-water bottle."

"She isn't hard with that young son of hers."

"That's true," Fitz agreed. "But motherhood breaks any rule a woman sets herself. And the softer she is with that kid, the harder she'll be with the rest of the world to make up for it."

"I'm very fond of her," said John.

Fitz glanced sharply at him.

"Oh no, not in that way. Even if I get over my prejudice against falling in love with other men's wives I should not fall in love with Athene Langridge."

"Why not?"

"What a damned idiotic question! As if one could give reasons for not falling in love. She happens not to be the kind of woman with whom I do fall in love. Besides, I was in love with a girl in Greece, and she was drowned last summer."

John was angry with himself for having said as much, but having done so he set himself to the task of telling the whole story. He was astonished, and somewhat shocked, to find that the tale was as easy to tell as some tragic legend of the remote past. No wonder he had said to Fitz last night that he was dead at the moment. He was dead. This was the proof of his mental condition.

"I'm sorry, Judge, I let you in for that," said Fitz.

"To-morrow if this weather holds we'll go out to the Galli," John announced to close further discussion of Athene Langridge.

The weather held fine over Christmas when, after ten days of long walks in the hills above Citrano and visits to Amalfi and Sorrento and Capri, Fitzgerald went back to Rome. Then the weather broke, with heavy gales from the west.

A week later came a letter from Rome:

Dear Judge,

I've had my orders and I leave here to return to Ireland within a few days. It was good to get a glimpse of you again. I'm no hand at all at writing letters, and I'm not likely to get down with a pen what I couldn't manage to get across by my mouth. But it's this way. What's the matter with you *is that you can't see the trees for the wood. You've been so busy running around to do your bit to keep the British Empire on its feet that there's nothing to show for it. Well, how the hell can there be? It's too big. You hadn't the luck to be born an Irishman. If you had been you'd have seen your road clear before you, and whatever happened to you personally on that road you'd have taken it and stuck to it. A small country and a worldwide religion. That's the happy combination, Judge. You've got to find one or the other if you can't find both. Now where will you find the small country? Scotland, says you. There's not a chance of it to my thinking, but if you can stir up Scotland, good luck to you. Meanwhile, the worldwide religion is at your elbow. You're living in a Christian country now. Why not take advantage of it? You can't write at present because you've got no definite faith. You can't do anything without that. If you were an honest-to-God atheist you'd have something more positive behind you. But how the hell can you worship the Great Perhaps? I count the large multitude of Perhapsers as half dead. That's why you think you're dead now. Just because you* are *a Perhapser. What's the good of your bloody plays? There's nothing behind them. You're like an old woman piddling about with a game of Patience.*

I never said anything about what you told me of that girl you lost, because it was no good saying anything to a Perhapser. It wasn't that I didn't feel for you, Judge, but what could I say? She's gone from this world, and perhaps there's nothing left of her in eternity, and perhaps there is. Do believe one thing or the other. Believe she still is, in which case if she loved you she's praying for your happiness now. Or believe there's nothing left of her, in which case forget her. But come to some conclusion.

Well, that's enough! I love you, Judge, because you meant a thundering lot to me at school when I was savage with misery. I'd sooner hear you were happy than any man I know. So forgive this letter.

Yours ever

Fitz

I've just heard that the fools are seriously thinking of trying to conscript us in Ireland. Let them try. Will nobody persuade the silly bastards who run Britain that the rest of the world thinks them silly bastards?

John sat down at once to write his answer:

TORRE SARACENA,
CITRANO
Jan. 15, '18.

Dear Fitz,

I perfectly understand how maddening my uncertainty is to a temperament like yours, but how is my uncertainty to be cured? I should be as happy as any man in Europe if I could achieve that assurance the lack of which you seem to suggest is due to nothing except my own deliberate and cultivated feebleness. Never for a moment have I been aware of any desire not to believe because the acceptance of a supernatural creed would interfere with the freedom of self-indulgence. And this I take to be a most powerful sub-conscious inhibition with many. I should sacrifice nothing I know of, were faith granted to me. I recognize the ability of the human will to overcome the seven deadly sins, but I cannot discover how the human will can acquire the three theological virtues. It seems to me that a man cannot believe, or hope, or love without the grace of God. But if that grace be withheld? I suppose you would argue that such a question implies in me such an obstinate retention of pride that until I can rid myself of it grace must be withheld because the channel is closed against it.

All I can say is that I have repeatedly prayed for faith and so far as I know expelled from my mind every thought that resists it; but I have never been granted faith. You must not suppose that my uncertainty is due to any encouragement of a careless or indifferent attitude. Perhaps I am a child of a generation incapable of withstanding the strain of so much fresh knowledge playing upon it, knowledge which, though it may mock the easy and complacent materialism of the nineteenth century, mocks equally the ancient dogmas of the Catholic creed.

But I do not want to argue, Fitz. All I do want to assure you is that I am not content with ambiguity. I have always envied you your clear horizon, and if I may use the word, perhaps *I shall one day behold one of my own. Meanwhile, my position is that I know humanity would be a better humanity if all of it accepted and carried out the mental and moral obligations of the Catholic creed. But that is not enough for me. I want more than pragmatic truth. If wholeheartedly I agree with you that Catholicism (which I regard as the same thing as Christianity) works, that does not prove to me its truth.*

In political matters I am much more positive. I know with absolute certainty that imperialism produces only a specious appearance of unity, because it is inspired solely by the spirit of greed, gain, and competition. I know that the only composition of a perfect state must be a society of perfect individuals, and I perceive that the universal tendency of contemporary evolution is to destroy the individual and that one method of destroying the individual is to destroy the small state which encourages the individual. I believed (for a very short time) that the intervention of Great Britain on behalf of Belgium was an expression of genuine virtue, but I have learnt that it was a piece of sentimentalism. The treatment of Ireland and of Greece has proved that. An Englishman saw a bully knocking about a small boy and intervened, that was Belgium. The same Englishman prevented his sister from living her life because he wanted her money to support his household, and when she tried to run away he did not hesitate to use violence. That was Ireland.

God knows when peace will come, but I *know already that when it does come whichever side wins the victory will be abused. One group of imperialisms will have defeated another group, and mark my words the rights of small nations will be heeded only as far as they are a convenience to great nations.*

Fitz, Fitz, the human spirit is in chains, and the chains have been forged by man for his own comfort and security. To win this war we are turning ourselves into Germans. We boast that we are fighting for civilization and we revert to the methods of those whom we proclaim the enemies of civilization. But why do I rail to you? Your sole aim at present is to free Ireland. But you have your dreams for that Ireland when she is free. You must dream that she will go back and pick up the strands of a pattern of life that was torn to pieces in the nineteenth century. Oh, the damage done to the spirit of man by Scotsmen like James Watt and Adam Smith, and even before that by Paterson when he helped Dutch William to finance his ruin of Europe by inventing the Bank of England. I sometimes think that since the Reformation Scotland has been the evil genius of England, the 'âme damnée' which John Knox sold to Satan. I believe that's why the Scotsman worships Burns. Burns bids him repent and shows the way to salvation. Burns restores his pride.

And Burns would have understood you, Fitz, when you dream of a country free from the usury of capitalism, of a country where the small man's life will be rich, where the fruits of the earth will be fresh and available and the good husbandman esteemed above the big business man, and . . . oh, I know I told you I feared it was too late to revive a vanished way of life and that the only end of your free Ireland might be a bad provincial imitation of the country from which she has cut herself free. I take that back. So far as Ireland is concerned I will renounce Perhapsism.

And now stimulated by your visit, which did me a power of good, I shall have another shot at writing a play I think worth writing. I hope you'll manage to keep out of Dartmoor this year. Geoffrey Noel who amused you so much has written a sonnet about you, but as I don't think it is really very good I shan't send it to you to be jeered at. I hope your Mother is well. Give her my love and salute Nora and Padraig.

Yours ever,
J. P. O.

The resolution to concentrate again upon writing a play was kept by John. Until the beginning of March he led a completely secluded existence in the tower, even discouraging Geoffrey Noel from coming to see him.

"I understand, of course, my dear man, that when the Muse desires to commune other tongues must be stilled.

Nobis non licet esse tam disertis,
Qui musas colimus severiores.

We who follow the stricter Muses must not chatter too much, to paraphrase Martial. Don't be afraid, my dear man, I shall respect your austere nuptials. I'm too much used to my own company, though I shall enjoy yours when you offer it. Did I tell you I had a postcard from

Francesco? He is hoping for a few days' leave. I must manage to send him a little money somehow, and Vanessa cut me even shorter than usual for my December money and then didn't send it till last week."

From the window of the tower John watched Noel making his way up through the rosemary under a grey January sky. Beheld thus he looked superb, the classic head defying the blows of fortune. Thus, the short legs were hidden by the scrub, the tripping gait was imperceptible.

The play was finished in the second week of March, and by the post next day a letter arrived from Captain Wade to say that if John's health might now be considered re-established there was an interesting job waiting for him.

"I don't know when we shall meet again, Athene," he told her in farewell.

"The war can't go on much longer now surely?"

"I don't see what will stop it. The Germans won't really feel the effect of the American armies until next year. However, I think we can count on its being finished by 1920."

"And you've no idea where you'll be sent?"

"None at all, but it will be to some place of which I have no first-hand knowledge; of that you can be sure. By the way, I telegraphed to Wacey, suggesting he should meet me in Paris if he could manage it."

"That'll be fine."

"I expect he'll wangle a spot of leave later in the spring."

"Do you think so? I don't think so."

"Dear Athene, what makes you so knowledgeable about leave?"

She ignored the question, and took his two hands in hers.

"Come back soon to Citrano, John. We shall all miss you terribly even if you have spent most of your time shut up in your tower like some old prisoner of long ago. And I hope the play will be an absolutely brilliant success."

"I don't think it will," he said.

"But you finished it?"

"Oh yes, I finished it."

" I think that's great. My, what an exquisite day!"

"How the March sun feels like May!" he quoted gaily.

Athene had walked across the courtyard with him, and waved her last farewells until he turned round the corner of the narrow alley over the walls of which peach-blossom was breaking in a line of rosy foam. A pity he should be going back to the war now when spring was here. She wondered, standing pensive on the terrace, whether he would meet Gabrielle Derozier on the way through Paris. Or was that all over long ago? How little she knew about him! She turned back indoors and, pulling open drawer after drawer in her bureau, found at last the small terra-cotta head of Minerva which John had picked up that June day in 1914 and given to her, telling her that she was more like her namesake than it. She could recall now the way he looked, and she had not thought again about that terra-cotta head until to-day. She wished she did know more about him, and that he could know more about her. It would make such a difference if she had a really intimate friend. She hoped Wacey would not succeed in meeting John in Paris. He would be so bent on convincing John that she was pining for him to come home. And John would see through it. She was sure he would see through it. When that Irish friend of his had talked so earnestly to assure her that he and her husband had spent a bachelors' evening together, John had tried to divert him from the topic. For what reason would he have done that except out of sympathy for her?

But the war must come to an end some time and so Wacey must come home some time. And that meant endless endeavours to persuade her by word of mouth to admit she believed that bill from Rome was a mistake of the chemist. There was not a letter he had written since he had been in France in which he had not asked her if she was satisfied that a mistake had been made. It would be easier to write and tell him that she was satisfied than be compelled to listen to his eternal repetitions of the lie. And pleading repetitions! Oh, the muddle, the muddle, the muddle people made of their lives by weakness! Wacey was weak, but in surrendering to his weakness she had been no less weak. However, the war was still going on, and perhaps a way out would be found at the end of it.

Indeed, the war certainly was still going on, as John found out when he reached Paris. He had been spared the long journey by troop train to which British officers had been condemned on account of the inability of some of them to behave themselves even like temporary gentlemen, as the sneer went, on their way through Italy. For this he had to thank the opportunity of conveying home a couple of bags from the Embassy in Rome. To be sure, the usual travelling female who attached herself to the Messenger as a tick to a sheep had attached herself to him; but he shook her off in Paris where Wacey Langridge met him, looking as well as it was possible for anybody to look in the khaki uniform of an American officer.

"Why, this is corking, John! But say, have you heard the news?"

"No."

"The Germans broke through the British lines yesterday west of St Quentin, and the Fifth Army is being driven back in confusion. They say Byng's Third Army will have to retreat too. It's queer you should have cabled me to meet you to-day, because my General was fetched from St Nazaire in a hurry. So I should have had to come anyway. They say we'll probably have to brigade some of our fellows with the French and British to help stop the rot."

"There's not likely to be a French or British rot," said John, a little stiffly.

"No, you don't get me. The situation's terrible. We can't throw into the line American troops that haven't completed their training unless they're brigaded with British or French troops. Which way are you crossing?"

"By Havre."

"That's all right. I doubt if you'd get through by Boulogne. If the Germans reach Amiens I wouldn't put it past them to reach Paris."

"Paris?" John echoed in consternation.

"Sure! We must hand it to the Boches."

"Paris?" John repeated.

"No, not Paris necessarily, but we must hand it to them for an offensive like this in the fourth year of the war. They've taken 16,000 prisoners and 200 guns already. Where will you stay to-night?"

"The Ritz, I think. You'll dine with me?"

"Sure thing."

Apprehension brooded over the Ritz that night. The voices of the diners mingled in one tense note, unbroken by a laugh. The waiters were absent-minded.

"Well, how did you leave them all in Citrano?" Wacey asked.

"All well and peaceful there. Athene sent you much love."

"She's beginning to worry when I'm going to have my leave. I tell her she can't expect to see me yet awhile, and any chance there might have been has vanished with this business of yesterday."

"I'm sure she quite appreciates that," said John. 'What shall we drink?"

"The drinks are on me to-night."

"You're my guest," John objected.

"No, John, the drinks are on me The dinner is on you. Waiter, put two bottles of the Heidsieck 1911 on ice." Then turning to John, he added, "I'm damned if I'm going to leave that champagne to the Boches."

John knew that Wacey would be happier in paying for the drinks, and he ceased to argue.

"We had news of you of course from my friend Fitzgerald," he said.

"Yes, wasn't it a queer thing meeting him like that and being able to put him wise to your whereabouts? I didn't see him on his way back. I hope he doesn't get into too much trouble. I never cared a lot for the Irish, but I took a liking to him. I suppose everything between you and Gabrielle Derozier is finished long ago, John?"

"She hasn't acted in any of my plays for a long time. Well, naturally, I haven't had any time for plays."

"She's a great actress. Shall you call around and see her to-morrow?"

"No, no. I can't cart these bags all over Paris," John replied, glancing down under the table to see that they were safely at his feet. John was glad of the excuse that the heavily leaded bags gave him. It was absurd of course, but somehow he did not fancy the idea of Wacey's writing to Athene about the dash he had made to see Gabrielle.

"You know, John," Wacey began when they were sitting over their coffee and *fine* in a secluded corner of the great hotel, "you know, this is the first time that Athene and I have been separated since we were married. I've loved her since she was fourteen years old, and I'm finding this separation pretty tough."

"I expect you do."

"And I know Athene's finding it tough. She's looking well, though, you say?"

"She's looking more lovely than ever."

"She is a lovely girl. Being her husband, I oughtn't to say it, but darn it, I don't see why a man shouldn't be proud of his wife."

"Oh, it's not a rule without exceptions," John murmured, turning in his embarrassment to jejune sarcasm and wishing that Wacey would talk about the German break through instead of about his wife.

"I guess most men when they find themselves fixed the way we're fixed on active service can't help themselves, but I just don't see any other woman. I don't take any credit to myself for being faithful to Athene. Don't misunderstand me there. I just don't see any other woman. Athene jollies me when she writes about the gay time I must be having, but you bet your life she knows I'm as safe in Paris as I would be in Citrano."

"Has there been an evening communiqué?" John asked.

"Not since the one we read. I wouldn't worry too much about that. Maybe it's not so bad as it sounded at first. I wish you could have seen Athene when she was fourteen. I don't believe there ever was anything so lovely. I just fell for her like that. There was lots of trouble with her father because it seemed kind of all wrong to have me seriously proposing to a daughter of fourteen. In fact I was forbidden the Gilmer house for quite a while. I had to wait six years for her."

"A very satisfactory achievement all the same," John observed.

"I'd have waited sixteen," Wacey declared fervidly.

John knew that he was being invited to ask if Athene had loved him since she was a schoolgirl, and he would have gratified Wacey but that it seemed as if Athene herself away over the Alps was forbidding him. So, lamely, he said he was sure Wacey would have waited.

"The only thing that worries me," the husband continued, "is that I can't hit it with a book. I don't give a damn for myself, but I know Athene would be tickled to death if I made a name for myself. You can't blame her. We're like that in America. That's why I prefer to live in Europe. However, I guess that when this war's over I'll have lots to write about, and maybe I won't be so critical of myself. I believe this war will put a hell of a kick into art all around."

"You do? I'm afraid I think just the reverse. I found when I got back to Citrano that plays didn't seem worth while. I have written one, but if I find a producer I'm dead certain it won't run a fortnight."

"Why not write a novel?"

"I should find that just as little worth while. Besides I never did see life in terms of a novel even before the war, and now . . . I don't know, Wacey. I believe we're in a bad period for any of the arts."

Fortunately Wacey was prepared to be argumentative on this subject, and the rest of the evening passed away without any more uxorious reminiscence.

That night the sirens sounded an air-raid warning, but there were no aeroplanes over Paris. The city was being bombarded by a German gun. So the Boches must have advanced even further than had been revealed by the communiqués. Yet for once neither of the High Commands had lied. The German gun was seventy-five miles away, and though the British were falling back in what was unpleasantly like confusion all was not yet lost.

When John had left the Rome bags at the Foreign Office he walked along to Captain Wade's headquarters. It was one of those grey, blighted, still days which so often follow the spring equinox, when like an old Prime Minister clinging to office winter lays a dead hand upon the youth of the year. The air tasted of verdigris and smelt of soot. The Thames was like an unwiped knife. The buildings on the Surrey side loomed through an ashen mist. On such a day even the view from Adelphi Terrace was drear.

While John was waiting to see the Chief, his mind, under the influence of the weather and the news from the western front, preoccupied with the depressing sameness of this *milieu*, James Yarrow came into the room.

"James! At last an exotic note in a bistre symphony!" he exclaimed.

"Do you know what the old man has in view for you?" Yarrow asked.

"Not a notion. Do you?"

"No, but whatever it is and wherever it is, put in for my services."

"I should say I would!"

"Because if I have to endure much longer the company of Carstairs, Osborne, Hargreaves, Browne-Pawson and Chorley," Yarrow declared, "I shall become a mental casualty. A condition of passive boredom I can stand. In fact it is sometimes even enjoyable like a narcotic. But I cannot stand boredom the only relief of which is acute irritation. Can you imagine what it means to have to sit at a desk opposite Osborne day in day out?"

"Very easily," John replied. "I did it for six months at the beginning of this infernal war."

"I'd forgotten that; but the world of war was young then. An adventurous future was still credible. Osborne's dull fishy eyes spoke of ocean deeps in those days: they speak now of nothing except human stupidity. And I see no reason at present why I should not be sitting at a desk opposite Osborne for another four years and having to listen to his fatuous comments on the extremely inadequate information which is now coming in from the Eastern Mediterranean, unless the Germans bring the war to a speedy end by sweeping right across France and re-embarking the Yanks at St Nazaire. Have you heard the latest news?"

"Only what's in the papers."

"45,000 prisoners and 700 guns, the whole British line from the Scarpe to the Oise in full retreat, Peronne and Bapaume gone, in fact a major disaster, and only the beginning of it at that," Yarrow proclaimed with gloomy relish. "I see no chance for Amiens and very little for Paris itself. And we had such a lot to say about the Italians and Caporetto last autumn when we were throwing away thousands of lives at Passchendaele. I understand that a fog on the morning of March 21st is to be given the blame. Nobody murmurs a word about the fog in the brains of our High Command. I'm not fond of amateur strategists, but they do less harm than these professionals. The military mind escapes my analysis, but as far as I can make out it is composed of the pulp of obsolete textbooks, the discarded fodder of cavalry stables, the . . ."

But James Yarrow's analysis of the military mind was interrupted by a message for John that the Chief was waiting for him.

The pallid Punch's face beyond the paper-scattered desk regarded him intently for several moments.

"You don't look very well yet," Captain Wade observed at last.

"That's because I've been indoors for the last two months writing, sir."

"What at?"

"A play."

"I hope it will make me laugh," the Chief growled.

"I'm afraid not, sir. I've been in no mood to be funny since I left Lipsia."

"Humph! then I shall give your play a miss, Ogilvie. I think we want cheering up in these times. This is a jolly business in France. We'll have the Hindenburg Line running through Piccadilly in a minute."

"That might be to our advantage, sir. Whitehall would then become the front-line trenches."

The old man grinned sardonically.

"Or No Man's Land," he added. "Well, do you feel like returning to work of national importance? I want you to go to Ireland."

"To Ireland?" John gasped. It was as if the dormer-window in the Chief's room looking out across the Thames had been suddenly blown in by a gust of savage wind.

"You have an exceptional chance of doing some really useful work," Captain Wade pressed.

"I don't know why you say that, sir," John countered.

"Isn't one of the more prominent Sinn Feiners an intimate friend of yours?"

John was silent.

"Edward Joseph Aloysius Fitzgerald?" Captain Wade read from a paper in front of him.

"I know him, yes. He was at school with me."

"When did you see him last?" Captain Wade asked, looking up and fixing John with those eyes that behind the thick lenses of the dark tortoiseshell-rimmed spectacles had the hardness and colour of lapis lazuli.

"He stayed with me in Citrano over Christmas," John replied without hesitation, for he guessed that Fitz's visit had been reported to his Chief, and in any case if there was to be a battle between them then he did not desire to fight it on a lie.

"Yes, well, that confirms what was reported to me by the War Office," Captain Wade went on. His tone was grudging. He hated it when the rival military organization to his own was right. "I rather hoped you'd give me a chance to contradict them. What on earth induced you to harbour a fellow who'd been released from Dartmoor?"

"Really, sir, I cannot see what concern it is of the War Office if an old friend spends ten days in my house in Italy."

"It was a bit indiscreet."

"The indiscretion lay with our passport mandarins. They should have been able to prevent his travelling from Kerry to Rome. I did not know he was in Italy until he arrived at my door. Not that it would have made any difference if I had." John went on quickly. "Quite apart from Fitzgerald's having been an intimate friend since boyhood, my sympathies lie with the rebels."

"I know that."

The Chief tossed a sheet of paper across to John. It was the letter he had written to Fitz from Salonica on May 2nd, 1916, when the news of the Easter Rising first reached him. The sapient scholiasts of officialdom had framed his own sentiments in an inky polychrome of marginal notes.

"Have you just seen this letter, sir?" John asked.

"No, this is the second reading of the bill. I made my observations on it nearly two years ago."

John found a marginal note in green ink:

> *This officer's services have been most valuable and are likely to remain so. H. M. W. 14/5/16.*

"Thank you, sir," John said, with a smile. "But you'll admit that my prophecy was only too completely verified?"

Captain Wade grunted.

"That's as may be. As you have these disreputable friends the question now is what use we can make of them."

"I'm afraid, as far as I'm concerned, none, sir," John answered firmly.

"In view of the intention of the Government to impose conscription upon Ireland, and this business in France will hasten the decision, Sir Claude Verity attaches considerable importance to accurate information about the progress and strength of disaffection."

"I'm sure he does," John said. "But if Sir Claude Verity is the man selected for the task let him find his own spies."

"Now, don't talk in that silly way, Ogilvie. You know perfectly well that I have to obey orders . . . just as *you* have to obey orders."

"You can't expect me to obey an order to spy on one of my best friends. You couldn't demand that from your own son," John answered hotly.

"I'm not asking you to spy on this fellow Fitzgerald. What I'm suggesting is that your friendship with him will give you an exceptional opportunity to reach an opinion about what is going on in Ireland."

"That means spying on friends of my friend. It seems to me a distinction without a difference. Besides, even if I knew nobody in Ireland I wouldn't spy on the rebels. They have my sympathy. I should have thought I made that clear in this letter," John said, as he pushed it back across his Chief's desk.

"Then after five months' leave, which you'll admit was a generous allowance, you've come back to tell me you refuse to obey my orders?" the Chief asked, staring coldly at his favourite officer.

"These orders, yes, sir," John replied firmly. "It is fairer to you and to myself to tell you that right out than to go over to Ireland and pretend to obey them. Give me a desk in one of the sections here at 41 Adelphi Terrace for the rest of the war, and though I'll hate the job I'll work at it as well as I can. Would you do what you're ordering me to do, sir?"

"Certainly," the Chief snapped. "Personal considerations mean nothing in our service."

"I'm afraid I remain an amateur, sir. I am lacking in professional ideals."

"Yes, well, don't start trying to be sarcastic or I shall get annoyed," the older man growled. "Am I to understand you expect me to tell the War Office people that an officer whose actions I have always supported against any complaint of their irregularity from the authorities now refuses to obey *my* orders? In other words, Ogilvie, do you expect me to look a damned fool?"

"I'm sorry, sir, but your order is impossible for me to carry out," John repeated.

There was a long silence. The pallid Punch's face glowered at the wall of the room opposite his desk. John gazed out of the dormer-window at the monotone of the blighted March day

"Very well. There's no more to be said at present," Captain Wade grumbled at last. "I'll have to think over what course I shall have to adopt."

John left the old man with a heavy heart, for he knew that his refusal had wounded him. Downstairs James Yarrow asked him what chance there was of something more amusing than the sight of Osborne trying to understand what a simple telegram meant.

"None," John snapped. "Look here, James. I'll be staying at my father's house, 57 Church Row, Hampstead. Ring me up, and we'll dine together somewhere."

John had left his luggage at Waterloo. There was the usual difficulty of persuading a taxi to go as far as Hampstead.

"War's war, guv'nor," one driver muttered with a sententious surliness which angered John.

"Bloody little you know what war is," he retorted hotly.

"It isn't only them in uniform as knows," the man grumbled.

John had already repented of his loss of temper. "All right, we won't argue. Drive me as far as the Charing Cross tube station."

When John started to lug his bags toward the entrance of the station the driver jumped down from his seat and called after him.

"All right, I'll drive you up to Hampstead, sir," he volunteered, relieving John of his bags as he spoke. "It's the blooming heartbreaking job we have to get petrol," he explained. John nodded and smiled.

"I'll carry the bags in," said the driver when they reached the house in Church Row. "Back for a bit of leave, sir?"

"Leave's over, I'm afraid," John told him. "Thanks so much for driving me up."

"Thank *you*, sir," said the driver, eyeing the half-crown his fare had added to the usual sixpenny tip.

His stepmother had just finished lunch when John entered the long eighteenth-century drawing-room whence the five tall windows looked across to the row of old houses opposite, unmarred by even a Victorian intruder.

"John dearest!" Elise exclaimed. "If I'd known when you were arriving I would have waited lunch."

"I don't want any lunch. Really."

"But, John, you must."

"No, really."

He threw himself down into an armchair covered with a brown and yellow chintz.

"You're not ill?" Elise asked anxiously.

"No, no, of course not. Just a bit tired, that's all. It's a tiring journey nowadays. Where's Prudence?"

"At school."

"Of course! I forgot she had been granted her heart's desire at last."

"Yes," said Elise, with a smile. "And I'm afraid she's already regretting it. But she became too much for poor Peachey. Didn't she write to you?"

"Yes, but I didn't answer her last letter. I let all my correspondence go to pieces while I was working on this play."

"And you've finished it?"

"Yes."

"Pleased with it?"

He shook his head.

"I expect it's splendid really," she said. "What's it about, or is that an unfair question?"

"Cowardice."

"What?"

"Cowardice. I finally came to the conclusion that the only drama to be extracted from war was to be found in its destructive effect upon personality. But I was given another theme to-day."

John related what had happened at Adelphi Terrace that morning.

"Oh, but an impossible suggestion!" Elise agreed.

"Yes, but what a study of the destructive effect of war upon personality if I had been willing to fall in with it," John added.

"This war, this war!" she sighed. "The news from France is dreadful. John, do you think it can go on until September year?"

"It's no use pretending that this latest German success is likely to shorten it," he answered.

"David will be eighteen in September year."

"Yes, but don't forget they wouldn't be likely to send him out to France for at least another six months. That would bring us to March 1920. I don't think it *can* last till then."

John stared out at the grey monotone of sky above the roof opposite. It seemed to prolong itself into a weary, endless future.

"You're not looking at all well, my dear. I'm going to ring and have some soup warmed up for you. You can drink it in here."

"It's only the fag of the journey, and perhaps a little emotional reaction after the shock my old man gave me. Where's Mr Justice Ogilvie?"

"At the Old Bailey."

"I wonder what it feels like in a wig to condemn people to death in these times. They ought to put His Majesty's Judges into khaki. You know, Elise, I can't help thinking that we ought to have shown some signs of reasonableness last autumn. I believe we could have secured reparation for Belgium, and Alsace and Lorraine for France, and Trieste and the Trentino for Italy if we had offered to restore all the German colonies. Of course now, with the success of this new German offensive, we *must* hold out. But don't let me go on talking about this infernal war. Will you think me very dreary if I go up to my room and lie down for a while?"

John was dozing when about five o'clock the door of his bedroom was cautiously opened.

"My god, it's you," he exclaimed, sitting up. "I thought it was a bad dream!"

"John! Don't be so rude," his young sister expostulated.

"Look at yourself!" he told her.

Prudence was wearing the dress of thousands of schoolgirls all over Britain—that shapeless navy-blue tunic cut square to show the top of a white blouse, beneath which black cashmere stockings emerging from navy-blue knickers completed the outrage on girlhood.

"Well, everybody says I'm getting more and more like you all the time."

"No such luck for you, my lass," her brother jeered.

"You're only joking, I know," she said, sitting down beside him on the bed. "You'd be jolly glad to have my complexion anyway."

"You conceited little brute! I had a complexion worth two of yours once."

"Ah, once. You haven't now, though. You're quite white except for a sort of dirty colour where the sunburn hasn't quite faded."

John seized a pillow.

"No, pax, pax! I take it back. Oh, John, I am glad to see you." She threw her arms round him. "I didn't mean a dirty colour really, but I don't think you're looking very well. You aren't ill are you?"

"Just tired."

"Poor John."

"And how do you like school?"

"It's simply frightful. I can't tell you how frightful it is. I got into a frightful row this morning with Miss Weekes because I spelt 'probably' p-r-o-b-e-r-b-l-y."

"I'm not surprised. You ought to have been flogged."

"Don't be an ass. They don't flog you at St James's."

"They did when I was there."

"You weren't at St James's Girls' School."

"Oh, you're at the Girls' School? I thought by your knickers you were at the place I was."

"You're not supposed to see my knickers."

"Well, I can, and a pretty grim sight they are."

"I can't help it. It's because I'm growing so fast."

"I never heard of anybody growing out of her knickers."

"John, you just misunderstand me on purpose. Not out of my knickers. Out of my djibba."

"Out of your what?"

"My djibba. We call this a djibba," she explained, tugging at her tunic.

"How do you spell that? G-i-b-b-e-r? Jolly good name for it."

"No, d-j-i-b-b-a—at least I think so. John, are you coming down to tea? That's what I came up for?"

"You greedy little brute. I thought you came to see your handsome and distinguished half-brother."

"So I did. John, I do love you. I wish you were all my brother. David's getting pretty sidy. He hardly pays any attention to me now. I think Etonians do get sidy after they're sixteen. Don't you?"

"The wretched youth was proberbly ashamed of your knickers."

John had got off the bed and was brushing his hair.

"Come on, your hair's quite all right. You're as bad as David. He puts Flowers and Honey on his hair."

"What kind of flowers? Dahlias?"

"John, you are such an ass. Flowers and Honey is the name of a patent hair-lotion. Didn't you know that?"

"I can't know everything. I'm not Miss Weekes."

"She's frightful. She's always breathing on her glasses."

"I'm not surprised, if she has to read handwriting like yours."

"You never answered my letter," said Prudence reproachfully.

"I know. I was a lazy hound. Come on downstairs." He pulled her to him and kissed her. "Great Scott, what have you got on those two rats'-tails of yours?"

"It's Flowers and Honey. I bagged some of David's."

"No wonder Miss Weekes breathes on her glasses," said John. "She must be looking to see who left a bad lemon-sponge lying about the class-room."

"I wish I hadn't gone to school," Prudence sighed.

"Well, you've done it now. Let me see, you'll be fifteen in May. You've got another good three years of it."

"I don't think Mother will make me stay all that time. But perhaps it won't be so bad when I'm older. I hate being a new girl. I'm the only one this term except one. Irene Andrews her name is. I don't like her much. She wears a ring round her teeth, and she's a year younger than me."

With this piece of information Prudence danced ahead of John into the drawing-room.

"Dear child, this isn't the school gymnasium," her mother reminded her, a coldness in her tone.

Prudence made a wry face at John behind her mother's back. Later when she had retired to homework John remonstrated with Elise.

"I don't think it's quite fair to take it out of Prudence because she's younger than David."

"What *do* you mean, John?"

"Isn't that fundamentally the reason? You resent the thought of her security. If David were her age, he might feel sure of escaping even this eternal and infernal war."

Elise laid down the tambour-frame on which she was working, and looked at John.

"I really don't think that's fair, my dear. Prudence is very young for her age at present, but she'll be developing fast presently, and she does require a firm hand."

"No doubt, but she's such a lovable kid, and I think it hurts her when you're cold with her."

"John dear, I think you exaggerate rather."

"I don't think I do. I can't help remembering twenty years ago when I was a good bit older than Prudence is now and when my father used to practise forensic sarcasm at my expense. Indeed, it wasn't until he married you, Elise, that he became comparatively human."

"He's very human with Prudence."

"Yes, in a grandfatherly way, but that's hardly enough for a child like her. I wish you'd let her come out with me to Citrano last autumn."

"This is very paternal of you, John."

"Well, I am old enough to be her father."

"Yes, I suppose technically you are."

John laughed.

"You evidently don't consider that my sense of responsibility is on a level with my years."

"What I do consider is that you're very much overtired and inclined to criticize imaginary misdeeds. I try to be strict with Prudence, yes. She can stand any amount of strictness, believe me, and I don't want her to suffer from the general slackness about children which is one of the signs of our national preoccupation with war. But that I am unkind to her or that I too obviously indulge my fondness for David I deny."

But John was in no mood to give way to mere assertion.

"I don't accuse you of deliberately favouring David."

"You haven't seen me with David for I don't know how long," Elise interrupted. "You haven't seen David since 1916. You never went down to see him at Eton last half. You always have accused me of being too severe with Prudence. It's just prejudice."

"I only criticize when I see you all again after an absence," John argued. "Which proves that each time it does make an impression on me."

"Now I've gone wrong with my pattern," Elise exclaimed, picking irritably at a woollen leaf stitched in the tambour-frame.

"I'm afraid I've upset your ladyship," he said at last, with an apologetic smile. He had noticed a grey strand in the beautiful light brown hair. He felt a sudden compunction in the realization that the resilience of youth had gone from her. And in another ten years he himself would be her age.

"Forgive my frankness, Elise," he begged, putting a hand on hers. "I was back in boyhood, and going off to homework, bored to death with the prospect of school."

"Prudence herself was so anxious to go to school.

And if I was really hard-hearted I should have sent her to Roedean or Cheltenham."

"That indeed would have proclaimed the Roman mother." John laughed.

"And surely she must pay for experience?" Elise continued. "I think it's never too soon for a child to get that lesson. At first I was hard-hearted and unimaginative because I wouldn't send her to school. Now when she has had a couple of months' experience of it I am to be equally hard-hearted and unimaginative because I do not immediately take her away. That seems to me an extremely weak method of education."

"Yes, I expect you're right," John agreed. "But if after a year of it she still hates the particular brand of female education which we are inflicting on women in the first quarter of the twentieth century, I do hope you won't ascribe to it a mystical value just because it is the conventional education of a young English woman of to-day. My own belief is that the mistake of contemporary female education is its foundation on a system of male education which is itself so vulnerable to criticism. This nonsensical idea of diverting the growing girl from thoughts of love by offering her lacrosse and hockey in exchange is due to the notion that the passive sex can be as successfully tired out as the active sex. Surely mental not physical occupation is what girls require? And this atmosphere of soured virginity which surrounds the teachers! It's most demoralizing because as a result the mind of the growing girl associates art and science and scholarship with frumpish sterility."

"What it amounts to is that if Prudence succumbs to the present system of female education she will have lacked the character to survive it and will be happier floating with the stream of fashionable convention, and if she rebels she will have something on which to harden her character early."

"Well, if ever I have a daughter she shall not go to school."

"You'll trust to finding the perfect governess? Or will you make a bargain with your future wife in advance that she shall devote her whole life to educating her daughter?"

"I shall educate her myself."

"How could I ask your father to educate Prudence?"

"I offered to have her at Citrano, and you refused."

"But you're not Prudence's father, John. You are her very attractive half-brother, and although over twenty years older you are not really old enough to take sole charge of her education. And now do stop arguing. You're looking wretchedly pale, and you'll have to talk to your father after dinner."

It was about seven o'clock when Sir Alexander Ogilvie returned.

"My dear fellow, I didn't realize you would have already arrived," he exclaimed cordially. "I shouldn't have dallied at the club, had I known. Why didn't you ring through?"

What a fine figure of a man he was, John thought, as he watched his father at dinner and listened to his narration of the gossip he had heard in the select corner of the Garrick he frequented. Seen thus by the kindly light of the rosy table-lamp he was as ageless as the portrait of some famous actor hanging on the walls of his favourite club. A portly man, but not more portly than dignity demanded. The advocate's eloquent mouth, fined down by some years of judicial caution . . . in his manner the easy self-confidence which success bestows . . . and to that added the stateliness bestowed by office. Yet this man free of the best-informed conversation in the country was as much at the mercy of rumour as the man in the front-line trench, and might have been lampooned by Swift as one of the foolish that mistook the echo of a London coffee-house for the voice of the kingdom.

"But you've just come from Paris," his father was saying. "What was the opinion there?"

"Very pessimistic."

The Judge shook his head, and refused the butler's attempt to refill his glass. Yes, a famous actor, his son thought. In that gesture of abnegation he was dramatizing the will of his country to face the worst. What a pity the average Englishman always acted so much worse on the stage than he did off it.

"Pessimistic, was it? Well, I was talking to ——," Sir Alexander mentioned the name of a distinguished General high in the councils of the nation, "and he told me the Prime Minister would probably achieve his ambition now of putting the British Army under the command of a Frenchman. X—— was extremely annoyed about it. He doesn't believe the rank and file will fight with the same confidence."

"It will be a miracle if the Prime Minister does succeed in unifying the command," John said. "But I don't think your informant need worry about its effect on the rank and file. The rank and file abandoned in 1914 any credulity in which they may have indulged themselves over British generalship."

"That's the rather superficial impulse to blame anything that happens on the nearest bigwig in sight."

"Like the criminal in the dock," John said, twinkling.

"No, perhaps 'bigwig' wasn't quite the word," his father smiled. "I don't deduce, however, from what as I say is usually an ill-informed estimate of the British general, that the rank and file will be any more inclined to trust a French general. At least we keep our generals clear of politics, which is more than can be said for our ally. But I'm sorry to hear that Paris is pessimistic. Certainly we have a nasty corner to round, but the Americans must make themselves felt soon."

"Perhaps not soon enough, though," John objected.

But the Judge had a store of exclusive information from people who ought to be experts which led him to suppose that his son's misgivings were unnecessary.

When about ten o'clock Lady Ogilvie was retiring to bed, and Sir Alexander and John prepared to move from the drawing-room to the Judge's library, she paused in the doorway to beg her husband to make John go off early.

"He's tired, Alec."

"We shan't be long. A short cigar and a whisky," the Judge promised reassuringly.

As long as John could remember, his father's library had seemed as much a part of him as the shell of a snail. It had expanded with the years like the owner, and this library at 57 Church Row was as much more impressive a background as Mr Justice Ogilvie was a more impressive figure than Sir Alexander Ogilvie, K.C. It was fortunate that he himself had expanded too during the last twenty years.

"I don't know how I should have faced your inquisition in this room when I used to have to convince you that there was a just cause and impediment to my having arrived home earlier than I did," he said to his father as they pulled their chairs nearer to the fire that was blazing under the carved overmantel.

"Was I such an unsympathetic parent?" the Judge asked sceptically.

"I think all fathers are unsympathetic to their eldest sons," John replied, disconcerting the Judge, who had grown into the habit of being agreed with. "I suppose it's a kind of protracted nervousness about the success of their first experiment. And the habit boys have of regarding grown-ups as beings who have passed beyond their own cribbed and cabined existence into freedom doesn't help."

"No, I suppose it doesn't."

"You wouldn't expect to be considered sympathetic by one of the unfortunate creatures whom it is your business to send to prison or the gallows. You wouldn't even expect to be considered human by any standard they have for measuring humanity."

"I believe I'm considered a merciful judge, John. You must remember I made my name as a defender of criminals."

"Yes, but you can't expect to be considered human when you sit there on the bench, dressed up like a cross between Father Christmas and the King of Hearts. In fact the whole preposterous masquerade with which the judicial office is surrounded is maintained with the deliberate object of dehumanizing the individual who fills it."

"Naturally the dignity and detachment of the Law must be preserved."

"Oh, they are, with complete success; but a judge cannot hope to strike the vast majority as a human being. I am compelled to recognize that *you* are a human being by the fact that you are my father; and my individual and comparatively rare experience compels me by analogy to recognize the common humanity of your learned brothers. At the same time, like the small boy who dreads the result of introducing his critical little friends to the home circle, I should even now be careful which of my friends I chose to behold you at home."

"A man does not change when he becomes a judge," Sir Alexander insisted.

"No, but other people change him. Luckily for the dignity of the Bench, I may add. Has it never struck you as absurd that a man who has devoted his career to persuading juries that black is white should be chosen to administer impartiality?"

"A Common Law barrister gains a good deal of practical experience of human nature, you know."

"Yes, but I wonder if the distorted use he makes of it

does not destroy the mental integrity which, for instance, the artist demands his experience shall give him. I'm afraid the lawyers have looked after themselves, as, being lawyers, they might be expected to look after themselves. They have fenced themselves in like a hieratic caste and made the exclusion of everybody else inevitable. They are the medicine-men of civilization. The priests held the world in chains once, but they were driven out by the lawyers, and the world has been more pitilessly enchained ever since. Imagine a bench of judges not one of whom had risen to the dignity by practice at the bar. It might be the salvation of modern society."

"Yes, well, of course, that's just sentimental anarchy," said the Judge. "Naturally, all of us who occupy positions at the head of our respective professions must surrender something of ourselves to that position, but I cannot see why a judge or a bishop or a cabinet minister should be denied the mental integrity of what you call an artist, by which I presume you mean a writer or a painter or a musician who indulges in art for art's sake."

"Not at all. By an artist I mean a man who indulges in art for truth's sake. The artist can only be compared with the scientist. You mentioned cabinet ministers. Do you seriously believe that a man whose career has been devoted to parliamentary manœuvre, to humbugging the electorate, to obsequiousness to his party and his party chiefs is thereby better qualified to hold a high administrative post? Surely the contemptible political intrigues of the last four years, during the greatest crisis in the history of the nation, is the answer to that. How can one believe in the mental integrity of politicians? We should count ourselves blessed when we can believe in their moral integrity."

"Well, look here," said the Judge. "Elise said I wasn't to keep you up. So what about bed?"

"Bed it shall be, in one moment," John promised.

"But first I want your opinion on a mental dilemma in which I found myself to-day. At least it wasn't really a dilemma, because I had no difficulty in making up my mind how to reply."

John told his father about the proposal of Captain Wade.

"Now inasmuch as I have transformed myself for the duration of this infernal war into an Intelligence Officer, it is clearly my duty to undertake the job of spying on my friend and his associates. It is, within the compass of an Intelligence Officer, equivalent to inviting you to condemn to penal servitude a man who had been from youth your intimate friend. You would surrender to your office and obey. I will not surrender. Which of us is displaying integrity?"

"I don't accept the parallel," said the Judge.

"Nevertheless it is a parallel in its humble way," John insisted. "And now I really will go to bed."

Sir Alexander sat on by the fire. The elfin chimes of the travelling clock upon his desk struck eleven. Soon Athene would have been dead thirty years, and yet how vividly she had lived to-night in her son.

"In our son," the Judge muttered.

Yet now with a second wife and another son, and a daughter, he beheld this pale man of thirty-five in naval uniform, vaguely and a little disturbingly like himself in set of bone and contour of face, return like a phantom from the past with the eyes and the smile of her who still held his own youth. One could vow, in hearing John talk, that his mother still lived to feed him with the energy of her own questioning mind instead of having died when he was scarcely seven years old.

David arrived home from Eton next day, and although

John was still feeling rotten he suggested they should celebrate the occasion with a theatre. After a grave argument whether to visit *The Bing Boys on Broadway* at the Alhambra or *The Lilac Domino* at the Empire, the decision went to the Alhambra.

"Perhaps it's my fault, but I didn't think it was very good," said John when they emerged into Leicester Square at the end of the performance.

"I didn't think it was terribly bad," said David.

Incredible, thought John, that when this infernal war began his half-brother was still in jackets. Now here he was as tall as himself and achieving in his first evening tails an excellent imitation of a boy at least eighteen years old.

"When I was a year older than you," he told this elegant youth of sixteen and a half whose curly light brown hair had been reduced to conventional order by Flowers and Honey, "I wore a discarded creation of Mr Justice Ogilvie's."

"Did you? That must have been rather foul," David commented.

"Built by Bunting's some time in the early 'nineties," John continued.

"I say how absolutely rancid!" David ejaculated.

"I wore it first at the opera. . . ."

"I'm not fearfully keen on opera," David interposed. "I once saw a very boring thing called . . . well, I can't remember what it was called, but I know it was very boring."

"I went to *Traviata* . . .," John tried to continue, but his brother's glances were measuring critically a Leicester Square *traviata* who in the dim nocturnal air of war-time was smiling at him from the edge of the kerb.

"Rather cheek the way these Polls grin at you," the boy observed austerely.

"I haven't heard that word since I came down from

Oxford," John exclaimed. "A good eighteenth-century word too. Polls!"

"Look out, I say, people will hear you."

"Apologies, David, I won't disgrace you again. . . . And at that performance of *Traviata* I ought to have seen your mother for the first time. She saw me. I was up in a box, but she was down in the stalls with the Judge" —it was always an embarrassment to John to have to speak about their father as "Father" to Prudence and David.

"Did you feel very sick when he married again?" the boy asked.

"Not in the least. Your mother exercised an entirely admirable influence over him."

"Still, I should think it was rather boring having a father as old as him suddenly getting married again."

"He was only forty-six."

"Well, that's pretty old, isn't it?"

"I admit I thought so at the time. Of course it doesn't seem quite so old when one's thirty-five oneself."

"Yes, you are getting pretty antique, aren't you?" David agreed solemnly. "We had an argument last half when middle-age began. I said if you took seventy as the average age, which I believe it is, you ought to divide it into four. Up to seventeen and a half a man's a boy, up to thirty-five he's a young man, up to fifty-two and a half he's middle-aged, and over fifty-two and a half he's old. Some people stuck out that eighty was a better average age nowadays for what I believe is called the expectancy of life, in which case middle-age wouldn't begin till forty and old age at sixty. But I pointed out that in that case you'd remain a boy till you are twenty."

"So you do legally."

"What about if you're in the army?"

"I don't think you can lay down a general law, David. Some people are middle-aged before they're thirty."

"Well, anyway, I think forty-six is much too old to start marrying again," David declared. "And when are you going to get married, John? You'll have to look out, or you'll settle down into a bachelor, though perhaps with all this taxation it might be best. Oh, I knew there was something I wanted to talk to you about. It's about this German drive. The news is worse than ever to-night. I think there's a good chance of the war going on for at least another two years, don't you? That means I still have a chance of getting to the front. I believe my best plan is to try for Sandhurst next summer."

"You're so anxious to be killed, are you?"

They were walking slowly up Charing Cross Road toward the Tottenham Court Road tube station, and David kicked a piece of banana-skin off the pavement to cover his embarrassment at a question which he thought exceeded the limit of intimacy allowed even to an older brother.

"I want to have done something in the war," he muttered. "All of us who just missed it would feel such fools."

"Much better that than perhaps not to be able to feel anything for evermore. And as a matter of fact I don't believe there's going to be this gap between those who fought and those who didn't. I thought so myself once, but that was when there still seemed to be something worth fighting for."

"I should have thought fighting to win was enough to fight for," David suggested.

"I wonder if it is," John murmured to himself. Then he asked abruptly if his brother had decided what profession he intended to aim at should the glory of a military life be denied him by the premature arrival of peace. "I assume you won't want to be a professional soldier in that case, for I can't imagine any drearier existence than to enter the army immediately after the end of a world-wide war."

"I don't know that I'm particularly keen on anything," David said gloomily. "Everything will be so boring."

Was this the mark of youth's exhausted vitality through these years of strain, or was it no more than the Byronic mood of adolescence? John knew that Elise would question him to-morrow upon his impression of David, but he had no heart to tease the boy into self-revelation.

"You'll find everything more amusing when the war stops," he assured him. "What about coming out to Italy with me next summer—or the summer after?" John added quickly, for he had been forgetting he was still chained to his commission.

His young brother looked round with a smile. "I'd like that awfully."

The next morning John went down again to Adelphi Terrace to find out what his Chief's attitude was. He had to wait some time to see him, and he fancied from the curious glances of Osborne, Hargreaves, Browne-Pawson and Chorley the prevalence of a comfortable feeling at Number 41 that a favourite had fallen. James Yarrow was nowhere to be seen.

"Well?" asked Captain Wade glumly, when at last he reached the room at the top of the house.

"I wanted to know if you wished me to start work?"

"In Ireland?"

"I am willing to go to Ireland, sir, on two conditions. The first is that I do not meet Fitzgerald. The second is that you accept the responsibility for the prejudice I am bound to import into the investigation."

"Conditions!" Captain Wade growled. "You temporary fellows have the most extraordinary notions of discipline. I set you a task. There is only one way to carry it out, and that is to the best of your ability."

"In a task like this it is surely my duty to warn you, sir, that I am the wrong person to carry it out. I have no right to waste public money and time without giving that warning."

"Are you well enough to go?" Captain Wade shot out, his nose and chin seeming to meet as he stared at his junior.

"I'm not feeling brilliant at the moment, but I've no reason to suppose I shall not be well enough."

"Come back after Easter and I'll decide then what to say to you. In my opinion you're ill."

John divined that the old man was anxious to believe that he was ill and thereby find an excuse to explain away to himself his favourite's defiance.

"Go and see a doctor," he barked after John as he was closing the door behind him.

Downstairs John asked what had happened to Mervyn Iredale and heard he had been sent out to a job in the West Indies. He then enquired for James Yarrow, and was told by Osborne that he had contrived to get himself a few days' Easter leave in the country.

"You people from the Mediterranean are pretty hot at wangling leave and cushy jobs," he added, with a note of resentment in his flat voice.

"That's because we never had time to let our bottoms get grafted on to our chairs in London, Obby."

"How was the old man?" Osborne asked maliciously.

"He told me to come back after Easter. Then he's sending me to Nicaragua. See you soon."

The picture of Osborne's dull indignant eyes and fatty scowl carried John to the end of Adelphi Terrace with a certain buoyancy and passing a telephone-box he decided to ring up Miriam Stern and ask if she would dine with him to-night. She was not in, and he told the maid to let her mistress know that he would call for her about half-past six. After this he went round to see his agent, with whom he discussed the play he had just written.

"But why cowardice?" asked Gosnell, a large beaky man in the late forties who, as the age for military service rose, had been taking an entirely new personal interest in the progress of the war. "Why cowardice, my dear fellow? We don't want themes of disillusionment. We've all got to pull together. Did you see the casualty list this morning? Shocking, isn't it? I'm afraid they won't pass me for active service. I hoped you were coming back from Greece with another *Maid of the Mountains*. And what leading man's going to play a coward? There's been a lot of nasty criticism as it is about some of our leading actors clearing off to the States for the duration. Some of those who had been playing to big business for three years are now cadets. And they don't like it. I'll see what the reaction is, but honestly, old man, I don't think there's a god-earthly chance of getting a production now. It's all against the mood of the moment. You *have* disappointed me. And I think it would be so bad for you. Your public won't like it. It's a slap in the face for a successful dramatist to come back from this great adventure and tell his public that a coward is a hero. Why, I doubt if the censor would pass it."

"I rather thought you'd take this line, Gosnell."

"Well, I do, Ogilvie. In fact if it weren't for those little bits of ribbon you're sporting, I'd call it rankly unpatriotic to write such a play at a moment like this. What's that one?"

"The Croix de Guerre," said John curtly.

"Let me see, it's the Legion of Honour, isn't it, that gets you through the French Customs? Pity you didn't get that. Dam useful for running down to Monte when the jolly old war is over."

"Surely the public must be ready by now to face up to

some of the unpleasant facts of war?" John asked, returning to his play.

"Not while a war is going on, Ogilvie. I daresay if you put this play aside it might get a good hearing when peace was signed. We'll probably all be feeling anti-war by then. It might even be really good box-office. But not now. Well, did you see this morning where the Germans have got to? Why those blasted Yanks couldn't have come in at the beginning I don't know. Yes, what I want from you is another *Maid of the Mountains*. Where's Julius Stern these days?"

"Over in America."

"Pity he turned so highbrow," said Gosnell. "You and he might have swept the musical comedy board. Well, so long, old man. And do think about writing something to cheer us all up. I'll talk to one or two people about this new play of yours, but frankly I don't think it has an earthly."

John reached Claremount Gardens about half-past five. Mrs Stern had not yet come in, but Anna was sure she would not be long now, and he went upstairs to wait in that room where orange damask curtains and creamy walls had replaced the sea-green velvet and grey distemper which used to haunt his youthful craving for beauty. The Steinway Grand was still in the same place, seeming like a live creature asleep. The visitor flung himself down into a deep chair, too much jaded to make even the effort necessary to stretch across and pick up the current issue of *The Nation* which was lying on a low occasional table just out of reach. He fell into an arid sleep, from which he woke with a start to see the window-panes like sapphires in the March dusk and the shadowy form of Miriam looking down at him. He jumped up, aware that his bones were aching and that his throat was painful.

"What's the time? I've come to take you out to dinner," he said, his voice appearing to ring out harshly to senses not yet perfectly co-ordinated after sleep.

Miriam switched on the light and hurried to draw the curtains in consonance with the regulations of war-time.

"John, I am so sorry I was out when you rang up. How lovely to see you! I've been over to Canonbury to visit a decrepit sister-in-law."

"Where shall we go and dine?" John asked.

Miriam looked at him critically.

"Would it bore you very much to dine at home with me?"

"Not a bit. Only perhaps . . ."

She cut him short by saying that Anna had some delicacy which she would be disappointed to find ignored.

"I won't be a minute. Here's a letter from Julius which you may like to read."

WABASH HOTEL,
INDIANAPOLIS
March 5, '18.

My dear Mother,

It's about time I sent you a line. I played here last night to a big audience. The Sibelius Concerto. I like the mixture of south and north in it. Queer thing, the disappointment of Sibelius's life has been that he wanted to be a great violinist, but did not begin till he was fifteen which was too late, though he did nothing for ten years except practise day and night. I started as a violinist and hoped to be a great composer. According to the critics I am *a great violinist. All the same, when the war is over I shall go back to composing. After all, I'm not very much over thirty. I don't really care for concert work. One feels like a piece of furniture being moved about from place to place.*

Leonora is with her people, waiting for me in New York. We both think she ought to be with Sebastian to prevent his being utterly spoilt by the old people. We plan to come over to Europe at the first possible opportunity after we get peace. I expect you're finding it somewhat irksome in London. I haven't heard from Emil for months, but have to admit he hasn't heard from me. And that goes for John Ogilvie too.

Oh, by the way I don't think I've told you that Leonora has been received into the Church. Poppa and Momma Blakiston were a bit frightened by the fact. I think they fancied their silver-stacked Fifth Avenue parlour would be overrun by the greasy Wops and the dirty Irish. However, they've recovered from it now.

I don't like bragging, but I must inform you that as a result of my concerts this winter I've handed more than 50,000 dollars to war charities. And is Poppa proud?

Momma whose roots stretch down to mingle with yours and mine, dear Mother, thinks half would have been quite enough to give away like that. The other 25,000 dollars didn't earn its value in gratitude, she said. Well, no more. The Sibelius Concerto is tiring. The composer of it may not have managed to become a violinist himself, but he meant that the man who played it should be! All love.

Julius

"I hope he *will* go back to composition," said John gloomily. "It may not be quite as easy as he thinks. Play me something, Miriam."

She sat down at the Steinway and asked what he wanted to hear.

"Chopin's Twenty-first Prelude. Oh yes, and the B minor Scherzo. And then some of Schumann's Noveletten. Oh, and all the things I love. It won't be dinner-time yet?"

"Not for an hour or more."

"Play to me."

He leant back with closed eyes. Ah, that exquisite

Prelude. It was a rippling stream which suddenly plunged down like a waterfall and all too soon became a rippling stream again.

"Once more that Prelude," he begged. "It's so short. I wish that phrase in the middle could last for ever."

And the moment it had been played it could not be held by the mind's ear. Like a waterfall it was untraceable in the placid ripples of the stream below. Like that August night in Cracow, not far from twenty years ago now, in which he had plunged with Miriam down from a flowing stream into the equable and placid stream of their friendship.

"Will Poland rise again from the ashes of this war, Miriam? Do you remember the tune of that trumpeter playing the hour at dawn from the top of the tower of St Mary's Church? Every hour for seven hundred years since the first trumpeter was pierced through the throat by a Tartar arrow. And the same broken tune every hour since, day and night, trumpeter after trumpeter blowing that same tune from the four windows at the top of the tower and ending always on the same wavering note, the last note blown by the watchman before the Tartar arrow pierced his throat."

Miriam Stern stopped playing to turn and look at John with amazement. This was the first time in eighteen years he had alluded even indirectly to that August dawn in Cracow.

"Play to me, Miriam. Play the Chopin Scherzo I like," he was muttering in the strange inward voice of one who dreams.

She rose from the piano and hurried over to where he was leaning back in the chair.

"John dear, are you feeling all right?"

"I'm feeling like death. My throat is closing up, I think." She put a hand on his forehead. It was dry and burning.

"Go on playing. Do go on playing, Miriam," he whispered fretfully. "The music gets in the way of this invading illness. Perhaps it will be able to drive it back. If my throat gets any worse I won't be able to go to Ireland, and that'll annoy my old man, who is a profoundly decent old man. Oh God, I feel like death. What can be the matter?" Miriam had rung the bell and was talking by the door to Anna. "Why are you talking instead of playing? It's the Scherzo I want now. Or if you like, the Prelude again. There's a phrase in the middle I never can keep in my mind the moment it has passed. Such a lovely bar or two of music, but they refuse to stay with me."

Anna had retired, and Miriam Stern was asking him if he would like to lie on the sofa.

"Well, really, do you know, I don't think I can get up out of this chair just yet," he told her. "It's odiously boring for you, but perhaps if you go on playing I'll be all right presently. I say, did I ask you something about Poland just now? Or was I dreaming?"

"You were wondering if Poland would rise again from the ashes of this war."

She did not mention Cracow, because she feared he might be embarrassed at the thought of letting the fever loosen his tongue, for fever it must be. If only Anna could make the doctor come at once.

"Is your throat very bad?" she asked anxiously.

"It's getting worse and worse," he muttered. "I really don't believe I'll be able to talk in a minute."

"Then don't try to talk, my dear. I've sent Anna for the doctor."

He did not answer. He must be very ill indeed, she thought, not to protest. She wanted to bathe his forehead, but when she moved toward the door he called her back.

"Play to me, Miriam," he called, it seemed like a sick child.

And perhaps that would be as soothing as anything. But not Chopin. Not something that would set his fevered mind racing back into the past. Not Schumann even. What should she play? And from girlhood came a sonata of Mozart, every note of it, though it had been her own father who had heard her play that sonata last, oh, more than forty years ago.

And when the sonata was finished and she paused for a moment, thinking to cross the room and look at John, he muttered again in that strange inward voice of one who dreams, "Play to me, Miriam."

So for another half-hour she played all she could remember of her girlhood's pieces, until the doctor came into the room.

"A wounded warrior?" he asked, looking down at the figure in naval uniform huddled in the armchair.

"Not wounded, Dr Kember," said Miriam. "But a very sick warrior, I'm afraid."

The Doctor, an agreeable plump little man with a shiny face, pursed his lips.

"Humph! I think I should like him to get over on the sofa while I have a look. Can you manage to drag yourself along, old man?"

After he had made his examination, Dr Kember took Miriam outside the room.

"I can't be sure yet," he said. "But I rather fancy it's scarlet fever. I'll come again in the morning, and if it is I'll get the ambulance to take him to hospital."

"But I could nurse him here. He ought not to go to his father's house where there are children?"

"Certainly not, if it can be avoided."

"Oh, easily. I'll ring up Lady Ogilvie in Church Row."

"Is he the son of the Judge? I didn't realize that. He's not staying with you?"

"No, but he can so easily. I'll arrange matters. You'll come in the morning?"

Miriam took the doctor's orders for the night, and came back to John.

"You have to stay here," she told him. "Now don't argue, my dear."

But he was too ill even to argue.

It was scarlet fever, and a severe scarlet fever of the septic variety. Owing to the demands of the war it was impossible to obtain the services of two nurses, and Miriam Stern herself assumed day duty, night duty being taken by a broad-bottomed, rosy-faced Cockney nurse in her early sixties, with the unusual and as it happened appropriate name of Widehose. The patient's temperature rose on two nights to 105°, but the delirium did not inspire violence. The floor of the room, which was Miriam Stern's own room, was thronged by Lilliputian armies marching, counter-marching, and fighting, and occasionally he would sit up in bed when an army disappeared under the toilet-table or behind the curtains, anxious not to lose sight of its evolutions.

"Nurse!" he shouted once, sitting up and fixing his fever-bright eyes, "I must warn these Poles."

"Of course you must, dearie. Warn away as hard as you like."

"They're rising! They're rising!" he cried in triumph, and before she could bear him back into the pillows he had leapt out of bed to plant a bare foot in the middle of a German division, the survivors of which scurried over his instep in confusion.

"Now that's just being a naughty boy," Nurse Widehose reproached him with jovial severity.

"But I think the Poles will rise all the same," the

patient told her as he suffered her to get him back into bed.

"Of course they'll rise," she assured him. "That's what a pole's for. Now look what you've done to your pads." She wrapped the cotton-wool round his knees and ankles and wrists, which were tortured by arthritis. "Your throat must be better if you can holler out like that. Perhaps you could bear to let me swab it."

"No, no," the patient muttered, for the Lilliputian armes had vanished for the nonce and he was back again with the pain. "No, spray it. I can't stand that blasted swab."

"Well, a little of what you fancy does you good, as dear Marie Lloyd used to sing. Open as wide as you can."

By day the delirium subsided, though there was one morning when Miriam Stern appeared to the patient she was tending like the shadow of herself, and the more earnestly he tried to restore this insubstantial shape to the reality of herself the more uncomfortably it eluded him. Sometimes he would succeed in focusing her face for a moment; yet though it was always her face it was never the same face, but wrinkled now with age or ivory-smooth as youth, or, most disconcertingly of all, broken up into cubes like a post-impressionist portrait; and if from these cubes he tried to compose her recognizable face the cubes would shift and fall into a new pattern like the glass in a kaleidoscope. However, during most of those first ten days, he lay in half a stupor while she read to him from his favourite poets. Letters came from his father and Elise, from Prudence, David, and one from Captain Wade the pleasure given to him by which was the first thing that led him to suppose he might be feeling better. The last worry he had been able to deal with practically before the fever seized him with full fury was his position at Adelphi Terrace, and he had managed to dictate a brief note which Miriam Stern sent off with a letter from Dr Kember. The Chief wrote him to say that he was under orders not to show himself until October, when, if the war was still going on as seemed more than probable, a job would be found for him. Thinking it over, Captain Wade added, he had appreciated the frankness which had kept John from letting him down by taking a job he knew himself incapable of carrying out properly.

By the middle of April, except for the slow business of recovering his strength, John was himself again. Over in France the Germans were still pressing hard; but the news that Foch had been appointed Commander-in-Chief of the French and British Armies in the field brought to these Armies a similar relief from fever. There was no obvious reason to these hard-tried men why the situation should suddenly appear so much more favourable. There was no relaxation in the German efforts to batter through. But rumour now went attired like a beneficent spirit of light. Foch had a plan. It mattered no longer that the enemy was still so potent. Foch had a plan. From that day in April when his supreme command was announced the British Army fought with a conviction of ultimate victory, no longer with a gallant hope of staving off defeat. Foch had a plan. It reached John in letters from friends at the front. Nobody had the faintest conception what Foch's plan was, but Foch had a plan. The very birds in the lime-trees outside the house seemed to be singing that Foch had a plan.

Even James Yarrow, who refused to consider the possibility of infection and made a habit of coming up to see John every day 'après le turbin' as he called his work at Adelphi Terrace, spoke about Foch's plan.

"But what is this plan, James?"

"I don't think any of our people have a notion, but I'm quite prepared to believe that he really has a plan. Everybody thinks we shall finish the Germans off by the summer of next year. I'm not an optimist, as you know, but I always have thought our main handicap throughout the war has been the High Command, and I believe we're going to win after all, now that the High Command has stepped down a pace. It's interesting, isn't it, to find the British nation at last willing to admit that the French have brains?"

Apart from the visits of James Yarrow, John spent all his time for the first month in the company of Miriam or Nurse Widehose, for it had been agreed that, with Prudence and David at home, it would be wiser not to run any risk of infection.

> *It's rotten,* wrote Prudence. *I'd love to have scarlet-fever, because then perhaps I could go away with you for your convalessence, and which would be simply topping. And now there are only eleven and a half days before school begins again. They say I'll have to play cricket next term, and I do hate games. I don't see why one should have to play games when they bore one, do you? Some girls like games but only because they like showing off to the games mistress who struts about looking very beefy, whistling and mooing all over the place. I* hate *her.*

John gave the letter to Miriam.

"Suppose you'd been chased about by a games-mistress when you were a child," he said.

"No, there were no games-mistresses in Warsaw. Yet this is a happier country than mine was."

"But when you were Prudence's age there weren't so many games-mistresses in England." John laughed suddenly. "I was thinking how Emil used to loathe games," he explained. "Fortunately, they weren't compulsory at St James's."

"I had a letter from Emil this morning."

"You never told me."

"It worried me a little. Read it, John."

BRITISH CONSULATE,
STOCKHOLM
April 20th, 1918.

My dear Mother,

I'm sorry to hear from you about John, but as I've heard no more I'm presuming that by now he is better. Give him my love.

I am so angry with the attitude taken up towards the Bolsheviks. It's preposterous the way we are even ready to encourage the Germans to intervene in Finland now that the Swedes have refused to let the "White" Finns buy arms. They're frightened of course of Bolshevism in Sweden. On April 2nd 40,000 German troops with 300 guns landed at Hangö. They have also seized the Aaland Islands and I hear that the Swedes to preserve their precious neutrality will withdraw. The amusing thing is that the Germans have deported all the British subjects on the Aaland Islands and to our protest they have replied that the expulsion of British subjects is a reprisal for the way the Allies treated German subjects in Greece during 1916. Tell this to John!

The Finnish Bolshevik Government has had to evacuate Helsingfors which was occupied by the Germans six days ago. Now if you please, it is proposed that Duke Frederick Francis of Mecklenburg-Schwerin shall become King of Finland. It's a scandal. Even the reactionary White Finns were Republicans. We however are more afraid of Bolshevism than of a Germanized Baltic, and I have very little doubt that we quietly encouraged the Swedes to back up this monarchist business. If they aren't careful they'll drive the Bolsheviks into killing the Tsar. And that will be an excuse when we've finished with the Germans to have a go at the Bolsheviks. I grow tired of reading this propaganda against them. How can one achieve a revolution of such magnitude without a certain amount of bloodshed? If the Allies don't manage to beat the Germans soon we shall have a revolution all over Europe. And indeed not before it is time. I do not see how capitalism can recover from the strain of this war, anyway. I do begin to feel hopeful that Communism will be established universally before I die.

It is difficult, indeed impossible really, to resign from the service so long as the war goes on, but I do not intend to remain an official for a day longer than is necessary, and to be frank with you I have seriously contemplated clearing over the frontier and joining the Finnish Reds. In fact if I were sure I should not be suspected of being a spy I believe I wouldn't be able to resist the temptation.

Fortunately perhaps for my future, I have become engaged to a young woman—Astrid Hellner. She is the only daughter of the Swedish philosopher and mathematician and has a brain herself. She is two years younger than myself. I say 'fortunately' because, although Astrid herself sympathises completely with my political and economic views, she thinks it is too soon to identify myself openly, and as people in England would think flagrantly, with this upheaval in Russia beside which the French Revolution looks parochial. She believes that I should waste myself by active participation at present, and as one is inclined to pay attention to the opinions of a woman whose personality has been strong enough to lead one toward a step one had never seriously considered, I have welcomed (I hope not too pusillanimously) the excuse to remain where I am. We shall not get married immediately because we feel that we do not want to begin our life together in circumstances which forbid our liberty of action.

Your affectionate son

Emil

"How like him," John commented, "to fill three-quarters of his letter with politics and divulge the really important news as an afterthought. But surely you are not worried about Emil's resolve to get married? It seems to me the best thing that could happen to him."

"No, that didn't worry me. It's this obsession with revolutionary theory. We have suffered so much from that in my family. It cost my brother Jan his life in Siberia. It cost my father exile."

"Yes, but that was Poland. Revolutionary theory in this country doesn't lead as far as Wormwood Scrubs, much less to Siberia."

"But how is he proposing to earn a living if he gives up the consular service?"

"He'll find a way," John said confidently. "I always thought his official career was for him a no thoroughfare. I'm amused by the way he announces his engagement to a young woman. It's so like him not to assume that we should expect it would be to a young woman. And the best of it is that the young woman herself is not very young if it comes to that. She's over thirty."

"That is a young woman, John."

"Not a girl, you mean? Yes, I suppose that's what he was telling us. I wonder what she's like. It sounds like the loves of the triangles."

"It's a relief to me that he *has* found a woman to love at last."

"You needn't have been anxious about that other tendency," John assured her. "He had it absolutely under control."

"Ah, John, I don't believe 'absolutely' can be used of any human body. It was always an anxiety, and it would have continued to be an anxiety as long as I lived."

John shook his head.

"Women regard that tendency with a perplexity, and sometimes a resentment, about the unknown which it doesn't deserve. The serious criticism that can be levelled against homosexuals is their easy lapse into promiscuous indulgence. They have, so many of them, the same apparent insensitiveness in sexual matters as too many women have, and if their tastes lie in the active direction they have, too many of them, the indiscrimination of wanton youth. The result is that if two homosexuals—I hate using this hermaphrodite of a word, but perhaps it is more justifiable than most Greek and Latin hermaphrodites—I was going to say that if two homosexuals find themselves meeting for the first time in a party composed of normal human beings they will be attracted to one another not by personal appeal but by sharing an eccentricity. This I have repeatedly observed. It has always recalled the way that youths who hear that a woman is easy game will run after her just because she is easy game."

"Does that stop with youth?" Miriam asked.

"Not always, but surely maturity without discrimination can be called premature rottenness?"

"And Emil was never promiscuous?" she asked, a little painfully.

"Never. Being honest intellectually, he never deceived himself, and his pride supported by his fastidiousness was too strong for his passions. I would vow that he has been completely ascetic for years now. I imagine that this ice-maiden he has found will be his perfect match."

"She may not be an ice-maiden, John."

"Oh, I think she is. However, whether she be or not, it's clear that Emil has found at last a woman. So let us rejoice."

"John, it always seems to me that of late years you have been inclined to laugh at Emil, rather."

"My dear, I'm not laughing at him."

"As if you rather disapproved of him, almost as if you resented him," she pressed.

"I'm a little frightened of him, I think," John admitted.

"He represents a phase of human development which I distrust. He has such a faith in human perfectibility that he is prepared to sacrifice humanity to achieve it. I suppose, as the domination of machinery grows, the world will gradually be at the mercy of these cold apostles of economic determinism. It's significant, I think, that so many of them are Jews."

"What is the significance?"

"Well, the Jews are the rubble of so many megalopolitan experiments, aren't they? Egypt, Babylon, Nineveh, Rome, the ghettos of the Middle Ages, and to-day. Bricks and mortar are their natural element. If this Zionist idea materializes in Palestine, they'll make a city even of that in due course. It's significant, isn't it, that the early Christians were subterranean city folk, subterranean and subversive in the mass until they began to escape from the trammels of ancestral Jewry? The Jews have been at the mercy of economic determinism since the Pharaohs. And I believe that the fundamental cause of anti-Semitism is the instinct of the Western individual to preserve his individuality. He is horrified by what seems to him the essential similarity of one Jew to another, and the dread lest their corporate influence should succeed at last in overpowering him. In parts of the New World you find a similar dread of the Chinese and Japanese. And you must admit it would be frightening when you had obeyed some atavistic urge to escape from the menacing East to the farthest West to find the East menacing you again from the other direction."

"But, John, that's surely a very different menace. That is the menace of numbers. After all, we Jews all the world over cannot number half the population of England! We could be assimilated so easily."

"I doubt that. I think it's too dominant a strain. I think that the fear of assimilation is another instinctive urge to anti-Semitism. A nation which lent itself to assimilation might easily become assimilated."

"Would you call Emil a typical Jew?" she asked.

"A typically fine flower, yes. But that doesn't say I want the world directed on its course by Emils."

"And Julius? How do you account for Julius?"

"That I cannot account for Julius is my chief hope at present of landing myself into the same mental security as he has found. There's one tune I promise myself in the piping days of peace, and that is an argument between the two of them. But I shan't allow them the support of their wives. For I suspect that dear Leonora will not be as much use to Julius as his ice-maiden will be to Emil."

"I don't know about that. Leonora loves him very deeply. And intelligently too. I haven't shown you her last letter to me. It came by the same post as Emil's, and I must say it was more reassuring to me than his."

"I really do not think you need fret about Emil."

"But, John, if he gives up the service what will he do?"

"I told you I'm sure he will find plenty to do. Do not worry."

"One begins to worry at my age, John. The middle fifties are the anxious time when old age is within sight. I suppose the body is beginning to weaken and in that weakening we begin to dread dependency. One's happiness is no longer at one's own command when age comes. We become dependent on what others can spare from their happiness. Oh, I expect, indeed I am sure that one adapts oneself and probably discovers in doing so a new kind of happiness, but from now for another ten years I shall find it hard not to worry about other people."

"You're feeling the effects of nursing me through this ridiculous fever."

"It's ridiculous now, is it? It wasn't ridiculous three weeks ago. Dr Kember wondered for two days if you would pull through."

He put out a hand as white as hers in the April sunlight that streamed through a budding lime-tree into the music-room, where he was now sitting up for the best of the day.

"I'm not being flippant really," he added. "Show me Leonora's letter."

She fetched it from the walnut escritoire that stood between the windows. The rustle of the papers, the chirping of the sparrows in the lime-tree, and the crackle of the fire seemed to combine in a melody above a silence so deep as to sound like a ground bass.

"They are back in their New York apartment," Miriam said, as she handed him her daughter-in-law's letter:

My dear Miriam,

I do hope you won't mind terribly if I call you that. I feel Mrs Stern is all wrong somehow, and I think it would be silly to call you mother. I ought to have written much more often during these anxious times, but it's just a foolish thing like that which makes one postpone writing and when one does write makes one all stiff and awkward, and to-day I'm so happy because Julius is back from this concert tour and so I feel I must write with all the love I'm feeling in myself. You know Julius has given from the proceeds of his concerts the sum total of 65,000 dollars to the American Red Cross and other war charities. Everybody says it's the most wonderful thing to have done, and I'm so proud of him that I could just swim out of the window and float right across Central Park. I know you were anxious what the effect of taking up concert work again might be on his music, and I was anxious too, but I do honestly believe it has given him more strength for the future. I have never seen him look so well and never heard him sound so well since I met him first in the fall of 1912. I wouldn't have thought I could love him more than I did, but I do love him more and more all the time. And Sebastian is growing so cute, I'm just dying for you to see him. We think over here that the war will be over next year when our troops can really let the Germans know what it means when we do start.

I believe Julius wrote to tell you that I had been received into the Church. I am terribly happy about that because though I knew he wanted it I knew he wouldn't have me do it just to please him. But it was his example which showed me the truth. He's so wrapped up in religion, but not so as to make other folk feel it's anything less than his own music. I don't know if I'm explaining what I'm trying to say. I mean, so many people who become religious make it uncomfortable for other folk because they make them feel they're kind of not playing up by not being just as religious themselves. But nobody would feel they were not playing up if they couldn't compose a symphony. And that was the way I used to feel about Julius. His religion was something he just had *to give way to, and his music was the same. I know lots of wives grow jealous of their husbands' work. Well, I couldn't be that. I just wanted to do everything and say everything and be everything that would most help him, and yet at the same time never let him see that, because I knew if he did he would be angry. And he has been so sweet always in the way, more and more, he has taken me into his confidence. I believe I'm the happiest woman in the world. Anyway, there can't* be *any woman* happier. *And I'd wanted to tell you that so often, and now I have, and I hope you'll love me and think you're glad Julius married me.*

Your very loving
Leonora

John's mind went back to that morning in the May of 1914 when Leonora astounded him with the news that

Julius had gone to church, and when as they sat drinking their coffee together on the terrace of the Albergo Sirene she had told him of her happiness with Julius and asked him to try to find out from Julius if he was as happy with her. He remembered that note in her voice which had filled him with a sudden immense affection for one who had always seemed so self-sufficient and hard and bright, lovely and trim like a little golden humming-bird, preoccupied only with extracting the honey from life. He remembered too how Leonora had told him that morning she was scared of meeting Miriam, and how he had told her they would both love one another.

"That marriage is a complete success. Let's hope Emil has chosen as well," he said to Miriam as he handed back the letter. "And let's hope I choose as well if ever I do choose marriage . . . again," he added quickly.

"You have not yet talked to me about Zoe," said Miriam.

"There is nothing to talk about, my dear. It was a dream from which I had to wake, and who can talk about his dream?"

"But you are able now to think about the possibility of marriage?" she pressed.

"Oh yes, but only as one thinks of a possibility which exists but seems infinitely remote from one's own probable experience."

"I wish you would get married, John."

"I wish I could, when I read a letter like that of Leonora's. And yet I suppose all the pleasure that letter gave you does not outweigh the apprehension you felt when reading Emil's announcement. And you pretended it was Emil's revolutionary theories which agitated you, not his approaching marriage. You showed me Emil's letter before you showed me Leonora's. But they came by the same post."

"John, John, nobody knows better than you what Emil means to me."

"And you think his snow-queen will bury him with her soft flakes and make a snow-man of him so far as you're concerned."

"John, I beg you not to laugh at Emil. It hurts me. It really does."

"Well, I'm going to be brutal and say that I think he should be laughed at when he adds almost as a postscript to a long letter about Red Finns and White Finns and his contempt at the notion that we should expect the Bolsheviks not to murder on the grand scale the news that fortunately he is engaged to a young woman. And I'm sure the best thing for your peace of mind is to laugh too. I think you'll like the ice-maiden so much that she will become the prop of this old age about which you are beginning to have what I believe should now be called an anxiety-neurosis."

Although John appeared to laugh about it, he knew that Emil's abrupt news of his engagement had disturbed the maternal jealousy of a first-born son, and that this was more difficult to allay when she could form only her own idea of what her future daughter-in-law would be. He understood that it had been the contest with this jealousy which had made her declare her relief that Emil had found at last a woman to love. He must persuade her to come with him to Citrano when he went back there as he was planning to go early in June.

John's convalescence moved along without a check. Nurse Widehose had already left at the time Emil's letter arrived from Stockholm. He had enjoyed talking to her during sleepless hours of the night. She had been like a fat old-fashioned novel of long ago, into which he could always dip when in the mood and escape from the pressure of the war which burdened the mind as an undigested weight of unpalatable food burdens the stomach.

"Well, you certainly gave *me* plenty of war and no mistake," she had told him. "Who you *weren't* fighting is what I'd like to know. The Poles seemed to worry you most, and it was only after a bit I found out there *were* such people. I thought it was poles like barbers' poles you were worrying your poor head about. And then there were the Greeks. Oh, dearie me, were they or were they not a trouble? I wish I could remember the quarter of what you said. I'm sure it would give you a rare good laugh now. But it was Greek to me, as the saying is. Anyway they were all over the place. And by what I can make out as quarrelsome a set of people as anybody could meet even at a prize fight. Oh, and the Irish! What the Irish weren't going to do to us! Shocking, really. Tut-tut-tut! And I've known some very nice Irish nurses in my day. Exceptionally nice, they've been. And good at their job what's more, once you got it into their heads that time's time and not a moveable feast as the Prayer Book says. The patients always liked the Irish nurses. Well, they were always so merry and bright. Oh, I haven't got a word to say against the Irish, and it's my opinion if they'd have been given Home Rule when they first asked for it a lot of unpleasantness would have been avoided. But of course people were upset by Parnell and all that divorce business. It's not that lots of people wouldn't like to get divorced if they could, but it's always seemed something the rich can do and others can't, and that always sets people's backs up. Besides, when a man's a Member of Parliament, well, he's a Member of Parliament, and should behave as such. I don't say that's my opinion, because a nurse sees the whole world undressed, as it might be said, but other people don't like to think an M.P. can slip upstairs to the bedroom of another man's wife. Oh, there's no doubt all that scandal did in Home Rule for Ireland."

"You remember the Parnell business well?"

"Remember it? I should think I did. I won the hospital sweep on the Derby that year, and I gave up the idea of marriage for myself."

"Not on account of the Parnell business?" John exclaimed.

"Oh, no. But it had been going on too long. Oh, yes, too protracted altogether. Short and sharp, that's the best for an engagement *or* an illness. I met my young man in '79, and he wasn't by any means too young then. Seven years older than me, and I was twenty-five, being born in the first year of the Crimean. Regular old war-horse, aren't I? Well, in 1890 I was thirty-six, and his lordship forty-three, with a bald patch on the top of his head you could have stood a teapot on."

"Was your young man a juggler?" John asked, grinning.

"Certainly not. He was a commercial. He travelled for Benham & Benham's candles. I was speaking in a manner of speaking. The bald patch was as big round as the bottom of a teapot. Where was I?"

"About to give up the idea of marriage."

"That's right. Well, I was getting a bit tired of being pushed on from Christmas to Easter and from Easter to August Bank Holiday and from August Bank Holiday to Michaelmas, year in year out. And in the October of 1890 I said to him, 'Fred,' I said, 'you've pushed me on to Christmas once too often. Here's your ring, and if you take my advice you'll tie it round the neck of a new-born baby girl, and perhaps by the time she's grown up you'll have settled whether you want to live in Turnham Green or Tooting.' "

"Couldn't he make up his mind between them?"

"Oh, he was building a love-nest for two in every suburb round London. 'You ought to have been a bird, Fred,' I told him once right out. 'You could have flown round with straws in your mouth to your heart's content. Pity you can't marry my new hat instead of me,' because I had a hat that autumn with a lovely red-and-blue bird going right round, and the beak sticking out over the brim ever so saucy. Oh, it *was* a smart hat. All the other nurses were jealous of it. I was at the great Southern Fever Hospital then."

"And what did Fred say when you gave him the go-by?"

"Didn't say a word. Just put my ring in his top right-hand waistcoat pocket the same as if it was a railway ticket, and turned on his heels. Oh, it's always been my firm belief he'd been working up to get that ring back for a long time. Yes, it was just deliberate, because soon afterwards he got engaged to another girl, and he'd have hated to spend money on another ring if he could get mine for nothing. He was mean, was Fred. Very mean. I never did really like him."

"Then why *did* you stay engaged to him for eleven years?" John laughed.

"Really I don't know. I suppose it was a change from nursing. But I must be fair to Fred in one respect. He was never ill. I will say that for him. Never an ache or a pain all the time we were engaged, and an appetite like a horse. Just his hair began to go on the top, that was all."

"But surely you could have met plenty of other men who weren't ill?"

"Only the doctors. And I wasn't up to their style. Oh, I'm not ashamed of it. I came from quite humble people. My father was a jobbing gardener who had a cottage in the North End Road and which his father had lived in before him. He sold penny packets of seeds when he wasn't planting lobelias and marguerites and geraniums in window-boxes. One thing, though, I will say. We were real Cockneys. Widehose & Son, Nurserymen and Seedsmen, founded 1818. That's what we had above the cottage door. And I've always thought that's what gave me the notion to become a nurse."

"1818! A hundred years ago!"

"That's right, just a hundred this year. Oh, dear me, I wonder what my poor old dad would have said if he'd have lived to be blown up by a Zeppelin. Well, he wouldn't have believed it. Nothing aggravated him more than Fifth of November squibs and crackers. I've seen him take his best fork to a Guy when some young varmints pinned a Catherine Wheel to our door which he'd had fresh painted only six months back. Poor old boy. He turned up his toes in the spring of the Diamond Jubilee. Got pneumonia potting up wallflowers in a biting east wind. He was only just turned seventy-two. But my mother's still alive."

"Really!"

"Oh, yes, eighty-eight, and as bold as you like. She can remember Queen Victoria coming to the throne. It made a great impression on her when she was a little girl, and nothing would content her but she must go to the funeral. 'Well, that's that, Alice.' Alice was me, of course. 'That's that,' she said. 'And now let's hope the Prince of Wales'll settle down and be a bit less wild.' I really had to laugh. Oh, well, times have changed since the old Queen's funeral, haven't they? We thought the Boer War was something to wave flags about then, but where would old Kruger be to-day? Nowhere in a manner of speaking."

A queer experience it was, this exclusion from the present brought about by illness, this voyage back into the past conducted by an old woman's garrulous tongue.

"You were born in October 1882, were you? I was twenty-eight then, but I hadn't taken up monthly nursing at that time, or I might have brought you into the world. Pity you should have lost your mother when you were so young."

"She died in the February of the year after you broke off your engagement, nurse."

"Fancy that now. I remember it well. A nasty cold spring, and none too nice a summer neither. But you mustn't start talking about your mother now. It's time you turned over and went to sleep."

The old nurse had shaded the lamp and settled herself down in an armchair by the fire as usual; but that night, whether her book was dull or whether reading was seeming a waste of time, she had started knitting instead. The click of the needles, the tempered and circumscribed radiance in which she sat, the glow of the fire through the woven wire of the high guard, and the mention of his mother carried John back to the house in Westminster where he had spent the first six years of his existence. Thus had his mother sat when he had had croup. And hark, thus sang a kettle then above the click of knitting needles. How safe the surrounding darkness had seemed when his mother sat there in her small tent of light, how rich therein the yellow silk daisies embroidered on the smocked breast of her brown velvet dress!

John made a sudden resolve. When he was quit of this fever he would go down to Cornwall for a couple of weeks before he made the long journey to Citrano. It was absurd that in all these years he had never had the curiosity and the energy to visit Nanphant, and the Cornish land from which half of him had sprung.

Thus, it was owing to Nurse Widehose that John found himself with his father on the platform of Paddington Station on a morning in May. John had let his people know of his plan, and it was Lady Ogilvie's idea that the Judge should spend the few days of the Whitsuntide recess with his son in revisiting the home of his first wife.

John was surprised by the suggestion, but rather pleased.

"I'm glad you don't play golf," he said to his father, as they watched by the door of their compartment the middle-aged gentlemen in tweeds escaping for a few days from the war under the impression that they would return to London refreshed by a surfeit of exercise.

"I've always regretted of late years that I never did take it up," Sir Alexander observed.

"I never shall," John prophesied confidently. "Look at that old buffer in checks, with a complexion of imperial purple. He must have a heart, with a face like that. He oughtn't to be swinging clubs about like a Zulu. Why doesn't he play marbles, if he *must* play with something round? How do you account for this human passion to play with spherical objects? Is it because man was made in the likeness of his Creator? Or does it derive from his monkey ancestors and their coconuts?"

"Exercise is good for people," said the Judge. "It's good for the liver."

"I wonder. It drives a lot of bile into the system. It's not the bad temper on the links, but it's the brooding afterwards on the might-have-beens of their play which is so bad for them. Golf is a favourite game of civil servants, and I'm convinced that most of the worst gaffes in this war have been made on Mondays by civil servants suffering from week-end golf. I'm sure I should never have got through this go of scarlet fever if I'd been a golfer. Extraordinary people the English. They spend their youth playing games like cricket and football to develop the team spirit, and then when they grow up, and a little team spirit would be really useful for the commonweal, they cultivate the ferocious individualism of golf."

They had settled down in the railway carriage by now, and the train was leaving the station with the dignity that distinguishes the Great Western trains.

"This German conspiracy in Ireland is a serious business," Sir Alexander observed, laying aside his *Times* presently. John picked up the paper and read Lord French's proclamation calling on all loyal subjects of His Majesty to aid in crushing the conspiracy to enter into treasonable communication with the German enemy. He read also that numerous arrests of prominent Sinn Feiners had taken place.

"I don't believe in any plot that was not hatched in Dublin Castle," he averred. "I suppose this was why they wanted to send me to Ireland. The Government have not produced a shred of evidence that the fellow landed from a German U-boat was in communication with any of the leading Sinn Feiners. No doubt it was hoped I would provide some material for them."

"It's hardly likely that the Government would arrest all these men without evidence," said the Judge.

"People like Henry Wilson and French and those rats in the Castle are capable of anything."

"But there's no doubt this man Dowling did land from a submarine last month," the Judge pointed out. "He was sentenced to penal servitude for life. He was one of Casement's Irish soldiers corrupted in a German prison camp."

"Dowling may have been landed, but that doesn't implicate the Executive of Sinn Féin. It's obviously a worked-up sensation to justify the Government for taking stronger measures, and obtain support for their conscription policy."

"I think you let your prejudice carry you away. We don't do that kind of thing in this country."

"You officials are beyond me," John declared. "Apparently you do genuinely believe that we are incapable of deceiving the public by manufacturing a plot like this. You still believe that the Gunpowder Plot wasn't worked up by the English officials of the time. And if we ever are proved to have done something disgraceful without any possibility of evasion we convince ourselves that it all happened such a long time ago that perhaps it didn't happen at all, but that in any case it couldn't happen nowadays."

Sir Alexander shook his head with what he believed was the tolerant smile of a man who in the course of his experience in the criminal courts had achieved a philosophic charity toward the worst extravagances of human weakness and folly.

"I'm afraid you'll have to go a long way, my dear John, before you find officials such as we have in this country. My experience at the Bar and on the Bench has at least taught me that."

"Yes, because your conscience demands as much self-deception in order to justify your career. You cannot afford to recognize that the technical justice you administer may be a violation of true morality."

"We have to discover what truth is before we let that remark pass unchallenged."

"There was a judge before your day, Father, who asked what truth was."

Sir Alexander had missed the reference, by the upward movement of his bushy white eyebrows.

"Pontius Pilate," his son reminded him.

"Ah, but he was a military judge," Sir Alexander retorted, smiling. "We have never had a high opinion of the court-martial."

"None of you professional lawyers uttered a word of protest against the Dublin courts-martial held by Sir John Maxwell in May two years ago," his son pointed out.

"What I don't understand," Sir Alexander went on, "is why you have this passion for Ireland. Have you any ultimate justification for your attitude, which I am bound to say, superficially perhaps, appears to me just—er—wrong-headedness? I say, superficially, for perhaps you have some reason which I have not yet appreciated."

"That's a large question," John replied. "Are you prepared to face a discourse above the noise of the train?"

"I hear you perfectly well. Judges are deaf only when they want to be."

"No, now I come to think of it, I don't recall any instance of a judge retiring from the bench under the threat of deafness," John agreed. "One or two had gone off their heads before they were persuaded to retire, but certainly I recall no judge who at any time admitted to deafness."

"And these Great Western trains are wonderfully quiet," Sir Alexander added.

They had been passing through the dreary landscape that marks the approach to London from the west. It had never been a beautiful countryside, but once upon a time its orchards on the flats of the Thames Valley had possessed a sort of cosy charm. Now most of the orchards were derelict, and the railway line on either side was bordered by ugly little factories or dumps of burning rubbish. Some fields pretending to be pasturage were labelled with hoardings that proclaimed them to be eligible sites for more factories.

"Why on earth didn't they use this land for their hospital for mechanized transport?" John asked. "Instead of looking round for six hundred acres of the finest cornland in the neighbourhood and using that at a moment when every acre that will grow corn should be used. There's your official mind working at full voltage."

"You're talking about the Slough Dump?"

"We shall see it presently from the train. I wish it

could be preserved as a memorial to what machinery has done to man, destroying his body in war and in peace his mind. There it is!" John exclaimed, pointing to the north side of the line, where on that desecrated tillage the foul relics of mechanical warfare were accumulating every day. "And will accumulate," John railed, "until the end of the war. I suppose one of those bastards of Mars we call profiteers will buy the lot at a bargain price, and thus deprive us of this super-souvenir of the war."

"But you were going to explain to me your championship of Ireland," Sir Alexander reminded his son, as he lit a cigar. He was not prepared to defend the obscenity of the Slough Dump.

"England still treats Ireland as the potential menace she used to be to her military and naval security in the days when France was her almost permanent enemy, or if not France, Spain. It might be called an inherited fear. Poland has been a similar bogy both to Prussia and Russia. And apart from both Ireland and Poland being Catholic countries there seems a resemblance in character between the two nations. Now, whatever Poland may be to Prussia and Russia, Ireland is no longer a conceivable menace to England."

"Wait a minute," Sir Alexander interrupted. "What about the Easter Rebellion which was inspired by the prospect of German assistance? And in spite of your scepticism I must add, what about the latest plot we're reading about in to-day's papers?"

"Oh, I agree that the Germans with the help of submarines might land a certain amount of munitions," said John. "But that's not a serious threat, and you can take it from me that the prospect of German assistance had nothing whatever to do with the Easter Rising. That was the act of men who were willing to sacrifice themselves in order to regenerate an Ireland which they believed was in danger of succumbing to the corruption of English parliamentarianism. But I don't want to be led away from my attempt to explain my theory about Ireland by what, if that theory be correct, has no bearing on the matter. I only mentioned the ingrained English feeling about the Irish menace to explain the blindness and indifference of the British public to what is happening in Ireland. I've no desire to justify what you call my passion for Ireland by raking up the interminable history of English cruelty, greed and oppression, all of which were inspired by fear. The fear of Ireland's being used as a French strategic base during the eighteenth century, as a Spanish strategic base during the seventeenth century was only the development of an earlier fear which must have dated back to the succession of invasions that made the Englishman the composite breed he is to-day. I won't go back into pre-history, and I'll ask you to accept Celtic as a generic name for the population of these islands when the Romans came. I'd rather go back to old fashioned ethnography and call it Celt-Iberian, for I'm convinced that the peculiar characteristics we associate with the so-called Celts are in fact Mediterranean characteristics. At the other end of Europe, in Greece, there was a similar mixture of race. Well, the Romans conquered Britain except for the mountainous parts of Scotland and Wales. Now, the Romans did not reach Ireland, but their fear of the Caledonians and the Cymri was their fear of the West. Then came the Saxons who preserved that fear of the West. Then came the Danes who had a shot at Ireland, and were badly defeated in the West. There were the Norsemen too, who were finally defeated by the West. Finally came the Normans who were so nervous of the West that they could feel no security until they had attempted the conquest of Ireland. Later on came the conquest of Scotland by England, and the salvation of Scotland by the willingness of the Celtic elements to be led by Bruce the Norman. The point

I want to make is this almost continuous dread of the West which has haunted the other half of these islands for two thousand years and more, due to the paradox of their having always been invaded from the East. That dread culminates in the sixteenth, seventeenth, and eighteenth centuries in the dread of Ireland's use to a Continental foe. Remember that the defeat of the Armada was a blow to Irish and Highland hopes. Macaulay couldn't discover any enthusiasm for its defeat north of where the red glare on Skiddaw roused the burghers of Carlisle. And you will note that the bloodiest oppressors of Ireland were the English statesmen with strong foreign policies like Cromwell or Castlereagh. The nineteenth century discovered a new way of dealing with Ireland and the Highlands, and that was to drive the people to emigrate. The old fear lingered."

"Perhaps there is something in your argument."

"And still lingers," John went on.

"Well, as I said, it's hardly surprising, when we hear of German submarines landing emissaries to stir up disaffection at a moment when this country is engaged in a life and death struggle."

"But there are no longer any real grounds for the fear of these imbecile English—I say English, but of course I include the whole crowd of Anglicized Scots from Aberdeen down to Dover. The English simply have to give Ireland the amount of separation that the Irish themselves demand, and the danger is gone."

"You mustn't forget the problem of Ulster."

"The problem of Ulster is simply a problem of two counties in Ulster, indeed when it comes to it of one city—the city of Belfast. There would never have been an Ulster problem if the Conservative Party had not seen a hope of getting back into power by creating one. I regard Carson, Bonar-Law, and F. E. Smith as political ruffians on a level with Catiline."

"Without going quite as far as that, I do think their behaviour just before the war was marked by a most dangerous irresponsibility," Sir Alexander admitted.

"But don't let me get off on the subject of those three tragic clowns," said John. "The point I want to make about the danger of Ireland being used as a strategic base for operations against Britain is that it has been removed by the new conditions and alignments in Europe. You cannot imagine our fighting France again?"

"No, certainly not."

"Or Scandinavia, or Holland or Spain?"

"No."

"Or fighting Italy or Greece or Portugal for the first time?"

"No."

"But Russia, yes?"

"Certainly."

"And unless Germany is paralysed completely, another war with Germany is possible, even inevitable?"

"I suppose it would be," Sir Alexander admitted.

"In other words, provided we win this war, and the Allies agree to share fairly the fruits of what maritime power has brought them, there is no reason why these maritime powers should fear one another any longer. The struggle for empire should be over. But all the maritime powers have still to fear the East. If Russia and Germany get together after this war the centrifugal force will be tremendous, and the maritime nations really will have to look out. Suppose Bolshevism reaches Germany, which seems to me an extremely likely result."

"And a highly unpleasant result," observed Sir Alexander. "But how does Ireland come into this disagreeable conjunction?"

"Because I believe the essential spirit of the British Isles has been preserved in Ireland," John replied firmly.

"The Englishman and the Southern and Eastern Scot owe their superiority to the Germans to that Celt-Iberian blood which through the centuries mixing with theirs has been the prime civilizing influence, to that and the influence of the west wind, and even where the east wind rules it is an east wind purged of Asiatic dust by the sea. The effect on the Anglo-Irish of living in Ireland is proverbial. If the West Briton could have detached himself from the political dependence on England which gave him his material ascendancy in Ireland, he would be indistinguishable from a genuine Irishman by now. And, to my thinking, what happened to the English in Ireland, happened to the English invaders of Britain. The Cumbrians, the Welsh, and the Cornish . . ."

"Ah, the Cornish," the Judge interposed quickly, with the air of having made a sudden discovery.

"Why do you say that?" his son asked.

"I'll tell you later. Go on."

"The steady Cumbrian, Welsh, and Cornish re-infiltration softened the Saxon, and so in turn the Dane and the Norman, until we have the amalgam that to-day we call British, and by that very word we admit that the Celt-Iberian owners of the soil have reabsorbed their conquerors, though gaining from them certain qualities which in the result have made us the dominant race we are. But in due course, as I see the way Europe will develop after this war, that mongrel race will require revitalizing from a purer source if it is to resist the peril from the East. This then in a word is why I attach so much importance to a free and contented Ireland. I regard it as a fount of inexhaustible Western life. I fore-see that the time will come, not perhaps that I shall live to see it with my body, when all the maritime nations of Europe will become a confederacy to resist annihilation by the swarming myriads of the Eurasiatic continent. But it is difficult to put into words what is really an illumination of the mind from within. The logical process is obscure, but I feel in my very soul the supreme importance of releasing Ireland from the bondage of English materialism so that it may destroy that materialism."

John leant back, and was silent. His voice had competed too long with the rumble of the train. The Judge was silent too. He was hearing the voice of John's mother:

"*Alec, while John is young I want to be sure he has a chance of considering some of the illogical ideas that his mother entertains in her crack-brained Celtiberian head.*"

"Yes," he said aloud, after a long silence, "Yes, it is your mother over again. It is from her you have inherited that illumination of the mind from within. That's why I exclaimed just now 'Ah, the Cornish!' "

"I expect it is," John agreed. "I have always wanted to think it was a throwback to ancestors on your side, but I suppose they compounded with God for the good things of this world too long ago. Has it ever struck you that the probable reason for the lack of anti-Semitic feeling in England has been the Scottish menace?"

"I can't say it has, but I should be inclined to look for it myself in the influence of the Bible over the people of this country."

"Call it a combination of both," John suggested. "The English have identified the immigrant Scots with the Chosen People."

"Well, you know my views, John. I think it's unwise, and indeed dangerous, to try to create barriers between two portions of the same island. I believe I have a dim notion of what you're driving at in your theories about Celticism. Possibly my Highland grandmother handed on something to me. But I don't accept your apocalyptic view of Europe's future. Bolshevism is a menace no doubt, but the Germans are at root a practical people, and I find it much easier to believe in the likelihood of their exploiting Russia after the war than of their letting themselves be exploited by Russia."

"So much will depend on what kind of peace is dictated," John said. "I dread the exacerbation of war, and the dictation of a strategic peace when we have won."

"You have no doubt we shall win?" Sir Alexander asked.

"None whatever. I only wish it could be an honourable draw."

"No, no, John, that would be fatal. The Germans must learn their lesson. Any peace by arrangement will only mean the possibility of a new war as soon as the Germans have recovered from the strain of the present struggle. The Germans must know that they have been beaten."

"In fact they must be treated like burglars?"

"What?"

"They must be given a long sentence of penal servitude, and be always liable after that to preventive detention. Well, of course, that's the simplest solution of the problem of the criminal, but it's a lazy solution. However, never mind about that. It is a solution, and I should not dread it if I were less distrustful of British greed. The trouble is that after this war the country will be in pawn to the banks, and the insurance companies, and the building societies, and all the many devices of capitalism to control the public's money. Do you think they won't regard the reconstruction and re-establishment of Germany as a profitable investment? The French will squeal of course, but that won't stop British finance. I make that prophecy now."

"The bedrock of our future policy must be Franco-British friendship," the Judge declared. "That I consider vital."

"At the moment, yes," said John. "The liaison isn't over yet. The war has still to be won. But when it has been won John Bull will feel that it wasn't a true marriage. John Bull will tell La Belle France what a wonderful time it has been while it lasted, and what a memory it will be to look back on. At the same time John Bull will make it clear that the liaison must stop, and the respectable life of peacetime business taken up again. And when La Belle France screams for settlements and asks what's to happen to the children like Belgium and Serbia and perhaps Poland and Bohemia, John Bull will shake his head and say that the worst of loose women is that they are so hard and mercenary, and he will seriously contemplate marriage with Germania who by that time will be seeming nothing like such a termagant as La Belle France. What is more, the moral cowardice which holds Britain in a palsy will make it afraid to face up to French rage at being jilted and consequently the marriage with Germany will not be acknowledged, and thus the prose of married intercourse will have all the poetry of an illicit and clandestine love-affair."

"An ingeniously sustained metaphor, John, but I doubt if it has much more to it than a rather perverse ingenuity. Nothing is easier to criticize than the incidentals of British policy, but the awkward fact remains for our critics that we always win the last battle and that what appeared in process as laziness, evasiveness, ambiguity, and even rank dishonesty is seen in the result to have been the only policy which would have achieved what was best all round."

"All round?" John echoed.

"Well, if you like, best for Great Britain," his father admitted, a little unwillingly.

"I agree about the infallible instinct Britain has for being good to itself. It is like a great big dog which goes round resting its chin on people's knees and gazing up sentimentally into their eyes and asking to be patted and admired and told what a noble animal it is, always ready to plunge into torrents and rescue children or lead blind men along or collect money for charity at railway stations or defend the house against robbers, but all the time the noble animal's nose is twitching slightly because somewhere the door of a larder has been left open."

"Ah, one can jeer at British methods, but look at what they effect."

"They won't effect anything in Ireland, and that's where we started," said John. "And the chief resentment England feels against Ireland is the way Ireland has always seen through every profession of good-will, every assurance of good intention, and every promise of generous behaviour. However, let Ireland win her freedom, and I believe this war will have been worth all it has cost in blood and treasure because I believe that England in another generation will be revitalized."

"Allow me now to indulge my habit of summing up," said the Judge. "In the course of this conversation you have claimed that the freedom of Ireland—I use the word 'freedom', though I think it is a deplorably loose word—that the freedom of Ireland will revitalize Britain and enable Britain in alliance or federation with other maritime nations to meet the menace of a Bolshevik Russia and Bolshevik Germany in alliance, bursting out of the heart of the Eurasiatic continent to gain breathing-space. You suggest that the inhabitants of these great inland spaces suffer from a periodic outburst of claustrophobia, I gather?"

"So it seems to me."

"Very well. At the same time, you forecast that after the war Britain will shake itself free of the embarrassments of the French alliance and try to achieve a much closer alliance with Germany. I do not understand how you reconcile this forecast with your expectation of a Germano-Russian alliance."

"I put that as an ultimate alliance. I do not believe that an Anglo-German alliance will last because I do not believe the Germans will allow themselves to be exploited indefinitely by British financial interests. I believe that British finance will be unable to handle the world after this war. It is as much out of date as bleeding in medical practice. It is indeed curiously like bleeding in the way it works."

"You surely don't think that the communistic theory will establish itself in economics?" Sir Alexander asked.

"I don't know enough about it," John replied. "But superficially I can't help seeing that it may be the economic salvation of the world, though I distrust the Russian kind. We must face the fact that something is seriously wrong. We should not have had this war otherwise. It's monstrous that, when the world is materially rich enough to support every living being in as much comfort as his imagination can create for him, the vast majority of human beings are existing in perpetual anxiety about their material future. If communism can allay that anxiety communism must triumph."

"And atheism, eh?"

"I don't see why the one should imply the other. All great revolutions encourage atheism, chiefly because the professionals of religion are always reactionary as a class. And for my part I am less afraid of the man who says there is no God than of the man who worships a false God, or worst of all, creates a God after his own private image of petty humanity."

John picked up Hudson's *Wild Life at the Land's End*. The Judge returned to his *Times*, the perusal of which he supplemented in due course with a glance at the *Daily Chronicle*. He did not consider the *Daily Chronicle* a good paper nowadays, but it was associated with that exciting period in the 'nineties when success was carrying him along faster and faster and it used to seem that by calling himself a Liberal and reading the well-written book reviews in the *Chronicle* he was in the van of progressive thought. The loss of Athene had made him much more dependent on the society of his two favourite clubs, the Reform and the Garrick, and the *Chronicle* brought back the atmosphere of that period, degenerate and blatant rag though, in his opinion, it had now become.

A comfortable city, the London of those days, the Judge recalled pensively, laying aside his papers and staring out at the buttercups and streams of Berkshire. Back from the foul air of the Old Bailey to his chambers in the Temple, the misted dusk of a fine October day stealing across the gardens from the river. The sound of footsteps after the heavy surge of the city traffic. His clerk's discreet good-night as he slipped round the door. Hackett had been dead now nearly ten years, passing from life as unobtrusively as once upon a time from his chambers. What a clerk he had been! And then that walk along the Strand to turn up into Long Acre and reach the Garrick. Hardly a theatre left of the old theatres. The Lyceum and the Savoy and the Adelphi, that was all, for the new Gaiety was not the old Gaiety, and Terry's was one of those cinema places now. Gone the Opéra Comique. Gone Toole's. Gone the Globe. Gone the Vaudeville. Gone the New Olympic, but that was in Wych Street. And how much else gone! Clare Market, Booksellers' Row, the Lowther Arcade, even Exeter Hall. A cosy narrow Strand in those days with that faint aroma of gas, horse-droppings, greasy harness, nosebags, oranges, violets, and tar which was London. And the sudden hum of the traffic as one turned up Bedford Street or Henrietta Street or any other side street. And so many familiar shapes at the club gone too. Not to be wondered at in all the years that had passed since he was elected a member. Yes, the decade between the death of Athene and his marriage with Elise had been a generous helping from the hand of Fortune. It had seemed for a long while that he would never enjoy life again without Athene; but the ache had passed and the years had been crowded with hard work and prosperity and agreeable companionship, and just when John's growing up was making him realize that he was in danger of being left behind in the nineteenth century he had met and loved and married Elise. Strange that Elise should have been so insistent upon his travelling down to Cornwall with John. And yet perhaps it was natural she should be anxious for him to identify himself with John's impulse. She might have been afraid lest John should criticize his father for never having once suggested such a journey in all these years. Looking back now to that selfish decade of the 'nineties he must reproach himself with not having taken John down to St Pedoc. He had thought of it once or twice, but the embarrassment he used to feel with John in those days had always prevented his making such a gesture without a selfconsciousness which might have ended in his doing more harm than good.

The buttercups and streams of Berkshire had passed. The spare downs of Wiltshire now bordered the sky. Once Athene sitting opposite to him in a railway carriage had said of these downs that they seemed to race the train like huge green hounds. John had been with them. That was in the May of '87. John would have been four and a half, and he himself, good god, he himself had been nearly ten years younger than John was now.

"I suppose you don't remember that visit we paid to St Pedoc in the year of the Jubilee?" he asked.

"Vaguely, but my visits to Cornwall run together in a blur. I can't disentangle them," John replied.

"Do you remember your grandfather?"

"I remember his velvet coat and the saffron cake he used to give me, and vaguely what seemed a huge house."

"It's not a very large house, but it would have seemed huge to you after our house in Westminster. I've always regretted I did not take you down after your mother died. Perhaps I dreaded meeting your grandfather. Your mother's death broke him up completely. And, oh well. . . . I regret much when I look back at your childhood, John. I understand children so much better nowadays."

"You've had more practice," John reminded him.

"I wonder when you'll think about marrying."

"You will certainly make a most accomplished grandfather," John told him with a smile.

"I was thinking about your tragedy in Greece."

"If I find a woman I want to marry I shall marry," John said remotely, as he picked up his book again. For the rest of the long journey there was no more than desultory chat about any topic the landscape suggested. They alighted in the late golden afternoon at Gwinear Road and changed into the little train to Helston.

Pendarves House was square and grey, built at the opening of the nineteenth century out of the profits of privateering to replace the dwelling which had served this branch of an ancient Cornish family for the previous three centuries. It stood at the head of a sheltered valley which sloped down to a small cove on the eastern side of the Meneage, about half a mile beyond the few white cottages of St Pedoc Churchtown that clustered round a badly restored mediaeval edifice surrounded by stunted pine trees.

"The motor-car has destroyed much of the peculiar fascination of this country," Sir Alexander observed to John as the rusty Ford they had hired in Helston turned aside from Goonhilly Down, a wild tract of cotton-grass and Cornish heath, to enter the drive of Pendarves House, the deep tawny surface of which glinted in the sun like bronze. "When we used to come here thirty years ago there was no railway as far as Helston, and at the end of a long drive Goonhilly Down used to seem the most desolate waste imaginable. Now a car will drive across it in a quarter of an hour!"

The Judge had telephoned from the inn where they had put up to warn the present owner of Pendarves House of his kinsmen's visit, and he had replied with an invitation to lunch.

"I should imagine Henry Pendarves was about fifty now," said the Judge. "His father was an oldish man when he succeeded to the estate on the death of your grandfather."

"What does one call a fifty-year-old third cousin?" asked John. "I can't call him 'Henry'. I'm not sure if I could call any man 'Henry' without feeling he would suppose I was laughing at him. I think I shall call him 'Cousin Pen'."

"You'd better make up your mind quickly," said the Judge, "for there he is, if I'm not mistaken."

They saw a tall lanky man leaning against one of the columns of the porch and watching the appearance of the car through a pair of glasses.

"Ah, how are you? how are you?" he asked, in the brusque way of a very shy man trying to hide his shyness. "I see you got hold of Sam Hockin's car. Good morning, Sam. Fine weather."

"Oh, 'tis handsome weather, sir, sure enough."

"Come in, come in, won't you. William John will look after you, Sam. Better drive round to the stables. Very glad you were able to manage lunch. Wish you could have come last month, though."

"Last month?" Sir Alexander repeated, throwing a quick glance round the room into which their host had brought them, for this had been the study of old John

Pendarves in which on that April evening in 1881, not far from forty years ago, he had looked up from his book to hear that his daughter and the young barrister from London were engaged.

"You'd have seen my daffodils," the host explained reproachfully.

"I remember the rhododendrons here," Sir Alexander observed, in the hope that the rhododendrons of a previous generation would compensate for the loss of to-day's daffodils.

"Yes, there was a wilderness of wretched American rhododendrons all round the house. They gave my father no end of trouble. However, he managed to root them all out at last, and then, as you see, replanted with clumps of bamboo. But I have been planting the best new hybrids every year for some years now. Not here. Down in the valley."

At this moment Mrs Pendarves came into the room, a fair, breastless Englishwoman of the 'county' type whose shoes looked as if they had been put on by the blacksmith and whose clothes looked not as if they were being worn but as if they were hanging from a hook on a bedroom door.

"I am so glad you were able to come to lunch."

"Henry dear, why did you bring them into your potting-shed? I call it Henry's potting-shed," she explained brightly to her visitors, "because this is where he keeps all his gardening books. Shall we wander in the garden for ten minutes before lunch?"

She led the way out to the wide undulating lawn at the back of the house.

"Yes, I'm bound to say that this is an improvement on the tangle of shrubberies I remember," Sir Alexander admitted. "The view is magnificent."

"It is *rather* wonderful, isn't it?" Mrs Pendarves sighed.

Below the lawn the valley was wooded, and a sea of

turquoise blue filled to the brim the gorse-golden cup made by the slope of the cliffs at the end on either side.

"But I do wish you'd been able to come last month," Henry Pendarves insisted. "Of course during the war the Truro Show has suffered, but there were some remarkable flowers. My friend and neighbour Geoffrey Vivian had a beautiful display of his new Poeticus *Lovelace* which I regard as the finest flower of its class yet raised. Form, colour, size, solid texture, and . . . and! . . . the red margin of the eye, which is the fiercest we've seen yet, does not bleach! The sun doesn't affect it. That's a triumph. 'Well, Geoffrey,' I said to him, 'you've had a triumph. I don't remember any flower that deserved its F.C.C. better. That perianth of *Lovelace* has the texture of a gardenia.' I told him frankly I was envious, but he said my Incomparabilis *Entente Cordiale* was quite as great a triumph and ought to have had an F.C.C. instead of an A.M."

"Henry dear," Mrs Pendarves interrupted, "Sir Alexander is a Judge, we know, but he may not be a judge of daffodils, and he may not appreciate the subtle difference between a First Class Certificate and an Award of Merit."

"I'm sorry, I'm sorry," Pendarves blurted out, and he stood silent, thrusting his long neck out at intervals like an uncomfortable bird, for only when he could talk about his daffodils could he escape from the shyness that enclosed him.

"Yes, *rather* a wonderful view," his wife sighed again. "I *do* hope you don't regard Henry as an intruder," she went on, turning suddenly to John, who looked completely surprised by the question, for his mind's eye had been straining to recapture childish impressions of this house, the only result of which had been that such faint memories as he had cherished had now vanished in the presence of the place itself.

"Why should I? If my mother had been my grandfather's son I shouldn't have come into the world."

At lunch two jolly freckled girls in their early teens were added to the company. The two sons of the house were at Sherborne.

"Have you any idea how long the war will last?" Mrs Pendarves asked the Judge. "We're rather out of the world in St Pedoc."

Sir Alexander bowed courteously.

"I'm afraid that prescience is not demanded of a Judge, but I understand we have hopes of making an end of the business next year."

"I was talking to our Vicar after church this morning," Mrs Pendarves went on, "and he tells me that his boy, who's in the Duke of Cornwall's Light Infantry, wrote to him last week not to be worried by the news from France, because Foch had a plan. It seems rather odd to me to put our wonderful men under a French general, but this war has turned everything topsy-turvy. That's Sir Richard Pendarves who raised a troop of horse for King Charles."

This remark was addressed to John, who had been looking across the table at a cavalier hanging over the fireplace—the common ancestor of himself and the daffodil-lover.

"One's ancestors all manage to look very much alike, don't they?" John commented. "It's a pity that the only comparatively permanent residents of a house should possess so little life."

"Henry was painted by a clever young artist at Newlyn just before the war," Mrs Pendarves told him.

In the drawing-room after lunch they looked at this portrait, which represented the present owner of Pendarves House contemplating a vase of daffodils.

"It's all right of me," said the subject. "But he made

a mess of that group of my Ajax *Saffron Maid*, which received an A.M. at Vincent Hall in 1913. That's not the right shade of yellow. It always annoys me when I look at it."

"But your *Saffron Maid* will still be in gardens when you have gone," John asserted gravely. "And posterity will be able to look at the living flowers."

He was startled by the effect of this remark on his kinsman, for his sallow cheeks flushed, his dark eyes sparkled, and so far forward did he thrust his neck that one waited for a loud cock-a-doodle-doo.

"That's kind of you, Ogilvie . . . well, I think I might say, John . . . after all we are cousins . . . both sprung from the same stock . . . very kind of you. I don't think I got as much pleasure from the F.C.C. the R.H.S. gave me for my giant Leedsii *Mont Blanc*. . . . I say, I wish you'd put in a week or so with us when Sir Alexander goes back on Tuesday . . . that is if you must go back, Sir Alexander . . . or why don't you both stay here to-night? . . . Sam Hockin can fetch your bags."

"Yes, do, Sir Alexander," Mrs Pendarves urged.

But the Judge shook his head. He thought they must go back to the Inn, though there was no reason at all why John should return to London with him. In truth the Judge could not have borne to stay in this house, for changed though it was, it was haunted for him by the poignancy of former youth and happiness.

So Sir Alexander went back to town by himself, a little anxious because there were rumours of a severe air-raid on the night of Whit Sunday.

"That's something we escape here, thank goodness," said Mrs Pendarves, when a telegram came from the Judge to reassure his son about the household in Church Row.

John enjoyed his stay at Pendarves House. His young cousins Jennifer and Christabel drove him in a jingle all over the Meneage, and though they deplored the fact that it was not a motor-car, John himself was grateful for being able to visit the villages and the coves, the sands and lonely churches and dark painted cliffs of that strange and remote peninsula, in a rhythm of time closer in accord with its immense past. In the course of these excursions they visited a minute cove called Nanphant, at the head of which, sheltered from the southerly blast by a great bastion of green and black and blood-streaked serpentine, was a small house covered by a pink ivy-leaved geranium. And before the house, in a lawn of vivid grass, was an iris-fringed pool which, said the girls, would later be full of crimson water-lilies.

"Well," John declared, "if ever I get married I shall try to secure that house for my honeymoon, and I will sit under that tree, the name of which, like most of the trees I see in Cornish gardens, I do not know, and read poetry to my bride."

"It's called Benthamia Fragifera," said Jennifer.

"And in the autumn it has fruits like enormous strawberries," added Christabel.

"And the man Nanphant belongs to does let it," said Jennifer.

"Yes, because he drinks, and when he's here all the time he drinks more than ever," added Christabel.

"His name is Corfe," said Jennifer.

"Edmund Corfe," added Christabel.

"He's a painter," said Jennifer.

"But not a very good one," added Christabel.

"And *do* you think you will get married, Cousin John?" Jennifer asked.

"I haven't the faintest idea, Cousin Jennifer."

"I hope you will, John," said Christabel. "But it was Mother who said we were always to call you Cousin John. It isn't Jennifer's fault. Only she's more obedient than me."

"No, I'm not," Jennifer contradicted indignantly. "*You* don't think I am, do you, John?"

"Copy cat?" Christabel cried disgustedly. "*I* dared you to call him John, and you daredn't."

"Well, you shouldn't say I'm more obedient than you are," Jennifer told her younger sister. "Because I'm not."

It was a pity Prudence was not here to enjoy the company, the weather, and the countryside during these idle May afternoons. Yet Jennifer and Christabel believed themselves injured by their father's refusal to let them go to school.

"You're a pair of young duffers," he told them one day when they were sitting on a grassy slope of cliff and gazing across the gently breathing expanse of Mount's Bay. "You don't realize the advantage of having a governess."

"But Miss Viney's so dull," they proclaimed in unison.

"Nothing like so dull as most schoolmistresses," he assured them.

"But even if the mistresses were dull the other girls wouldn't be dull," Jennifer expostulated.

"Don't you believe it. My young sister Prudence moaned and groaned until my stepmother sent her to school—a day-school too—and now she's kicking herself because she can't go back to her governess."

"But Prudence was in London. We wouldn't want to go to school if we lived in London," Christabel pointed out.

"It's so dull down here," Jennifer went on. "We don't see anybody. We can't go to theatres or to cinemas. We can't look at any shops."

"You can look at the Atlantic."

"The Atlantic!" Jennifer expostulated. "As if one wanted to sit and look at the sea all day."

"We haven't even had a good wreck," Christabel sighed. "William John found a barrel of spirits in our cove, and we helped him roll it up out of sight of the coastguards, but that was the only exciting thing that happened all last winter."

"And that wasn't *very* exciting," Jennifer said.

"Except when Mr Mavor preached about the evils of drink after Willie Lugg saw a merry maid on Good Friday morning sitting on the Bushel of Wheat, which is a rock you only see at a very low spring tide," Christabel babbled. "And old Mrs Lugg got in some frizz and walked out in the middle of the sermon on Easter Sunday because she said she came to church to hear *Christians Rejoice* and not have her son called a heathen because he'd gone wrinkling on Good Friday as he'd always belonged."

"And she and Willie both go to Chapel now," Jennifer said.

"But did Willie Lugg see a mermaid?" John pressed. "And was she combing her hair?"

"No, she was picking bits of seaweed out of the end of her tail," Christabel told him. "I think he must have seen her, don't you, Jennifer?"

The other girl threw a quick suspicious glance at their cousin to see if he was laughing at them.

"We haven't seen a merry maid, but other people have," she said at last. "Ernie Champion saw one when he was out fishing on a moonlight night, and she climbed into his boat and he was so frightened that he nearly jumped overboard."

"He would have done, he said, if he hadn't been afraid the merry maid would jump in after him and drag him down to the bottom of the sea," Christabel added.

"I think he was very wise," said John. "Obviously the mermaid would have had it all her own way in the water."

"You're not laughing, are you?" Christabel asked, a little anxiously.

"Certainly not. I'm thinking more than ever what a

pair of coots you two girls are to be wanting to live in London."

"But it is dull here, John," Jennifer protested. "These are only things that happen very, very seldom."

"Never mind, I'd swap all the shops and theatres in London to see one mermaid."

"Mother said you wrote plays. Isn't that tremendously exciting?" Jennifer asked.

"Oh, it must be," Christabel said earnestly. "Fancy hearing what you'd written being said on a real stage. Mr Mavor wrote a play for the children to perform the Christmas before last, and if one of them said a word wrong he got in a frightful rage."

"Yes, but the Vicar's play was nothing," Jennifer scoffed. "Father said afterwards he'd never spent such a deplorable evening."

"Yes, but you know he hates Mr Mavor," the younger sister put in.

"He doesn't hate him, Christabel. Only he thinks he's silly. He says a Cornishman ought to understand his own parishioners better and not try to teach them to copy the ways of foreigners."

"I certainly agree with your father," said John. "Hence my sympathy with his refusal to let you go to school."

"But he let Hugh and Richard go to Sherborne," Jennifer pointed out.

"Well, you see, the trouble is that boys have to make careers for themselves, and school is supposed to be the best preparation for making your own way in this world."

"Girls have careers too," Jennifer argued.

"Yes," said John, "but owing to this being a comparatively modern notion there's no tradition of a school education for girls, and it's no handicap not to have been to some recognized school. In fact the famous girls' schools are considered a legitimate subject for mirth."

"It's all very well for you to talk," Jennifer argued, "but you've been to school and you've lived in London and you've written plays and you're old."

"Old? Do I seem very old?"

"No, you don't seem *very* old," she went on. "But you are old, because mother said what a pity you were so old."

"Why a pity?"

The two girls looked at one another, and forthwith laughter floated out across the silver-blue expanse of Mount's Bay.

"You'll promise not to be angry if we tell you?" Jennifer asked.

"Of course not."

"Swear," Christabel adjured.

"I swear I won't be angry."

"Well, she said to father that it was a pity you were so old because you would have been an ideal husband for one of the girls."

"That's us," Christabel shrieked in an ecstasy of delight.

"She didn't know we could hear her," the older sister gasped in helpless merriment.

"It's just as well I am such a Methuselah," said John, "because if you'd been a little older and I'd been a little younger, I wouldn't have known how to choose between you."

"Yes, but neither of us might have chosen you," Christabel pointed out, with a triumphant laugh.

"Not if I'd offered to take you to London in the fastest motor-car you can imagine?"

"I wish you weren't so old," Christabel sighed.

"Wouldn't it do as well to wish that you were older?" he asked.

"Yes, but think how old we should have to be!" she exclaimed.

"Ah well, it's very jolly as it is," said John. "And to-night I shall go and look for a mermaid."

"You might get pisky-led," Christabel warned him. "Jimmie Bray was pisky-led once. He was coming back from Helston one Saturday night and just before he came to St Pedoc Churchtown the piskies caught him up and swung him three times round the church tower, and then they took him across Goonhilly Down and dropped him in the middle of Deadman's Pool, and on Sunday morning he woke up hearing the bells ringing for church, but he was afraid to go because his face was scratched with brambles. He said he wouldn't go through such a night again for more than a thousand pieces of gold."

"Did he see any of the piskies?"

"You can't see them. They're too tiny. There are millions and millions of them and they catch you up like a wind."

"Then I shan't go and look for a mermaid," said John. "I shall spend the evening talking to your father."

He enjoyed those evenings with Henry Pendarves in the room that his wife called 'the potting-shed'. The talk was almost entirely about flowers, but his kinsman was able to give life to his discourse, and John used to lie back in a battered old armchair and ask himself if existence held a greater pleasure than listening to an expert talking with complete assurance on his own subject. And during the mornings when the girls were at work with Miss Viney it was another pleasure to accompany Henry Pendarves round his garden, and find that every flowering shrub and herbaceous plant had an individual history.

"But I do wish you had come last month before the daffodils were finished. You'll have to come down another time at the beginning of April. Next year I'm expecting some grand new flowers from the crosses I made in 1912."

"Do you always have to wait seven years for a daffodil sown from seed?"

"Oh, it may be as much as ten years before you really know what you've got, and with some kinds a much shorter time. I started with Cyclamineus hybrids only three years ago, and I'm hoping for some results next year."

They were standing in one of the small greenhouses, the single shelf running round which was covered with square terra-cotta seed-pans full of green stems of various heights.

"And I've been working at the jonquils for a year or two," he said, running his hand lovingly along the top of some minute strands of what looked like young grass.

They moved on to another house where small pots held miniature shrubs about three inches high.

"I've started on rhododendrons," he revealed in the whisper of a man confessing to a fearful disloyalty. "I always swore I wouldn't, but they get you in the end. It's a secret, though. I haven't told anybody except my gardener that I've started on rhododendrons. William John knows. And now you know. But I'm not going to tell anybody else. I want to surprise 'em in Truro."

John asked when he might expect the first flowers from his new rhododendrons.

"About fifteen years from now. Perhaps fourteen, but I doubt it. And of course I may get nothing worth showing for twenty years or longer."

John expressed some dismay at the patience involved.

"Ah, but don't forget my daffodils give me something every year now. I started with them before I was married. But anyway that's the great advantage of raising flowers or even of ordinary simple gardening. The older you grow the better your garden is. Think what an exciting time I shall be having with my rhododendrons when I'm seventy. Every year something new and something better. Besides, I amuse myself with kniphofias, and I've been tackling Chapman's freesias, and I told William

John the other day I had a dam good mind to work on gladioluses. That's a two-year job."

"Mere lights o' love compared with your marriage to daffodils and your bigamy with rhododendrons," John commented.

They passed out of the house with the rhododendron seedlings, the door of which Henry Pendarves locked behind him with the air of one emerging from the vaults of a bank.

"I'm glad we've made friends after all these years of losing touch with your people. I'm afraid old John Pendarves, your grandfather, felt it a bit when he was dying and knew the place must pass to a junior branch, but I think he'd be pleased with the way I keep the place going. He had hopes of reviving the language, but it had been dead too long. Still, though we've lost our language, we keep ourselves clear of the English, except that ass of a vicar of mine. I gave him the living because he was a Cornishman, and all he's done is fill the place up with cockney ideas. Deplorable! Deplorable! I'm a little worried about my two boys too. I can't get either of them to think about anything except motor-bicycles and motor-cars and all that kind of muck. And the two girls would be as bad if I let 'em. Why the women all want to be men is beyond me. There's something wrong with a country where that's happening. In one way I made a mistake in marrying a foreigner."

"A foreigner?" John echoed in amazement.

"Ethel came of a Devon family. Oh, I don't mean to suggest we don't get on together splendidly. But racially it's a mistake. I'm sure all these motor-car, motor-bicycle notions come from foreign blood. She used to hunt a lot too before I married her. And Hugh spent the winter holidays with some friend of his, and he started hunting. And I heard one of my girls say she wished she could start hunting. We shoot foxes in this part of Cornwall if they're a nuisance. We don't hunt 'em, though I hear that up in the east of the Duchy they have a pack. Let 'em start a pack in the Meneage," challenged Henry Pendarves, "and by G——, I'll shoot the first hound that crosses the boundary of my land!"

"I fancy you're safe from hunters here," said John, thinking of the wandering Cornish heath three feet high. "I wish you were as safe from golfers."

"Infernal fellows," his host agreed. "But we haven't got 'em just round here. There again! My two boys are for ever getting over to the links on the towans above Gunwalloe. And I make no doubt Jennifer and Christabel won't be happy presently unless they're playing that numskull game."

"I find, Henry, that we have much in common besides a long ancestry," said John.

"I know. I know. We mustn't let this drop. I don't make friends easily. But I knew when you understood what I feel about my daffodils that you'd understand the way I felt about a lot of things. And you're going back to Italy soon?"

"Very soon now. I feel rather a fraud taking such long leave from my job, but after all the war *may* go on for another couple of years."

"Yes, I daresay. Too many people interested in keeping it alive," Henry Pendarves agreed. "Ethel is getting anxious of course about Hugh, but in her heart she'd be proud to say he was out in France. *I* wouldn't. If the lad was killed I wouldn't be proud, because I wouldn't think he'd been killed to save any of the things I think worth fighting for. I don't want to save Cornwall for tourists and golfers. I don't want to save Cornwall for the trawlers owned by a lot of fat business men who have ruined our fishing grounds and deprived us of the pilchards which have been ours for centuries. I don't want to save Cornwall for the Great Western

Railway shareholders. We lost our language. We lost the old faith. We lost our king. But we kept our old way of life and old way of thought; we shan't keep either long after this war. And what angers me is that the people of this country are being deliberately corrupted by the press and the pulpit in the interest of money. I've nothing against the *people* of England except their stupidity in not seeing the way in which they're being exploited by these big-business blackguards. Have you ever noticed that Cornwall, Wales, and Scotland always return a majority of Liberals? And Ireland has gone one better by returning Home Rulers. Isn't that voting Liberal the last flicker of the Celt's revolt from the alien culture that has been forced upon him? And what I complain of is that these damned men of business can't even run their own business. Look at our tin-mines. Oh, the war has helped them a bit, but that won't last. After the war you'll see Cornishmen going off again to work in the tin-mines of Bolivia. But I won't rail any more. I keep my mind off politicians or I should go melancholy mad. Don't think I talk like this every day. But you understand my point of view."

"Perfectly, and I can't tell you how warm a thought it will always be to think of you in St Pedoc."

"You know, when your father rang up from Helston and said he wanted to call on us, I don't mind admitting I didn't take to the notion. I always do curse that telephone, and I wouldn't have had it put in if Ethel hadn't insisted on the advantage of it for housekeeping. Strangers make me nervous at the best of times, but when they're kinsmen one doesn't know how the devil to deal with them. . . . I met your mother once. She was a beautiful girl, and I was a clodhopping boy at the time. She was staying near Bodmin, where we lived then. It was before your father came on the scene, and I got it into my head that she resented the entail. So I suppose I was sulky and shy. I don't know why, but I always got it into my head that she withered, away from Cornwall. Athene Pendarves! Her mother was a Trefusis. She died young too."

That night John wrote to Athene Langridge:

PENDARVES HOUSE,
ST. PEDOC R.S.O.
SOUTH CORNWALL
May 31, 18.

My dear Athene,

You'll be thinking me a churl for not writing before, but almost as soon as I reached London I went down with a rather bad go of scarlet fever, the result of which is that I have been given another agreeable stretch of leave. So I'm preparing to get back to Citrano by mid-June at latest. I'm hoping to persuade my friend Mrs Stern to come with me. She has been nursing me with great kindness. I saw Wacey on my way through Paris. He was in very good form, and full of the fighting spirit like all your countrymen. I wish they weren't, to tell the truth, for they may keep the war going because it's still a new toy. I'm staying for a few days at my ancestral home and feeling extremely Celtic and remote from the tormented present.

My friend Fitzgerald has been arrested again, I fear, though I am not sure yet. However, I'll give you all my news when we meet, because I don't want to waste ink to amuse some buffoon of a censor. Small men are Titans in these days—behind the lines. Remember me to all Citrano friends.

Ever affectionately,
John

Do not fear for the health of Arthur Gilmer. I am no longer leprous. I hope he's flourishing.

Three days after writing this letter John returned to London. He was accompanied to the station by Jennifer and Christabel, who had the exquisite pleasure of driving to Helston in Sam Hockin's rusty Ford. Their journey back would be made by the horse-bus, after lunch with friends.

"Good-bye, sweet cozes, and thank you for being so amiable to me. I'd kiss you both if you weren't so young and freckled."

"Oh, you *are* cheeky," Christabel gasped. "Just wait till you come back."

"Yes, wait till you come back!" Jennifer called after him as the little train puffed out of the station.

John sat back in the carriage, wondering why he had been so foolish as never to visit before the land in which half of himself was rooted.

Citrano was a scene set in an empty opera-house when John reached it with Miriam Stern in the third week of June; but the spirits of Don Alfonso Massa, Don Augusto Di Fiori, and Don Rocco Picarelli were buoyed up by the rumour that Citrano had been chosen as one of the places to which British officers convalescent from wounds or illness could be sent from the Piave front. On top of this it was said that a few Neapolitan families, who deprived by the war of their usual *villeggiatura* had experimented with Citrano as a holiday resort during the previous summer, had sung the praises of their experiment so loudly all over Naples during the winter that judging by the enquiries for accommodation Citrano was presently likely to be thronged. In fact the Hotel Excelsior and Imperial was now to be open to the extent of its capacity, and there was already talk of erecting another big hotel as a cistern for the torrential influx of which Don Alfonso, Don Augusto, and Don Rocco dreamed in the future. The end of the *miseria* which had threatened to ruin Citrano during the first three years of the war was in sight.

Meanwhile, the little resort lay like a ripening peach on the sunny window-ledge of a quiet room.

"Was there ever a lovelier view?" Miriam asked, when they leant in turn over each side of the castellated parapet that ran round the roof of the Torre Saracena. Northward, the white and blue and pink and yellow houses of Citrano scrambling up the cliff under the big hotel that was reduced to an impertinence by the majestic bastions and wooded gorges of Monte Sant' Angelo beyond. Eastward, across a level stretch of sand, the tumbledown little port sheltered by the promontory on which the green-tiled dome of the Church of Our Lady of Citrano shimmered against the mountainous line of the Salernian Gulf fading into the haze above the marshes where once bloomed the rose-gardens of double-bearing Paestum around those temples of travertine. Westward, the sweep of limestone cliffs rising sheer for a thousand feet, and seaward the islets of the Sirens, and beyond a Capri now dimmed to a ghostly blue. Southward, the wide empty glittering expanse of the Tyrrhenian.

"Lovely, lovely," she murmured. "And what spices in the air! John dear, this is the most delicious treat."

"But I must get hold of a piano as soon as possible. I ought to have hired one in Naples on my way through."

But it proved unnecessary to go to Naples, for Margarita said that her father had a piano, recently bought.

"It can be a very good pianoforte," Fofo declared, when he had led John to the mysterious hinterland of his shop and shown him a cottage Bechstein.

"I wonder if it's much out of tune," said John. "The tone is very good."

Fofo shrugged his shoulders. He did not pretend

to be a musical expert. John decided to make the purchase and get a tuner over from Naples. The instrument was a bargain. So it should have been, for it was the cottage Bechstein which Julius Stern had bought in 1914 as a present for Sister Franzeska and the Sisters of St Elizabeth to celebrate his baptism in their chapel. Sister Franzeska and the four German nuns had been sent back to Breslau after a period of internment, and Fofo had bought the sequestrated property of enemy subjects cheap. It was a pity John did not know the history of the piano, but he had never heard of Julius's gift.

"This is what I used to dream of when Salonica was seeming too foul to be endured much longer," he told Miriam when, sitting by the southern window of the library and gazing into the face of the full midsummer moon, he had listened for an hour to the music of Chopin. The play of Miriam's fingers across the black and white notes was like the rippling of the moonlight on the sea.

Geoffrey Noel who had been dining with them asked if Mrs Stern ever played any Debussy, and when she played for him some of the Preludes he wriggled in such paroxysms of emotional and aesthetic contentment that if he had been sitting in a shallower armchair he must have landed on the floor.

"Really Debussy gives me . . . m-m-m . . ." But he could not express what Debussy gave him, and lit his pipe instead, while away somewhere in the night a grillo's silver shrilling challenged the moon.

At the north window stood Athene Langridge, the golden curtains behind her seeming to break into flame along the silken line of her frock. She was lost neither in the music nor the moonlight at that moment, for she had fancied she saw an unexpected light in the Villa Allegra, and a sudden apprehension of fire had seized her, with Arthur's safety threatened.

"That tango frock of yours looks like fire from here, Athene," John observed.

She turned round startled.

"Oh, John, how you made me jump!" she exclaimed. "I was just foolishly wondering about fire."

"Not at the Allegra?" he asked, with a teasing smile.

"I know you think I'm a fussy old hen, but I just get caught up by these crazy ideas, and," she turned to Miriam, "you understand, Mrs Stern?"

The older woman rose from the piano and drew her from the window back into the glow of the room.

"I understand very well, my dear," she said.

"Now, now, Miriam, don't pretend you were ever as anxious about Emil and Julius," John protested.

"You didn't know me when they were small, John."

"Thank goodness, I've no children to worry about," Noel mumbled.

"I believe you worry every bit as much over Francesco, Mr Noel, as I do over Arthur," Athene laughed. "And now I suppose if I say I must be going along, John, you'll declare for ever and a day that I left your perfectly good party because I saw a lamp in a window and thought the Allegra was burning."

"Athene, it's not yet midnight. That's a wretched hour to break up a Citrano party."

"Why, John, I know it is, but I've grown so middle-aged this last year."

"Well, dear lady, if I may offer you my escort home?" said Geoffrey Noel, rising from his chair.

"There you are," John protested, "you've broken up the party with a vengeance."

When Athene and Noel had gone, John asked Miriam if she was too tired to play any more.

"You're voracious to-night," she said, seating herself again at the Bechstein.

"I know, but *hoc erat in votis*, this was in my prayers on

how many vile jangling dusty nights in Salonica, and on the beaches of Gallipoli, and beyond the fever in Lipsia."

"What shall I play you now?"

"That Mozart sonata you played to me when I was ill in London."

When she had finished and closed the lid of the piano, he asked her abruptly what she thought of Athene Langridge.

"She's lovely to look at. Quite lovely."

"Does that mean the extent of your approval?"

"No, of course not, but she doesn't reveal very much at a first meeting."

"I'm very fond of her," he declared firmly.

"In love with her?"

"Good heavens, no!"

"Beginning to be in love with her?"

"No, no, certainly not. I don't fall in love with young married women."

"You have a book of rules?"

"Don't be absurd, Miriam. Remember I've known Athene now for over five years. One doesn't begin to fall in love with a woman five years after meeting her."

"It sounds like a natural law when you put it like that," she told him. "But I've never been able to convince myself yet that one can lay down laws about falling in love. It may be true you met her five years ago, but you didn't meet her alone, I fancy, until last autumn."

"But her husband is a friend of mine. Moreover, they're devoted to one another. I got to know her better because she's less self-conscious when . . . when . . ."

"When her husband's not with her?" Miriam suggested.

"Now I've given you an entirely wrong impression of Athene," John said, a little irritably. "And really it's your fault. She is a perfectly ordinary young American woman with a good-looking rather weak husband and an amusing small son. I was first interested in her because of her name."

"Well, John dear, I shall say no more until I've had a chance to see more of her. And as you're not in the least in love with Mrs Langridge I shall be able to be delightfully frank, shan't I?"

"I hope you will be frank. I'm always frank with you."

"You say that with a trace of huffiness, John. So let an elderly lady retire, and forgive her if she has misjudged your interest in her answer to what was evidently the most casual of questions."

He jumped up.

"Miriam, I really am not in the slightest bit near to even playing with the idea of being in love with Athene Langridge. But she does—well, she baffles me. I can't make out if there's any real depth behind that manner of hers. She's been a puzzle for a long time."

"John, John, I must go to bed quickly, before I start arguing with you how dangerous it is for a man who disapproves of falling in love with young married women to allow himself the indulgence of being perplexed by them."

And with this Miriam Stern vanished from sight down the spiral staircase.

"Good night, dear lady," Geoffrey Noel was saying to Athene Langridge five minutes later at the door of the Allegra courtyard, just as their host of the evening was trying to make up his mind to tear himself away from the moonshine and go to bed himself. "Charming dinner, wasn't it? She really played beautifully," and humming to himself a phrase from one of the Debussy Preludes, Noel tripped homeward over the cobbles.

Athene was about to switch on the lamp in the square

entrance hall, when the door opposite opened and a figure in khaki stepped forward from the lighted sitting-room.

"Wacey! Why didn't you let me know you were coming?"

"I sent you a telegram from Rome? Didn't you get it? Hell, I'll have to make a fuss about that."

"But why not cable me from Paris?" she asked. "You know how much I hate to be caught suddenly unaware. In your last letter you said there wasn't a chance of your getting down to Citrano this summer."

"Well, come on in," he said. "You don't need to stand there in the hall."

"I'll go along the corridor first and see if Arthur is all right."

"Oh, Arthur's fast asleep. I peeped in at him. I've only been back half an hour. I'd have come down to the Torre Saracena, but knowing you hate surprises so much I didn't want to make you mad by suddenly breaking into a party."

She had followed him back into the sitting-room, the french-windows of which were wide open; guessing that he wanted her to come out on the terrace, she sat quickly down in a chair.

"If you sent me a telegram from Rome, why would I have been surprised?" Athene asked. "Why would I have gone to a party at all?"

"Well, as you were at a party, naturally I guessed my telegram hadn't reached you."

"How long are you going to stay here?"

"I believe I can put in a full week. Say, Athene, I have something for you."

"Wacey, you know I don't want you to spend your money on presents at a time like this," she said as his hand went to the pocket of his tunic."

"Don't worry, dear. I haven't brought you any presents. It's only this."

He handed her an envelope. It was from the chemist in Rome.

"I don't want to read this," she said distastefully.

"Ah, come on, read it, and you'll see it was all a fool mistake by Ferraro. When I told him what he'd done he was horrified. Read it, and see what he says."

"At your prompting," Athene commented, eyebrows slanting to a sharper angle.

"You might read the darned letter before you roast me for an imaginary crime," he said reproachfully.

"No, I won't read the letter, Wacey. You won't deny, I suppose, that you've just seen Ferraro in Rome?"

"Sure, I saw him. I couldn't get square with you until I saw him. Hell, it hasn't been so funny for me all these months, fixed as I was, and unable to straighten anything out. And now," he went on in the voice of a man who has touched the ultimate depths of human disillusionment, "you want to hang me without waiting to see if you might be doing me an injustice."

"I wonder you haven't more pride," she exclaimed with dark resentment. "To take Ferraro into your confidence!"

"Pride nix," Wacey retorted, "I'm not going to see my married life broken up because I'm too proud to have a fellow write and tell you he's made a mistake. Ah, come on, dear, read Ferraro's letter."

She looked at the envelope in her hand, tore it twice across, and put the pieces on the small table beside her chair.

"I don't want to revive or extend the humiliation," she said coldly. "I suppose you didn't telegraph from Rome because you didn't want me to know how long you were spending with Ferraro in working out an explanation."

Wacey looked up at the ceiling in despair at the power of suspicion over a woman's mind.

"I did telegraph from Rome, Athene."

"Yes, just as you were leaving, with the result that it hasn't been delivered yet."

"I know. I'm going to make a complaint at the post-office to-morrow morning."

"Will you persuade one of the Margiotti girls to write you another letter?"

"It's useless, I see, to reason with you in your present mood."

"Useless," she agreed.

"And so because of a fool mistake by a clerk you'll believe for the rest of our lives that I was imbecile enough to do something I couldn't ever have dreamed of doing?"

"I never knew until now that there was any limit to your dreaming."

He bowed his head in ironical gratitude.

"Thanks for so charitable an opinion. You'll pardon me, dear, won't you, if I suggest that you don't believe me because you don't want to believe me?"

"Oh, Wacey, don't play the injured innocent," she begged wearily. "I'd so much rather you admitted that, through my fault if you like, you meant to have a wonderful time in France. I can understand in a way. I know I've never been able to give you what you hoped for. But be honest about it. That's all I ask."

"I am being honest, Athene. That's the whole trouble. I wouldn't be feeling as wretched as I do if I had something to reproach myself for. I could take my medicine. It's coming up against a stone wall like this that's getting me down. For you to disbelieve me like this shows you don't love me any more."

"I never have loved you," she cried desperately. "Not in the way you wanted me to love you."

"You wouldn't let yourself," he argued. "You got it into your head that it was undignified to be human."

"Wacey, why must you always believe what you want to believe?"

He laughed bitterly.

"That's a good one to pull. Why, the whole trouble between us just now is that *you* are believing what you want to believe. Oh, I know what it is. You think I won't make good as a writer. You resent my lack of ambition. Well, perhaps you're right, but why take advantage of this fool mistake of Ferraro's clerk to put me in the wrong? I'll admit I've wasted my time. The trouble was you made life so darned pleasant that I was content just to enjoy it in your company. Forget what I said just now about your dignity. I know you can't help being cold. You're made that way. But don't think it has made any difference to my happiness with you."

He left his own chair to come over and sit on the arm of hers.

"It's lucky I didn't come down to the Torre Saracena when I arrived, or you might have had to kiss me for the sake of appearances," he said in that soft Southern drawl.

She sat frozen.

"Won't you kiss me, Athene?"

"There are no appearances to keep up here, Wacey."

"Well, I wouldn't say that," he murmured. "You see, I found you'd moved my bed out of our room, and of course when I arrived Assunta was a bit agitata, and the first thing she and Maddalena did was to put it back again. I couldn't very well tell them to leave it where it was, could I? You don't want the servants making a story about my return all over Citrano. Besides, I thought that when you read Ferraro's letter you'd forget what you wrote me last October."

"*How* long are you staying here?"

"I won't have more than four or five days."

"And nothing can be settled now," she said, to herself rather than to him.

"I don't exactly know what has to be settled," he answered, "but whatever it is, it certainly cannot be settled now. I'm part of the American Expeditionary Force now. And they've a way of settling your affairs for you. I guess they've settled quite a few things for lots of folks."

"Let's go to bed," she said abruptly.

He jumped up with alacrity.

"Did you have a good evening at John Ogilvie's? When I saw him on the way through Paris in March he wasn't expecting to be back so soon."

"He had scarlet fever. He's here with his friend Mrs Stern."

Wacey raised his eyebrows.

"Oh, he has a lady friend with him, has he?"

"Twenty years older than himself."

"And what did you think of that Irishman Fitzgerald? Did he tell you we met at the theatre where another lady friend of John Ogilvie's was acting?"

"Oh, yes, I had a certificate of your perfect behaviour as a husband."

"Sarcastic, eh?"

"Not in the least."

As Athene turned to leave the sitting-room she told Wacey that he had better gather up the torn certificate from Ferraro. "For I suppose you don't want the maids to talk about the contents of *that* round Citrano?" she asked coldly.

"They wouldn't learn anything from it," he answered. "Look, let me read you what he says. I can piece it together."

"Is that necessary? Don't you know the letter by heart?"

He sighed, put the fragments in his pocket, and after closing the windows of the room, followed her down the corridor.

When the light was out Wacey flung open the lattices to flood the room with moonshine. So light was it that he could see through the drawn curtains of the mosquito-net Athene's brown hair upon her pillow.

"Athene," he began tentatively.

"What is it?" she interrupted, in a voice that sounded like a snapped icicle.

"I guess we'll bathe to-morrow morning, eh?"

"If you want to bathe, Wacey."

"You bet your life I want to bathe. It isn't too light for you with the moon, is it?" he asked.

"You might pull the shutter round so that it doesn't shine on my face," she replied to his undesired solicitude.

He seized the excuse to stand close by her bed and moved the shutter to various angles, gazing the while intently through the netting lest in those dark eyes he might fancy a softer gleam; but she turned over on her other side and nothing was left except the brown hair, the unresponsive brown hair.

It was about eight o'clock next morning that John woke to the sound of his name being called from below the window of his room. He was astonished to see Wacey Langridge in a bathing-wrap among the stripling cypresses which Wacey himself had had planted for him three years earlier.

"When did you arrive?" he exclaimed.

"I had a few days' leave and reached here last night."

"Why didn't you come round last night?"

"Assunta told me there was a festa going on at the tower and I didn't want to show up in uniform and cast a gloom over everything. I only reached the Allegra half an hour before Athene came home. Come on down and have a bathe."

After the bathe John invited Wacey to have coffee, which they took on the roof of the tower in the perfection of an early June morning.

"You haven't changed much from the way I arranged the place," Wacey observed.

"No, as I told you in Paris, there was hardly anything to change."

"It's a corking place," said Wacey. "I grew kind of in love with it myself. We didn't lose a cypress, and they've come along fine."

"Wasn't Athene surprised by your arrival? It must have been your light she saw from the window. She was worrying if the Villa was on fire. That's really what sent her home so early."

"Yes, she was a bit surprised. The darned post office never delivered the telegram I sent her from Rome."

"She hates unexpected visitors," John said, with a smile which drew a quick glance from Wacey.

"Oh, you've discovered that, have you?"

"Yes, I was at tea sometime in the winter when Mrs Heighington paid a sudden call. You'd have thought it was a billeting party of German troops." He laughed in enjoyment of the memory. " 'I cannot think why people want to call without letting one know they're coming,' she spluttered. 'I don't see why Mrs Heighington should assume I must be dying for her company.' Oh, I tell you, Wacey, I wouldn't look in casually at the Villa Allegra for anything."

"She's always been like that," said Wacey. "I used to jolly her and say it was because she was afraid of being caught with the wrong frock on, or her hair not done."

"And how long are you staying?"

"Why, I guess I can't manage more than three days."

"That's a miserly allowance, for so long a journey."

"Yes, but I've a hunch things are going to happen presently, and I don't want to be away."

"Foch's plan?"

"It's my idea we'll see the shape of it next month. Say,

John, you'll come along and bathe with us about eleven, and come back and lunch afterwards."

"No, no, Wacey. If you've only three days in Citrano neither Athene nor you will want to be spending them in entertaining other people."

"Why, certainly you must come along to lunch. You have a friend staying with you?"

"Yes, an old friend of my boyhood."

Miriam Stern appeared on the roof at this moment, and Wacey was introduced to her.

"Pleased to meet you, Mrs Stern. I've just come along with a message from Mrs Langridge that she expects you to lunch with us to-day."

"How kind of her, Mr Langridge. I'm in the hands of my host," Miriam replied, turning with a question in her face.

John was aware that the real reason for his not wanting to lunch at the Allegra was his dread of Miriam's watching, with an amused eye, the efforts of Athene to overcome her self-consciousness as a hostess, which was so much more acute when Wacey was present. He continued, however, to protest against accepting the invitation on account of the intrusion it would be on a family reunited for so brief a time.

And thus it was for the whole of Wacey's stay, which so far as it was possible in this quiet midsummer season became a continuous party at the Villa Allegra.

"A strange couple," Miriam commented to John. "They're so polite to one another. I think there must be something gravely wrong with that marriage. Their performance is like figure-skating on thin ice. It makes the spectators feel a little nervous."

"They were just the same together when I first met them crossing from New York five years ago."

"What a pity," she said quietly.

Nevertheless Miriam admitted a week or so later,

when Wacey had gone back to France and she had had an opportunity of talking to Athene alone on the terrace of the Allegra on various occasions, that she was beginning to be fascinated herself by Athene's personality.

"Merely to sit and look at her is a joy to me, John, now that she has lost her superficial shyness with me, and can at least appear outwardly tranquil. And it is a beauty which becomes so perfectly this classic land. The other day when we made our excursion to Paestum I saw her leaning against one of those great honey-coloured columns and I could have fancied that she had survived miraculously from ancient Poseidonia. Oh, how I enjoyed that experience! What is that line you quoted from Virgil?"

"Biferique rosaria Paesti—the roses of double-bearing Paestum."

"No lovelier rose than Athene Langridge can have bloomed there long ago, though I would not call hers a second blooming."

"You mean?"

"I mean that she has not yet flowered to the full for the first time. She is a sleeping beauty, John. I wonder if she will sleep too long, as so many other women have done . . . as I did, John, myself. And yet how I have rejoiced for that late waking!"

"Do you remember that the first time I came to tea in Claremount Gardens you had Hymettus honey?" he asked, seeking to direct her mind to another point in the past.

"Had we, John? How clever of you to remember! That must have been sent me by my friends the Vondels. Charming Dutch people. Udo Vondel was the Netherlands consul in Athens. They were always asking me to go out and stay with them, but it could never be managed. So Paestum was my first experience of Greece." She hesitated. "And your Zoe, John! Forgive me, my dear, but I could not help thinking about her and you the other day."

"There is a couplet in Propertius about Paestum:

Vidi ego odorati victura rosaria Paesti
sub matutino cocta iacere Noto,

which means, I have beheld the rose-gardens of scented Paestum about to bloom lie blasted by the south wind of the morning. That's another way Fate deals with roses. They wake too soon sometimes."

"But you won't let that arbitrary stroke of Fate affect you too long, John?"

"No, no. She will remain young and lovely in my memory. You know, when I came back from Greece last autumn I had intended to ask you to come out with me to Citrano then, but I did not do it, because in the mood of frustration I was in I dreaded lest you should hint that my love for Zoe was like my original passion for the war. I couldn't have borne to be reminded that had Zoe lived and had I married her I might have found she was the emotional expression of so much zest for action and adventure, and that when the background faded from my everyday existence she might have faded with it."

"I hope I shouldn't have done that," Miriam said, dismayed by the implication of such insensitiveness.

"Oh, it would have been my fault. With you as audience I must have railed against the madness of this long protraction of the war, and you're too sympathetic an audience not to feed any mood. I still feel that the war should somehow have been stopped last autumn, and I believe we shall pay in the end for the complete victory at which we are aiming and which we now seem certain to attain, but I am no longer in the mood to rail. I worked off a good deal in that play I wrote, which, by the way, my agent writes to say is considered impossible to produce.

It is held likely to have the unpatriotic effect of chastening the mind of the theatre-going public, who must be preserved from the faintest tendency not to triumph over its about to be utterly defeated enemies. The excellent Gosnell asks why the devil I don't get down to something that will occupy people's minds with the bright side of life."

"I can't help sympathizing with Mr Gosnell."

"Nor can I, to tell the truth, which shows that I must be so much better that I ought to write to my old gentleman in Adelphi Terrace and report myself fit for action again. I shan't, because experience has taught me that an officer behind the lines looking for a job of work is a pest compared with the officer trying to dodge a job of work. So perhaps I'll set about concocting some elegant trifle for the London stage."

"I think that's an admirable idea, John."

"By the way, I never told you, did I, that my first leading lady, with whom I was sharing a villa at Sorrento, concocted an elegant trifle of a scene because she vowed I was interested in Athene Langridge?"

"As long ago as that?" Miriam exclaimed.

John stared at her. Then he laughed.

"Oh well, if you're determined to believe that I'm falling in love with Athene it's idle to protest."

It was soon after this talk that a letter came from Emil to say that he was expecting to be back in England for a while shortly, and his mother prepared to return immediately.

"But he may not be at home more than a day or two," John expostulated.

"If it were only one day I must go back. Especially now that he's engaged."

"He's not likely to bring his snow-queen with him across the North Sea."

"No, but I want to hear about her."

"You have a lively hope. I can imagine how much you'll hear!" John mocked.

But nothing he could say would detain Miriam Stern in Citrano.

John tried to persuade Elise to let David or Prudence or both, with or without herself, come to Citrano, but she would not agree to any plan. The war was at last looking as if it might be over by the end of next year, but she could not bear the idea of being parted from David and the problem of travelling with him in war time was too complicated to face. Besides, there was Alec to consider. As for Prudence it would be too unsettling a holiday. She seemed to be growing resigned to school. And anyway the notion of a child of fifteen crossing the continent at a time like this was unthinkable.

So John, feeling more full of energy every day, tramped over the hills above Citrano, rowed and bathed along the classic coast, and entertained a series of British officers who were enjoying short leave from the recent successes on the Piave front. The news from France was good. Foch's plan became daily more evident and nearer to complete fulfilment. A spirit of optimism pervaded Citrano. The Neapolitan discoverers of a new resort sang and screamed to one another in the moonlight. Mandolinatas were audible in many a corner. The marina was a parterre of bathing costumes. Fofo's was crowded. The Hotel Excelsior started a band. Everybody danced *il fox*, the favourite tune of the young Neapolitan bloods being *Oh, you beautiful doll*. John, because he was finding frivolity such a temptation, was able to derive from that temptation the necessary incitement to concentrate on another play, and that a farce. Even a farce became a serious matter when one refused an invitation to an amusing party because one had to finish that second act.

Among the best of such parties were those given by

Ivan Sidorovich Ostápov, who alone remained of the pre-war group of political exiles. The others had made their way back by way of Switzerland when the Russian Revolution began. He had quarrelled with his lean friend Olég Dmietrievich Acatsátov who had tried to steal his favourite mistress, Lia Leibovna Braude, the pale young Jewess with hectic cheeks, and there had been one or two shooting incidents which had almost involved the expulsion of the whole colony even before Italy entered the war in 1915. However, Acatsátov was back now in Russia, and reported to be an influential official of the Cheka. Lia had remained in Citrano with Ostápov, who was not the austere stuff of which Bolsheviks were made. The years of war had but made him more jovial and more vinous than ever. His curly fair beard was more bushy; his vivid blue eyes twinkled more brightly.

"But I thought you were too fervid a rebel against the existing order to dally here like a recreant Bacchus," John said to him one afternoon.

Ostápov's laugh overflowed from the brimming vat of his well-being.

"I am not such a fool as to give up the known for what is still the unknown. My villa is my own, and what is more important—my view is my own." He indicated with the goblet of red wine he was holding in his hand the big plate windows of the untidy studio, through which over a boscage of olives the myriad diamonds of the Tyrrhenian winked in the sun. "I have enough to buy wine for myself and wine for my friends. I have enough to buy food and clothing for Lia and myself."

"But why did you pose as a leader of the Revolution?"

"Listen, my friend, and I will expound to you the anatomy of revolution. The progressive man is discontented because his fellows have not reached the point which he has reached. Youth is naturally discontented because it arrives in a world of older men thinking in the terms of the previous generation. Education is the device by which the previous generation puts a brake on youth. The majority are duly restrained because education is reinforced by religious prejudice and armed with the threat of economic failure. In other words, youth must accept the education of its predecessors or fail to establish its economic security. Education, however, is never powerful enough to restrain a minority. This minority in revolting against its education begins presently to desire to revolt against the social scheme which produces such an education. This minority thus steps beyond the problems of its own education and, inspired by discontent, observes immense numbers of human beings who ought to be discontented with their servile lot apparently unaware that the remedy lies in their own hands. This minority becomes a revolutionary minority. Of such are university students, poets, and constitutionally sentimental liberals. On most of them the economic struggle exercises such a deadening influence that they surrender to what seems the inevitable, and in due course grow to regard the revolutionary fervour of their youth as a pleasant extravagance, like love-affairs with village maidens. They mistake loss of virility for wisdom, lack of desire for prudence."

At this point Ostápov drained his goblet and poured himself out another.

"Here let me interpose an observation which has no bearing on the theme under discussion, but partakes more of the nature of a personal confession. There was a time when I kept four mistresses and under the vile goad of female concupiscence was driven to regulate severely the quantity I drank unless I wished my ears to be tormented by the taunts and reproaches of disappointed women. Now I keep one mistress and am able to drink four times as much wine, thus adding four times as much to the treasure of my contentment. Yes, and now I come to think of it, perhaps providing myself with the necessary philosophic detachment to observe the phenomenon of revolution from a safe distance. Where had I reached when this excellent wine inspired that grateful parenthesis?"

"You had reached the decay of revolutionary vigour," John replied. "We have observed it in poets like Wordsworth, Browning, Swinburne, and many another. Revolutionary poets whom the gods love die young, like Shelley and Byron."

"We now reach the fanatics," Ostápov continued. "These are frequently men incapable of expressing themselves except by action, whether it take the form of organization or violence. Frequently too their activity has been thwarted by the failure of the economic machine to employ their services, and this disappointment nourishes their fanaticism. Fanatics are produced all the time. Nature is prodigal. When the period is unfavourable to them they either wither through frustration or they go mad and perform a deed of violence, in which case they pay the penalty. But when the period is favourable these are the men who make revolution practical. They become the leaders, but the strange thing is that the leaders of a revolution never seem to survive it long. They are thrown away like used matches. Of all the comrades I have fed and sheltered here there is only one who may survive what is happening in Russia. That is Vladimir Ilyich. Lenin you know him as. Why, he was in this studio that night your Jewish friend played the violin and I had to shoot the Aeolian harp in the pine-tree outside."

"Was Lenin here that night?" John ejaculated in amazement.

"He was playing chess in a corner. Yes, Lenin may survive the revolution, but not the rest. Others take the places of those who lit the bonfire, and the trouble is that those who lit the bonfire are blinded by the light of it, and therefore do not see the approaching shapes of those who will take their place. Besides, they think that because they can destroy with ruthlessness they can rebuild with efficiency. And that is one reason, my friend, why you find me in Citrano like a recreant Bacchus as you say. I have studied the anatomy of revolution. I know what happens to organs that have served their purpose. Revolution is only evolution at a moment of high speed. It was necessary for the benefit of my body that I should keep my mind young. Therefore I consorted with the comrades; but I am not bound to lose my mind by sacrificing my body, which is always liable to occur in revolutions. Acatsátof was my friend, but he wanted to apply the principles of communism to my mistresses. I allowed it up to a point, but Lia was more than I was willing to surrender. Therefore we quarrelled, and since it was I who had the key of my own door it was I who had the better of the quarrel. I know Olég Dmitrievich. Back in Russia my bourgeois behaviour over Lia would have made me suspect as a traitor to the revolution, and I should have landed in a cellar with my head in a pool of blood round me instead of a pool of wine. I remain a firm believer that during this century the future of mankind for some five hundred years will be redirected from the intense individualism that was created by the Protestant Reformation toward communism, but I shall take no active part in the process. A long-sighted father invested his money in Scandinavia. A grateful son enjoys in Italy the fruit of such paternal perspicacity. I spent some time in Siberia after the abortive revolution of 1905. It did not turn me into a prosperous and conservative man of business, but it developed certain epicurean tendencies often discoverable in the man well covered with flesh. For the rest of my life I intend to drink to the health of the revolution, and wish it well from the bottom of my glass; but at a distance, my friend, at a distance that will be perfectly safe provided that the imbecilities of statesmen do not provoke revolution all over Europe."

"Then you do not hope to see communism become world-wide?" John asked.

"Ultimately, yes, because I do not see how otherwise the progress of man can continue; but the process must be gradual or the remedy might be worse than the disease it seeks to cure. If the experiment succeeds in Russia similar experiments will follow in other countries."

"You speak of the progress of man, by which I presume you mean his material progress?"

"What other progress is conceivable?" Ostápov replied. "Man lives by his belly. The grandeur that was Greece depended on the safety of the corn ships from the Black Sea. The glory that was Rome was bound up with the prosperous voyage of the corn ships from Alexandria. What is progress except movement along the path that leads toward the greatest comfort for the greatest number in the longest life attainable?"

"You dismiss the possibility of eternal life?" John asked.

Ostápov turned down an empty glass in answer.

"You spoke just now of re-directing the future of mankind from individualism for the next five hundred years. Why do you postulate a limit? Why do you not look forward to an interminable development of communistic man? To a world of super-bees and super-ants?"

"Because one of our remote progenitors developed gills. Because we must breathe out and breathe in. Action and reaction. Ebb and flow. In my study of history I fancy I detect a rhythmic pulmonary process in which each breath takes about five hundred years. For instance in 490 B.C. the individualistic Greeks defeated the Persians and repulsed their vast denationalizing bureaucracy. About five centuries later the Roman Empire was beginning and individualism was fading under imperialism. Within another five centuries the Roman Empire was collapsing under the onset of the barbarians and handed on its mission to the Catholic Church. By the year A.D. 1000 another epoch was beginning during which the Catholic Church tried to evolve the dualism of spiritual and temporal rule in the conception of the Papacy and the Empire. Some five centuries later the combination of the Renaissance with the revived influence of individualistic Greece, the discovery of the New World, and the Protestant Reformation, brought about the individualistic epoch in the last century of which we are now living. The motive force for the change which will decide the next five centuries has been the conquest of individualistic man by the machine he has invented. What are dangerous toys for individuals will be conquered in their turn again by communistic man. That I prophecy with complete assurance, but I am not able to foresee what will be the problems of two people looking out at the Tyrrhenian Sea in the year 2418."

"I like your theory," said John. "But how does it apply to China? Or India? You confine it to Western man. I seem to detect a recurrent pressure from the East, as if from the heart of Asia humanity was for ever trying to get back to the foreshore on which I understand from a protoplasmic globule man has evolved. Your own Russia is the East impinging on Europe. Perhaps why Christianity alone of the Eastern religions imposed itself on Europe was that it was a Mediterranean religion. It is significant that the only other oriental religion which had contact with the sea was Mohammedanism, and that it was the only one which seemed at one time to threaten Christianity."

"Only by force of arms," Ostápov pointed out. "It did not threaten it mentally. But Mithraism! We have only to look at the caves of Mithras all along these coasts, in which mariners used to worship secretly, to realise that at one time the religion of Mithras must have been a serious rival to Christianity."

"Never seriously, I fancy," John replied. "The Mithraic cult must always have been an exotic import. The centre of it was too far away. After all, the centre of Christianity was Rome itself."

"You believe that?"

"There doesn't seem any question about it. I am not putting forward papal claims by that remark. The fear of Christianity in Rome must have been tremendous, or else why the persecutions? The devotees of Mithras were never persecuted in an organized scale."

"The Jews have been persecuted," Ostápov argued. "And even though I am a good Marxist and have a Jewess who is the love of my life, I think with reason."

"I suppose they seem a disruptive force through their solidarity and simultaneously their capacity for permeation. They have the resistance too of a sappy twig which one tries to snap off and then twists round and round and finally abandons, beaten."

"They *are* a disruptive force," Ostápov declared. "That is why so many Jews are leaders of the Revolution. But make no mistake, my friend, it is not because they believe that communism is the solution of the world's economic perplexity, but because they believe that their brains and fundamental contempt for those who are not Jews will enable them to exploit communism to their own advantage. I think the Roman fear of the Christians was because the Christians were Jews to the Romans, and for the city which had blotted out Carthage to see itself in danger of being undermined from below by more Semites must have been intolerable."

"The communistic theory may be all right," said John. "But it seems to me that in order to give it practical effect it will require an immense bureaucracy, and an immense bureaucracy must end in a despotism of the one to avoid a despotism of the many. Constantine, who by the way came in the middle of one of your five hundred year cycles, used Christianity to establish his own despotism."

"Constantine was only a development from Augustus. I did not say the change happened immediately: it was always a slow breathing in and breathing out. Constantine transferred the seat of the empire to Byzantium. Who knows if Moscow will not be the capital of Europe at last?"

"And come to grief like Constantinople?"

"After more than a thousand years, my friend!"

"Byzantium had been dead for five hundred years when the Turks took it. But what do you foresee in Russia? A Jewish Napoleon?"

"Ah no! I foresee a Russian Napoleon who will know when and how to use the bureaucracy built up by the Jews."

"I think the fulfilment of your prophecy will depend on the peace that is made after this war," John said.

"Then I can feel sure I am right, because statesmen who were imbecile enough to enter on such a war will certainly not have grown the brains during such a war to be able to make a sane peace. Therefore all I can hope is that my father's investments in Scandinavia will provide me with wine and food to live out my days in this epoch which is beginning to crack up, and that my mind will remain clear enough to appreciate what is happening all round me when it begins to crack in every direction."

"How old are you now?"

"Now I am forty."

"You may have some difficulty in preserving your Epicurean detachment for another forty years."

"If life becomes not worth living it is in one's own power to decide whether one will continue to live."

Ostápov drained his glass again and loosed a mighty

guffaw. At that moment Lia appeared in the entrance of the studio. The pallor of summer was heavy on her cheeks.

"Come here, ghost of Russia. Come here, my love, and drink with me upon my knee," Ostápov shouted. "Are you not glad to be here with me alive?"

She stared at him blankly, not understanding the English, but he murmured some endearment in Russian. She glided in a swift movement across the floor and threw herself down beside Ostápov, resting her head upon his knee.

"You see?" he said, opening his arms in a wide gesture. "She is content. There are times like this when I find it very difficult not to marry her."

"Ivan Sidorovich, where did you learn to speak English so well?" John asked.

"For five years, my friend, I was looking after a branch of my father's business in Newcastle."

"Were you? How did you like England?"

"I could not bear it," he replied simply.

John laughed.

"But what I find so admirable in the English is that when you tell them you cannot bear their country they think it is a splendid joke. In all my prophecies I never forget, my friend, that any of them may be hopelessly wrecked on the rock of British complacency. And then I console myself by saying that the Romans must have been just as complacent, but even their rock fell to pieces in the end."

"But how much was built of the fragments!" John reminded him.

"The Roman Empire was something much greater than the British Empire, my friend."

"You won't persuade me to contradict you, Ostápov, but then I am not such a believer as you in the value of material progress. You should give your vote to the

British Empire, in which I would argue you must include the United States if we are to speak of the influence of that Empire on the progress of humanity. Indeed, after this war I think that Washington may occupy the position of Rome, and London turn into a Byzantium expiring slowly from the efficiency of its bureaucracy. I can even imagine, within a comparatively short space of time, the destruction of Washington by Russian warplanes—the paradox of the West being attacked by the East from the West."

It was soon after this talk that Ostápov gave a party in the Villa Dioniso to celebrate the vintage. No more wine was likely to be drunk at it than at any other of his parties; but the impression in Citrano was that he intended to hold something in the nature of an orgy, and when John asked Athene over a glass of vermouth at Fofo's whether she had accepted the invitation she told him she had decided not to go.

"Oh, but you must come!"

"Why, John, I met Mrs Heighington and she said she thought it was disgraceful to allow aliens to throw parties like that during war-time."

"Mrs Heighington!" he jeered. "I'll bet Ostápov never invited Mrs Heighington to one of his parties. So she was only telling you that the vintage this year is all sour grapes. Really, Athene, you must come. Geoffrey Noel is going, which ensures you an old maid for chaperon. And those three agreeable and absurd English officers staying at the Sirene. But the star guest is Olensky."

"Who is Olensky anyway?"

"They say a marvellous dancer. You really must come."

And she gave way.

It was a warm starry night at the end of the first week of September when the guests began to arrive at the Villa Dioniso. Some deplored the setting of the young moon which Venus had dogged down the green sky of dusk into a placid glimmering sea, but the heady scent of the crushed grapes that pervaded this air seemed more potent in the dim starshine. All day caryatides had swung down the alleys, bearing on their heads the loaded baskets to pour them into the vats wherein boys and girls treading with purple-stained legs and feet deep-dyed had shouted and laughed with zest over their labour.

The caryatides had shouted too as their dusty feet slapped the cobbles of the level alleys, shouted in the raucous dialect to one another and to the gatherers they passed in the already dishevelled vineyards and to the *contadini* and *contadine* they met Bacchic jests that would many of them have been ancient jests two thousand years ago. The need to preserve the balance of the loaded baskets gave their bearers a carriage no sculptor could have embellished. The chin was held high. The generous breasts were strained taut against the stuff of the dress by one uplifted arm: the other arm was crooked upon a swinging hip. Up and down across the vineyards or through the alleys the line had moved all day beneath that hot blue sky of summer's end. Their blouses were patterned with sweat. On the white walls of the shallow-domed casettas hung the red and green peppers: along the arcaded balconies were spread the split figs. From the cactuses the prickly pears had been plucked and, scraped of their spines, they stood in the window-sills to win from the sun a richer yellow. Most of the fruit had been gathered. There was little now hanging on the trees except the persimmons waiting to be softened by the colder air of November. Yet all this fruit in its gaudy piles and rows—gourds and tomatoes, sorbs, plums, pomegranates, figs and peppers and prickly pears—could not exhale a scent perceptible through the fumy must rising from the fresh grape-juice.

And when the guests of Ostápov arrived at the Villa Dioniso some declared that merely from the starlit air of the vintage they were already feeling drunk.

"That is a base and cowardly evasion of the night's responsibilities," he proclaimed, and he pointed to them in the shape of demijohns standing in a row, white and red wine alternating.

The studio was not too crowded. The departure of the exiles had saved the owner of the Villa Dioniso a good deal of room. During the four or five years prior to the Revolution it was seldom he was not accommodating at least half a dozen with bed and board, and often twice as many as that. There was besides Lia another Russian girl called Eva Zvonskaya, she too a Jewess, though her high cheek-bones and flattish nose rather indicated a Tartar origin. She was a gentle creature with a gentle voice, the tone of which suggested a continuous state of astonishment at being still alive in this difficult world. A young Russian painter who had been studying in Rome with a scholarship and now found himself cut off from supplies had come to Citrano in the hope of earning enough money to live by painting portraits of the rich foreigners. This young man, whose name was Matrássic, had engaged himself to Eva, and in the hope of providing her with a not too indigent matrimonial existence had sacrificed all his modern aesthetic theory to the flattery of his sitters and the achievement of their recommendation. He had already had a notable success with Mrs Heighington, from whose fifty years he had brushed away a score.

"Perhaps it is a little flattering," she would declare modestly to the visitor to whom she had shown the portrait, which occupied a sort of Louis Quinze easel in her drawing-room beneath what Geoffrey Noel called a hymeneal veil. "But where I think Matrássic is so clever is the way he manages the light so as to bring out the best of one."

It was reasonable for Matrássic to expect that with the increase of visitors to Citrano when the war was over he would be able to maintain Eva in comfort, possibly in what both of them would consider luxury. He was a small man with a shock of fuzzy hair the shape of a blowball, which when he was white promised to give him the appearance of a seeding dandelion. In spite of his surrender to commercial portraiture he remained an earnest little man, voluble on the subject of what painting ought to be. The only commission he had received to paint in the way he wanted to paint was from Ostápov, for whom he had done a picture of Lia, in which she was seen to resemble less a woman than a hock-bottle with a pigeon's egg balanced on the top of it.

"*Dio mio!*" Ostápov had gasped. "So that's what Lia looks like! It explains why I love her so much."

Yet Lia's portrait painted under the inspiration of Matrássic's aesthetic theory was living flesh compared with his conception of his own fiancée's essential self. Poor Eva to her lover was a decrepit pine-cone into the top of which somebody had stuck a triangular morsel of cheese. Nor was the essential self of Eva further illuminated for the spectator by the portrait's being labelled *Étude in C sharp minor*.

"I don't know—m-m-m—I think it's rather good," Geoffrey Noel had mumbled. On the strength of having had his translation of a sonnet by Herédia published in the *Saturday Review* when Frank Harris was editor, he had preserved a warm feeling for modernity in the arts.

"Yes, but you have *horror feminae*, dear Noel," John had retorted. "If I painted Francesco looking like a half-picked wishbone you'd soon return to Velasquez, or even Joshua Reynolds."

Matrássic was not the only exponent of significant form in the studio that last night of the vintage. There was a plump carroty-headed Dutch painter, who must have made an impression even on the fortune her father had made out of the war by the amount she had spent on ultramarine in trying to achieve a plausible representation of the seascapes round the Bay of Naples and the Gulf of Salerno. There was a Norwegian sculptress, with plaits to her hair like sticks of barley-sugar and cheeks like raspberry ices. She specialized in male nudity, which set a problem to the *parroco*, who having succeeded in forbidding the maidens of Citrano to sit for painters felt he ought to make an attempt to stop the young men from sitting naked for sculptresses. He was unsuccessful and had to console himself by ordering a great ribbon embroidered with the maxim *Ubbedienza Al Papa*, which he intended to hang across the main street of Citrano at the next elections.

There was no violinist in the studio that night to take the place of Zlata Pocráss, who had returned with the comrades to Russia, but there were two or three to play the piano, a rather tinny Erard semi-grand for which Ostápov had been paying a monthly rent for five years.

When Athene and John arrived, the party was already in full swing. The air was thick with the smoke of Macedonia cigarettes, though they no longer cost thirty-five *centesimi* a packet as once upon a time. Several of the guests were wreathed with vine-leaves, among others Major Wascoe of the King's Own Herefords and Captain Hatch of the Huntingdons. Lieutenant Portman of the Westmorland Fusiliers felt he was not yet old enough to carry off that kind of thing. Moreover, he had had an early mishap as a reveller by treading on the frock of Eva and causing her to utter a shriek of hysterical dismay which had set Matrássic's shock of hair bristling with indignation at what he had supposed was a piece of amorous presumption on the part of the pink-faced young barbarian in khaki.

"Ah, here you are, here you are at last!" the host bellowed. "Red or white wine? I'm not offering anybody whisky. We are worshipping Bacchus to-night, not the Corn Goddess. Mrs Langridge, I want to present to you Román Alexandróvich Olensky who has promised to dance for us."

Román Olensky had not yet made his début as a professional dancer at this date. He was a young man of family who had been trained in the school of the Imperial Ballet but had been called up for service when war broke out. Interest had secured for him an appointment as an extra attaché to the Russian Embassy in Rome, where he still was, wondering like the rest of the staff there when it would have to be closed. Not that he had anything to worry about, for he had caught the eye (and won the heart, so it was whispered) of Bodísko, the famous impresario of the ballet, who had vowed to make him as famous as Nijinsky or Massine when life should flower again after the war. Bodísko was with him to-night.

"Sergei Sergéevich Bodísko," Ostápov proclaimed in a tone of rich vinosity, yet not so fruity as to disguise an unbecoming bourgeois pride in the introduction.

John shook hands with a small man whose fine features, piercing grey eyes, imperial, and up-curving moustache, and parchment skin suggested an ambassador.

"You have that charming tower, Mr Ogilvie. You are wise. It is my fancy to build myself a villa in Citrano. Capri has become so *affiché*. Amalfi is so banal. And Sorrento . . ." He shrugged his shoulders and offered John a cigarette. "Who is that beautiful woman talking to Olensky?" he asked, lancing a bright suspicious look across the studio. "Ah, an American lady. *Elle est belle—très très belle*. And you remain here for the winter, Mr Ogilvie?"

"Not unless the war is over next month," John replied.

"*Ah, cette guerre*. It lies upon the world like a stone. Will you be so kind as to present me to that American lady?"

And within a moment or two of the introduction Bodísko had somehow steered the young dancer to the other end of the studio, leaving John and Athene together. Geoffrey Noel came tripping up to them in a hurry of excitement.

"Did you notice the extraordinary likeness to the dancing faun?" he gulped, and then blew vigorously down his empty pipe, gazing the while from clouded eyes at Román Olensky, who had just flung himself on a divan where Bodísko interposed himself like a well-trimmed hedge between the dancer and the Norwegian sculptress.

"I hope the Midnight Sun is not going to get hold of him," Noel puffed indignantly.

"I don't think you need worry," said John. "She can't jump over Bodísko. I wish she'd ask the Major to sit for her."

He called to the pink-faced Fusilier subaltern.

"Oh, hullo. Good evening, Mrs Langridge," said Portman. "This is rather jolly, isn't it? But I'm afraid I struck rather a low note just now."

"Why, when was that, Lieutenant Portman?" Athene asked.

"Oh, didn't you see? I got into trouble with that little dark girl over there."

"With Eva Isáacovna?" John said. "What did you do? Tickle her knee?"

"No, no, no, Ogilvie. I trod on her skirt. And by Jove, she shrieked out at the top of her voice. I thought that queer-looking bird with the hair was going to pull a gun on me. But I'm enjoying myself no end. This is a topping sort of Bohemian sort of show if you know what I mean. I'm simply loving Sitrano, or is it Chitrano? My Italian's rotten. And I've been out here since January."

"I say, Portman, do you think you could persuade the Major to sit for our Norwegian sculptress?"

"I don't know, but I'll ask him if you like. Who is she?"

"Her name is Norem. That tall blonde on the divan."

"He's an awfully good-natured fellow. I expect he'll oblige."

"But this is none of your Sam Browne and field-boots stuff," John went on. "She'll want him to sit with nothing on."

"Good god!" the Fusilier gasped. "Do you mean . . ."

"Starkers," said John. "Not even vine leaves allowed."

"I think you'd better ask him, Ogilvie. Or wait a minute. There's Hatch. Hatch!"

Captain Hatch, a dark wiry man, drew near.

"I say, Hatch, you see that tall blonde on the divan?"

The Captain put up a monocle and identified her.

"Look here, Hatch. She wants Major Wascoe to sit for her. She wants to sculpt him."

"Good old Tubby," Hatch drawled.

"Yes, but she wants him to sit with nothing on."

The Captain's monocle dropped with a tinkle on one of his buttons.

"Nothing on?" he echoed aghast, patting his close-cropped black hair as if a spent bullet had whizzed over his skull.

At this moment the subject of so much amazement, a bald major still wearing a wreath of vine leaves, his face shining with good fellowship, approached the divan with a bottle in either hand and offered the sculptress the choice between red and white wine.

"She'll ask him herself if he grins at her like that," Captain Hatch predicted gloomily.

"My god, she has asked him," Portman exclaimed.

His excitement was prompted by the sight of the Major slowly melting from an upright position to the floor.

"You haven't hurt yourself, I hope," Ostápov bellowed as he plunged across the room to help the Major to his feet.

"Didn't—spill—a—single—drop," said the Major, beaming at the company from two glazed but still resolutely genial eyes. "Don't—suppose—I—could—do that—again—if—I—tried," he declared, with the excessive caution of drunken speech.

Nevertheless his surmise was wrong, for no sooner had Ostápov and another guest raised him to his feet than he melted back on to the floor. "And—again—I—didn't—spill—a—single—drop. Not—one," he repeated, his face by now resembling in its puzzled innocence the face of a baby who has sat down abruptly when learning to walk.

"I say, Hatch, do you think we ought to get him off to bed?" the Fusilier asked anxiously.

"No, no," John protested. "He's just beginning to enjoy the night. A little more wine and our sculptress will be able to use him as a model for a bambino."

"My Italian doesn't run to that, old thing," said Portman.

At this moment somebody at the piano struck up *Oh, you beautiful doll*, and the company taking partners danced round and round the Major, who sat on, smiling at the compliment and joining in the dance to the best of his imagination by making the bottle of red wine dance a 'fox' with the bottle of white wine.

"Aren't you bad, John!" Athene said, as they danced together. "But I'm crazy about the Major. I think he's a lamb."

Everybody was dancing except Bodísko and Olensky, who had vanished from the studio. Even Geoffrey Noel was dancing, under obvious protest, with the only woman in the room left without a partner, a solid Scotswoman of forty-five with a furry chin who was gathering material for a book on the Normans in the Mediterranean, and had thereby caused an immense amount of trouble to British Consuls and Vice-Consuls called upon to extricate her from the hands of the Italian police who naturally supposed from her Glasgow accent that she was a German spy.

Ostápov was dancing with his own Lia. Portman was dancing with Eva, who was watching his big field-boots all the time as a matador the horns of the bull. Matrássic was dancing with the Norwegian sculptress.

"Forgive me, Athene, for being coarse, but Matrássic looks exactly like a small woolly dog lifting its leg against a lighthouse."

"John, you're thoroughly bad to-night."

"I'm extremely happy," he replied.

At the end of the dance they found themselves stopping by a small divan under the farthest window of the studio, where they sat down together. The warm air of summer's end still faintly perfumed with must was an exquisite refreshment.

"Extraordinarily happy," John repeated with emphasis. "Perhaps it's the good news from France. At last there seems an imaginable end to this infernal war. You may yet have Wacey home for Christmas."

"You too, John—if you really have to go back to England."

"That's certain. I shall have been idling for a year presently. Oh my, how glad I was to see you in Naples that October day last year!"

"I was glad to see you."

He turned sharply to look at her, for there was a vibrancy in her tone he had never heard, a low vibrancy which made the breath catch for a moment in his throat.

She was leaning back against the cushions piled in the angle of the wall, and the turn he had made was toward the direct gaze of her deep brown eyes.

The tobacco smoke seemed to swirl into a vast question mark. The chattering voices became as impersonal as the cheeping of sparrows gathered in a sycamore. John felt he was receding into a world of which he and Athene were the sole inhabitants.

"This is a terrifying privacy," he murmured, unsure like one upon the margin of sleep whether his words were audible.

"What did you say, John?"

He jerked himself back into a party at Ostápov's studio.

"I didn't really say anything. I was thinking how well that frock became you. It was clever of you to wear black to-night."

"Where was the cleverness?"

He nodded toward the company.

"You guessed it would be polychromatic."

"And so you credit me with all that amount of far-sighted vanity?" she asked. "Well, isn't that discouraging?"

"You are vain. You've a right to be vain—a duty indeed. Even Bodísko, who should be a connoisseur, exclaimed to me at your beauty. In fact he feared for his Hylas. Didn't you notice the way he whisked him out of the orbit of your eyes?"

"Poor man, he didn't realize how little he had to fear," she laughed. "But here he comes, and where is the young man?"

Bodísko had drawn aside the host for a confabulation.

"*Signore! signorine! signori!*" Ostápov shouted a moment or two later. "*Olensky mi a fatto un gran complimento. Signore! signorine! signori! Olensky va ballare nel mio studio. Evviva il maestro!*"

"*Viva! Viva!*" everybody cried. "*Viva Olensky!*"

"I didn't quite get that," said the Fusilier, who in wandering round the room had found himself anchored by Ostápov's proclamation off the divan on which John and Athene were sitting.

"The young Russian is going to perform a *pas seul,*" John explained.

"Conjuring tricks? Oh, strong stuff! I'm rather hot at conjuring tricks myself. Got the right type of hand, they tell me." He held out a capacious palm like the pink quilted inside of a work-basket.

"But Olensky isn't going to conjure, Portman. He's going to dance."

"With a parcel? That's a new one on me."

There was no time to allay the Fusilier's perplexity, for at that moment with the bound of a panther Olensky landed on his toes in the middle of the floor. He was dressed in green tights and a short green doublet cut with a circular flair at the bottom and trimmed with purple grapes, his green cap cut in the shape of a vine leaf. No greater tribute could be paid to the young dancer's grace of movement, beauty of figure, and ease of technique than to say that his audience were not embarrassed by the spectacle of his *bacchanale* danced to the tinny Erard's accompaniment of Glazounov's music.

"I saw Pavlova and Mordkin dance to that music eight years ago, and their *bacchanale* was nothing like so good as this," John told Athene. "I wouldn't say that he was as good as Nijinsky, but I cannot imagine a dancer as good as Nijinsky. This, however, is nearer than anybody has come to Nijinsky."

Everybody in the studio was gazing spellbound at this lovely animal which leapt and twirled and slid and kicked and swayed in the middle of the smoky studio, at this green tourbillion spinning upwards toward the domed ceiling and touching the floor again as light as a leaf. The only person that did not sit motionless was Bodísko, who was pacing round and round the room, his eyes fixed upon the dancer in the way that lion-tamers will move round a cage. That the impresario was the only man in evening dress added to the illusion that he was an intrinsic part of the performance.

"What a hurdler, eh?" the Fusilier ejaculated in admiration.

"Look at Tubby," said Captain Hatch. "He doesn't believe it's real."

Major Wascoe of the King's Own Herefordshire Regiment was following Olensky's leaps with the expression of the little boy blowing soap-bubbles in Millais' picture.

"I think I can make a wonderful nude of him," the Norwegian sculptress murmured dreamily.

"I doubt it, Miss Norem," said John. "I think you'll find that Monsieur Bodísko will throw the clothes on faster than you can pull them off."

"Excuse me, sir," Miss Norem replied with cold dignity, "I never am pulling the clothes off my models."

"John," whispered Athene reprovingly. "You're incorrigible to-night." And as further evidence of it, when Olensky had retired to doff his costume and when the guests, their superlatives exhausted, were wondering who was going to break the spell cast by Olensky, John called for a recitation from the Scotswoman investigating the behaviour of the Normans in the Mediterranean.

"Now who told you that I recited?" Miss MacCracken challenged.

"You recited to Major Wascoe the other night."

"My god, old thing, do look out. It's a frightful business," the Fusilier muttered warningly.

"Well, what will I recite?" Miss MacCracken asked.

"*Young Lochinvar*," John suggested.

"Get along with you, Mr Ogilvie, as if I'd recite that!

I'll give you the Agincourt speech from Shakespeare's *Henry V*," she announced.

"Very unpatriotic of you," John observed, "considering that the Scots were fighting on the side of the French."

But Miss MacCracken was off, and when the speech was finished the audience clapped enthusiastically, less from admiration of Miss MacCracken's performance than from relief that it was finished.

"Monstrous!" Geoffrey Noel puffed. "It's worse than dancing with her. She's surely not going to recite again!" he added in horror.

But Miss MacCracken *was* going to recite again. She was going to recite, *How do the waters come down at Lodore?* And once started she might have continued to recite for the rest of the evening if one of the pianists had not started to play a 'fox'. In his anxiety not to be left again with Miss MacCracken as a partner, Geoffrey clutched the Norwegian sculptress with the desperation of a mariner who to avoid a watery grave clambers on an iceberg.

It was two o'clock when John and Athene left the Villa Dioniso. Their host was insistent that they should wait until dawn, which was the earliest moment he could accept as reasonable. However, they were firm, and Geoffrey Noel seized the excuse of their departure to escape from Miss MacCracken's discovery that he dabbled in rhyme.

"Impossible woman," he puffed indignantly as he jigged along beside John and Athene. "She actually proposed paying me a visit and reading me some preposterous doggerel she has written about Bohemund."

"Who was Bohemund?" John asked.

"Some crusader apparently. Scott and water! Not even Scott and soda! I hate these mediaeval enthusiasts. 'My dear lady,' I told her, 'the most welcome fact about the Normans is that they are no longer in the Mediterranean.' "

"I hope that silenced her."

"Do you know what she had the impertinence to do?" Noel bubbled. "She tapped me on the shoulder with her fan and called me crusty. Crusty! The sort of thing women in old volumes of *Punch* were supposed to say. I shan't go to any more of these Citrano parties. These unattached females are a menace."

"Never mind, Mr Noel. You'll have Francesco back when the war is over," said Athene.

"And I'm very worried about him. Carlino wrote to me this week to say that Francesco was hanging round some horrid little hussy up there. I cannot think why boys want to get themselves tangled up like that."

Geoffrey Noel's domestic anxieties carried them as far as the piazza, where he turned off along the street that led to his small house. John and Athene decided to take the steps down to the beach and walk back to the Villa Allegra across the sand. He took her arm lest she should slip on the uneven steps, and when they reached the level he did not drop it. They moved through the starshine in silence, bewitched by the long sighs of the glimmering sea. There was no scent here rising from the trodden grapes, but the salty tang of the glimmering unharvested sea. This progress across the beach seemed the continuation of their evening's dancing, and as in a dance both leaned toward each other as if to follow the rhythm of an unheard tune. And like dancers in strict accord the mind of neither strayed beyond that plenary awareness of the present which seldom comes to human creatures except in the eternal present of music. Then John, distracted for an instant by the flight of an urgent meteor across the firmament, caught his foot in a small mound of loose sand and in stumbling let go of Athene's forearm which had been resting in his palm. She put out her hand to save him from falling, and as he recovered himself they came face to face. She was so close that he could feel her heart, so close that he could hear the quickening of her breath.

And in the starshine, dark as a carnation her mouth was his.

They walked on in a trance, the stars dimmed by the brightness in their own eyes, the sea muted by the waves beating inside themselves.

It was not until they reached the foot of the columned steps leading up to the Villa Allegra that either spoke. Then Athene said:

"This has happened."

"Does it end here?" he asked, pausing in a swift thought, for the wings of the future had fanned him.

"It is you who must answer that, John."

She walked on up through the garden, and he followed her. When they reached the terrace she stopped.

"Let's sit and talk awhile here."

The thatch of genista shut out the zenith, and they were sitting beside one another on long wicker chairs. The parapet along the front of the terrace, with the starry sky beyond it, suggested that they were sitting on the deck of a steamship where sitting thus beside one another how many lovers had said good-bye to love at the end of how many voyages.

"We met first on a steamer," John murmured, prompted by the fancy that had struck him. "How well I remember the first time I saw you. You came into the dining-saloon for lunch and I *was* so glad your husband had invited me to cocktails before dinner. And I remember when the *Princess Sophia* was passing the Azores, you came up on deck in a green coat that matched the green island we were passing in the blue dusk. That was March 1913. I was thirty, and next month I shall be thirty-six."

"*I* shall be thirty next April," she sighed.

"What a long time we waited!"

"You were very much otherwise engaged when we first met," she reminded him.

"I must hand it to Gabrielle, though," John said reflectively. "You didn't know that you were the cause of our separation."

"John, don't be so foolish," she exclaimed reproachfully.

"The indirect cause, yes," he insisted. "Don't you remember when we lunched here, and poor Gabrielle was so rude to Claudia Sharpe? It was just before a terrific sirocco, and we wrangled over you. Gabrielle accused me of a flirtation with you on the voyage across. Well, I realized after that—we both realized indeed—that the liaison could not last much longer. We didn't quarrel, though. We just knew when we said good-bye that April in Rome that we should never take another villa together in Sorrento or anywhere else."

"When I was just twenty-four," she half sighed.

"Are you thinking now what a long time we waited?"

"I was thinking of many things all muddled together into one," she replied, putting her hand on his. He leant towards her and drew her hand up to his lips, holding it to them in a long kiss.

"Do you remember when we went to Cantone that June of 1914 and the picnic when I found that terra-cotta head of Minerva? I gave it to you because you were more like your namesake."

"I still have that little head. It's on my dressing-table."

"I remember that for a moment I had a strange fancy I was alone with you on that headland among the myrtles and the rosemary. Perhaps if the Archduke had not been assassinated that June . . ." He broke off.

"What?" she whispered.

"Oh no," he exclaimed impatiently. "That sort of speculation is the worst kind of sentimentality. I would not change all these years for to-night. I never told you I was engaged to a girl in Greece and that she died. I wonder why I didn't tell you," he went on meditatively. "I suppose it was because you always shied away from any conversation that ever trembled on the verge of intimacy. I am suddenly aware that this is the first time you and I have ever done more than chat to one another. Did you ever love Wacey?"

"No. I never loved him."

"But you would not have admitted that to me as a friend?" John pressed.

"I don't suppose I would."

At that moment she turned her head anxiously.

"What's the matter?" he asked.

"I thought I heard Arthur call. His nursery window is along there."

"You'd better go and see if he's all right," John told her.

She hesitated, listening.

"Go along," he urged. "We've lots of things to talk about. Go and make sure that Arthur is asleep."

He jumped up from his chair and gave her his hand to rise, and watched her vanish like a shadow through one of the french-windows of the *salone*. Then he sat down again and gazed up over the parapet at the stars. On what voyage was he starting to-night? '*Does it end here?*' '*It is you who must answer that, John.*' That night he had finished his play. Eight blank pages had been covered with dialogue and directions. If he had written those last pages the night before, almost every word might have been different, but the end of the play would have been the same because he had determined that already in his mind. What dialogue and directions would be written on the blank pages of Athene's life and his before he went back to the Torre Saracena? And on them would depend the end of something which had happened because a shooting-star of unusual brilliance had distracted his attention at the moment that what was left of some child's sand-castle stood in his path. Otherwise he and Athene would have parted a quarter of an hour ago, nearer to becoming intimate friends than they had ever been since first they met, but no more than that. Now . . . he sank into a reverie, and so quietly did Athene come back from the *salone* that until her hair fell about his face as she leaned down to kiss him he was not aware of her return. She had changed out of her frock into a soft negligé of silk and lace, and by the way she had let down her hair he divined with what proud simplicity she was leaving to him the answer to that question he had asked at the foot of the steps up through the garden.

"But you wouldn't run away with me, Athene," he said.

She had sat down again in the long wicker-chair beside him in this ship steering for their future, and by the sudden dry creaking he knew she had clutched the arms in a moment of apprehension.

"You haven't asked me to run away with you, John."

"And I'm not going to ask you, because if you said 'no' I should be jealous of the reason and if you said 'yes' I should spend my time wondering if you were happy."

"You mean Arthur?"

"Exactly."

A silence fell.

"I hadn't thought of running away," she said at last. "It wouldn't have entered my head to make such a demand of you. It happened. I suppose for some time now I have thought it might happen, but you mustn't think I thought it would happen. You don't think that, John?"

"Darling darling Athene, never. We were both surprised by love like two lovers in an old tale."

"And you know I count myself yours?" she turned to ask frankly, eagerly.

"I know that. But I must be as frank with you. I couldn't share you with a husband."

"You wouldn't share me. I would be all yours," she whispered.

"Oh, yes, in your mind, no doubt; but even this war will end one day. Wacey will come back. You could not deny him what is his right, and I couldn't stand that."

"I am justified in refusing Wacey what you call his right," she said firmly. "Before this happened I would have died rather than let him touch me again. And Wacey himself knows that. Maybe if I had not found out something last October I wouldn't have allowed myself to fall in love with you. Or at any rate I don't think I would have let you discover that I did love you. So you needn't believe I'll share you with somebody else."

"But even so Wacey will be coming back, and you know that whatever your private relations he is not going to let the world think you are anything except a passionately devoted wife. I have always discouraged Wacey from talking to me about you, but if he were to do it now I simply couldn't stand it. Nor could I stand an intrigue —all the ignominious little subterfuges which it involves, the pretences, the hypocrisies. We are both too old for them. They would end by killing our love. Stolen fruit may be sweet enough, but stolen fruit can go rotten."

"So this is the end, and you have given me your answer, John," she said, in a lifeless voice.

"On the contrary, if you love me it is only the beginning. You won't run away with me, and if you would I wouldn't run away with you. But if you have the courage to let me run away from you, and if I have the resolution to do it, you have presumably the evidence to divorce Wacey, in which case we can get married."

"Yes, I suppose I have the evidence," she said slowly.

"Even if you have not, surely you can make Wacey realize that your life together is finished and that you are entitled to your freedom."

"I wonder," she murmured half to herself.

"You must try. And, Athene, I shall leave Citrano to-morrow."

"John!"

"It's the only possible step. I only hope that my dallying here through the summer will not make Wacey suspect me, because there is none so obstinate as a weak and jealous man. Remember that from now onward we cannot hide from other people that we are in love with one another. We have a secret. Against that there is no armour. Up till now we have been perfectly natural. To-night we danced together almost every dance, but nobody cast a curious glance because we were able to be completely natural. Do you think if we went to a party to-morrow night we could dance like that without betraying ourselves? If we danced together we should betray ourselves. If we avoided dancing together we should be equally marked. If you knew how much I long to throw everything to the wind at this moment and go heedlessly forward . . . but Athene, if you are to win this battle you must be able to tell Wacey when he asks you—and he will ask you—that between you and me there is nothing."

"Wouldn't that be a lie? So far as I am concerned there is everything," she affirmed.

"Athene!" he cried in desperation. "I can't argue with you *and* myself. If you talk like that I shall have no strength to plan for the future. You must know how difficult it is for me not to let the future go to hell instead of talking to you like a prudent governess. Do you want to marry me?"

"John! How can you ask that?"

"You know Wacey better than I. If you leave Arthur out of it, are you convinced that he would divorce you over me?"

In a sweep, from the moment Wacey had told her, a fourteen-year-old girl, that he was going to marry her as soon as her father gave his consent, until he had wept across her bed the night before he went back to France a few weeks ago, Athene saw their life together, and seeing it knew that John was right.

"Then we part now," she said in a voice dry with grief, "until I am free?"

He held her in his arms.

"If you find I am wrong and that you want to give up all to be with me, I shall not argue any more, Athene. I can write to you freely at present; you can write to me; but I may not be able to write to you later. But remember it all lies with you. If you find it intolerable, come when you will the moment the war is finished. We are sacrificing a fortnight now at the most, for I had to go back as you know at the end of September. I think when I am gone, darling darling Athene, you will be glad I went like this. And now kiss me once again."

"I shall be thirty in April," she lamented.

"Well, it's a very good age to marry for the second time," he assured her.

From the window of the room at the end of the villa rang a childish voice:

"*Mamma, dove stai? Perchè stai fuori sulla terrazza?*"

John released Athene from his arms and drew back into the shadow of the thatch.

"Mark the omen," he whispered, as she hastened from him back into the *salone*. "Why do you stay outside on the terrace?"

As John went down through the rosemary toward the Torre Saracena he felt as if he were returning to it after an absence of many years.

A week later John walked into 41 Adelphi Terrace.

"Good god," exclaimed Captain Wade. "Have you got a tame genie?"

"Why do you ask that, sir?"

"Because I telegraphed to your castle in Italy an hour ago to ask if you were well enough to come back at once, and here you are already. Are you all right again?"

"Perfectly fit."

"Then I want you to go to Ireland."

John stiffened.

"Now don't put on that living picture expression. Wait till you hear what I want you to do in Ireland. The Government plan to hold a General Election before the year is out. That means of course an Election in Ireland. They want an intelligent report from an outsider—by which I mean a fellow who has had nothing to do with Dublin Castle—upon the prospects of that Election. Most of the likely Sinn Féin candidates are apparently in jail over here. We've released your friend Fitzgerald, and he ought to be able to help you with the right kind of pointers and introductions. Now get that expression off your face for God's sake. I don't want you to report anything that will compromise anybody. You can be perfectly frank with this friend of yours. If he decides to have you shot from behind a hedge we'll pay for your funeral. One thing the Government want to know, and that is the likely influence of the women's vote. This will be the first election in which what I personally consider the disastrous experiment of giving the votes to women of thirty and over will be put into practice. Why a woman of thirty should be considered any less incompetent than a woman of twenty-nine to drop her political opinion into the ballot-box I'm damned if I understand. However, the wise men of Gotham have decided to give women the vote, and that's that. What are you grinning at?"

"At the notion that the woman of thirty is considered to have reached years of discretion, though for private reasons of my own I should like to believe it."

"Well, there's your job," said Captain Wade. "Any observations?"

"It sounds harmless enough, sir. But what guarantee have I that no use will be made of my report by the elements in the Government that desire to crush Ireland by any means they think serviceable to their purpose?"

"I'll be quite frank, Ogilvie, and say at once that I wouldn't trust any politician not to play a dirty trick if he were sure of not losing any votes thereby. I haven't a high opinion of human nature in general, but I look upon the average politician as a pimp. And I think that pimps are just a little worse than most men. It will be interesting to see if when we get female politicians we shall find them on the same level as bawds. However, that's by the way. The only guarantee you have that your report will not be used by the powers that be for their own purposes is your own wit. I was asked if I had a man of judgment who could make this report by means of his contacts in Ireland. I at once thought of you and telegraphed, as I say, an hour ago. You needn't worry about your wild Irishman. Several deportees have been sent back. There won't be any obvious connection between the return of Fitzgerald and your arrival. My notion was that you could pay him a visit in the ordinary course of friendship. Your report will have to be judged in the end by the accuracy of its forecasts. You should be able to achieve that without injury to anybody. If your report proves all wrong I shall be damned for recommending the wrong man."

John pondered for a few minutes.

"Very well, sir," he said at last. "I believe I shall be able to get what you want without involving anybody. When would you like me to start?"

"The sooner the better, though I don't suppose they'll have the Election till November. We feel pretty confident now of finishing off Fritz in the spring."

"What's your own opinion, sir?"

"Well, I'm not fond of prophesying, Ogilvie. But this time I really do believe that we're in sight of the end. About time too when the police go on strike."

"That must have been a comical business."

"In point of fact it was comical. Damned comical. But it shook up the politicians. Most of 'em went to bed and dreamt they were swinging from lamp-posts. There never was a strike settled so quickly. I went out and had a look at their procession. They marched about seven thousand strong from Westminster to Tower Hill. There was a piper leading them. The public were staggered. Fancy seven thousand policemen swinging their way through London."

"In uniform?" John asked.

"No, no. They all got into mufti. They might have been burglars on strike."

"We shall have the judges going on strike next," John laughed.

Downstairs John enquired for James Yarrow, and was told he had gone to the Ministry of Food. They arrived together that night at the Savoy.

"Why on earth did you go to the Ministry of Food, James?"

"National Ration books," he said gloomily.

"I should have thought Rational Nation books would have been more useful," John said.

"Sez you!" Yarrow nodded.

"Ah, James, you're learning American? But now you're at the Ministry of Food—though I still don't understand why—you can tell me whether it's true that old perambulator hoods are used in the manufacture of margarine. I was told once that they were a chief ingredient."

"If you knew what went into margarine you'd never travel without a cow," Yarrow replied sombrely.

"You still haven't told me why you went to the Ministry of Food."

"They wanted extra people to deal with these ration books. White for adults. Green for children. Pink for adolescents. Blue for manual workers. Red for travellers. And inside, yellow for sugar, blue for butter and margarine, red for meat, fawn for lard, and green for reference. They printed forty million for adults. My god, it was like living in a rainbow."

"I suppose I must get hold of one of these ration books," John said.

"You won't get anything to eat if you don't," Yarrow warned him. "But listen to this from the Prime Minister:

"The message which I send to the people of the British Empire on the fourth anniversary of their entry into the war is 'Hold Fast'.

"We are in this war for no selfish ends. We are in it to recover freedom for the nations which have been brutally attacked and despoiled, and to prove that no people, however powerful, can surrender itself to the lawless ambition of militarism without meeting retribution, swift, certain, and disastrous, at the hands of the free nations of the world. To stop short of Victory for this cause would be to compromise the future of mankind.

"I say 'Hold Fast' because our prospects of Victory have never been so bright as they are to-day. Six months ago the rulers of Germany deliberately rejected the just and reasonable settlement proposed by the Allies. . . ."

"What was that?" John interposed.

"I don't remember. Destruction of various 'isms', I expect. . . .

"Throwing aside the last mask of moderation they partitioned Russia and enslaved Roumania. The great autocracy of Prussia will still endeavour by violence or guile to avoid defeat and so give militarism a new lease of life. We cannot seek to escape the horrors of war for ourselves by laying them up for our children. Having set our hands to the task, we must see it through till a final and lasting settlement is achieved. In no other way can we ensure a world set free from war. Hold fast!"

"What do you think we shall do with Germany?" John asked.

"Build it up again as soon as we can to make a market for ourselves," Yarrow replied.

"But supposing the Germans won't do business with us?"

"Go to war again and make them," said Yarrow. "Do you know what I think is the major mercy of Providence?"

"Sleep," John replied without hesitation.

"No, a greater mercy than that is the fact that although the Germans are as mentally dishonest as the English they are stupider. If the Germans were as clever as the English the only mercy of Providence worth gratitude would be death. Well, hurry up with dinner. They serve nothing after half-past nine."

"What an authority you're becoming, James, on the bureaucratic life. We'll go round to the club afterwards. I'm staying there till I go to Ireland the day after to-morrow. I wish you were coming with me."

"I don't," said Yarrow. "It's bad enough tackling contemporary life with a modern mind, but when it's tackled with a mediaeval mind . . ." He shook his head gloomily.

John was not sorry that the family in Church Row were still away for the summer holidays. And he was positively glad that Miriam Stern was out of town. He wanted a little time to elapse before he told her about Athene. To Athene he wrote that night:

> *I wonder if any man ever had a more difficult effort of will to make than I made six nights ago when I tore myself away from you; but I know that no effort in all my life came anywhere near it. My loved Athene, I hope*

that by now you are telling yourself that what I did was the best to do. I await with extreme anxiety a letter from you and am hoping I may receive one before I leave for Ireland the day after to-morrow where I expect to stay for a time with Edward Fitzgerald. I have a job to do in Ireland, and oddly enough when I arrived my Chief had just telegraphed asking me to come back at once. So we should have had only six more days together, and instead of writing to you at this moment I should have been parting with you after six days which would have added for both of us to the agony of such a parting.

I know too well that this separation is worse for you than for me because I am able to occupy myself with matters outside the routine of my ordinary existence, and also because I am away from the place which is now haunted for you by a memory. Nor do I forget that I have to leave you to carry through what may be a task of unbearable painfulness. I console myself by the certainty I feel that you could not leave Arthur and hope to be happy, and the equal certainty that if you find it impossible to endure this separation you will decide for yourself about that impossibility and that if then you come to me you will come with your mind fortified against all regrets. I beg you to keep this alternative always before you and to feel sure that the moment I am free from the fetters of this war-time service I am free to devote my life to you. I did not ask you what grounds you thought you had for divorcing Wacey, but I have been thinking that probably the best thing for you to do will be to go back to America for legal advice, and take the necessary proceedings there. If only the war were finished you could go at once, but of course as things are that is out of the question.

Opinion here believes the war cannot last beyond next spring, and I am optimistic enough to think the same.

That would mean you could go back in June perhaps, which if all went well would give us a hope of being married before the end of next year.

I do not think either of us should lament the amount of time we have wasted since first we met on board the 'Princess Sophia'. Neither of us knew until six days ago that we were meant for one another. Love is such a confounded mystery, anyway, that it's idle to speculate why it took us both so long. I suppose I was so busily engaged in wondering why I liked you so much in spite of your apparent determination to remain aloof even from friendship that the possibility of ever falling in love was beyond imagination. Now, of course, I tell myself I must have loved you all the time, because it is *difficult to believe that two people who love as we love took more than five years to reach that state. Yet it is reassuring in one way, because what comes slowly lasts long. I cannot even bring myself to write about the depth of my love for you. It seems an impertinence to a self-evident fact. Time-worn endearments and tender apostrophes are equally beyond my pen. You are Athene. I can add nothing to that simple assertion. I would as soon try to inform the world that the Parthenon is beautiful.*

Fortunately for me (and I pray you share this good fortune) I am certain that we shall be married. Therefore I am serene. Love came like a revelation, and so with it came perfect faith.

The moon is bright over Citrano now and all my faith in the future does not avail to keep me from sighing at this moment to be sitting with you and looking out across that sea. Good-night, my loved Athene.

A letter from Citrano reached John on the morning of the day he was leaving for Ireland:

My darling,

I cannot pretend that I am not longing for you and that I do not miss you. That will last until we are together for always. All the same you were right to go like that, and I am grateful for your strength of mind. It gives me now a feeling of security, and I look back now to your resolution in a delicious kind of luxury. I have had so much of softness and irresolution. I believe I'm hard myself. I'm sure I would horrify lots of people by what they would think my cold-blooded determination to settle my future as I am determined it shall be settled. I started a letter to Wacey to-night with the intention of telling him he must understand that all is finally at an end between us, but on reflection I thought I would wait a month because I don't want him to find such a letter coincides with your departure from Citrano. I'm not at all underestimating the difficulties before me. I am thankful, for your sake, that you are not married. I ask myself if I'm being too selfish in asking Wacey for Arthur as well as for my own freedom, and I do not think I am indulging in self-deception when I say that I want to keep Arthur for his own sake rather than mine. After all, half of him is myself and I cannot bear the thought that he might be brought up to develop the other half of himself. Wacey is what he is largely because he was spoilt as a child. He cannot turn his back now upon the easiest way.

When I stop to think that three days ago I saw no way out of the life before me and that now the path ahead is already clear and straight, last night seems a dream from which I shall presently wake up. What I wish most poignantly is that I had been able to be yours when I was twenty and that I should not have to wait until I am thirty to become yours. Of this be sure, dearest one, I will not wait beyond that, unless I am compelled to wait by the war. Nothing else will keep me from you.

Already I am feeling sick at heart for the time when you can no longer write to me. Mercifully that has not arrived yet and I can hope for a letter in about a week. This letter carries all the love of your

Athene

Fitz was waiting for John at Killorglin station with a battered old Ford car.

"Judge, I'm glad to see you, but you're lucky to see me, for I'm only back here from the Parkhurst Hotel a couple of days. I'm one of the German conspirators. Oh, begod, if you British aren't the playboys of Europe!"

"I suppose it was a complete ramp," said John.

"A ramp, do you call it? It was the bloodiest fake that even Dublin Castle and the military worked between them. Ten jokers with fixed bayonets from the barracks in Tralee arrived in a lorry on the night of May 17th and took me off. 'What's this for, boys?' I asked. Devil a word could I get out of them, and begod, it's the truth I didn't know till I reached the Parkhurst Hotel that I was being given free board and lodging because the Germans were going to invade the West with my help! They arrested about a hundred and fifty of us, and they hadn't enough evidence to bring a solitary one to trial."

The ancient Ford was rattling through the main street of the market town, which was thronged with people, cattle and geese. A small military patrol was trying to make its progress through the congestion appear dignified. Fitz braked with a screech, and putting his head out of the window called "Sergeant!"

The sergeant approached suspiciously.

"I'm Doctor Fitzgerald of Tinoran by Lake Caragh, sergeant."

"Yes, sir?"

"And I've reason to suspect that the German Emperor will be landing from a submarine in Lake Caragh to-night. Will you report that to the Commanding Officer, sergeant."

Before the sergeant's mouth had shaped itself to utter a crushing sarcasm in retort the Ford had leapt forward, honking. A dozen geese advancing in single file stepped simultaneously to the right and delivered a unanimous hiss at the car.

"The geese are quicker than the sergeant," Fitz commented, with a delighted laugh.

Soon they were out on a great bronze expanse of bog, under high fleets of cumulus breasting majestically the huge sky, and through the car's smell of mildewed leather and petrol the air a-blow through the flapping celluloid windows was noticeably sharp and sweet.

"The old flivver can still move," Fitz said proudly.

The wide level of the bog ended in hills, and the road began to wind. Here and there in a patch of cultivation wrested from the stony hillside stood a whitewashed cabin buttressed by a stack of winter turfs. John asked the use of a platform that was standing where two roads met.

"That's for the dancing. The Kerry dancing."

John felt a sudden added bitterness against the attempt to coerce this country. Three centuries and more of almost incessant persecution, and now once again under martial law.

"The maddening thing is that if only the English people were given the facts they would never stand for this exploitation of a nation in the interest of a political party," he exclaimed. "It's not the English people but the English ruling caste which is the enemy of your country and of their own country. Some wretched Hyde Park orator ranting against that caste's oppression of the poor has more justification in the eyes of intelligent and civilized men than such cold-blooded egotists."

The car was running now along a woodland road, and the water of the lake flashed in lustrous blue between the trees.

The car swung round through a gate, crackled down a short drive, and pulled up before a stucco house standing on the top of a grassy tree-scattered slope that ran down to the gravel strand of Caragh, on the farther bank of which above a narrow level of vivid green cultivation wooded cliffs rose steeply. Within the hush that succeeded the stopping of the car the lapping of the water was faintly audible.

"And this is Tinoran," Fitz announced, leading the way into the entrance-hall. "And this is Nora whom you meet at last."

Nora was much as John had fancied her—a crimson-cheeked black-haired girl of about twenty-four with deep smoke-blue eyes. The youthful Padraig who was to be two years old next month was clinging to her skirts.

"Was the crossing very rough, Mr Ogilvie?" she asked in a shy soft voice.

"Ah, Nora, don't embarrass the man with your company manners. Call the poor fellow John."

They moved into the sitting-room, where old Mrs Fitzgerald rose from her seat in the window. She put her thin hands on John's shoulder and looked fondly at him.

"Well, well, who'd have thought we would be having such a grand pleasure as this, John? Such times as these, such times as these," she sighed.

"You look just the same, Mrs Fitzgerald," John told her, but he did not really think so. She could not be much more than seventy. Yet she looked ten years older. Indeed, as he cast an eye round the room and marked the dilapidated furniture, the faded wallpaper, the worn upholstery and the threadbare carpet, she seemed as old as her background.

"Don't criticize the poor wild Irish," laughed the owner of Tinoran. "We left this room as my grandfather, God be good to him, left it."

To-day the lake was a vivid blue, and the bright sunlight was unkind to this shabby room; but on a grey day it would take on a pastel beauty of subdued colour and make all the other rooms beside this lake appear in contrast garish and intrusive.

"I was thinking how wise you were to leave it like that," John said.

Fitz addressed a boisterous remark in Irish to his son, who replied firmly,

"I won't. No, I won't!"

"Well, if you're going to be rude, for God's sake be rude in your own language," said Fitz. "I marry an Irish-speaking colleen, and damn it, she can't make her son speak her language."

"Edward, Edward," his mother protested. "I wish *you'd* be more careful with the English you use."

"Edward dear, he doesn't understand you when you try to talk to him in Irish," said Nora, and turning to John she added, "Edward's accent tastes terribly of English."

"Well, will you oblige your father by shaking hands with this gentleman?" Fitz said to his son, who at once advanced and performed the courtesy with a grand air.

"Why the hell you couldn't have done that when I asked you to in your own language, St Thomas Aquinas himself would be puzzled to explain."

"Edward, I must beg you not to teach him to behave like a corner-boy," his mother protested again. "You never used to swear like that all the while."

"I learned to swear from your own husband, ma'am," said Fitz.

The argument was interrupted by the entrance of a buxom woman with a high colour to which powder gave an artificial look.

"Ellen!" John exclaimed.

"So the famous dramatist has not forgotten the face of the poor actress even if he has forgotten her talents, to which the provincial press has been testifying for the last eighteen years," she said, her grey-blue eyes twinkling as she shook John's hand.

"In justice to myself I've not had a play running since before the war," he pleaded.

"He's not a dramatist at all just now," Fitz put in. "Didn't you know he was Lord Nelson's understudy? He's been dancing the hornpipe all over the Mediterranean for king and country, and standing up for the rights of small nations, and putting civilization on the map of Europe. Lieutenant-Commander J. P. Ogilvie, R.N.V.R. Don't laugh, Ellen, I've seen it on the envelope."

"We are the boys of Wexford," sang Ellen, with a wink at John.

"Augh, you're no better than a dirty little West Briton," her brother jeered.

"And what's happened to Connie Fenwick?" John asked.

"She's still on the stage. She's been married seven or eight years now. An actor of course. I haven't run against her for a long time. But do you remember her young brother Rupert?"

"Of course, a red-haired kid."

"Well, he was in front at a show I was playing in at Birmingham last winter and he sent a note round to ask me out to lunch next day. He's a captain and got the D.S.O. and the M.C. and was twice badly wounded. He couldn't go back to France."

"That must have pleased his father."

"Oh, old Mr Fenwick died a year or two before the war began. But you're right, John. He would have been proud of his boy."

"That's enough of the British Army," Fitz interrupted. "When you've been dug out of bed with a bayonet for conspiring with the Germans, the British Army is a sore subject."

"Jesus, Mary, Joseph . . . Holy Family give us peace," the old lady murmured, clutching her rosary. Her thin voice sighed across the faded room like the wind in the reeds of Caragh.

"Now, Judge boy, what about a day with the grouse to-morrow?" Fitz asked. "It means a hard tramp behind the dogs and not more than a couple of brace probably, with half a dozen hares, but the tramp will do you good."

"I'll tramp without a gun, Fitz. I don't want even to try to kill anything," John replied. "I never did enjoy killing birds and animals, but now the notion of taking the life even of a gnat revolts me."

That night at half-past nine Fitz rang the bell in the sitting-room and told John to go along to his den off the surgery, where he would join him after rosary.

"Mayn't I stay?" John asked.

"Sure, you can stay."

Joe MacCarthy, the bandy-legged gardener, and Bridget Sullivan, the round-faced maid-of-all-work, came into the sitting-room.

Pater noster qui es in coelis, sanctificetur nomen tuum . . . Ave Maria, gratiae plena, Dominus tecum, benedicta tu in mulieribus . . . sancta Maria, Mater Dei, ora pro nobis peccatoribus . . . gloria Patri et Filio et Spiritui Sancto . . . fiat voluntas Tua . . . panem nostrum . . . et benedictus fructus ventris tui, Jesus . . . nunc et in hora mortis nostrae . . . sicut erat in principio, nunc, et in saecula saeculorum. . . .

Century after century these words uttered by numberless millions now dead . . . night after night, day after day . . . and night after night, day after day being uttered still . . . sorrowful mysteries, joyful mysteries, glorious mysteries . . . never a moment when somebody somewhere on this green earth was not rapt in contemplation of those fifteen mysteries of the Christian creed . . . *let us contemplate in this mystery how the Blessed Virgin Mary, when the time of her delivery was come, brought forth our Redeemer Jesus Christ at midnight, and laid Him in a manger, because there was no room for Him in the inn at Bethlehem* . . . no room for Him in Downing Street . . . no room for Him in the Wilhelmstrasse . . . no room for Him at the Quai d'Orsay . . . no room for Him at the Consulta . . . no room for Him in Vienna or Petrograd . . . no room for Him in Washington . . . no question in a tormented Europe that this Divine Babe could not answer . . . but there was no room for Him . . . no room save in the hearts of the meek, the lowly, and the humble . . . *Pater noster qui es in coelis . . . dimitte nos debita nostra sicut et nos dimittimus debitoribus nostris* . . . forgive us our trespasses as we forgive them that trespass against us . . . Holy Mary, Mother of God, pray for us sinners now and in the hour of our death . . . as it was in the beginning, is now, and ever shall be. . . .

The evening rosary was told. Joe and Bridget beamed a good-night and slipped through the door. Old Mrs Fitzgerald, candle in hand, went up to bed. Ellen and Nora sat down to read and sew for awhile together. Fitz and John sought out the small room off the surgery where a turf fire was glowing and the bottle of Johnnie Jameson stood on a low table between the two worn leather armchairs which old Dr Fitzgerald had bought when he first came to London in the 'seventies.

"And what is the real reason for your being in Ireland, Judge?" Fitz asked when the glasses had been filled and the fire had been stirred to flames.

"I've been wondering why you haven't asked that already," John replied, and forthwith gave the explanation.

"You shall read my report," he promised his friend, "and if there is anything in it which you feel might cause trouble it shall be taken out. What decided me to accept the job finally was my belief that I might do some good."

Fitz pondered for a moment or two.

"They're so damned suspicious of wandering busy-bodies—forgive the description, Judge," he murmured to himself at last.

"I'm not surprised," John said. "Well, it lies with you, Fitz. If you can't allay these suspicions I'll get back and let them know in London that my stay here would be a waste of time."

"Augh, I think it'll be all right. But John," he asked sharply, his eyes narrowing to what seemed a single pale-blue point of fire, "you're not playing a double game, are you?"

John shook his head in despair.

"If you are going to suspect that, Fitz, how do you hope to convince others? I can't argue about it. If you believe me capable of betraying our friendship you must believe it, and I'll clear off back to England to-morrow."

"I don't believe it, Judge. But the country's lousy with informers, police spies, and Government agents. We seem to have frightened them this time."

"And what will be the result of an election if it is held later on this autumn?"

"Sinn Féin will sweep the polls," Fitz declared confidently. "Then if the British Government admits itself beaten there need be no more trouble."

"I expect that's what we'll be telling Germany presently," John said. "I only hope that what is called the verdict of the polls will not be reversed by the court of appeal, or in other words the central office of the Conservative Party. I wonder if even you, Fitz, realize the extent to which Ireland has been sacrificed to party advantage, or how much the prevailing Irish view of the English is coloured by the fact that the struggle has always been with the English ruling classes."

"Don't forget I was at an English public-school," said Fitz. "The English middle classes take their orders from above not below, and indeed with the growth of the civil service you can call *them* the ruling classes now. They hate Ireland because Ireland is a riddle to the English civil servant, for which he can find no answer on a buff form. Ireland is the monkey-wrench in the works. There's more than the central office of the Unionist Party we have to deal with. There is a natural antipathy."

"On both sides?" John asked.

"I think the English hate us much more than we hate them, because fear is at the back of the hatred. But fundamentally the trouble is that we spoil the pattern. We won't play the game, which of course is cricket. Yet, damn it all, this wonderful game which is supposed to foster and demonstrate to an envious world all the English virtues requires an umpire at both ends of the pitch to prevent a dishonest catch or a foul ball."

For six weeks John travelled about the country, and by the end of the experience he had no shadow of doubt that whether a General Election were held this autumn or early next spring there would hardly be a constituency which did not declare itself in favour of separation from England. He was less successful in arriving at what the country proposed to do with its independence when it was achieved. Coercion in fact had destroyed in the mind of the average Irishman everything except the passion to be free from it. And this, John wrote in his report, was a dangerous condition to have set up, because it meant that, if the verdict of the country at the elections should be disregarded, purely destructive forces would be at once released, the sole object of which would be to fight coercion by violent means.

John found everywhere among the Unionist minority a complete failure to appreciate the profound moral transformation of the country by the self-sacrifice of the leaders of the Easter Rising. For them political agitators, the bane of Ireland, had stirred up the peasants to believe they still had a grievance, but anybody who knew the Irish peasant as well as they did knew that the last thing the Irish peasant wanted was a government which would make it impossible for the owners of country houses to remain in the country. 'Home Rule' was just a catch-phrase nowadays. Mistakes had been made in the past by people who did not understand Ireland as they did, people in fact who were not, as they were, proud to call themselves Irishmen. Home Rule had seemed an easy remedy for that kind of thing, but nowadays with the opportunities given to the country people to acquire their own holdings there was no real discontent. It was stirred up by agitators who, resentful that they were not gentlemen themselves, could not bear the influence over the people enjoyed by gentlemen.

"I mean to say," a retired colonel in Connemara assured John, "there's nobody quicker than one of these fellows to recognize who doesn't come out of the top drawer. You get these clean, fine, strong, temperate, hurly-playing country fellows, and by gad, when I served with a regiment like the Munsters and Royal Irish we could march round most English regiments, and stand heat, cold, and wet like salamanders. That sort of chap doesn't want Home Rule. He laughs at it. He knows jolly well that Home Rule will drive the money out of the country."

"From what I gather, colonel, it's no longer a question of Home Rule but separation."

"They've been pulling your leg. There's nobody like

the Irish for pulling a stranger's leg. Separation? Preposterous! Why, the country wouldn't last a year without English protection. Look here, Ogilvie, I'm seventy-five. You wouldn't think it, eh? But I am. I could have commanded a Brigade in France, but they had no use for my services. Too old, they said. Well, I don't know. They dug out much more decrepit specimens than me. So I've had a lot of time on my hands since the war. And after a day's fishing I'd get around and talk to the fellows. They like it when you can talk to them naturally. And believe me, Ogilvie, in their hearts they do not want Home Rule. Well, look what a fellow who knows the best pools can earn in a season. Of course, since the war there haven't been quite so many of us, but the good man can do very well for himself even now. And he knows which side his bread is buttered. Did you really say it was a question of separation now?"

John confirmed his statement, and the old colonel again laughed heartily.

"That's the kind of bogy these fellows at the Castle produce to keep their job. Mind you, that Easter business was a bit nasty. But it was handled wrong. It was taken too seriously. I may not be fit to command a Brigade in France, but I tell you this, Ogilvie, if I had been G.O.C. the whole business would have been over in twenty-four hours. It was a piece of fanatical play-acting, and it should have been treated as such. You see, I'm an Irishman myself, and so I know."

But John became more and more surely convinced that men like this did not know what had happened to Ireland in the last two and a half years.

At the end of October he returned to Tinoran.

"It *is* a long way to Tipperary, Fitz," he said. "We'd been driving through a thick grey mist since morning, and when we reached the heart of Tipperary it faded away and those rich rolling pastures were touched by the loveliest golden light I ever saw. They were golden-green as chrysoprase. I felt I was looking at a world such as Blake beheld in his visions. And there was the paradise of the heart's desire of which every man who sang that song was dreaming. And it *was* Tipperary. But it *is* a long way from Piccadilly and Leicester Square, and it's still further from Downing Street, I'm afraid. I confess I should like to have wrapped Lloyd George in his bardic robes and whisked him to Tipperary this morning and dismissed him with a warning not to betray the West."

"And what have you learned about the next election, Judge?"

John tossed his report across to his friend.

"You certainly won't have to reproach yourself with not having warned them what they must expect," Fitz commented when he had read through what John had written. "I wonder how long they'll leave me out of jail. The people round here are such patriots that, begod, they'd sooner die than consult a Unionist doctor."

John was loath to leave Tinoran, for in this exquisite autumn weather Caragh dreamed in beauty, the fern on the higher slopes ruddy as a fox from the dews of the morning and the leaves of the birch-trees spun gold.

"I'm sorry you're going, Judge, but I'm glad you've seen this Christian country. You might remember that, when you wonder what Ireland intends to make of her freedom."

"Remember what?"

"Remember that it is a Christian country and will keep the Faith."

"I wish it could be kept without bloodshed and violence," said old Mrs Fitzgerald. "Holy Family, give us peace . . . peace. God bless you, John."

He turned to Ellen.

"Now be sure to let me know your address if you go

to England, because if this last play of mine gets put on soon, as my agent writes hopefully to say he thinks it will be, I promise you a part."

"I'll believe it when I hear my first cue," Ellen told him.

Fitz tried to make his son say farewell in Irish, but Padraig was obstinate.

"I won't. No, I won't."

"He's like the old Orange flute," John laughed.

"I don't know what in hell's biting him," Fitz lamented.

"Edward, it's your Irish he doesn't like," said Nora. "He thinks it's all wrong. He speaks it to me beautifully. Good-bye, John. Wouldn't it be nice now if you were coming instead of going?"

"It would be grand," he agreed as he got into the hired car which was to drive him to Dublin, with a week on the road in the counties of Cork, Waterford, Wexford, and Wicklow. It was a morning of utter serenity, and as John leaned from the window to wave a last farewell to the group standing by the porch of the stuccoed house, the walls of which were stained by damp to the semblance of a faded panorama, he could have fancied that house and people and grassy tree-scattered slope beside Caragh had been drawn down into the golden-wooded depths of that watery mirror, to live for ever thus in a lake of amber.

The wind was blowing a full gale from the west a few hours later, and that night as he lay awake in the bedroom of a Cork hotel and listened to the rattling of the windows the picture of that group of people beside Caragh was always in his mind until the vividness of its tranquillity defeated the noise of the tempest and he slept.

John's last call before he reached Dublin was at Aughavanagh, where he was to have a talk with Captain William Redmond, who was back from France for a few days. The house in the recesses of the Wicklow Mountains made an impression upon him of almost violent melancholy. Originally it had been built as a barrack for English troops to overawe the disaffected countryside after the Rising of 1798. It was a long ivy-clad house with some thirty windows looking out on a large lawn surrounded by a thick belt of trees. On one side a squat tower muffled in ivy and apparently windowless had presumably been built as a blockhouse and powder-magazine. The uncanny thing about the building was its shallowness and the large area of blank wall it presented to the open moorland on which it backed. Such windows as there were on this side must have been loopholes for defence once upon a time. In front of the main door was a white glazed porch such as may be seen in front of suburban villas. In the angle made by the tower and the house was growing a large Crinodendron, the flower-buds of which would be able to weather the winter in this moist western air and swell to half-tralucent great hexagonal rubies in the spring. John would not have been able to identify this Chilean beauty but for his visit to Pendarves House in the summer.

The road up from the village of Aughrim was rough and steep, and as the car reached the top blue mountain hares scampered away over the moor on either side. A pair of hoodie-crows upon a stone dyke flapped off croaking. A flock of winter curlews rose, whistling their alarm. The impression was of interrupting a wild life caught unaware. A motor-car in this remote fastness was evidently a surprising novelty.

Redmond was a dark burly beaky-nosed young man in the uniform of the Irish Guards. He was the sitting member for Waterford, to which constituency he had been elected after the death in March of his father broken-hearted.

"Not because I was a Nationalist," he told his guest, "but because I was my father's son."

"And will you be elected again if there is a General Election this year?" John asked.

"I shall be elected, but I doubt if another Nationalist will be elected outside Ulster. The country has gone mad, but it was driven mad by the folly of the British Government."

They discussed the political future, and the melancholy of the house pierced John to the marrow like the dank of a charnel-house.

"My father bought this place after the death of Parnell," said Redmond.

Of course! This had been Parnell's retreat before John Redmond's, and another broken heart had haunted this barrack. Cursed by the peasantry it had been built to overawe, abandoned for a long while, lived in by Parnell, bought by his most faithful follower, and for nearly another generation the centre of how many deferred hopes, how many bitter disappointments, how much rejected loyalty, how much wasted effort and solitary endeavour, no wonder this house lay heavy upon the mind with a sense of human frustration that was almost intolerable.

They ate that mountainy mutton for lunch, meat which gave back in its juices the fragrant moorland air; and after lunch they went along to the great vault of a kitchen where it had been cooked and congratulated the domestic staff. Afterwards Redmond loosed from the kennels two or three Irish setters and they wandered up beside a burn that ran behind the house.

"The promised land," said Redmond, pointing to the wide vale outspread far below the mountains. It was such a landscape as delighted Umbrian painters. The gale dying had left behind a wash of lucid air in the clarity of which the details of remote distances appeared as exquisitely diminished as a much nearer landscape appears through the wrong end of a telescope. The trees and towers and villages were reduced to the farthest background of an Umbrian painting, and the radiant light and shade of the celestial blue in which they reposed offered the background of serenity meet for a Nativity or Annunciation in the foreground.

"And your father did not reach it," John said, divining the allusion.

They went back to the house and looked at relics of Parnell's fights in the 'eighties. Crude prints of this or that convention in Australia or America hung on the walls. Bearded delegates and whiskered delegates in top hats crowded together at the Chicago convention, and below in the margin their numbered profiles in miniature assisted the identification of individuals whom time by now had lumped together into that composite figure, the Irish malcontent. All the eloquence, all the cheering, all the harps of Erin tied with green ribbon, all ground slowly down to dust by the mills of the Parliamentary machine.

"There's not often such warmth in party politics as the loyalty of your father to Parnell," said John. "And the English might have had the same loyalty if they could have appreciated it."

"They might," Redmond nodded.

He crossed to a cabinet stacked with bundles of letters, through which he searched while his guest turned over albums of old gramophone records which were lying about on a kind of sideboard.

"My father brought those back with him from his American tour in 1910."

With their lilac and almond-green and buff and pale blue and scarlet and white labels these records of famous singers, which had cost as much as five dollars apiece some of them, exhaled an air of frivolous luxury beside the prints and the scrapbooks and press-cuttings of over forty years of political life. Yet those discs were melancholy too, for they seemed in this haunted barrack doomed to an eternal silence as utter as the bearded and bewhiskered delegates in their tight frock-coats who thronged the musty prints upon the walls.

"I'm afraid the spring of the gramophone is broken," said Redmond.

But John closed the album hastily. The sound of Caruso's voice in this room choked by the past would have been frightening.

"Here's a typical letter," said Redmond. "My father wrote to the commanding officer of the Irish Brigade in 1914 for a commission for Gavan Duffy, who had travelled all the way from Australia to join up. This is the answer he received on Christmas Day:

> "*I make it a rule never to recommend a man, and especially a colonist, without an interview or a recommendation from someone I know, based on recent personal knowledge. Even this rule does not save me from an occasional bibulous fire-eater. Only the other day a gentleman whom I interviewed on the recommendation of a most reliable gentleman and ex-soldier, and got made a captain, came drunk to mess on two consecutive days.*"

"Incredible!" John murmured.

"And even more incredible when you think that the despised colonist is the grandson of the Prime Minister of Victoria, and the nephew of the Chief Justice of Australia. But look at this letter. After my Uncle William and Stephen Gwynn had joined the Irish Division into which the Irish Brigade had grown by the beginning of 1915, I thought that as an M.P. of twenty-nine it was up to me to follow the lead of M.P.'s over fifty, and my father asked for a commission for me. Read the reply from the commanding officer."

John read:

"Politicians are apt to forget that I alone am responsible that I get my division fit to take its place in the field, and that when it gets there it will not disgrace the British Army and its country, and that I, therefore, cannot go on indefinitely sacrificing military to political interests.

"What did you do?"

"I enlisted. I was given a commission later in the Dublin Fusiliers and transferred to the Irish Guards."

"And were wounded," John added, looking at the thin golden stripe, "and won the D.S.O.," he added with a glance at the ribbon.

"The point is the way my father was treated," said Redmond. "If he had not been sacrificed to English party warfare Ireland to-day would be a united nation with all the Home Rule it wanted. I was in Ireland on leave at the time of the Easter Rising. I'd been to the Fairyhouse Races and was held up by the rebels at a barricade outside Dublin, but I drove through them and caught the last boat from Kingstown. The rising was a mortal blow to my father, and for a time his attitude towards it was the attitude of Ireland as a whole; but the shootings against his advice turned the country right round. Those lads achieved their purpose. They offered their lives to recall Ireland to a sense of her nationhood. And they succeeded. But what will Ireland do with her nationhood?"

"Won't that depend on the extent to which England opposes it?"

"I'm pessimistic."

"Naturally." John felt inclined to add "because you are surrounded in this house by the sense of failure," but he substituted "because you see the movement being carried so far beyond anything that Parliamentary Nationalists dreamed possible."

"I suppose I'm prejudiced by my inheritance,"

Redmond admitted. "I cannot believe that Sinn Féi
can build solidly."

"I have an intimate friend who is a prominent figur
in Sinn Féin, and his theory is that after Parnell wa
hounded to death the Parliamentary Nationalists decaye
under the corrupting influence of Westminster."

"My father kept outside Parliamentary friendships."

"Yes, but the influence is insidious," said John. "
defy any man to hold out for ever against the magic i
the atmosphere of British government. It affects every
body. After all, the British Empire *is* a tremendou
affair and the long tradition of Parliament *is* overwhelming
Parnell nearly broke it, but he was up against one of th
superlative masters of what other nations call Englis
hypocrisy, and Gladstone broke *him* on the rock o
respectability. I suppose it is the instinct of self-pro
tection which forbids the British to forgive anybody wh
is found out. They have usually so much to concea
that the man who allows himself to be found out let
them down by suggesting their own hidden weaknesses
I do believe my friend Fitzgerald may be right when h
declares that the Parliamentary Nationalists had begu
to think that the process of achieving Home Rule ha
become more important than the object in view."

"That was not true of my father," Redmond insisted.

"I daresay not, but I think it was true that, in his attemp
to achieve the isolation which, learning from Parnell, h
believed was vital to the leadership of a political party
he succeeded in isolating himself from the new spirit o
youth in Ireland. Your father who was held up by Sin
Féin as a perfect example of the Anglicization of Irelan
was for years regarded in England itself as a dangerou
revolutionary. He *was* once upon a time revolutionar
in his own date, but isn't it the fate of most revolutionarie
to forget that the wheel they start revolves faster as i
grows and so to be left behind by the speed of what the

have created? This friend of mine as long ago as 1900, speaking in a debate at our old school, St James's, told a Nationalist M.P. who was speaking as a visitor that the Parliamentary Nationalists had outlived their utility, to the curse of Irish Independence."

"But my father never considered complete separation was feasible."

"Parnell did," John reminded him. "I must say that if I were an Irishman I should have little use for mere Home Rule. You feel that your father died broken-hearted because he saw the ruin of his life's work, but history may relate that the ruin of his life's work was its crown of glory."

"Sinn Féin will never cover it with glory," Redmond prophesied bitterly.

"But aren't you, too, perhaps prejudiced, Redmond? It's difficult to appreciate Sinn Féin from the Irish Guards. I have just travelled all over the country and I cannot express the enthusiasm I feel about Sinn Féin. This revivification of Ireland, and I hope, presently the revivification of Poland, seem to me the best result of this war, which, by the way, judging by the news in this morning's paper looks as it if might be over now before Christmas."

"The war won't be over in Ireland. The war will begin in Ireland after the General Election."

"You mean to say the British Government will not accept the verdict of the polls, which to me seems certain. I should go so far as to prophesy that three-quarters of the country will vote for Sinn Féin."

"You don't suppose the British Government will accept an Irish Republic?"

"I don't know; after all this talk about the rights of small nations, they may have to. When do you go back to France?"

"I'm leaving to-night."

Even Fitz's contempt for Parliamentary Nationalism

might have been softened by the atmosphere of Aughavanadh, John thought, as he leaned back in the car on the way to Dublin. That lonely tragic house haunted by the frustrated hopes of two patriots . . . he shivered in the autumnal air, for it was already late afternoon and the November sun was but a ghost at this hour. He pulled Athene's last letter from his pocket to bring back the warmth of hope:

I am so glad you have been enjoying this visit to Ireland. It's useless to pretend that I can follow Irish politics. We always feel in America that the Irish are never satisfied whatever happens, but your last letter was so full of lovely descriptions of lovely places that I forgot about the politics and wished for nothing except to be driving with you on and on for ever through such places.

I have written at last to Wacey to say that it is impossible for me to continue the pretence of the last years when he comes back, and that he must release me. I do not expect a satisfactory reply, naturally. But at least when he does come to Citrano we can begin to discuss the problem of the future without a moment's delay. I sound very hard, don't I? But I am really miserable on his account because he is incapable of standing up to the responsibility of his own character. He is happy in his weakness. I shall never persuade him that he is responsible for what has happened to make our marriage an impossibility. It will be my hardness, my selfishness, my pride, my unforgiving nature, my refusal to believe him. It will be his misfortune, nothing else, that I for no valid reason have decided to cut free. That will be the wearisome part of what I have to go through, so wearisome that I know before the endless arguments have finished I shall be tempted to confess myself the cruellest female that ever lived. Oh, how wise you were, John, to go away that night! You have no idea how that effort you made has fortified me. Geoffrey Noel met me in the piazza yesterday and said, "Really, dear lady, you look as determined as the goddess after whom you were named. I'm thankful I'm not Paris." Poor Noel, there is more weakness. How he can tolerate the ignominious existence on his wife's contemptuous and wayward charity I do not know.

But fortified as I feel I become very tremulous when I think of what has to be endured before we meet again. But I miss you, my loved one. Every minute of every hour. The news from France makes me wonder if the war may not be over by Christmas. And in Italy too they are doing splendidly. Oh, how far far away you are, and always the sick dread that soon you may not be able to write to me. Thank God, there is not an instant in which I do not feel the security and assurance of your love. Yet we have not talked together of love for even so much as an hour in all the time we have known one another. Known one another! Why, neither knew the other until last month. And now I cannot believe there was ever a time when we had not met. The maestrale is blowing to-night, and the stars are brilliant. Oh, so *brilliant. That intelligent interest we take in geography when our lovers are far away tells me that the north-west wind is blowing from your direction as I sit here writing to you from the Allegra. I dislike wind from any direction as a rule because I don't like my hair to be blown about, but the gratifying discovery that this maestrale is blowing from where you are has taken me out into the garden to breathe it in. How black your tower looks against the sky, so black and empty—like my life, John, till you came into it. And now after sitting and dreaming over this page without writing a word for quite twenty minutes the lamp is going out and I can only write that I am always*

Your Athene

John avoided the Shelbourne Hotel because he did not want to be irritated by the conversation of subalterns. He went instead to a small family hotel recommended to him by Fitz. Tired after the amount of driving he had done that day and the emotional drain of the time he spent at Aughavanadh, he went up to bed soon after he had finished dinner and added to his report some notes of his talk with Captain Redmond. About two o'clock he switched off the light and soon afterwards fell asleep. He woke suddenly from a dream in which he was walking through a roofless ivy-clad ruin, aware that a great owl was gazing at him but unable in the eerie way of dreams to know why or to discover where in the vast roofless ruin the owl was perched. The impression of the dream was so strong that when he woke he felt that the owl was in the room, and thrusting out a hand to switch on the light he touched, not feathers, but the hair of a human head. He recoiled for a moment in dismay, but recovered enough wit to switch on the light just as the figure of a man reached the door of the room.

"Stop where you are if you don't want to be plugged," he shouted, feeling vaguely that he was still in the middle of a bad dream.

The figure turned to show a thin tallowy furtive face beneath dank black hair.

"What the hell are you doing in my room?" John demanded.

"Please, sir, I made a little mistake," a whining Dublin voice answered. "I tought it was Captain Smit's room, sir. I'm sure I beg your pardon, sir, and hope you'll excuse the little interruption. I'm sure I'm very sorry, sir."

Suddenly John saw that his report was lying on the floor beside the bed.

"So that's what you wanted, was it?" he exclaimed.

"I must have knocked it over by mistake, sir. You gave me such a fright, sir."

"Who's Captain Smith?"

"He's a British officer, sir."

"In this hotel?"

"Yes, sir."

By this time John was out of bed and the wretched intruder was cringing against the door.

"Get away from that door," he said sharply. "I want my dressing-gown. Now take me to Captain Smith's room," he went on when he had put on the dressing-gown.

"He won't be in to-night, sir."

"Look here," said John, "I've had about enough of you. Who sent you up here to pinch my papers?"

"It was all a mistake, sir. I came to the wrong room."

"Who sent you?"

"Nobody sent me, sir. It's true what I'm after telling you."

"Are you from the I.R.A.?"

"Glory be to God, no sir! I'm loyal. I'm known well at the Castle, sir."

"You're known at the Castle, are you?" John asked. "What's your name?"

"Michael Duggan, sir."

"Do you know Major Brinsley Rossiter?"

Duggan hesitated a perceptible two or three seconds.

"No, sir," he replied at last, looking away from John's eyes.

"It wasn't he who sent you to steal that packet of papers?"

"I don't know the gentleman, sir."

John glanced at his watch. It was two o'clock.

"Do you live in this hotel?" he asked.

"Yes, sir, I'm the night porter, sir. That's why I made the little mistake, sir. I was after forgetting Captain Smit wouldn't be in to-night."

"Well, get to hell out of my room. I'll see what Mrs

Kavanagh has to say about you in the morning."

John returned to bed, but he was too angry for a long time to sleep, and when he got up next morning rage was still lying on him like an undigested meal of the day before.

The landlady, undulating in bombasine, was equally indignant.

"I wouldn't have had such a thing happen in my house to anybody and least of all to a friend of Dr Fitzgerald's. Well, that's the end of Mike Duggan, the dirty blackguard! And a British Government spy at that," she went on in a low voice after a glance to right and left along the lobby. "Perhaps you'd step into my office, Mr Ogilvie?"

"Too early in the morning for me, thank you."

"Not just a small sensation? It would do you good after such a night and all."

"No, really, thanks. I'll have one with you before I leave for Kingstown to-night."

"You're leaving us so soon? Pray God you'll have a safe crossing to Holyhead, but ever since the *Leinster* was sunk last month I can't hear of anyone crossing to Holyhead without a shiver. The hundreds of poor souls that were drowned! And little children too! My brother's wife's uncle lost a grandchild. Just a lad of sixteen going to work in England. It's terrible the way the British do be taking the bread out of the mouths of Irishmen so that they have to go to England to find work. Dreadful things we've suffered in Dublin, but it'll be all for the best in the end. Yes, indeed, a man might be forgiven if he'd gone into a guest's room for the good of his country, but to go sneaking in at the bidding of the British . . . augh, it's the greatest disgrace I've ever known . . . it would have killed my husband if he was alive, God rest his soul! Ah, just wait, my bold Micky, till you come sneaking back for duty this evening, and it's you that'll wish you'd never so much as heard of Mrs Lawrence Kavanagh. The blackguard! The dirty spying rascal! And such a gorgeous morning too. I'm sure you'll enjoy walking about in what the British have left us of dear old Dublin."

John reached the Castle about eleven o'clock, and after a series of encounters with red-capped military police, staff-sergeants, black-coated clerks, and a ha-ha fence of subalterns he penetrated to the office of Major Brinsley Rossiter, seconded for special duties from the Princess of Wales's Flintshire Regiment.

A narrow-headed man, with grizzled red hair receding from a forehead the freckled skin of which seemed to have been stretched unnaturally tight by pressure exerted upon the deeply indented temples on either side, looked sharply up at his visitor from pale eyes, while freckled fingers stroked the bristles of a small carroty moustache.

"Sorry to keep you waiting, Commander Ogilvie, but I'm pretty busy this morning," he drawled.

"You were damned busy last night too, weren't you?" John asked, pulling forward a chair and seating himself uninvited opposite the Major.

"I'm afraid I don't quite get you. I understand you wanted to see me on an urgent matter."

"So I do," John snapped. "I want to know what the devil you mean by hiring the night porter of Kavanagh's Hotel to steal my report on the present state of Ireland?"

Major Rossiter stroked the side of his jaw as if searching for a bristle which had escaped the razor that morning.

"I'm afraid I don't quite follow you, Commander Ogilvie."

"I thought you were an Intelligence Officer?"

The Major stopped stroking his jaw and opening his mouth slightly tapped with two fingernails on his upper teeth, while he contemplated his visitor from cold pale eyes.

"I'm on special service, yes," he said at last.

"Then if you can't follow me, why not try using your brains?" John asked.

There was no frown or wrinkle of the tight-skinned forehead, but the thin mouth tightened.

"If you've nothing better to do than waste my time by being rude, perhaps you'll let me get on with my work," the Major suggested.

"You don't admit that you employed Michael Duggan to break into my room last night?"

"I don't know what you're talking about."

"You know why I've been in Ireland for the last six weeks?"

"I've no official knowledge of your existence."

"Look here, Rossiter, what's the use of quibbling. You know perfectly well that I was sent out here on a special mission. Otherwise you wouldn't have been interested to read what I wrote. You took a chance. A damned silly chance, I may add, as one who has had some experience in trying to get hold of other people's papers. . . ."

"I find all this rather boring," the Major cut in.

"That's of no importance to me. You wanted to know if I was going to say anything in my report which would reflect on the way things were being run in the Castle. That wasn't my business. But when I get back to London to-morrow I'll add a pretty forcible footnote to say what kind of information particularly interests the Castle."

"I tell you, Ogilvie, I have no official knowledge either of you or your mission."

"Do you admit you tried to get a glimpse of my report?"

"I admit nothing."

"It's a queer thing that when I asked this very inefficient spy whether he was in the employment of Major Brinsley Rossiter his manner gave him away at once. I thought at first it was an I.R.A. fellow, but poor Mike Duggan was horrified at such a suspicion and assured me he was well known at the Castle. That's when I asked him if he was employed by you. So you didn't want to see my report?"

"Why the devil should I?" the Major yapped. "If I wasted my time reading every report written about the state of Ireland by wandering experts I should be kept pretty busy. But now we've started I'm going to make a complaint, Ogilvie. I'm going to complain about Spicer butting into our show. His sphere of action was clearly established before the war. Why doesn't he stick to enemy and neutral countries?"

"I thought you were treating Ireland as an enemy country," John retorted. "No doubt that's what's caused the overlapping. Well, I don't suppose I'll see you again, Rossiter, either officially or unofficially, and so I'll take this opportunity of saying what a bloody rotten Intelligence Officer you are. Good morning."

By the time John reached London the attempt to get hold of his report had turned from an intrigue into a joke, and it was as a joke that he related the incident to Captain Wade.

"What is my next job, sir?"

"Unless you want to stay in the service with me I should think your next job would be your own work. The war won't last into next week. Mind you, I think it will be a mistake if we let 'em have an armistice. We ought to march into Germany and show 'em that they're beaten, and when I say Germany I mean Berlin. That's where an unconditional peace ought to be dictated, but I expect the wise men of Gotham will know better. They're very busy now trying to wind up the watch on the Rhine and keep an eye on the political barometer at the same moment."

"My weather forecast from the west won't cheer them up."

"You sound pleased," Captain Wade grunted.

"I'm not distressed."

"Well, if I do want you, Ogilvie, you're going to stay in town for a while?" his Chief asked.

"Certainly, until I can get out of this uniform, and then I fancy my new play will be put on soon after Christmas. So I shall look for a small furnished flat somewhere and probably stay in London till the spring."

"All right. Keep in touch with me, and don't get influenza. It's carrying people off at the rate of eight hundred a week in London at present."

John managed to secure a small unfurnished flat at the top of Queensberry Mansions in Charing Cross Road, from a disabled officer whose wife had just left him.

"That's the second, old man, since I joined up with the First Hundred Thousand in August, '14. I divorced the first, but this one can do what she likes about it, the lawyers aren't going to have any more of my gratuity, and that's a fact. You'll pay a month in advance, I suppose? You don't mind me asking, but these are funny times."

"I'll pay you three months in advance if that's any convenience," John offered.

"Well, we didn't think much of the British Navy out in France, but my opinion of 'em's going up. Well, I hope you'll be comfortable here. The porter's a bit of a bastard, but most of the flats are let to tarts, and in fact when I think of the way my wife played me up with that fellow pulling twelve quid a week for walking the floor among a lot of munition workers I wouldn't say this flat hadn't been let to a tart while I was in hospital. Reserved occupations? He wasn't very reserved in his occupation of my little ball of worsted."

"George Fettering? That's right?" John asked, as he handed him the cheque.

"Couldn't have spelt it better myself. Well, good-by-ee! Oh, and about the plug. It's quite all right. Only it wants a bit of knowing sometimes. If it's true what they're saying about an armistice you may be able to find a plumber soon. And remember what I told you about the porter. He's a bastard. I'll leave the keys with him, and clear out by Saturday."

Walking down the stairs of Queensberry Mansions, which were an old-fashioned block of flats without a lift, John wondered what would happen after the war to Temporary Lieutenant George Fettering, and hundreds like him. At the bottom he stopped to speak to the porter, an elderly man with a heavy grey moustache, dark and damp at the edge. He was garbed in a frayed and stained green uniform, and squinted.

"I shall move in on Monday afternoon," John told him. "What's your name?"

"My name is Sayers," the porter replied pompously, wiping his moustache with a grubby handkerchief and sucking a fragment of food from a tooth.

"Well, see if you can find a respectable woman to come every morning, give me breakfast, and tidy the flat."

"Is it a single tenant?"

"Of course."

"Oh well . . ." He paused to extract another relic of his lunch. "Yers, well, I wouldn't say as my wife mightn't oblige you. On'y I warn you. If Mrs Sayers comes in and finds she has to get breakfast for two, it's the last you'll see of her. She has very strong feelings, Mrs Sayers has."

John felt he was safe in giving satisfactory assurances on this point, so satisfactory apparently that the porter touched his cap to him when he walked out of the entrance to the flats, a salute which obviously startled one of the female inmates who was walking out at the same time, for her rouged baby mouth opened like a mullet's as she stared in astonishment first at John and then at the elderly porter.

John was still up at Church Row on Monday morning, November 11th. He was with Lady Ogilvie in the drawing-room, the five long windows of which looked out at the trim Georgian houses opposite through a drizzle of rain. Sir Alexander was away at the Assizes of some ancient burgh. David was at Eton. Prudence was in bed, a threatening cold having secured her relief from school, which in these days of influenza was a much easier manœuvre than usual to effect.

"This suspense is terrible," Elise sighed. "Surely, surely nothing can go wrong? You don't think there is a chance the Germans will refuse to accept our armistice terms? Now that the Kaiser has gone . . ." She broke off, and went to the blurred windows as if somehow the answer to her question would be vouchsafed from the grey November monotone without.

"That was an act of courage," John observed. "But I suppose as he will be made the scapegoat it will have to be considered cowardice."

Elise turned away from the window.

"If anything goes wrong," she cried, "the war may last another two years!"

"Oh, that's quite impossible," John assured her. "We may decide for reasons of policy to march into Germany, but that could only delay their surrender for two or three months. Hark!" He dashed across the room and flung up the window, leaning out to listen.

"Maroons!" he shouted. "You can hear them. The armistice must have been signed."

Windows all along the street were opening. People

leaned out. Shopkeepers and their customers were hurrying into Heath Street. The grey November monotone had become dawn, and the drizzling rain was soft as dew.

Prudence appeared in a quilted dressing-gown. "The war's over," she gasped. "Oh, my poor David, he'll be frightfully disappointed!"

"Go back to bed, foolish child," her mother commanded.

Two tight plaits flapped upon a protesting back as she swung round and disappeared.

"Oh, John, isn't it wonderful?" Elise cried, and the tears which had been ruled so strictly for the last two years were free at last.

"Well, I think I'll leave you to rejoice alone," he said, leaning over to kiss her cheek. "I see the car's waiting to cart me and my luggage down to Queensberry Mansions. I'll come up to dinner some day later in the week."

As he passed along the passage Prudence called to him from the landing above.

"Are you going now? I do wish I could come with you, or else I wish you could come up and talk to me in bed; but you mustn't catch my cold in case you get influenza. John, you will take me to the theatre as soon as I'm all right, won't you? I do want to see *The Lilac Domino*. I say, damn!"

"What's the matter?"

"They'll probably give a holiday at school because the war's over, and I shan't get the advantage of it because I'm absent already. Stinking luck!"

She sneezed violently.

"Go back to bed, you disgusting Niagara," John adjured. "And when you're well we'll celebrate."

"Oh, cheers for you! And I'll tell you a marvellous story about a girl who lost her . . . oh, gosh, do I hear the voice of dearest mamma?"

The quilted dressing-gown fled.

"Which way will we go, sir?" asked the chauffeur. "This armistice has properly stirred things up. Everybody's making for the West End."

They took the road down by Fitzjohn's Avenue, and John told the man to stop at Claremount Gardens.

"Miriam, isn't it sublime?" he cried, embracing her. "I'm just off to my flat. We'll have dinner together soon. And I heard this morning they're going to put on the last play I wrote by February at latest."

"John, you look as young as when you first came to this house," she said, staring at him.

"We can begin to live again now, Miriam. We must get Julius and Leonora over. We must get Emil back."

He hurried away.

Outside the house he found three young women each carrying a small Union Jack.

"Excuse me, sir," said the chauffeur, a little doubtfully, "but these three young persons wish to be given a lift."

"Pack in behind," John told them. "Where do you want to go?"

"Everyone's making for Buckingham Palace," said one of the girls. "But we don't mind where we go, do we, Maudie?"

"No, I don't mind. I'll go anywhere," Maudie answered. "That's all right for you, Ethel, isn't it?"

"Quite all right," Ethel agreed. "I'll go wherever you and Gwen go."

The girls bundled into the back of the car, giggling.

"What would my father think of his touring Daimler now?" John murmured to the chauffeur with a chuckle.

"Oh, I don't expect he'd object, sir. Sir Alexander's very broad-minded, and a war like what we've been through doesn't come to an end every day."

"This is an occasion when I regret horses, Crafford."

"You're right, sir," the elderly chauffeur sighed. "Biggest mistake ever made, it was, to go and invent these motors. Why, we wouldn't never have had aeroplanes if we hadn't had these blessed motors first. It put the idea in their head, as you might say. Yes, we should look just to rights now driving down to the West End behind our old bays. I think Sir Alexander himself would have hung on to horses a bit longer, but her Ladyship was terrible took up with cars from the first."

"Are you girls all right?" John asked, turning round.

"We're fine," they replied in chorus.

Then they giggled again.

"It's a lovely car, isn't it?" Maudie observed appreciatively, whereupon her two companions on either side prodded her.

"What are you both punching into me for, you soppy things?" Maudie demanded indignantly.

"Don't make personal remarks," Gwen told her.

"Personal yourself. You haven't half got a nerve, young Gwen," Maudie retorted.

"Is it your car?" Ethel asked.

"It's my father's," John told her.

"Does he let you take it out?" Maudie exclaimed enviously. "You are lucky, aren't you?"

At this moment they overtook a taxi full inside and loaded outside with people waving Union Jacks and singing the choruses of the last four years.

Gwen, Maudie, and Ethel waved triumphant flags back, and Gwen put her head out of the window to let a jeer at the slowness of the taxi float back to the occupants. John told Crafford to stop at the post-office by Swiss Cottage, and as he got out of the car the taxi was passing the Daimler in its turn to the accompaniment of cheery insults from both sets of passengers.

It was to send a telegram to Athene that John had alighted. He pondered for a while to find a message that would not intrigue the Citrano post-office too much.

It is over earlier than we had hoped and life will begin sooner, he wrote finally.

"Name and address of the sender, please?" the clerk demanded.

"The name and address don't matter," he replied.

"I'm sorry, but no telegrams can be sent to any place abroad without the name and address of the sender," she insisted. "That's a war-time regulation."

"I thought the war was over."

"We have had no notification that the regulations in force for telegrams despatched to places abroad have been altered yet," said the clerk primly.

John surrendered.

"Aren't you glad, though, that the war is over?" he asked, with a smile.

"It doesn't make much odds to me," the prim little clerk answered. "I lost my fiancé and my two brothers. Eight-and-six, please, for the telegram."

"I'm sorry," he said lamely.

"That's quite all right," she replied, without bothering to look up at him.

On the pavement outside the post-office John found the three girls in the middle of an argument with a very fat man who had tied a Union Jack handkerchief round his bowler like a pugaree.

"Certainly you can't come in with us. It's not our motor for one thing, and for another you're too massive," Maudie was telling him.

"Massive's right," Gwen added.

"We don't want any Russian steam-rollers in with us. The war's over," snapped Ethel.

"So hop it," Maudie concluded, "because here's the gentleman to who the car belongs."

The fat man raised his decorative bowler and bowed gravely to John.

"Excuse me, sir," he said with immense solemnity. "I always raise my hat to the Royal Navy, and on this auspicious occasion I should be highly honoured, very highly honoured, if you would drink the health of the United Kingdom of Great Britain and Ireland with me, Captain. Fullalove is my name. . . ."

The girls shrieked ecstatically, and the fat man shook his head. Then he produced a bottle of whisky from his pocket, and when John begged to be forgiven for refusing a drink he took a heavy swig himself.

"The Silent Service!" he gave, and followed the toast with a rousing hiccup.

"Oh, you rude thing!" Ethel exclaimed.

"Anyone would think you was a baby in arms," said Gwen indignantly.

"Take no notice of him," Maudie urged snappily. "We want to get down west. Come on, Jellicoe."

This was to John. And as they looked back they saw Mr Fullalove standing rigidly at attention, his bottle serving as a musket.

All the way down Avenue Road the three girls babbled merrily on, their excitement rising the nearer they got to the heart of the West End the more crowded grew the thoroughfares. Lorries full of cheering passengers, taxicabs swarming inside and out, British, American and Australian soldiers, plenty of bluejackets, old and young, rich and poor, men and women and children, all carried along the streets on a tidal wave of joy.

"Let me see, you girls want to go to Buckingham Palace," John said.

"We don't mind where we go really," Gwen answered for the trio. "It looks as if anywhere would be good for to-day. Only Maudie and Ethel was staying up with me for the Sunday, and we overslept and it was too late to get to the factory. So we were going to take the day off anyhow. We're in munitions."

"I reckon we'll be out of munitions to-day any old way," said Maudie.

The car had reached Oxford Street by now, and John asked if this would suit his three passengers as the starting place of their day's amusement. He had half decided to take them with him to Queensberry Mansions while he unloaded his luggage and then escort them to the neighbourhood of Buckingham Palace; but he came to the conclusion that to arrive at his new flat for the first time in the company of three munition workers might prejudice the porter. The three girls did not mind where they were put down.

"I reckon we shall be walking round the houses all day, so it doesn't matter where we start," Gwen said. "Thanks ever so for the ride."

Maudie and Ethel echoed their thanks, and jumping out of the car with their Union Jacks they joined the crowds upon the pavement. Before the car could move on in the jam of traffic John saw them arm in arm with three Anzacs. He was sorry to see the last of them, for they were the expression of all that was most lovable in this great swirling city.

"You've chosen a funny day to move in," said the porter of Queensberry Mansions when John arrived. "I don't know how this luggage of yours is going to be got up to the top flat." He eyed the elderly chauffeur pessimistically.

"It's impossible to leave the car," John told him. "We shall have it full of people before we know where we are. There's not much luggage. You and I can manage, Sayers. You'd better get back to Hampstead now, Crafford. I shan't want you any more."

Temporary Lieutenant Fettering had left the flat in good order, but John found that the telephone had been cut off.

"Yers," said Sayers, breathing stertorously from his

exertions, "some people expect something for nothing every time. Of course he had his 'phone cut off, seeing as how he never paid the bill from the time he came into the Mansions."

"He was away most of the time at the Front, wasn't he?"

"A lot of people found the Front a nice excuse to behave as they liked at home," Sayers observed severely. "Well, by what we can understand, though, mind you, I don't believe what the Germans say any more nor I believe what the papers say, still it looks as if the war has come to an end, and which finishes the Front as an excuse for neglecting everything else."

"Well, you get the telephone fixed up as soon as possible," John told him. "Ask Mrs Sayers to call me with a cup of tea, a boiled egg, and toast at ten o'clock. No butter. I'll settle with her about future arrangements."

"I hope ten o'clock will be convenient for Mrs Sayers," said her husband dubiously.

"I hope so too," John agreed, "because if it isn't I shall have to find somebody else to look after the flat."

The porter pondered this announcement for a second or two.

"I expect it will be all right," he said at last, "seeing as how Mrs Sayers is always very obliging. You're in the Royal Navy, I see."

John nodded.

"Well, perhaps you can explain something as has been puzzling me for a long time. And a lot of other people come to that. How is it the Royal Navy hasn't done better in this war?"

"I was under the impression it had done a good deal," John answered.

"Yers, because you're in the Royal Navy yourself. Charity begins at home, don't it? But it's my opinion, and I'm not the only one with that opinion, it's my opinion as the Royal Navy's been a wash-out. What about this battle of Jutland?"

"What about it?"

"Well, I reckon, and a lot of my friends does too, that the Germans won this battle of Jutland in spite of what the Admirality give out to the papers. A lot of guff and gup, that's what me and my friends reckons the Admirality give out."

The noise of cheering crowds in Charing Cross Road came thinly up to this top flat. John walked across the sitting-room and opened the window to give the sound volume.

"You hear that?" he asked.

"Certainly I can hear it," Sayers replied. "You'd have to have cloth ears not to hear it."

"Well, you wouldn't hear that this November morning if the fleet had lost the battle of Jutland."

"That's your opinion," said Sayers obstinately. "But that doesn't say it's got to be my opinion, does it? Well, I'll ask you another straight question. Did you ever see one of them submarines?"

"I never actually saw one myself."

Sayers laughed in hoarse triumph.

"No, nor thousands more like you in the Royal Navy. But the pore bloody merchant sailors sore enough submarines, didn't they? Yers! There you are, that's what I'm trying to tell you. On'y you're obstinate. See? I don't blame you, mind. It's what you're paid to be, seeing as how you're *in* the Royal Navy and can't help yourself. But if you ask me who won this war, if it *is* won and which we aren't shore of yet, if you ask *me*, it was the Army as won this war. It don't get called the Royal Army. Oh, no. Never mind, if Royal means doing nothing, and saying nothing because it hasn't got nothing to say, then the Army's better as it is. No, the Royal Navy's been a bit of a disappointment, and it's no use pretending anything else," Sayers concluded gloomily.

"I think what you want is a drink to cheer you up," John suggested, offering the porter one of those green ten-shilling Treasury notes which pledged the country's credit in the interest of the Banks.

"Thank you, sir," said Sayers, belching faintly in his excitement. I'm always glad to be helpful where I can. And I'll let Mrs Sayers know about to-morrow morning. Mind you, I'm not saying as everybody's a better man just because he happens to be in the Army instead of the Royal Navy. In fact some of these tempory lieutenants and what not are no better in khaki than what they was out of it. Everything about 'em's tempory. Look at the fellow you've took on this flat from. Tempory Lieutenant, yes, and a tempory wife and a tempory telephone. And as for his cash it wasn't even tempory. Well, Mrs Sayers isn't one to mince words, and Volga Round that's what Mrs Sayers called Fettering. 'Lieutenant?' she said to me. 'You mark my words, Elf, it's more Left than Tenant you'll find Lieutenant Fettering.' But she's a quick-tongued woman, Mrs Sayers is. Always was too. Her father kept a stall in the Caledonian Market, and it don't do to be slow in the uptake there. You'd find yourself sold for a dressmaker's dummy by the sheeny at the next stall if you started in to be tempory in the Market. Well, good morning, sir, and anything I can do to help I'll do it."

When he had unpacked, John decided to go round to his club. The most cantankerous of the older members had wintry smiles to-day. They were looking forward to a second helping of butter, and to getting rid of the waitresses who for two years had been profaning the mysteries.

"You can't even go down and pumpship," one of them

grumbled, "without a damned girl waiting to give you a message as you come up again."

The porteress had a message for John.

"Mr . . . well, sir, it sounded like Groundsel, but I don't think I can have got the name quite right."

"Gosnell, I expect."

The porteress smiled with relief.

"Yes, I expect that will be it. He wanted you to lunch with him at the Royal Automobile Club, and if you can't would you please ring Gerrard 8 5621."

John's agent was waiting for him in the fidgety atrium of the R.A.C., with the look in his eyes that agents wear when they hope that an author is going to be sensible.

"What's the matter, Gosnell?"

"Everything's grand, old man. There's nothing the matter at all. But I thought it would be a good thing if you met the chap who's putting up the money for *All Or Nothing*. It's Turner Rigden. You've heard of him?"

"Vaguely," John replied. "Who is he exactly?"

"He's made a packet in the war. He was Deputy Controller of Paper at the Ministry of Waste. He's just acquired the controlling interest in the *Sunday Journal*. He'll be in Parliament presently. He's the Coalition Candidate for South-East Kensington. He's a big man, and unlike so many of these big business men he's a generous man in private as well as in public. You'll like him. He's keen as mustard on *All Or Nothing*."

Presently John was introduced to a neat little man with a pink face and a trim golden-brown moustache who might have been forty, though the network of fine lines round his merry and aggressive eyes suggested at close quarters that he was probably quite ten years older

"Well, I'm glad to meet you, Commander Ogilvie. Now what are you going to have? Dry Martini? Right. The better the day the better the deed, eh? Gee! I liked that play of yours. I nearly bust myself laughing.

It ought to be a riot. And what business we're going to do next year! It's going to be terrific. Terrific! What a boom! Well, you know war isn't pleasant, but there's something to be said for it. Picking up the broken pieces and all that. Say, you must come down to my little place in Sussex. I've been going in for Irish wolfhounds. Did you know I'd been going in for Irish wolfhounds, Gosnell?"

"I knew you went in for Jersey cows."

"Oh, of course. I've got the finest herd of them in England. Say, Commander Ogilvie, you've got a crackerjack agent. You writing fellows want good men with good business heads to look after you, and you certainly have got a good adviser in Mr Gosnell."

John was wondering faintly where this spruce little man with the pink face and merry blue eyes hailed from. Was he Canadian? Or was he assuming a few stock Americanisms to cover up a provincial origin? The burr might be West Country.

It was about half-way through an expensive lunch that John realised why they were drinking champagne, the excuse for which had been the armistice.

"I've always been interested in art, Commander Ogilvie, but of course a business man like me never gets much chance to what one would call really cultivate the mind," said Mr Turner Rigden, with that wistful backward glance at an earthly paradise so many business men affect in the hope of leading a listener into believing that malicious fortune dragged them past the entrance against their will. "I know you artistic johnnies, you artistic guys, have an idea we business men only think of making good, but I tell you here and now that most of us, most of us would sooner have written Gray's *Elegy in a Country Churchyard*. . . . I always remember that poem because I belong to the Stoke Poges Golf Club . . . than, well, anything you like . . . win the battle of Waterloo as

Wellington said. And the ironical thing about me is that I've made most of what little money I've made out of paper . . . you heard I'd bought the *Sunday Journal*, Gosnell?"

"I heard you'd acquired a controlling interest, Mr Rigden."

"Controlling interest be damned. I bought the whole bloody caboodlum. Lock, stock and barrel. And the *Sunday Journal* is going to hum. But that's not what we've met to talk about to-day. And now I'm going to tell you a little romance, Commander Ogilvie . . . say, do you attach a great deal to that naval handle of yours, because it makes a hell of a mouthful in the middle of a good lunch."

"So far as I'm concerned it fell off at eleven o'clock this morning," John replied.

"That's good, we'll forget it. But drink up, Ogilvie. You're drinking nothing. Charles, put another on the ice. Yes, I want to tell you about this little romance. My duties for the Ministry happened to take me up to the North of England last month and I went to a show in Sheffield. The play wasn't much good, but there was a little girl playing a part in that show who's the best actress I've seen in years. May Lavender her name is. Ever heard of her? But of course you wouldn't. That's the whole point of my little romance. Nobody has heard of her. But I said to myself when I walked out of the theatre after the performance that if that little girl didn't become a London star my name wasn't Turner Rigden. Now, don't you misunderstand me, Ogilvie. I'm a married man. I've got two nice girls of my own and the finest wife that ever stepped. May Lavender is pretty. . . . I'm not much hand at description, but take it from me she's pretty . . . definitely . . . good carriage and figure and all that . . . fair . . . lovely voice . . . but what took me was her talent. I told her at lunch next day that as soon as

I found the right play I was going to make her name . . . and she was so grateful. Well, I'm a hard man of business . . . or so they say . . . but I don't mind telling you, Ogilvie, I was touched by her gratitude. She burst into tears. She did really! Broke down in the middle of lunch and sobbed like a child. It was in a private room. Not that there's anything in that, but I've always made it a rule during my war work never to give the faintest excuse for criticism. And at the Ministry of Waste we had to be particularly careful about that because our chief job really was to criticize every other Ministry for what they were spending. Do you know I took two inches off every bit of toilet paper used in public conveniences throughout the country? And yet my Labour opponent in South-East Kensington tries to hint at every meeting he holds that I've made money out of my war work. I'll say this for Louis Matheson, the sitting Liberal member, he's never done that. I told my agent to send a circular round to every voter telling them what I'd done to save toilet-paper, but he said it was risky now that women had the vote. Women are funny creatures, he said, and they might take offence. He said he'd know better what you could do with women after the next election, and advised me to stick to the Union Jack and warn the electors what had happened in Russia. I daresay he's right. Here, I wish you'd drink up that champagne, Ogilvie. We don't finish a war every day."

"I'm so fascinated by your account of the Ministry of Waste," John told his host with a smile.

"He's pulling my leg, Gosnell. That's the worst of these writing fellows. I'll bet you he has a line about me in his next play. Well, to come right down to business, Ogilvie, as soon as I was back in town I got in touch with my old friend John Gould and he told me he'd just been reading this play of yours and that he didn't think the part suggested for him was quite what he wanted, but that the woman's part was wonderful. There you are! There's my little romance in a nutshell! But I wish you'd not leave your glass standing. Gosnell says he's sure you'll raise no objection to an unknown actress being given the lead. What's your reaction?"

Turner Rigden emptied his own glass and sat back in his chair.

"I'm perfectly agreeable," said John.

"God damn it," the Deputy Controller of Paper exploded, "that's the kind of way I like a man to talk. And you told me Ogilvie might be a little difficult," he went on, turning reproachfully to the agent.

"I didn't quite say that, Mr Rigden," Gosnell protested. "What I said was that playwrights often had their own ideas."

"Well, that is being difficult, isn't it? We used to get fellows with ideas in my department at the Ministry, and all it led to was trouble all round. And the worst of the lot were the fellows who'd been invalided out of active service. To hear them talk you'd have thought business men like myself who'd volunteered to do their bit were downright shirkers. However, the war's over now, and if the Coalition Government get back at the General Election we can look forward to a big boom. Yes, sir."

"You handled him beautifully, old man," Gosnell whispered to John as they followed their host to the smoking-room. "I couldn't have handled him better myself. We shall get a good production."

When they were sitting over coffee two men passed their table. The first was a dour-looking heavily-built man with a swarthy face and great tufts of hair growing from his ears, who passed grunting his recognition of Turner Rigden. His companion was sleek, with lank carroty hair and a pair of greenish eyes peering benevolently through gold-rimmed spectacles. He stopped for a moment.

"Hello, Turner," he enquired in an oily tenor. "All well with you?"

"A1, Willie. So the war's over."

Rigden introduced the newcomer as Sir William Tufnell, who beamed his acknowledgments.

"Yes, the war's over, Turner," he murmured in a voice that was not so much unctuous as larded. "I suppose I oughtn't to say so in front of one of you fighting men, but we were just a teeny bit disappointed at the Ministry. You see, we had a new gas we were going to try out next week, and we did want to know what it could do. However, we must be thankful the war is over. Good-bye. Good-bye, Turner."

"I haven't congratulated you on your K.B.E. yet, Willie."

"Oh, thank you very much, Turner. It was a great surprise. But it was a G.B.E. I was rather greedy."

With a roguish smile, Sir William Tufnell moved on to overtake his companion.

"A s——," Turner Rigden observed. "But a clever s——. Hard as hell's front door-step. He's in chemicals. But he gets no pleasure out of his money. Notice the way he was playing pocket-billiards all the time he was talking? Nervous colitis, that's what makes him fidget with himself like that. And what gives him colitis? Worrying about halfpennies he lost at school. Did you see who was with him?"

"I'm not familiar with the *grands seigneurs* of big business," John replied.

"That was Lord Eccleston. I'm putting it low, Ogilvie, if I say that Eccleston has made four million in the last four years."

"Has he, by Jove?" said John. "His gains compete numerically with our casualties."

"Now don't get bitter, Ogilvie. Bitterness is a mistake. I've taken some nasty knocks in my day, but I never made the mistake of getting bitter. And look at me! Say, how old do you reckon I am?"

"You might be forty."

Turner Rigden chuckled with gratification.

"Fifty-three next March! And I celebrated my silver wedding last June. Yes, bitterness is a mistake. And Eccleston is a big man. I don't grudge him a pound of what he's made. Willie Tufnell's another pair of trousers altogether. Just a greedy swine who when he passes a blind beggar takes out a penny, looks at it, and puts it back in his pocket because he would have liked to help the poor man but realizes that indiscriminate charity does more harm than good. Mean, Ogilvie. Mean and greedy. He'd sooner lick his own dirty plate than give a drop of gravy to the kitchen sink. I'm greedy myself, but by G——, I'm not mean. See here, Gosnell, you asked a two hundred and fifty option on *All Or Nothing* until the end of November. Well, I take up that option here and now and I'll send you a cheque for five hundred pounds in advance of royalties. Is that a deal?"

"Of course," said John.

"Laconic, that's what you are. Laconic," Turner Rigden repeated with enthusiasm. "That's a good word, isn't it? I only came across it the other day looking up in the dictionary what laches meant in law. Now do *you* know what laches means, Ogilvie?"

"Something to do with negligence I should guess."

"Gee, aren't these writing fellows marvels?" Turner Rigden apostrophized. "Well, come on, just one more brandy to drink the health of our production. I'm in treaty for the Sheridan Theatre, Gosnell. It's going to be just one big wow! We'll have a little supper at the Savoy one night soon and you shall meet your leading lady, John. I'm cutting out 'Ogilvie' here and now. And as for me, I'm Turner to my friends."

The party broke up, and as John watched the little man

getting into his big beige Sunbeam car, a cigar at a jaunty angle in the corner of his mouth, he thought how much Turner Rigden himself, with his pink face glowing above his brown suit, resembled a plump and expensive cigar, the band of which was furnished by his gold cigarette-case, gold card-case, gold lighter, gold pencil, gold pen, and gold toothpick.

"A good afternoon's work," commented Gosnell, his beaky nose confronting the beflagged crowds in Pall Mall with the majesty of an eagle which has killed its lamb. "We're going to make a lot of money out of Turner Rigden," he murmured dreamily. "I hope this little pet of his *can* act."

"It doesn't much matter," said John. "I don't attach any importance to this play. I want you to get busy again over *What It Was Really Like*."

"Oh, for . . . oh, put that unfortunate bit of self-indulgence out of sight and out of mind, Ogilvie. Look at all these jolly people celebrating the armistice. You don't suppose they want a realistic play about the war, do you? They want to forget it."

"Many people don't forget so easily," John suggested.

"Yes, but not enough of them to fill a theatre for six months. Well, I think I'll go back and close the office. Nobody expects to do any work to-day. But in the morning I'll get after Turner Rigden with that contract," the agent announced in the tone of a detective who has his man.

That evening John dined with James Yarrow at a French restaurant in Soho, where the proprietor produced dainties one had come to believe were no longer to be found on this war-tormented planet. Bélanger was eloquent on the necessity of making it impossible for the Germans ever to let loose the dogs of war again, and thought that the simplest way of ensuring perpetual peace was to sterilize every German male. As a young man he had fought in the war of Soixante-Dix and had recognized then that the Germans were the main obstacle to the achievement of a better world.

John suggested that the Germans might be civilized by a merciful peace.

"One cannot civilize the Germans, monsieur," Bélanger replied in swift French. "They are wild animals, and because the English love animals so much I am afraid the English will make the mistake of being kind to the Boches. Good dog, good dog, that is very nice, but we cannot say 'Good Boche, good Boche,' and pat his head. You have not known in England what it is to be overrun by the Germans twice in less than fifty years."

"I agree with Monsieur Bélanger," said Yarrow. "There are no bad Germans, there are just Germans."

"Yes, but we've got to do something with them, James. We've got to live with them in Europe somehow," John urged.

"*Pardon*, I have told you what must be done with the Germans," the patron interposed.

"But you can't sterilize a nation of sixty millions," John objected.

Bélanger shrugged his shoulders.

"Then it will all begin again, and perhaps again after that, and at last we shall be so tired, we French and English, that we shall say anything for a quiet life, and the Germans will be the masters of Europe. Perhaps we are all dead, but our poor children and grandchildren will suffer. No, no, we have now an opportunity, and it is better we make an end of the Germans for ever."

"My notion would be to recreate Poland and Bohemia," said John. "Join Bavaria and the rest of Catholic Germany to Austria, make Hungary independent, and isolate Prussia."

"The Italians would object to your Austrian plan," Yarrow said.

"And nobody would object if the German race died out," Bélanger pointed out. "So why are you so soft-hearted? The Germans use their women only for breeding. We should not deprive them of the pleasures of love, for we should leave them the kind of love they prefer."

When they left the restaurant the two diners stood on the pavement, listening to the noise of the rejoicing populace.

"It has suddenly occurred to me, James, that we are not celebrating our victory to-night but the fact that the war is finished. I think that's a good sign for the future sanity of Europe, don't you?"

Yarrow nodded sardonically.

"Wait till you see the election address of the Coalition. You'll feel less optimistic about European sanity then. Well, I'm going home to read *Bouvard et Pécuchet*. I want to arm myself with Flaubert against the horrors of human imbecility."

"Nothing can be more stupid than the war, James."

"Except the peace," Yarrow answered. "Why should you suppose that the demagogues who have led us through the war will be less stupid because they are now tired? The only chance for a wise peace would be to call in men who have taken no active part in the prosecution of the war. I should like to invite a Swede, a Dutchman, and a Spaniard to draw up the terms of peace."

"Do you believe in this idea of Wilson's for a League of Nations?"

"It would be all right if there was universal disarmament and the League of Nations maintained a police force, but what chance is there of disarmament so long as imperialism continues?"

"What will happen in the next twenty years, I wonder?"

"An americanized England, a balkanized Europe, and a communized Asia."

"Thanks, that's a very cheerful forecast on which to sleep. Well, good-night, James. You're bound for Bloomsbury, I'm making my way to Charing Cross Road."

But when John reached Queensberry Mansions he found the antics of the nocturnal crowds so amusing that he walked past his destination and reaching Trafalgar Square stood watching the great bonfire which had been lighted by Australian troops. Thousands of people all happier than they had been for many weary months, thousands of people who would all wake to-morrow with lighter hearts. No doubt the exultation of relief would not endure for long. The problem of readjusting the country from war to peace was likely to be much more complicated than that of adjusting the country from peace to war. These munition workers with silk stockings who excited the resentment of elderly taxpayers might be wishing soon, with the wages, or worse with the wageless unemployment, of peace that they were back at war again. The very soldiers might sigh sometimes in the cold future for the heat of war. They would feel, and how justly, that the country which had claimed the right to exact death from them was morally bound to ensure them a decent life in return. John's mind went back to that smoking-room of the R.A.C. after lunch. Rats and lice in France and Flanders: leeches at home. From the moment that men were conscripted for service in the field wealth should have been conscripted. While these business men were helping the country to win the war they should have been kept on a salary and their businesses run for the benefit of the country. The desire to stop the war should be at the back of everybody's mind. It might have come to an end last year then. Yet the Germans were obstinate, and they had remained outside the great tradition of European culture. Perhaps Bélanger was right. Perhaps there was no way to deal with them except as barbarians. Perhaps this complete collapse was the best thing that could have happened. If the Germans had granted the armistice instead of being granted it, all Germany to-night would be rejoicing because the war had been won, not because the war was over.

Over! Problems and perplexities enough, national and personal, but at least they could be faced without that hideous prior claim on every form of human activity of getting on with the war. Over! Now the future of Athene and himself might be uncertain, but it was no longer vague. She would be sure to telegraph if Wacey were coming home. She had already told him by letter what that home-coming meant. What capacity for resistance did Wacey possess? She knew what a hold over Athene he had in their son, and with his refusal to face facts he might hold out indefinitely. In none of her letters had she revealed what was the evidence on which she hoped to obtain a divorce. She might have fancied it was more potent than it was. Undoubtedly the wisest course she could take would be to return to America at the earliest possible opportunity. Over! At any rate she would be able to travel again, and although the ships from France and England would probably be crowded she would have a good chance of securing a passage in an Italian liner. He must write to-morrow and urge upon her the necessity of booking now, if it should be necessary, without waiting for Wacey's return. Let him follow her to America, and let the issue between them be fought out there.

Preoccupied with his own thoughts and jostling his way through the crowd without being aware of anything except a succession of flushed excited faces, John reached the corner of Whitehall and Northumberland Avenue. Here he paused for a while to watch an eightsome reel that was being danced by four Highland soldiers and their girls, or rather being danced by the men and pranced by the girls, to whom it was clearly an unfamiliar dance.

Suddenly John heard a shrill cockney voice exclaim:

"Why, it's Jellicoe! Fancy meeting you again!"

And there were his three companions of the morning. Only Gwen still retained a portion of her Union Jack, and twelve hours of wandering round the houses, a good part of the time in drizzling rain, had left them bedraggled.

"We were waiting for a bus," Ethel informed him. "We *are* tired."

"Lean on me, darling, I'll rock you to sleep," a young man in a burberry, standing near by, suggested.

"Don't pay any attention to him," Maudie enjoined scornfully. "Indispensable? Not to us."

John asked if they were going back to Hampstead.

"No fear," Maudie replied. "We're going home to Camberwell. Gwen's coming back along with us, aren't you, duck? We just shook off three fellows who well thought they were going to put it across us. They wanted us to go back with them to their flat."

John enquired if they would like to be driven home in a taxi.

"If we can get a taxi," Gwen said doubtfully.

"Of course we can get a taxi," Maudie put in. "Camberwell isn't like Hampstead. It's in reach of earth."

"It is nice of you to drive us home," Ethel said. "We really are tired, and my sister would go on all night if anyone would go on with her."

"Well, why not?" Maudie challenged. "I like enjoying myself. When I marry my Bert I reckon I'll wish I'd enjoyed myself a bit more."

"Are you two sisters? I didn't realize that," John said. "You're not much alike. Ethel so dark and Maudie so fair."

"I'm not so dark as all that," Ethel declared indignantly. "I'm not a coon. Besides, Maudie touched up her hair."

"*Touched* it up?" Gwen, who was red-haired herself,

echoed sarcastically. "Yes, some people *is* very heavy-handed."

"All right, bricktop," Maudie jeered. "Anyway, my dad didn't ring the fire-alarm when I was born like yours did. Or so your mother told me. She's got ever such a nice mother, Gwen has," Maudie explained to John. "You know. Keeps you in stitches all the time at the stories she tells."

The four of them were walking down Whitehall, looking out for a passing taxi.

"And so you're engaged?" John asked Maudie. "When are you going to get married?"

"Never," Ethel cut in, "unless she stops playing him up the way she does. Here, listen, she promised her Bert she'd be back in by six, and go to the pictures with him. I bet he isn't half wild. I lay he thinks she's got off in the armistice."

"Good job too," said Maudie. "If you don't play up a fellow when you're engaged to him he'll play you up when you're married. Or that's what I think. Are you married, Jellicoe? No? Nor even engaged? No? Girls, do you hear that? Admittance free."

"All the nice girls like a sailor, all the nice girls like a tar," Ethel sang, "for there's something about a sailor . . . There's a taxi! Taxi! Taxi!"

"How far do you want to go?" the driver demanded suspiciously.

"Only to the South Pole and a few yards farther on," Maudie replied.

"Willow Crescent, Camberwell," said Ethel more practically.

"And I'm coming back to Trafalgar Square," John added, to encourage him.

"Go on over Westminster Bridge and then down to the right along the Kennington Road and turn off to the left just before you come to Kennington Park and then we'll tell you where the Sleeping Beauty lives, Dick Whittington."

"Funny, aren't you?" observed the driver to Ethel, who had given him these instructions.

Maudie winked at John.

"Ethel had two Guinnesses with those fellows who wanted us to go back to their flat."

"And you didn't have three, did you, young Maudie?" Ethel retorted. "Oh, no, it's only a rumour."

They bundled into the taxi. Gwen and Maudie pulled John down between them on the seat, and Ethel leant back on one of the front seats with her heels resting on the door. "Oh, girls, isn't it lovely to recline again?" she sighed.

"Well, take your massive limbs off the door," her sister cried. "I want to shut the window. It's cold. I bet you half a dollar my Bert's waiting for me at our place."

Maudie's forecast was correct, and when the taxi pulled up before 12 Willow Crescent it was Bert who came down through the front garden to greet the truants.

"You're a nice one," he proclaimed indignantly. "Wherever have you been all night?"

"Now, don't start in arguing, Bert," Maudie commanded. "You'll hear all about it."

"We've been in the armistice," Ethel put in. "And we've brought Gwen Price back with us."

"Cheer-o, Bert," said Gwen, getting out of the taxi. "I've been looking after Maudie for you and keeping her from straying."

"Well, goodbye, you girls," John said. "Perhaps we'll meet again some day."

"Oh, aren't you coming in?" the girls protested in a chorus of thwarted hospitality. "Oh, come on in. It's armistice!"

John hesitated, but they insisted more loudly.

"But the taxi. I can't keep the driver waiting, and I may not get another."

"He can come in too," said Ethel. "You'd like a drink, wouldn't you?"

The driver said he didn't mind if he did, and the party followed Maudie and Bert toward the door. John saw that the front garden was full of tombstones, crosses, and urns, and was able to read by the light of the street lamp that Frederick Hanshaw executed every kind of memorial in stone with prompt and personal attention to his customers.

In the parlour they found, besides Mr and Mrs Hanshaw, two young men in khaki.

"Charlie!" his sisters cried. "Whenever did you arrive?"

"Got to Victoria this morning. Syd and I got eight days' leave and found the war was over when we walked out of the station."

"That's right," said Syd, a solemn and lanky young man who was evidently feeling a bit overwhelmed by the arrival of so many people at nearly midnight.

"Well, what a day!" Maudie began. "We started off this morning from Gwen's place in Hampstead and this friend of ours gave us a lift in his car to Oxford Street. Oo!" she ejaculated, putting her hand up to her mouth in dismay. "I don't know your name—we've been calling him Jellicoe."

John introduced himself and was cordially invited by the tombstone-maker to a seat beside the fire. The host was a burly man, his square face finely dusted with minute particles of stone which set off his fresh complexion like powder. Mrs Hanshaw was a little dark bird-like woman obviously the mother of Ethel.

"Very kind of you, Captain Ogilvie, to give these girls a lift home."

"Yes, indeed, though they ought to have been home long ago," Mrs Hanshaw added.

"We wouldn't have been home now, Mum, if we hadn't

seen Jellicoe again by accident and he offered to drive us home in a taxi. This is the driver. . . ."

"Take a seat, Mr . . .?" the head of the family paused.

"Mr Baker's my name," said the driver. "Thanks, I don't mind if I do."

He was a middle-aged man with the soured expression that taxicab-drivers acquired during the war, but when Mr Hanshaw was heard to instruct his son to fetch in two more jugfuls and Mrs Hanshaw bade Ethel go and help her brother with the glasses, Mr Baker relaxed slightly in his chair and drummed upon the table with what he probably supposed was an expression of benevolence.

"What do you think of my young man, Jellicoe?" Maudie asked, indicating Bert Finningley, who coloured up and loosened his collar.

"Really, Maudie, what things you do ask!" her mother reproved. "You'd make *any*one feel embarrassed *you* would."

"He's one of the indispensables," Maudie giggled. "What a scream! Yes, you may be indispensable to your country, lovee, but watch out you don't think you're indispensable to Maudie Hanshaw."

"I can't help it, can I, if they kept me at home?" said Bert. "Think I wouldn't sooner have been out at the front?"

"I wouldn't," Syd Walker burst out, and then blushed deeply.

"If you ask me," said Mr Baker, "fellows out at the front was a lot better off nor fellows at home. A lot better off. Try driving a taxi when you can't get petrol without signing your name on about twenty blooming forms and can't get what you want even then, and when you pick up a fare living out at Hampstead say . . ."

"There you are, Gwen. What did I tell you?" Maudie interrupted. "I told you you lived at the top end of nowhere."

"Hampstead's not so far as all that," Gwen argued in defence of her native place.

"It's a blurry long way, miss, whichever side of Regent's Park you take—pardon my French, m'm. . . ." This to Mrs Hanshaw.

"Oh, she's used to French, Ma is. If you want to shock Ma you want to talk Spanish," said Maudie, twinkling.

"I never knew such a girl," Mrs Hanshaw sighed, with a look at her husband that threw the blame of Maudie entirely on him. "Go on, Mr Baker, you were talking about Hampstead."

"Well, as I was saying," the driver continued, "you get a fare as wants to go to Hampstead from Chelsea perhaps and you may have the petrol to get you back to your rank in the Strand. Or you may not. You might try and explain, and what do you get? Rudeness. Right-down rudeness. Told you didn't know when you was well off and why wasn't you out in the trenches. The next blurry war we have I'm going out with a R.A.S.C. lorry, and come back a blurry sight fatter nor what I am now staying at home."

Luckily for Mr Baker's pent-up resentment accumulated through four years of war, Charlie and Ethel Hanshaw returned at this moment with the beer and the glasses.

"Well, I know I shall be glad when my boy gets back for good," Mr Hanshaw declared. "He's come through without a scratch, thank God, but look at the way it broke into his work. He was with me in the business, Captain Ogilvie, and you can't go off for a year and a half to a war and expect to keep your hand in at lettering. And a small private business like mine isn't so easy to keep going these days, when there's all the time more and more people dealing with these big stores and whatnot. My grandfather started this business when Camberwell was just a village you might say, by the osier beds. He bought a ninety-nine-year lease of this house in 1848. Well, that runs out in 1947, and the way they're pulling down old property I reckon they'll pull down Willow Crescent. I sometimes wonder whether I did right to put Charlie in the business. He's twenty-one now. In 1947 he'll be just the age I am now, and I'm wondering if he has to move our premises whether the business will stand it. It's dropping slowly all the time."

Mr Hanshaw lit his pipe again and puffed meditatively, with an eye on the future written in the glowing heart of the fire.

The young people were talking among themselves in corners of the snug parlour. Charlie and Gwen, Maudie and Bert, Ethel and Syd. Mr Baker was sipping his beer with relish. Mrs Hanshaw was nodding.

"It's damnable the way the small men are being pushed out," said John at last. "England will wake up one day and find too late that England no longer exists. I'm afraid this infernal war has speeded up the process. We've had to surrender so many of our rights and so much of our dignity as private citizens to win this war, and I doubt if we shall recover either our rights or our dignity. Mind you, I think that in their own interest the big business combines will try to maintain a higher level of wages among the workers because they want to give the workers a larger purchasing power, and I daresay that superficially the average worker will be better off than before the war, but what I dread is the loss of individual independence. In the long run that must destroy us."

"I'm just of your opinion, Captain. Why, my boy there prefers a wage as a skilled workman to being his own master. He may be better off in one way, but he'll be the servant of others and he'll learn to think like a servant and act like a servant. What we aimed for when I was young was independence, but nowadays the young people seem to enjoy being ordered about provided they get well paid for being ordered about and don't have no responsibility. Take my two girls there. They've done nicely out of the war. They've been drawing good money now for the best part of three years. All right. It's over! They've got to come down to earth. Well, take Maudie there. She's twenty-four. She's been thinking for the last two years that perhaps she'll marry Bert Finningley. He's a decent steady young fellow working in Tufnell's big chemical works, making poison-gas by what I hear for the last twelve months. He'll probably keep his job and go back to making something a bit more useful than poison-gas, and he and Maudie'll get married, and that's that. But they can't raise a family and leave 'em a business. Any son of theirs'll just have to look forward to becoming a what to my mind's no better than one of these slaves you read of in history books. I can work all day and all night if I've the mind. But these fellows can only work when they're told, and take their holidays when they're told. There's thousands of them all reading the same trash in the papers, all going to the same trashy pictures, all thinking what's thought for them. None of 'em with an independent notion in his head. Well, by the way I look at it in another ninety-nine years you'll hardly be able to tell 'em apart. Just sheep. I'm a Londoner myself and perhaps I don't understand sheep, but of all the miserable animals I ever saw give me a sheep."

"Here, don't make us gloomy, Dad," his elder daughter adjured. "It's armistice night. Anybody would think, to hear you preaching, it was last Sunday week, and wet at that. Don't let him go on talking, Jellicoe. He's terrible if he can get anybody who's too polite to tell him to shut up."

Mrs Hanshaw woke up with a start at this moment.

"There, now you've woken your mother up," said the tombstone-maker.

"She wouldn't have wanted waking if you hadn't sent her off to sleep joring, joring, joring," Maudie retorted.

"I must be going anyway," said John.

The girls declared that it was a shame to go so soon, but he saw that the driver brightened at this announcement and held to his resolve.

"Well, it's been a great pleasure to meet you, Captain," said Mr Hanshaw. "And I hope you'll call in and give us some more of your company some time. Does this armistice mean you'll be finished with the Navy?"

"It certainly does."

"And you go back to your work whatever that may be."

John guessed that the tombstone-maker wanted to know what this was and he told him that he wrote plays.

"Theatrical, eh? Well, I should think that was a very interesting job."

"Do you mean you write plays they act?" Gwen asked.

"Not at the moment, but they'll be acting one early next year."

"I bet he doesn't half have a time with the actresses," Maudie cried. "Naughty boy!"

"Maudie," Mrs Hanshaw protested. "I really won't have you saying things like that. The Captain will wonder where ever you was brought up. And he'll be right."

John made his farewells and promised to come and visit 12 Willow Crescent again. He promised, too, to send tickets for his play when it was put on next year. The girls escorted him past the examples of their father's craft to the taxi.

"Wouldn't Bert be mad if we all got in and drove back with Jellicoe to Trafalgar Square?" said Maudie. "I bet the armistice is still going on as merry and bright as ever."

But Gwen and Ethel were not prepared to indulge her

energy further, and John drove away from Willow Crescent alone.

Maudie had been right in supposing that the armistice was still merry and bright. The West End seemed as crowded as ever, but John resisted the inclination to wander about any longer and at Queensberry Mansions paid off his taxi.

"Sometimes you have quite an unexpected treat," said Mr Baker. "That was a very good glass of beer we got in Willow Crescent. I haven't had a better glass of beer than that not since the blurry war started. Yes, you get a bit of pleasure in life once in a way. Good night, sir. But not often, mark you," he leaned out from the taxi to add as he drove off, and presumably relapsed into an habitual misanthropy.

John was still asleep when Mrs Sayers knocked at the door of his room next morning at ten o'clock.

"Come in."

The knocking increased in volume.

"Come in!"

The door was opened wide enough to admit a woman's head, which seen thus suddenly on the edge of sleep might have been mistaken for the head of a black Minorca hen. Two beady eyes took in the contents of the bedroom, dwelt suspiciously for a moment on the second pillow, which John had a habit of pulling down beside him in a double-bed, and finally fixed themselves on John himself.

"Your brekfuss," announced what was presumably Mrs Sayers.

"Bring it in, will you?"

The porter's wife hesitated.

"Well, I had set it down on the floor outside." She still hesitated, but then abruptly the hen-like head darted down, the door opened, and Mrs Sayers, tray in hand, advanced into the room.

"Good morning, Mrs Sayers."

"Good morning," she replied grudgingly. "And in fack it is a better morning that what it was last night."

"Were you celebrating the armistice?"

"I never celebrates," Mrs Sayers generalized sombrely. "If I celebrates once in two years that's azaggerating. Some people can afford to celebrate morning, noon, *and* night. I can't. A glass of port wine at a fren's funeral is the most I celebrate, and I'm too busy to be going to frens' funerals every day of the week. Well, there's your brekfuss, and that's a *fresh* egg. I've dusted out the sitting-room, and I'll come up in an hour's time and do your bedroom. Mr Sayers spoke to me of your requirements, and I'm willing to oblige prervided . . . prervided," she repeated sternly, "it's strickly understood I'm looking after a single gentleman, and by single I *mean* single, tempory and otherwise. Perhaps you take my meaning?"

"I think so, Mrs Sayers."

"Since Mr Sayers took on as porter to these flats, Mr . . . I didn't get your name exack . . ."

"Ogilvie."

"Ogilvie? That's a foreign name, ain't it?"

"It's a Scottish name."

"It may be," Mrs Sayers commented oracularly. "And perhaps it is. But it's what I would call a foreign name. Still, now the war's over I daresay we can be less particular about foreign names. As I was saying, since Mr Sayers took on as porter to these flats, I've seen sights I hadn't thought could happen. I wouldn't digrade myself by repeating to you what I seen, Mr Ogilvie," she continued with salacious relish in her undisclosed memories. "But I made a strick rule not to enter one of these flats if there was a woman inside. *In* her cloves or *out* of her cloves. And which is all the same to the class of women who lives in these flats. Well, I think we understand one another now, and I hope we'll continue without unpleasantness on either side. And you'll find that egg perfeckly fresh."

John could almost have believed that Mrs Sayers was prepared to add 'because I laid it myself' as, scratching the door-mat back into place with the heel of her left foot, she retired hen-like from the bedroom.

Eleven days after the signing of the Armistice, Lloyd George and Bonar Law put out their manifesto soliciting the country's support for the Coalition Government at the General Election to be held in the middle of December:

Thanks to the patient valour of the Hosts of Freedom, the knell of military autocracy has sounded for ever in the continent of Europe . . . our first task must be to conclude a just and lasting peace, and so to establish the foundations of a new Europe that occasion for further wars may be for ever averted . . . the care of the soldiers and sailors whose heroism has won for us this great deliverance is a primary object of patriotism . . . land on simple and economical bases for men who have served in the war, either for cottages with gardens, allotments or small holdings . . . the land of the country if properly cultivated and used, could have yielded food to a much larger extent . . . the war has given a fresh impetus to agriculture . . . the Government regard the improvement of village life and the development of rural industries as essential . . . reform is urgently required in the constitution of the House of Lords . . . a Second Chamber which will be based upon direct contact with the people . . . so long as the Irish question remains unsettled there can be no political peace either in the United Kingdom or in the Empire . . . one of the first obligations of British statesmanship to explore all practical paths towards the settlement of this grave and difficult question, on the basis of self-government . . . two paths which are closed—the one leading to a complete severance of Ireland from the British Empire and the other to the forcible submission of the six counties of Ulster to a Home Rule Parliament . . . it is a source of pride to be of this age and to be members of this nation . . . right earnestly do we trust that the united temper, the quiet fortitude, the high and resolute patriotism of our nation may be long preserved into the golden times of peace.

In case this lengthy prospectus by two political share-pushers for an earthly paradise should be too long-winded for the female voters on whom the Coalition Government was relying for their support, the quick-witted Welshman issued a snappy programme on the eve of the Election. This pocket guide to the new world designed by himself and what Fitzgerald had once called that pudding-faced Scotsman Bonar Law, was (1) Trial of the Kaiser, (2) Punishment of those responsible for atrocities, (3) Germany to pay the cost of the war, (4) Britain to be reserved for the British, socially and industrially, (5) Rehabilitation of those broken by the war and, with an almost Messianic generosity of promise, (6) a happier country for all.

On a drenching December morning Mrs Sayers appeared with John's breakfast dressed in a black jet-fringed mantle which her mother had worn at the two Jubilees and the funeral procession of Queen Victoria, and she herself at the funeral of King Edward VII and the coronation of King George V.

"Are you going to record your vote, Mrs Sayers?" John asked with amicable inquisitiveness.

"Certainly I'm going to vote," she replied haughtily. "And in fack I shall have to ask you to wait for the flat to be done out until after I come back from the poll."

"And for whom are you voting?" he pressed.

"Meaning no disrespeck, Mr Ogilvie, that's my business. I wouldn't tell not even Mr Sayers that. I packed off more than enough of those Nosey Parkers as call theirselves canvassers. *They* don't know and *nobody* doesn't know who I'll give my vote to. I have my own opinions, but I'm not like one of them low-minded Volga suffragettes. I keep my opinions to myself."

Whether Mrs Sayers was one of the women who, in some districts outnumbering the men by twenty to one, signalized their achievement of the franchise by returning that disastrous influence over the future of Europe, that amalgamation of enriched patriots, was not to be ascertained, but her unusual agreeableness on the day the result of the Election was announced led John to fancy that she had supported the Coalition Government. His own depression was faintly lightened by the victory of Sinn Féin. In his report he had in fact slightly underestimated the probable completeness of the defeat of the Parliamentary Nationalists. In four only of the nine counties of Ulster did the Unionists contrive a majority, and in two of these only a bare majority at that. Three days after the Election the Chief Secretary for Ireland observed that the Irish question would be settled peacefully or bloodily within six months.

President Wilson was less cynical about the future. On the last day but one of the year he told the citizens of Manchester he believed that men were beginning to see, not perhaps the golden age, but an age which at any rate was brightening from decade to decade and would lead them some time to an elevation from which they would be able to see the things for which the heart of mankind was longing.

"Who *is* this President Wilson?" Mrs Sayers was asking. "He opens his big mouth very wide about this, that, and the other. I don't hold with these Americans myself. We had one of them in Queensberry Mansions six months back. Nasty n'ya-n'ya way he had of talking. 'Your voice wants oiling,' I said to him once when he was trying to teach me my own business. I reckon this President Wilson is another Knowall. Just another Kayser if you ask me. Pity they can't all keep theirselves to theirselves like what I do. 'President Wilson looks forward to Golden Age.' That's what was printed in my morning's paper. In course he looks forward to it. After our money, that's what he is in my opinion. And these dirty Irish, they're another plague. Murderers, that's what *I* call them, and I wouldn't show them no more mercy than what I would the fellow who drowned them poor women he married in a bath. Fifteen years Mr Sayers and me have been man and wife, and when I've had occasion to take a bath I've sent him out of the house. Just because you're married it doesn't say you've got to lose all common decency. Well, if you ask my opinion I'd say the Irish was worse than the Germans. That's where I like this Boner Lore. He hates the Irish like what I do myself. And this Carson too, he's another who hates 'em."

"But Carson is an Irishman himself," John pointed out.

"There you are. Set a thief to catch a thief, they say, don't they?"

"I'm afraid you're prejudiced, Mrs Sayers."

"In course I'm prejadist and proud of it. I been a staunch Conservative ever since I can remember."

"So now I know how you voted on December 14th," John laughed.

"Clever, aren't you? But perhaps not so clever as you think. Nobody knows where I put my cross and nobody never will. So I suppose you're one of these Radicals. Yes, they can call theirselves Liberals and try and mislead simple folk, but that don't *make* them Liberal. Well, I'm sorry you're a Radical, because in many respecks, as I've said to Mr Sayers more than once, you're a cut above the usual riff-raff we get in Queensberry Mansions. I told Mr Sayers as much right out when he first took on the job of porter here. 'Well,' I said, 'I've had some queer things happen to me since I left my home as a girl in Wych Street in the autumn of the Golden Jubilee to go out to service with a greengrocer in the Theobald's Road, but nothing so queer as to find myself married to a man with the keys of a common knocking-shop.' Oh, yes, I told him straight out. I didn't mince the word. And he looked a bit took aback because usually I'm very careful about words I will use, as you may have noticed. But when you finds yourself in a disgosting place like Queensberry Mansions you may have to use a disgosting word to speak your plain meaning. Mansions! There's a blaspheemious name to give it. Shocking, I call it, to take a word right out of the Bible and give it to gay flats. There now, keeping me talking about politics and whatnot, I forgot to give you this telegram, and which came this morning. I expeck it's New Year Greetings."

"Of course. I forgot. A happy new year, Mrs Sayers," John wished her.

"Well, I forgot too till this telegram come to my mind. The same to you, Mr Ogilvie, and many of them."

John tore open the telegram. It had been sent from Naples:

Don't write till you hear from me
Athene

So Wacey must be home. John wished that Mrs Sayers would leave him to meditate alone upon the news in this telegram.

Yet it was not Wacey whom Athene was meeting in Naples on that New Year's morning. It was Wacey's mother, of whose arrival from America Wacey had notified her by telegram only on the previous day. He must have cabled to his mother to reserve a passage the instant he received Athene's letter telling him that their life together must finish. He was counting as he had counted from earliest childhood upon his mother's being able to extricate him, when all else had failed, from the muddle into which he had got himself. She had not foreseen that counterstroke when she wrote to him, and he had skilfully allowed her no time to prepare her own riposte.

It was an angrily preoccupied Athene who drove down to the Immacolatella at noon, after an almost sleepless night in the Santa Lucia Hotel. A courier sat beside the driver on the box of the *carrozza*. At last the boat he engaged succeeded in getting clear from the swarm of craft round the wharfside, and Athene was rowed out to the liner which according to custom would discharge her passengers with their cabin luggage before berthing. She was dressed that morning in a coat and skirt of deep maroon facecloth severely cut and suggesting a kind of military defiance as she went up the ship's ladder on the port side and hurried along to the purser's office. She had hardly had time to ask if Mrs Stewart H. Langridge was aboard when she heard her name called behind her, and turning saw her mother-in-law.

"Why, Athene darling, isn't this kind of you? I didn't expect to be met in Naples. I was going to send you a telegram just as soon as I landed and come right along to Citrano. Dearest child, how very well you're looking!"

Mrs Langridge put a hand on each of Athene's shoulders and gazed fondly at her daughter-in-law.

"What a welcome sight for old eyes sore from gazing all day for nearly a fortnight at that ugly old ocean!"

"Did you have a good crossing, Mrs Langridge?"

"Why, yes, I suppose for the time of year it was a wonderful crossing, and of course we gained a lot of perfectly lovely weather by the Mediterranean route."

"The Mediterranean can be pretty nasty in December,"

Athene said, clinging anxiously to those commonplaces of voyagers' conversation for as long as she could and wishing that her heart would stop beating with such disconcerting insistence.

"Don't I know it can!"

"I've a shore-boat waiting, and we can go through the customs with your cabin trunks right away. We'll send the hotel-courier to clear the baggage from the hold later."

"But I haven't one trunk in the hold," said Mrs Langridge. "I didn't want to clutter you up with a whole lot of burdensome stuff at your sweet little Villa Allegra."

"Then we can go right back to Citrano to-night," Athene said.

"Sure."

This tall woman with the gentle voice and soft white hair and clear-cut profile so like her only son's could intone that monosyllable with a truly frightening inevitability. In her grey travelling-cape she seemed to annihilate the future with the pervasiveness of a creeping sea-fog.

No attempt was made by Mrs Langridge to bring the conversation round to the reason of her departure from home, but that reason haunted the back of every remark, and the most trivial Atlanta chit-chat with which she sought to entertain Athene during the drive from Naples seemed weighted with an ominous intention.

"I saw your dear mother the day before I left. I have a letter for you from her. She and your dear father are so proud of the lovely baby boy with which dear Vera and Hugh presented them just a year ago. Your father is looking so well. They're all hoping so much you'll be able to visit them for a long stay this year. Why, my dear, I haven't yet wished you a happy, happy 1919!"

"Thank you, Mrs Langridge. And you too."

"We should be so happy now that the war is over, and

all our dear boys coming back from Europe. No news yet when Wacey will be released from his duties?"

"None yet."

Mrs Langridge patted her daughter-in-law's knee.

"It's been such a difficult time for you, honey."

"How is Mr Langridge?"

"Oh, grandpa is fine. The war took him out of himself. And of course he was terribly proud Wacey was so much in the thick of everything. He was anxious to come over with me, but I was afraid you might find the two of us a little overwhelming. Dear grandpa, he's wild of course to see Arthur. And so am I indeed. You must remember we haven't seen the little man since he was two, and now, why, dear goodness, he'll be eight in four months' time."

"You haven't changed in six years, Mrs Langridge."

"I'm not any younger, dear, that's one sure thing. Sixty-four, you know. And grandpa will be seventy next fall." She looked at the passing scene. "Oh dear, how little this old Europe changes! Let me see, it's nine years now since grandpa and I stayed with you in Switzerland, and we toured Italy afterwards before we went home. It just seems the day before yesterday. You'll see big changes in Atlanta, and as for New York, well, I find a different city every time I go there."

It was not until the third evening of her arrival that Mrs Langridge reached the reason for her hurried departure from Atlanta in mid-winter. At first her mind had seemed entirely taken up by an attempt to conquer the heart of her grandson. Arthur was not inclined to be easy. Under the influence of candy he consented to give up talking to his grandmother in Italian, but for most of the first day he held out.

"I do think, Athene darling, it would be wise to take him across to America soon," said Mrs Langridge, whose almost imperturbable gentleness had been slightly ruffled by the prospect of having a grandson speaking English with an Italian accent. "And indeed," she added, "I can't help feeling it would be wise all round to make the trip as early as possible this next spring. I wouldn't think they'd want to keep Wacey in France longer than that . . . and now, dear, as we're alone . . ." She looked over her shoulder.

"The maids don't understand English," Athene assured her. "And anyway they're at the other end of the house." She tried to speak casually, but she fancied, the way her pulses were throbbing, that her mother-in-law must be noticing this agitation at the prospect of the struggle between them now at hand.

"I had a letter from Wacey before I left home in which he hinted that there had been some little misunderstanding between you and him which had cast a cloud upon his happiness while he was away . . . away serving his country."

"Mrs Langridge, I don't want to seem rude or unsympathetic, but I wish you wouldn't talk as if Wacey's serving his country had anything to do with the matter. He wanted to go to France and I was perfectly glad he should go. I wouldn't have wished him to do anything else."

"No, dear, you misunderstand me. I wasn't trying to suggest that Wacey was . . ."

"Doing anything else except serve his own inclinations in serving his country," Athene cut in sharply. She must make it clear as soon as possible that this was not a petty domestic squabble which could be cleared up by the intervention of a smooth-tongued mother-in-law. She would not allow herself to be manœuvred into a defensive position.

"Why, I apologize, dear, for dragging in my foolish old sentimental patriotism," Mrs Langridge went on gently. "You're perfectly right. That has nothing to do with your two private lives. Nothing at all. It was blundering of me to talk like that. But the misunderstanding . . ."

"It was not a misunderstanding, Mrs Langridge," Athene interrupted defiantly. "It was a revelation of Wacey's character."

"I don't know what the trouble was exactly. But certainly poor Wacey believed it was a misunderstanding."

"Wacey can convince himself of anything he wants to believe," Athene asserted.

"Why, I know . . . dear little boy, don't I remember his funny little ways? . . . I know poor Wacey will occasionally let his own good intentions persuade him that some little thing he has neglected to do was done all the time . . . but surely, dear, the two women he loves best and"—she stopped for a brief instant and let her grey eyes rest on Athene—"who love him best can make allowances?"

"For lying?" Athene challenged.

Mrs Langridge shook her head in mournful reproach of so positive, so aggressive a word.

"As I don't know what the trouble was I can't well argue about that, dear."

Athene was tempted to fling the ugly fact at this gentle-voiced woman who all through her life had been sealing over ugly facts as she had read once that bees will build a a waxen tomb over a dead mouse in the hive. She restrained herself, however, for she knew that if once the discussion were to revolve round the fact which came to her knowledge on that October night the fundamental divergence between Wacey and herself would be lost sight of and the effect it had on herself entirely misapprehended. She knew that Wacey must have hinted successfully at trouble to bring his mother hurrying across the Atlantic like this, and she decided to let her see at once that it was not a false alarm.

"The particular misunderstanding, as Wacey calls it, only brought matters to a head, Mrs Langridge. It is possible that if something which occurred in October year had not occurred I might not have written to tell Wacey this last October that I wanted him to give me my freedom. I consider that he did something then which released me from any obligation to him, but it would be foolish to pretend I did not welcome the release. I do not love Wacey. I have never loved him. I won't go into the question of why, when I was a girl of twenty, I married him. You know better than anybody how difficult it is not to indulge his weakness. I was fond of him. I am still fond of him. But I cannot live with him on the terms that he would want me to live on, and I could not stand the strain of watching Wacey's pretence to the world that we were living on those terms. It has cost me mortification enough even when we were still living as man and wife. I always hated that side of marriage. If we were having this talk before Arthur was born you would have assured me that most women felt like that at first, but that one settled down. You cannot assure me of that now. I have been married too long. It is impossible for me ever again to live with Wacey as his wife. His absence in France has made an open break unnecessary so far, but that must come, and the kindest thing you can do, Mrs Langridge, is not to plead for Wacey because that may lead me to say things which I don't want to say."

"But you've always been such an ideally happy pair," Mrs Langridge insisted. "Everybody has believed it to be the perfect match. Forgive me, dear, for saying so, but you are acting hastily and perhaps unwisely. You forget the disturbing influence of this dreadful war. You have been separated for fifteen months. When you meet again . . ."

"Wacey was home on leave last July. I had no doubts about our future then," said Athene. "Please, dear Mrs

Langridge, do not try to argue me out of this resolve. It has been taken deliberately, and nothing, nothing will ever shake it. The kindest thing you can do is to convince Wacey of my unchangeableness and persuade him to release me before his resistance makes me bitter. I am willing that he should have Arthur for three months every year until he comes of age. That is the most I will agree to."

"And grandpa and I were planning to come back with you to Europe after your visit home this year."

Athene shuddered inwardly. Had she needed a final spur to ruthlessness this suggestion would have provided it.

"I'm sorry, Mrs Langridge, that you are disappointed, but my mind is made up."

"I suppose hardness does make for happiness," the older woman murmured sorrowfully.

"I'm sure you think me terribly hard. But if I can be blamed it is for my softness. I agreed to marry Wacey because I was too soft not to be upset by his wretchedness when I refused him time after time. I was too soft not to leave him when I realized that he never intended to make the effort to be independent, when he played around year after year with the notion of writing books, when he tried to spoil Arthur, oh, please don't make me list a long catalogue of grievances . . . it just can't go on any longer. I don't suppose you believe me when I tell you it's breaking my heart to make your long journey across the Atlantic a journey for nothing. But can't you see how unpardonable it was of Wacey to bring you into this at all?"

"Well, dear, I'm not going to say any more to-night. What you tell me has been a terrible shock. You wouldn't expect it to be anything else. But I'm an older woman than you, honey, and I've lived through lots of queer disillusioning experiences, and I'm not convinced that this break-up of your married life is necessary. You owe it to Wacey to give him at least a chance to make up for anything he may have done heedlessly, for I know Wacey wouldn't hurt you deliberately. I know how much, how very very much my poor boy loves you."

"Please, please, Mrs Langridge . . ." Athene begged.

"Very well, dear, I'll say no more. Perhaps I'd better go off to bed and leave you to yourself. Oh dear, what sad things happen to people in this poor old world!" She rose from her chair and coming across to Athene she put her hands on her shoulders.

"I still believe we shall find a way out," she told her, and then like a grey wraith she faded from the room.

When Mrs Langridge was gone Athene sat down at her desk and wrote a long letter to John, telling him at the same time not to write to her until she telegraphed because she intended to do all she could to get Wacey down to Citrano so that the future could be discussed by the three of them together. At the same time she wrote to Wacey. She was determined that the 'misunderstanding' should not become the central point at issue.

It was not until the third week in January that Wacey arrived home, and the strain of living in the house with his mother without ever allowing the one subject that preoccupied the minds of both of them to escape into the open of conversation was exacerbating Athene's nerves. Her own irritation was increased by the consciousness of Mrs Langridge's pliable strength of purpose. This air of kindly imperturbable graciousness made Athene feel that her mother-in-law was wrapping her up in one of her own shawls of angora wool and suffocating her in the spongy stuff. She agreed with everything Athene said, and even obviously denied herself the pleasure of indulging Arthur as if by such restraint she could imply her willingness to recognize the faults of her own son.

To add a final vexation to Athene's state of mind two old friends of hers and Wacey's—Gaisford and Olive Carter—had turned up and were staying at the Excelsior.

He was an American painter settled in Paris, and Olive was a classmate of Athene's. Olive had a maddening way of drawing attention at every opportunity to the similarity of her life and her friend's.

"And it's so poetically appropriate," she gushed. "The olive was Athene's gift to Athens, and I was Athene's gift to Gaisford because if Athene hadn't married Wacey Langridge, who was an old friend of Gaisford since Quartier Latin days, I'd never have met him. So you see our destinies are all mixed up together. And Wacey and Athene have Arthur, and Gaisford and I have our precious Susan who's just two years younger, and so we say that it's evidently been decided by fate that Arthur and Susan should one day make a match of it." In this strain Olive Carter, whose Southern drawl was spoilt by the harsh timbre of her voice, would chatter endlessly in public.

But this was by no means the worst, for whenever Olive could find Athene alone she would insist on confiding in her the intimacies of marital experience with Gaisford and press Athene with questions about her own experiences with Wacey.

"My dear, aren't you longing for Wacey to come home? Gaisford and I will be just tickled to death to see you two lovebirds on the same perch again. Gaisford was only working on camouflage for the A.E.F., but even that seemed to make him mighty glad to be with me whenever he could. I guess poor Wacey's . . ."

The Carters were still at the Excelsior when Wacey did arrive in the third week of January, looking pale and tired. He brightened visibly to find them in Citrano and was prodigal with invitations to lunch and dinner and cocktails.

Mrs Langridge saw how much this hospitality was annoying Athene. One night, after the Carters had lingered on after lunch until dinner-time, and Athene, in response to Wacey's suggestion that they should stay and take pot luck, had said sharply that there wasn't anything in the pot, she told her son that the Carters were dear sweet folk but that it was possible to have too much of them.

"Especially in this wintry weather, son, when we can't all be out in the garden."

Olive Carter had managed to exasperate Athene particularly that day because on retiring to her bedroom to powder her nose she had looked meaningly at the single bed and said:

"My dear, you certainly are happy. Why, I don't believe I could sleep even with my beloved Gaisford in a bed that size."

She hoped Olive would not hint at her amorous fancies to Wacey. Sex-ridden creature, she was quite capable of doing so!

It was after dinner the same night that Athene, on hearing Wacey was due to return to France a couple of days later, decided that she must bring matters to a head by asking him if he had made any plans about the future.

"It's foolish to make plans while I'm still tied to my military duties," he answered. "There's more to do now really than there was before the armistice."

"You know what I mean, Wacey. I'm not asking you to name an actual date, but you haven't told me yet that you are willing to give me my freedom."

"I don't suppose it makes a lot of difference to you, dear, whether I'm willing or not. If you're determined to break up our married life you can do it."

"I wouldn't put it that way, son," his mother interposed. "Athene and I haven't talked a great deal together. We thought it wiser to wait till you could come along. But by what I understand from her something happened between you and her which hurt her. I don't know what it was. . . ."

"It's no use bringing that up, mother. Athene believes I'm lying about something and refuses to let me give her an explanation."

Mrs Langridge looked pleadingly across to her daughter-in-law.

"I'm sure, dear, you wouldn't refuse that," she urged gently.

"Mrs Langridge, I'm sorry if I seem unreasonable, but the kind of explanation Wacey offered could not convince me. It was not even plausible. And furthermore it would have humiliated me to accept such an explanation. I wish, Wacey, you wouldn't deceive yourself into supposing that even if I *were* convinced by your explanation I could change my mind now about the future."

"That's what I said, Athene. You are determined to break up our married life."

"That isn't the right word, son," Mrs Langridge began, but Athene caught her up.

"Mrs Langridge, I'm not worried about the word. If Wacey chooses to say I am breaking up our life together I accept his description. I do wish to break it up."

Wacey turned to his mother, with a shrug, as if he would indicate by the gesture the hopelessness of attempting to argue with a self-willed woman.

"And now, Wacey," his wife continued, "as I have admitted my determination to break up our married life, will you tell me if you are going to help?"

"What do you want me to do? Give you evidence of infidelity?"

"Son, son, don't talk like that. I'm sure that's the last thing Athene would want . . . or expect," his mother added in a low voice.

"Well, what other way is there?" he asked. "Desertion? You can't see Athene sitting patiently deserted for two or three years or whatever time the courts demand. It's easy enough to ask me to give her her freedom, but suppose I say I will? It's not so darned easy to do it."

Throughout her planning for the future Athene had held to the idea that the bill from Rome would provide her with a plea no judge would refuse to accept. Now suddenly she realized how flimsy such a plea might sound. If Wacey left the case undefended it might serve, but his vanity would never allow him to do that. To the end of his life he would cling to the explanation she had refused to accept. Wacey seemed to divine by her silence that she was baffled for the moment, and he took advantage of her hesitation.

"Where do you want to obtain the divorce?" he continued. "In Georgia, so far as I remember, it takes two juries to grant a divorce, but I'm not dead sure about that. It never occurred to me when I married you I'd ever be wanting a divorce, or I might have put myself wise to the matrimonial get-out in our State. I suppose you can go to Reno with collusion from me. But I don't see you hanging around in Reno for six months or whatever the time it takes to acquire a domicile. I'll do what you want me to do, dear, but it would help a lot if you'd tell me just exactly what you do want."

"Why, yes, Athene darling, I think you owe it to Wacey to let him know what you do want," said Mrs Langridge.

It was silly to repeat that she wanted to be free. She should have written to some lawyer and asked his advice. Divorce always seemed so easy when you heard of it among your friends. She sat silent, furious with her own ineffectiveness.

"Look, dear, I'll make a suggestion if I may," Wacey said presently. "It's no use pretending I want to see our marriage broken up. I don't, and you know I don't. Still, I'm not going to hold on to you against your will, if holding on means you're going to be unhappy."

"No, no, of course, you'd never do that, son," his mother put in eagerly, for she was seeing him as a not altogether unheroic figure when he talked like this. "And dear Athene knows you would never do that."

"All right, mother, I've worked out a kind of crazy scheme for myself." He did not feel that her admiration was helping him with Athene and he felt he could manage better by his own manner of approach to the problem. "My notion is this, Athene. I'm willing to clear right away for a year. I'll have to wait until I'm demobilized, but after that I'll go right off to the Pacific, and perhaps" —he was on the verge of saying 'write a book', but he stopped himself in time—"and perhaps stay there. That'll rest with you to decide."

"But, Wacey, you've been away now for over a year all except a few days last July, and I'm not likely to change my mind because you go away for another year."

"I'm just offering to keep out of your way a bit longer. So long as I'm out of the way I don't see what you're worrying about. You don't want to marry anybody else, do you?"

"That's being silly," she said very quickly to avoid giving a direct answer. She wondered if he would notice her nervousness, but he was so used himself to giving an indirect answer that he apparently did not notice it. "All the same," she went on, "it wouldn't be a very satisfactory position either for you or for me. The clean cut would surely be better."

"Well, you can call me nuts, but I've a kind of a fixed idea that if you won't rush things I may stand a chance. Oh, I know I make you mad, dear, by saying that, but it's how I feel and there's no sense in giving up a hunch without a struggle."

"Athene darling, forgive me for butting in," said Mrs Langridge. "I may be doing more harm than good, I know. Surely, honey, what Wacey asks is fair. I daresay some folks will gossip and speculate, but if you come back to America and stay awhile with grandpa and me and with Mr and Mrs Gilmer I don't think gossip will matter at all. It's terrible for me to realize that you two beloved young people haven't been as happy together as we all thought, but you won't refuse to give Wacey's suggestion a trial, will you? And in all this there's the question of Arthur to be thought about. I think it's the children who suffer most from divorce. Give Wacey's suggestion a year, and if at the end of that time you feel it's useless to patch up the poor old cloak, why, then throw it away."

"I cannot see the good of postponing what I know is inevitable," Athene said miserably. "It puts a strain both on Wacey and me. I'd so much sooner he felt himself free to find another woman. . . ."

"I'm afraid I'll never do that, Athene," Wacey broke in.

In spite of what happened in October year, this was true, Athene reflected, and she wished that she could feel touched by his love instead of irritated by it.

"I don't understand how you can go on being in love with me, Wacey."

She stopped abruptly. She had forgotten for the moment the presence of Mrs Langridge. The last thing she would do was to discuss their emotional relations in front of her mother-in-law.

"I'm going away off to bed now," the older woman announced, seeming to scent that her presence was hindering a freedom of talk which might lead to a reconciliation. "Oh, you two dear foolish children!" she exclaimed, gazing from one to another fondly, her grey eyes moist. "Well, I just can't believe it won't all come right in the end."

She floated away; but when she found the bulb in her bedroom had fused, she undressed in the dark rather than come back and interrupt what might follow from that question to her son, which by now Athene was regretting she had asked, for it had led to what she most desired to avoid—the long story of Wacey's love from the time he saw her under the magnolia in the garden of the house on Peachtree Street.

"Yes, yes, Wacey," she cried impatiently at last. "But if I haven't been able to fall in love with you after nine years of marriage how am I likely to fall in love with you now? If you drive me into saying that I married you because I was sorry for you, does that help? If I tell you that I am sorry for you now, does that help? I never had any will not to love you. It just hasn't been possible. If it's any consolation to you I'll admit that even if you hadn't given my pride that shock after you went away to France in 1917 I would probably have asked you to let us separate, once I had known what it was to be alone. There must be some way of getting a divorce that won't involve scandal and publicity. Other people manage it. If you love me you'll let me go."

"I am letting you go," he answered. "From what I can make out you've grown to dislike my company, and I don't intend you shall have to put up with it. If at the end of another year you still find the notion of life together repulsive, why, I'm willing to eliminate myself. I think I'm entitled to ask you to agree to this for the sake of my father and mother. I've been a disappointment to them in some ways, but my marriage to you has been their compensation for other disappointments. You see the way my mother came right over because she might help straighten things out a bit . . . well surely for her sake you'll agree to wait another year?"

"Why, I suppose I'll have to," said Athene limply.

Don't call me weak, she wrote to John, *for though I suppose I am weak it's really the weakness of a feeble kind of decency. I haven't the heart to hold out without any apparent reason for holding out except utter selfishness. I suppose this means the postponement of our marriage for at least eighteen months from now. I don't have to tell you that you must consider yourself completely free. If after eighteen months you still want me I shall be yours. But, believe me, I could not bear to think that you felt under any obligation to me. You are under none, John. Neither you nor I deliberately fell in love with the other. It is that which gives me the courage to believe that perhaps you will not forget me in what may easily prove in the end to be two years from the time we parted. But because I am foolishly credulous, my heart, do not think you have to indulge that credulity. If I have made a muddle and a mess of my life I have only myself to thank. If I love you now I have only myself to blame. I had planned beforehand to be so cold and unyielding, but all my good resolutions fell to pieces. When Wacey said to me, "You don't want to marry anybody else, do you?" I ought to have said "Yes", instead of turning the question with an evasive reply. And yet I don't know. I fear if Wacey thought I wanted to marry somebody else he would refuse either to let me divorce him or to divorce me. Oh, how often I have scoffed at the eternal triangle in French books and plays, and now here I am beating upon it myself. Wacey goes back to France the day after to-morrow. Will you write in a few days and let me know you do not despise me for this weakness? And remember, my loved one, that I release you—that is true, true, true, and you must believe I am in earnest about this. I should be disappointed, yes, but I should not be disillusioned if you found this long separation had been too much for you. There is a great difference between disappointment and disillusionment. And so, you are free. Believe that, my heart, and whenever you wish, with a clear conscience forget your Athene.*

Wacey did not ask Athene to see him as far as Naples

on his way back, but he was looking so pale and forlorn that she insisted, and he was even more zealous over the minor attentions and courtesies than usual, pathetically zealous indeed. The weather was abominable. Tattered icy draperies of squall after squall from the north-west were swept across the bay, and hailstones beat upon the windows of the car with such violence that they were heard above the racket of the traffic on the heavily cobbled roads. The upper half of Vesuvius was hidden in a swirl of livid vapours rent every now and then by flashes of lightning. Capri, Ischia and Procida appeared and disappeared like dark monsters in the murk. It was the *maestrale d' inverno* and therefore *tempo d' inferno*, the wintry north-west which is the weather of hell.

"I'm afraid I've dragged you out on a terrible day," he said.

"We're perfectly all right in the car," she answered.

These two remarks might have stood for the whole of their conversation during that drive to Naples. The two of them were as guarded as players in some game the point of which is the successful concealment of the vital word.

On reaching Naples they were met with the news of a railway breakdown further up the line, which meant that the first train for Rome would not leave until the early morning.

"You'd better go right back to Citrano, dear," Wacey told her. "I'll have to put up here for the night. I think I'll stay down in one of the hotels near the station."

She guessed at once why he chose to do that. The hotels by Santa Lucia were too closely associated in his memory with happier days. On an impulse Athene told him that she would wait over in Naples until tomorrow and go with him to a more agreeable hotel than was to be found by the station. So in the end they went to the Virgilio, where the manager and the porter and the head waiter beamed upon them.

"You have stayed at the Santa Lucia when you came at the beginning of January, Signora Langridge," said the manager reproachfully. "And I have felt very hurt when I hear of it. Now I find you your favourite room with the view you like so much."

"I don't think we need bother about the view to-day," said Athene quickly.

"You are right, signora. It is bad weather—very bad. Still, I think you will like your favourite room."

"Give the signora that room," said Wacey. "But give me a small room to myself, because I have to be up early to catch the first train to Rome. I ought to have gone right on to-night, but there's a breakdown on the line."

Athene smiled gratefully at him.

At dinner the head waiter was anxious they should try some champagne of which he spoke with enthusiasm, and so they drank it.

"It is good, yes?" he enquired anxiously when after watching them both out of the corner of his eye he decided that something was the matter either with the wine or with the guests. The arrival of Signor Langridge at the Virgilio once upon a time had been the precursor of much joviality.

"Yes, it's a good champagne," Wacey told him listlessly. "Will I have him put another bottle on the ice, dear?"

"Oh, I couldn't drink any more, Wacey," she begged.

"*Una bottiglia basta*, *grazie*," Wacey told the head waiter, who retired in discouragement. *Quella maledetta guerra!* It had changed everybody. One bottle of champagne was enough for Signor Langridge nowadays.

After dinner, Wacey suggested a film. The atmosphere of the hotel lounge where two or three English old maids were clicking away at their knitting under palms in pots was depressing. So they went to a Harold Lloyd picture, the first the Neapolitans had seen of that comedian. His art never earned a greater tribute than the smiles it won from Wacey and Athene Langridge that evening.

"I'm feeling pretty punk to-night," Wacey said when they got back to the Virgilio. "I hope I'm not in for a go of this darned influenza."

"You'd better go right up to bed, Wacey. I'll come along presently and see if you're all right."

A quarter of an hour later when she came with aspirin he declared he felt better.

"Do you think you ought to travel to-morrow morning?"

"But I must travel, dear. I'm still in uniform, you know. Well, thanks a lot for seeing me through what would have been a pretty dreary evening all alone. And this is good-bye for a long while perhaps. Thanks for agreeing to this extra trial. I'll write from Paris and tell you my plans as soon as I can fix them up. Good-bye, Athene."

"Good-bye, Wacey."

She could not keep the tears back. She could not help feeling miserable for him. She could not help remembering the eternal optimism of his attitude toward their life together. She could not help recalling brief illusions of happiness in this hotel when, because there had been a bunch of jolly friends with whom they had kept it up until dawn and because, let her be frank with herself, she had drunk enough champagne to blunt the edges of reality, she had been able to fancy she was at last responding to Wacey's passion.

"What are the tears for?" he asked.

"You don't think I'm enjoying making you unhappy?" she asked brokenly.

"I wouldn't worry about that if I was you. Anyway, you've offered me this chance to make good, and I've not given up hope yet. I've been dull to-night because I'm not feeling too good. Don't you worry about me. There's only one thing which is eating me all the while and that is that darned mistake over that bill. If you'd only believe it *was* a mistake. . . ."

She could fancy her tears were freezing.

"Don't let's talk about that again, Wacey. Please! And you'll write to me when you know your plans?"

"Sure thing."

"Good-bye, then, Wacey."

She bent over and kissed his cheek. Looking back for a moment from the door she caught his eyes, which had followed her form across the room. They were unnaturally bright, and the hungry look in them thawed the tears so fast that when she reached her own room she had to fling herself down upon the bed and weep and weep. The raging *maestrale* which had died down for a while at dusk was now blowing more fiercely than ever, and above the screaming blast the hailstones were sounding a demoniac tattoo upon the french-windows.

When Athene reached home the following evening she found Mrs Langridge so full of appreciation for her thoughtfulness in going into Naples to see Wacey off that in her embarrassment she was almost curt.

"But I do think it was so sweet of you, Athene honey, to venture all that way in such dreadful weather," she insisted gently. "Sonny was awful pleased. I could see that, and I just felt I wanted to take and hug you."

Luckily Athene's embarrassment was able to vent itself on the Carters, who were heard hallooing from the front-hall like hunters.

"Oh my, I do wish Gaisford and Olive wouldn't suppose that a day without their company for cocktails is a day lost," she exclaimed irritably.

"They mean so well, poor souls," said Mrs Langridge.

"Halloo, halloo, anybody at home?"

The round and rubicund countenance of Gaisford Carter appeared round the door of the *salone*.

"Ah, you are back. We thought it must be your automobile that passed along the top past the hotel," he said.

"Welcome, little stranger," Olive Carter shrieked amicably, pushing past her husband and hurrying forward to embrace Athene, who shied from her demonstrativeness like a deer.

"Gaisford and I decided we must come and cheer you up after the sweet sorrow of parting. We're going to take you back to dine with us at the Excelsior. So go and put on your pretties and we'll go right along."

"No, really, Olive, I don't think I'll come out again to-night," Athene demurred.

"Mrs Langridge, she ought to come, oughtn't she?" Olive appealed. "I just know what it feels like to be deserted by a perfectly adorable husband, and it's tarantella evening at the Excelsior. It's the first they've had, and I'm crazy to see a tarantella danced."

"No, really, Olive, you'll have to excuse me, I'm tired. I'd rather dine quietly with Mrs Langridge and go off to bed soon afterwards."

"Faithless Paris, cruel Paris, thus the poor deserted spake . . . oh dear, I can remember learning that in Tennyson and being so jealous because Maimie Ward recited it so much better than the rest of us. Can you remember that, angel child?"

"I don't know whether I remember it or not," Athene replied, in a fume of exasperation.

"Gaisford," said his wife, shaking her head. "Big You and little Me aren't popular to-night. We're the orphans of the storm. We wanted to do a kind action, and we've been discouraged. So, come on, let's make a stately and dignified retreat."

"You'd better have a drink now you're here," said Athene, grabbing desperately at her party manners and contriving to rescue a fragment of them.

"I don't believe I ever said 'no' to a perfectly good drink," Gaisford replied, plunging down into an arm-chair.

And it was an hour before the Carters left, promising to come around if the weather had cleared by the morning to take Athene for a walk.

"Well, grandma, I hope the weather won't clear," Athene said coldly when the Carters were gone.

Mrs Langridge fluttered with gratification at being called 'grandma'. Such a form of address was reserved for occasions when Arthur was present. This sounded to her the most spontaneous recognition she had yet received from her daughter-in-law.

"Poor souls, they dearly love you, Athene," she purred. "They only want to be kind and helpful."

"I shall throttle Olive Carter one of these days," Athene threatened. "I don't know why I ever imagined I liked her."

Mrs Langridge drew her daughter-in-law's arm through hers and patted her hand affectionately as they went into the dining-room.

It was ten days later on a pellucid February morning that a telegram came to say that Athene's husband was seriously ill and urging the advisability of her coming to Paris at once.

"Athene darling, you're pale, what is it?" the old lady asked.

"It's Wacey. He's very ill. We must go at once, Mrs Langridge. You'd better read the telegram."

They failed to catch the night-express from Rome, and

when they reached Paris Wacey had been dead six hours.

General Nicholson, whose A.D.C. Wacey had been, was grieved that a telegram had not been sent earlier.

"But the doctor didn't think there was any cause for anxiety until three days ago," he said, in a deep attractive drawl. "He came back from leave with a touch of influenza, but he argued it was nothing. However, after a couple of days I insisted he should go to bed, and then pneumonia set in, and his heart wasn't up to it. I'll miss him greatly, Mrs Langridge. He's been all kinds of use to me during the past year, and I'd grown very very fond of him. There isn't anything one can say at times like these which is any good to those who are left behind. It will be a military funeral. He gave his life for his country just the same as if he'd been killed in action. My other A.D.C. will look after both you ladies."

Athene was too anxiously preoccupied at first with Mrs Langridge to think about herself. She feared for a day or two that the old lady would die herself from the shock of Wacey's death. Her mother-in-law did not speak for forty-eight hours, and it was considered better she should not attend the funeral. Athene therefore did not attend, but remained with the old lady.

"Wacey was buried this morning, grandma," Athene told her, after she had sat through a day of silence in the little sitting-room. The hotel was crowded with hangers-on of the Peace Conference.

"Yes, dear, I know."

"Would you like to leave Paris soon, grandma, and come back to Citrano?"

"We'll leave as soon as you like, dear. There's nothing to keep us in Paris now. I'm afraid I've been very little help to you. I'm afraid I've been wrapped up too much in my own thoughts. Grief makes people selfish. But I've had my battle with myself, and I take humbly what God has sent for me to bear. I feel so much to blame."

"But, grandma dear, you have nothing to reproach yourself for."

"Oh yes, I have, honey," she said shaking her head. "I don't want to talk about that just now. Some day you and I will talk about it, but not just now. It isn't any use just now. It won't bring Wacey back because God has shown me now where I was wrong."

"But, grandma, you've not been wrong. Please don't think that anything you did or didn't do could have made any difference. You've enough to suffer without tormenting yourself unnecessarily."

Athene crossed over to where her mother-in-law was sitting upright in a chair by the table, and kissed her forehead. The old lady gripped her hand.

"I think, don't you, honey, that if we'd managed to reach Paris in time you and our dear Wacey would have made up your little differences? I think you'd have told him to hurry up and get well and come back with you to Citrano? I'm so sure you would, dear child. And I believe that might have rallied him. I think you really loved him all the time, didn't you?"

"Why, you know how fond I was of him, grandma."

The old lady sighed contentedly.

"I told him that, before you and he went off to Naples . . . why, it's hardly a fortnight ago! . . . and I *was* so pleased when you went to see him off. I just hugged myself when I saw you and him getting into the automobile together. Yes, I told him you loved him in your heart. And now"—she clutched more tightly Athene's hand—"and now we have to tell poor old grandpa. I believe I won't send him a cable. I believe I'll write him a letter when we're back in Citrano. Grandpa had set his mind on spending his seventieth birthday with Wacey and you and Arthur, and you know what grandpa's like when he's set his mind on something. Poor Wacey! He had his father's obstinacy and his poor old mother's weakness, and somehow they weren't mixed in the best way for the poor boy. But it's too late now to be sighing about that. I'll have to write grandpa soon, though."

"Wouldn't it be better if I cabled my mother and asked her to break it to grandpa?" Athene suggested.

"Why, yes, perhaps it would be. That's very thoughtful of you, Athene dear. But you always were thoughtful. Yes, I believe that would be the kindest way, because it wouldn't do for grandpa to hear the news from somebody else. I wonder if you'd come back home with me and bring Arthur? That would help grandpa a lot. He's never had to bear anything like this without me."

"Why, of course I'll come back with you," Athene told her. "We'll travel as soon as we can book berths."

"Well, I knew you'd say 'yes', Athene darling, but that doesn't make the way you've said 'yes' any less sweet . . . and the little difference there was between you and Wacey, that's always going to be a secret between you and me, isn't it?"

"An absolute secret," Athene promised.

"Because I wouldn't like other folk to know that it was ever anything but the loveliest marriage that ever happened. Perhaps we ought to have gone to see Wacey laid in the earth, but if I'd seen him lying under Old Glory I don't believe I could ever have looked at our beloved old flag again. But I think General Nicholson would understand, and that nice young Lieutenant was so fond of our Wacey, he'll understand why I couldn't have borne it."

"Everybody understood," said Athene, marvelling herself that Wacey's mother in that trance of grief had yet understood all that was going on.

Athene had written a brief letter to John from Paris. She wrote again when she and her mother-in-law were back at Citrano:

VILLA ALLEGRA,
CITRANO
February 8, 1919.

John, my dearest, I have secured berths in the Italian liner 'Principessa Mafalda' which sails from Genoa for New York on March 8th. It is an almost overwhelming temptation to ask you to come out to Citrano before we leave, but I know I am right to resist it, because it would be a terrible blow for Wacey's mother if she were to guess that I had loved somebody else. And the shock of Wacey's death has put her into that state of acutely heightened sensitiveness which would reveal to her the truth. Apart from my natural dislike of hurting her at such a moment I do feel I have a duty towards her and poor old Mr Langridge which I must fulfil to the best of my ability. Moreover, since for me the stroke of fate has made my future so much clearer I do not wish to take selfish advantage of it. What I said when I wrote to you about the difficulty of persuading Wacey to agree to a divorce holds good more decidedly than ever now. I want you to count yourself even more completely free than before. You will have time now to think over everything, and if next fall you know that you want me I am yours. I will come when you tell me to come any time after August, but once again please, John, remember, please please do, that no sense of chivalry, and above all no cowardice is to influence your decision. Write to me here before I leave, and write me in America c/o Lawton J. Gilmer, Peachtree Street, Atlanta, Ga. I expect I will be staying a good deal of the time with the Langridges, but I'd rather you wrote to my own home.

I am still dazed by this ending of one part of my life. You who knew and liked Wacey can understand the pathos of it all. There are moments when I reproach myself for ever having told him that everything was over between us, but one day I will tell you what exactly it was that I considered released me from any obligation, and you will understand that so far as you played a part in my future it did not injure Wacey in any way. That was done, by a strange coincidence, on the very night you came back from the war. And you know I agreed last month to wait a year before the question of divorce was raised. You have not written since, and now perhaps your answer will be easier for you. I do not know. There are black moments when I tell myself that no man could be as patient as I ask you to be, and then I remember that starry night of the vintage and I tell myself that the man who could behave as you did that night has all the patience in the world.

Oh, John, my dearest, poor old Mrs Langridge is such a tragic figure. I do not know how I am ever going to steel myself to take Arthur from her. And yet I cannot believe that she is the right person to bring him up. But that problem must wait. It has not to be solved yet. I lamented once that I should be thirty next April, because it was seeming so old for me to be coming to you, but to-day I feel I am going to be forty. Is there any strain equal to the strain of hurting other people when you know you are hurting and would give everything not to hurt them except the one thing they want and you cannot give? I do not believe that in the end the pretence of it is worth giving. And so, my loved one, my so dearly loved one, do not ever pretend with me. Do not mind hurting me if you cannot give me what you know I long for, without pretence. If our lives are to be joined let them be joined for ever in a perfection of mutual understanding. If the moment should come when you no longer want me, tell me so, and though it may tear my heart from me at the time I shall be grateful. I have lived now for nine years a completely false existence. My shadow has had as much substance as myself. You used to tease me about my party manners. They were the manners of the doll I had wound up to represent myself, and the best mechanical doll betrays its mechanism.

It strikes me in looking through what I have written that you may think I do really want you to come down to Citrano before I sail. John, I do not. Besides what I have written about the reasons against your coming I must add another, which is that I cannot play a part with you. You have felt the same about me, and that gave you the strength of will to leave me on that starry night. So I am in earnest about your not coming. And if I go on writing about it it is to indulge myself in the fancy of holding you in my arms again.

I have been so completely emptied of all emotion during the last five or six weeks that I am even faintly shocked at myself for talking about indulging myself. Dearest heart, do not fear that I will come into your life, if I am granted such happiness, mournful and temperamental and introspective. During these months I shall live for you, and if at the end of them you find you do not want me . . . but that's a question on which I shall not speculate or torment myself. I love you, my dear one, and how I long to be always

Your Athene

This letter reached John on the day after his play *All Or Nothing* had received its first performance at the Sheridan Theatre. He replied at once:

5B Queensberry Mansions,
Charing Cross Road,
London, W.C.
February 14, 1919.

My Athene,

Your letter from Paris was naturally a shock.

I was weighed down for a while by a sense of guilt. Inevitable in the circumstances. I was relieved to get your letter of the 9th from Citrano. You have been through a ghastly time, and I feel I have had nothing to bear except this separation from you. Your earlier letter telling me you had agreed to wait a year before asking poor Wacey to take any definite step agitated me only in so far as I was unable to write back at once and tell you how completely I understood and sympathized with what you had promised him. You could have done nothing else. I beg you to give up once and for all the faintest doubt that I shall find the time too long to wait. I am well aware of the danger of challenging fortune by asserting too much about the future. I am as superstitious as an ancient Greek about that. Still, in spite of the fashionable surrender to uncontrollable impulses gathered in the cradle, fermented in childhood, bottled in adolescence, and kept in the cellar of the unconscious for the heady destruction of one's manhood, I retain an invincible belief in the freedom of the human will and in man's ability with the aid of what professing Christians call grace to direct it safely through the impulses. When I tell you I am not prepared either to love anybody else or not to continue loving you I have confidence in my strength of purpose. I find it incredible that some magical female can suddenly cross my path and lure me from it. I find it equally incredible that the love I have for you at this moment can be killed by absence and delay.

As I have told you more than once, it would be easy to cultivate the romantic fancy that I have really loved you from the first moment I saw you on board the 'Princess Sophia', and I expect by the time we meet again, not to part, I shall be disinclined to give up this fancy. At any rate it provides me now with the kind of meditation on which parted lovers nourish their loneliness.

I am not going to say anything about poor Wacey now. We owe piety (in the Latin sense) to his memory, and you are showing your piety by your attitude toward his mother and father. I shall try to show mine by never allowing myself to grudge him a moment of your youth.

As this is presumably to be the only letter you want me to write you before you sail on March 8th I must try to give you news and my plans. In the first place 'All Or Nothing' was produced last night at the Sheridan, and is apparently a tremendous success. Wonderful notices this morning. My profiteer patron Turner Rigden already sees himself controlling half the theatres in London. The little actress he fell for has turned out to be a real actress, and the dim little provincial moon has blazed into a metropolitan star of the second magnitude with every hope of blazing on into one of the first magnitude. No brains. Nothing but the mummer's instinct. These queer plastic creatures! My patron Turner Rigden, who won South-east Kensington at the General Election by defeating Louis Matheson, a sad disillusioned Liberal, not to mention a Labour fellow as well, touches the sublime in magnificent absurdity. I am going to enjoy watching the profiteer's progress during the booming years of peace and reconstruction. It has hardly begun yet. He has now bought another profiteer's palace in Surrey with the appropriate name of Wickets, which with the help of an extravagant architect he is spread-eagling. He is still hesitating between a grouse-moor and a deer-forest, but I expect a yacht by summer, and a racing-stud next winter. The technique of spending rapidly-made wealth has been a fine art in America for a long time, but our nouveaux riches are still in the school-boy stage. Yes, Turner Rigden is going to become my favourite toy. I must persuade him to visit Citrano some day. It will be the most practical return I can make for what the place has given to me.

Julius and Leonora Stern announce their arrival at the beginning of April, and I count on persuading them to come to Citrano and take the Allegra for a month or two. I should find it more than I could bear to have unsympathetic strangers there. Julius's elder brother Emil whom you have not met has married a Swedish girl, and they will be in London in a few days. I myself shall go to Citrano early in April at the latest and wait there until we decide what to do. At the back of my mind is a plan to come over to America myself at the end of August. There's a faint chance of a production on Broadway for 'All Or Nothing'. Then you and I could travel back together and be married in England?

The Peace Conference is not going to be quite the simple affair it sounded when Clemenceau announced at the opening last month that there was no question of territorial or continental peace, but that it was to be a peace of peoples. The trouble is in defining what a people is. Every nation in Central Europe during the long ascendancy of Austria has overflowed its boundaries. I see we've already had to send a mission to find out what Poland is. I don't feel too optimistic about your President's League of Nations. It's a grand phrase, but I wonder if it will ever be much more. Nor does it argue well for the future of the Peace Conference that already Hymans, the Belgian Foreign Minister, has had to protest that the whole work of the Conference is being carried on by the Great Powers, and to demand representation on all the committees for the smaller States. His protest was backed up by quite a few. I was amused by Clemenceau's reply that the Great Powers if they liked could have made the peace without reference to the smaller States! Such candour is refreshing. One can fancy the kind of humbugging evasiveness with which a British or American President of the Conference would have replied.

Now we hear that the Poles and the Czechoslovaks have started a minor war on their own account in Austrian Silesia, and it looks as if the Serbs and Roumanians will presently start another. I hear rumours of extreme Italian discontent already. Well, we shall see. Meanwhile, we have the problem of Ireland, which the ineffable Bonar Law declares to be an entirely domestic matter. Suppose Germany had won the war. Wouldn't Poland have been claimed as an entirely domestic matter? Edward Fitzgerald writes that the Sinn Féin Government is functioning and runs its own law-courts where the judges just have time to sentence the criminal before they're arrested by the British authorities and sentenced themselves!

Paris is swarming with delegates, sub-delegates, the delegates of sub-delegates, experts and sub-experts, each with an attendant staff. The rush for jobs was terrific. Several bureaucrats were crushed in a Whitehall lift in trying to achieve a particularly luscious secretaryship, and so many chauffeurs have been imported to Paris that the motor-traffic in London is perceptibly less. As for books of geography, not one is to be found. The Peace Conference has bought up the lot.

Rumour vows that Lloyd George has agreed that Venizelos shall have a large slice of Silesia and that Cilicia is to have a plebiscite whether it is to be German, Austrian, Bohemian, or Polish. Meanwhile, the people of Germany and Austria are still being blockaded, which is an odd way of showing our appreciation of the way they have renounced the 'isms' against which we were fighting for nearly five years and bowed down to the golden calf of pluto-democracy. I wonder whether the new world achieved by Versailles will justify the twenty-six million casualties that laid the foundations and the starving women and children of whom it is to be built. No doubt the Germans would have behaved far worse in victory, but that's not a sound argument. Moreover, I dread the effect on British opinion of too harsh a treatment of the Germans. It will cause a revulsion because there is a fundamental decency among the British which cannot be indefinitely repressed. That will mean we shall encourage the Germans to suppose we are their friends. Then they will start again, and when we have to be unpleasant 'Gott strafe England' will be heard once more. The trouble is that the Germans despise the French just as they despise women, and therefore whatever the French may do the German consoles himself by thinking that when the moment is propitious he can deal with the French. He does not feel sure of being able to deal with the British. The longer one ponders over the German problem the more remote the solution seems. Perhaps the French are right, and the only way is to extirpate them. Or else persuade the Canadians to remove en masse to Germany, and plant the Germans en masse in Canada. That would be such fun for your native land!

I wandered off into politics because I wanted to go on writing to you, but I felt I could not at this moment say more of the intimate personal things that I am longing to say. My next letter will be waiting for you in Atlanta. Presently the situation will be reversed, for you will be in America in surroundings I do not know, and I shall be in Citrano where you will be able to picture me. Athene, my Athene, how much, how much I love you!

John

Emil and his wife came to stay with Mrs Stern, and on the night after their arrival John went up to dine at Claremount Gardens. He was immensely curious to meet the woman who had surprised him and everybody that knew Emil by converting him to the state of matrimony. He had laughed about Emil's snow-queen, but when he saw Astrid he saw what might have been a snow-queen. She was as tall as Emil himself, that is to say about five feet eight inches, lithe and slim, with high cheekbones in an oval face. Her pale flaxen hair parted in the middle above a high forehead seemed against the orange damask curtains of Miriam's room almost white. Her complexion was very faintly flushed like a Christmas rose or a wintry cloud in the east reflecting coldly the sunset, and her eyes were blue as the ice deep down in the crevasse of a glacier. She was wearing a long, tightly fitting dress of dead white silk as remote from contemporary fashion as the wardrobe of a Hans Andersen princess.

John was aware as he shook hands with her that he was being weighed up. He had never missed Athene quite so acutely as in that moment, being caught up in a sharp desire to have her beside him, herself as lithe and slim as this snow-queen and all the roseburnt south in her cheeks. It was the first time he had recognized his own incompleteness without Athene.

"I have heard so very much about you from Emil," Astrid said in English that was as delicately flushed with the hint of a Scandinavian accent as her own cheeks.

"He was almost secretive about *you* in his letters," John answered with a smile. "Yet I pictured you without his help as like what you are. Didn't I, Miriam?"

"Why?" Emil enquired, in the tone of an interested archaeologist slightly impressed by a colleague's theory about a piece of pottery.

"I suppose a kind of divination," John replied.

"Oh, is that all? You had no reasons," said Emil, losing interest in what was evidently nothing more than an idle speculation.

"It's nearly twenty years since I first came to this house," John told Astrid. "And Emil was then very much like he is now except that he was dressed as a schoolboy. You've shaved off your moustache, I see," he went on, turning to his friend.

"One has to maintain a moustache in the Levant. It is kept as an earnest of one's virility as an Englishman keeps a sporting dog. In Stockholm I could dispense with it, much to my relief. And incidentally I have dispensed with the consular service."

"What are you going to do now?"

"I am starting as a publisher."

"Just like that?" John asked. "Doesn't publishing require any previous knowledge of its mysteries?"

"I shouldn't have thought so, to judge by the books that are published. But as a matter of fact I am going to work for a year with X——." He named a famous firm.

"And the capital?"

"Oh, I have arranged about that," Emil murmured distastefully. He evidently did not enjoy being reminded that capital still existed. "Astrid has worked with one of the chief Stockholm houses. She is now going to work for a year with Y——." He named another famous firm of London publishers.

"We shall be quite excited when we begin for ourselves, John," she told him. "You are not minding, please, that I call you John? But I think it is very foolish to pretend with calling people misters when you know that so soon you will be calling them not misters."

"How right you are, Astrid! And what a charming name your own is. What does it mean?"

She turned to her husband.

"Can you say impulse of love? Is that good in English?"

"Admirable," John assured her.

"It is perhaps more a Norwegian than a Swedish name," she told him.

"You have returned as usual, Emil, when I have a

play running which you would despise, but you certainly bring me luck," John said.

"You have now a play being acted?" Astrid asked. "Oh, we must go soon, Emil, to see it. I like the theatre so much. What is your play called?"

"*All Or Nothing.*"

"*All Or Nothing,*" she repeated gravely. "It is symbolical, I think. Is it not?"

"Of English theatrical taste," Emil put in.

"Pay no attention to Emil," his mother said. "I went on the first night, and it is most witty and amusing."

"It is a comedy?" Astrid asked, disappointment tightening her lips. "I like less comedies. They laugh too much, I think, in comedies."

"I'm afraid *All Or Nothing* is just meant for laughing," John warned her. "But I have another play which I believe even Emil would find serious enough. That is to be performed on Sunday week for one performance. You must come."

"That is not funny?"

"Not in the least. It's about a coward in the war."

"Oh, that sounds so splendid," Astrid declared. "Yes, indeed, we must go to see that. You find, of course, that all really intelligent people are afraid in war and for that reason war must be bad?"

The prospect of a gloomy evening in the theatre evidently enchanted her. In fact, as they went down to dinner, John heard her laugh for the first time. It was like the tinkling of ice.

After the meal was over and when they were on their way back to the drawing-room John called Astrid to come and look at what had once been Emil's little room, what indeed was still Emil's little room should he desire to occupy it again with his dreams.

"This is where he and I settled, or rather unsettled, the whole world when we were young. We used to sit in those two chairs on either side of the gas fire and talk and talk and talk. Look at that picture." He pointed to the painting over the mantelpiece by Emil's grandfather. "The four men in black cloaks are sitting with their heads close together at the same table, and reading the same document by candlelight, and the young woman coming toward them with a tray of food is still pausing to listen anxiously by the door, and the old woman at the back is still blowing up the fire with a pair of bellows."

"*Poland 1863*," she read from the legend on the frame.

"The year of the last insurrection against Russian tyranny. When we looked at that in 1900 how little I guessed that within twenty years Poland would have risen again. I was always very pro-Polish. And Emil whose grandfather had had to leave the country because he was a Jew used to scoff at Polish aspirations."

"As I still do," Emil insisted firmly. "The most reactionary people in Europe. And the most feckless and incompetent."

"Well, we shall see. I'm bound to say, though, Astrid, that Emil was more often right than I in the discussions we held in this little room. It was here he foretold the certainty of the European War when I was lamenting the deadly dullness of an epoch which considered our war in South Africa a major excitement."

"I'm sorry you retain this prejudice against Poland, Emil," John said, returning to the subject, when they sat over coffee upstairs.

"Now, John, that's really naughty of you," Miriam told him. "Just a direct challenge to argument."

"It must have been the atmosphere of the little room at the end of the passage downstairs. It sang like the Hebridean maid of battles long ago."

'If this wretched broth at Versailles now being stirred by a hundred mediocre cooks produces Poland as a titbit," said Emil, "it will only have produced another tit-bit for the dogs of war to snarl over in the future."

"But what colourful rhetoric, dear Emil," John laughed. "Now I begin to realize how much the Russian Revolution has gone to your head. You know, you quite shock me when you talk like that. It's the kind of way I might talk myself. I expect a graver style from you."

"John, you're being extremely naughty," Miriam interposed, but not quickly enough to stop Astrid from asking him, eyes glowing blue, if he did not think that the Russian Revolution was the most important manifestation of the spirit of man perhaps for five hundred years.

"Very important," John agreed. "But its importance may be to evil. Perhaps my despised Poles will stem Bolshevism from spreading westward as once they stemmed the advance of Islam, checked the Tartar, and blocked Luther."

"I do not intend to argue with you," Emil proclaimed with a lofty indifference. "If you really think that the nation of mediaeval survivals now being pieced together again by the jobbers of Versailles will be capable of deflecting Communism your mind is a novelette."

"Well, as I said just now, we shall see. But I won't argue with you, Emil, partly because I'm not in a position to put up a positive creed against yours, and that would handicap me too severely. But I'm waiting with a good deal of pleasurable excitement at taking the chair for an argument between you and your Catholic brother when he arrives next month."

"Your brother is a Catholic, Emil?" Astrid exclaimed. "You never told me that. How strange! Is he intelligent? But perhaps not, because it is so easy to be a great musician and have no intelligence at all."

"Play to us, Miriam," said John.

"Now that is malicious of you, John," Astrid scolded. "You have tried to make me say something—how do you say it?—derogatory to Mrs Stern. I think that is quite malicious of you, yes? Please to play indeed, Mrs Stern, but please not to think that I was criticizing the intelligence of musicians."

"But you were," contradicted, John. "However, you wait till you hear Julius versus Emil. They have not met since Julius became a Catholic five years ago, and Emil does not know what lies before him. And the beauty of it will be that if Emil's dialectical materialism—I believe that is the phrase—should outfence Julius's Thomist logic, Julius will pick up his violin and turn the argument into a fugue, an exquisite orderly fugue in which dialectical materialism will be so finely ravelled up and then so equally finely unravelled that when the music stops dialectical materialism will have dissolved into zero. So don't underrate the intelligence of Julius, Astrid."

"But still I find it incomprehensible that an intelligent man can be a Catholic," Astrid insisted. "You agree with me, Emil?"

"Oh, *I* agree with you. But John is attracted to Catholicism. It is an emotional refuge," Emil replied loftily. "Besides, he has had no chance yet to learn anything about what is happening in Russia. The ignorance in this country is prodigious, as it is everywhere in Europe. But I'm not going to dissipate the clouds from John's mind to-night. So I shall echo his request and ask my mother to play to us."

"What would Astrid like?" Miriam asked.

"I would like Mozart, please."

So even that lovely highbrow from the North must ask for Mozart. What was it in him that held this time of ours in thrall?

A few days after this first meeting with Astrid, John invited Miriam to dine with him at Bélanger's restaurant in Soho.

"Well, what do you think of your daughter-in-law?" he asked.

"I think she's an enchanting creature, John. I love such utter earnestness and distrust of laughter when it goes with brains and beauty. And you were very naughty to tease Emil like that the other night. Just to pay you back I'll tell you Astrid's comment on yourself when you had gone. 'I like him so much, Emil, your friend, and I find it astonishing that I can like so much anybody who is so easily amused by things which are quite not worth while at all.' So that's where you get put in your place."

John laughed.

"She turns Ibsen's Lady from the Sea into a district visitor. But I've been kicking myself ever since that I did not ask you to play Grieg. I should have enjoyed the struggle between Scandinavian self-determination and international highbrow disapproval of such eminently bourgeois music. Oh, I'm going to get very fond of the snow-queen. She and my profiteer patron Turner Rigden are the best discoveries of the new world rising from the ashes of the war. If a phoenix in a cage wouldn't set all Heaven in a rage I should like to put them both into cages for my own amusement. Yes, I think you're very lucky in your two daughters-in-law."

"Emil is happy. Didn't you feel that, John?"

"Yes, for he has been set on fire by ice, which must be a most gratifying achievement for one of his temperament."

"I'm glad you think that, John. I'm glad you don't think it's a purely intellectual companionship."

"Indeed, very much the contrary. She has descended upon him from the North as once upon a time the golden-haired Dorians on the Mediterranean; or if you prefer it, he has won her as once upon a time some dark-eyed Tyrian or Sidonian trading for Baltic amber carried off a young priestess of the northern Apollo, sacred apple-bough in hand. I do hope they'll produce offspring. The mixture is a fascinating one to contemplate. After all, Leonora is a quarter Jewish herself, but Astrid is pure and essential Nordic. Have they settled yet where they're going to live in London?"

"They've found a house in Brunswick Square. Not the whole house, of course! The top flat of a converted house."

"Ah, the north-eastern confines of Bloomsbury. Very appropriate," John observed. "I expect Emil will make a success of publishing. There should be an opening for new publishers in the post-war conditions."

"John, you really mustn't laugh at Emil."

She spoke with emotion, and he tried to reassure her.

"My dear, I'm not laughing at him. True, it's difficult not to feel a faint exultation in the spectacle of the invincible overcome at last. You've not heard as much as I have during the last twenty years of Emil's contemptuous anti-femininity. I joked about his snow-queen, but in my heart I expected to be presented with a flat-breasted dun-haired female in glasses. It never entered my head that he was going to fall in love with a priestess of the northern Apollo."

"Surely you wouldn't have expected Emil to choose an ugly woman?"

"Why not, if as I supposed from his letter announcing his engagement he was taking her from the mathematical philosopher much as he would have accepted from Hellner one of his own abstruse works? I could never have suspected his father-in-law would have begotten anything more human than an isosceles triangle. And as it never entered my head that Emil himself would fall in love with a woman I saw no reason to presuppose beauty."

"Thank God he had found a woman to love normally!" Miriam exclaimed fervidly. "You don't know what a relief it is to me, John."

"But I always assured you that you were fretting unnecessarily about Emil. He had complete mastery over his temperament. And now he gets his reward. But I am still faintly amazed. I wonder what psychoanalysis would have to say? I suspect it would be attributed to his fondness for strawberry ices when young. Do you remember how fond he always was of strawberry ices? Sublimate a passion for strawberry ices and you find an Astrid. I must tell Emil my theory."

"No, no, John. You must not laugh at him," she protested.

"But Emil would be delighted, Miriam. Don't you yet realize that psychoanalysis provides the same kind of narcotic drug for Marxist intellectuals as they accuse religion of providing for the bourgeois. A dialectical materialist will sit in the inglenook, listening entranced while another dialectical materialist establishes the fact that much of his emotional experience is founded upon a longing in his own unconscious to retire back into the womb from the warm and comfortable darkness of which he had been expelled into an as yet uncommunistic world. If I could once establish to Emil's satisfaction that Astrid's attraction for him was due to his youthful passion for strawberry ices he might become Case 14 E—— S—— in one of Freud's note-books. . . . No, but seriously I am just as glad as you are that Emil has fallen in love with his snow-queen, and I do believe that they may humanize one another sufficiently to produce between them a human being. So rejoice, Miriam, for you would not enjoy being the grandmother of a parallelepiped."

Miriam Stern shook her head.

"John, John, your vanity was just a little piqued by Astrid's grave disapproval of your writing comedies, and by her evident intention to convert you from flippancy to the things that really matter."

"Perhaps it was, perhaps it was," he smiled. "But it was not just to get back in all good-humour at Emil and

Astrid that I asked you to dine with me to-night, Miriam. It was to congratulate you on your own perspicacity."

She raised her eyebrows in a silent question.

"Yes . . . over Athene Langridge. You were right—I was in love with her."

"John, and you have . . ." She broke off.

"No, I've not started a clandestine intrigue," he replied. "Her husband died just about a fortnight ago, and we shall be married next autumn. You are the only person who knows this, and you will remain the only person until just before we are married."

"Tell me about it, John."

So he told her the story.

"I wish I had managed to get to know her better," Miriam exclaimed.

"I don't think it was possible then to know her better," John assured her.

"I knew you were inclined to be interested in Athene Langridge, but you overestimate the range of my perspicacity, John. I never dreamed for a moment of marriage. Oh, how glad I am that you will both be spared the ignominies of divorce. However discreetly divorce is managed it always seems to me ignominious that the disposal of people's private lives should be at the mercy of the law. Well, my dear, is there anybody living who can wish you happiness from so full a heart as mine?"

John put his hand across the red-shaded table in the little restaurant and took Miriam's hand.

"None," he murmured.

Suddenly he looked up into her face with an expression of surprised perplexity. He had realized abruptly that the hand he held was that of a woman who was beginning to age.

She divined his thought.

"Yes, I shall be sixty in another four years, John. And there's one secret I want you to share with me alone."

"It shall always remain a secret," he promised.

"You will keep nothing from your Athene thereby," Miriam continued. "She was a little girl of twelve on that night in Cracow. Call *me* vain now, if you will, but I should not like her to look at me curiously, and I should not like to fancy that she was wondering to herself how such a night could ever have happened."

"It shall always remain a secret even from Athene," he promised again.

"And you should be glad I have asked that of you, John, because it is a token that I recognize the security with which you know your mind and the certainty of your intention. That is a joy to me."

"It may please you to hear that it was the inspiration of your resolution in the dawn of that Cracow night which gave me the strength of purpose not to stay with Athene on that starry night last September. It was only as I grew older that I was able to appreciate your strength of purpose, though the fact that it could endure as an example through my life shows that even at the time I must have had some notion of what it meant."

"I never doubted that, John. Not many women could have done what I did and won thereby the most precious friendship of her life unless the other person had had exceptional imagination. Dear John, I am so glad you have found the woman at last. You are thirty-six, you know. You have waited quite a long time—longer even than my darling Emil."

"Ah, but less virginally than he. Let us drink to his happiness."

"And to yours, my dear," she added.

A cable came from Julius at the end of March to say that he and Leonora had had to postpone their departure until the third week of April, and would come to Citrano at the end of May and spend the rest of the summer there if John could find them a furnished villa. John had already made sure of the Allegra, by telling Fofo to secure it for him when it was given up by Mrs Langridge. He decided not to wait for the arrival of Julius, but to go out to Citrano immediately, and by a sudden attack on his stepmother he secured her consent to the company of David and Prudence for the whole of their Easter holidays.

"Well," Mrs Sayers declared heavily, when John was packing, "I never thought as I'd be sorry to see the last of anybody in these flats, but I'm bound to say I shall miss bringing you your egg of a morning, not to mention feeling a bit aggravated to think as that Fettering will get the extra two weeks' rent you've paid him up to the end of April for nothing. Elf and me was only talking about it last night, and Elf felt very strong on the business, for if there's anyone Elf can't stand in this blessed world it's that Fettering."

In the course of five months the intimacy between John and Mrs Sayers had progressed to the point of her referring to her husband now as Elf instead of Mr Sayers.

"I wouldn't worry about poor Mr Fettering if I were you, Mrs Sayers. You won't have him back here. He intends to go in for pig-breeding in Berkshire."

Mrs Sayers snorted contemptuously.

"Well, if he can't make a success of pigging he won't make a success of nothing. That's a shore thing. But there, the country's in a bad state through and through. That's a nice business I was reading about what they call this here Slough Dump."

"The Slough Dump is certainly a scandal," John agreed. "But what particularly annoyed you as a voter, Mrs Sayers?"

"Why, paying an old ruffian aged ninety-two four

pounds a week to tinker about with all them motors."

"I didn't see about that."

"It was in the papers this morning. Yes, an old man of ninety-two who'd been pensioned off by the Great Western Railway in the year of the Diamond Jubilee, droring four pounds a week to-day. It was all in Parliament. A lot of nasty feeling it created in Parliament too, and I'm not surprised."

"I'm afraid if you're going to follow the country's finances you'll have a lot of unpleasant reading presently, Mrs Sayers. Wars cost money."

"Well, the Germans'll have to pay. They've had their bit of fun. Let them pay for it, and which in my opinion Lloyd George will make 'em pay."

"I doubt if it's going to be easy as all that even for Mr Lloyd George."

Mrs Sayers sniffed.

"He won't get my vote next time he asks for it if he don't make these Germans pay. Yes, and what's more, send the Kayser down for life."

"So you did vote for the Coalition in December," John said, smiling.

"Smart, aren't you? Still as you're leaving I'll tell you now that's who my vote did go to, and all the other women I know in this districk too. Here, and there's something else I read in the papers which give me a bit of a shock. Do you believe it's right they've got a way of telephoning now by this wireless business? That's a nice look-out for the world. The wireless telegrams was bad enough, upsetting the weather all through the war, them and the guns. But wireless telephones! How's a fellow like that Fettering to have his telephone cut off if there aren't no wires to cut him off with? Proper confusion, that's what I call it. And just because beer's gone back a bit nearer to what it was, except in price of course, Elf thinks everything in the garden's lovely. But that's a man all over. Give him his beer and his bed and his Sunday paper, and he's perfeckly content to turn over and snore hisself to sleep thinking if he'd only picked the other horse he'd have had five shillings to come in from the hairdresser round the corner, instead of leaving his wife a shilling short in her weekly money. Dreamers, that's what men is, and Elf he can dream the hind leg off a donkey just like the rest of them."

"It hadn't struck me that Alfred was a dreamer," John said.

"Dream? I reckon Elf could have been one of these Big Four as they call theirselves at this peace barny they're having in Versailles. The way they're carrying on, the peace'll take as long as the war what led to it. Big Four! And that Lloyd George about as big as a wurzit. And Clemensoo, there's another no bigger than a stinging midget. Wilson, he *is* a bit bigger especially about the teeth, and which aren't none of them his own by my reckoning. And that other with a comical name. Orlando! I saw pore old Dan Leno once in a play called *Orlando Dando*. Still, joking apart, it's high time this Big Four got a move on, the way the unemployment and prices is going up. And these miners starting in to strike. Disgraceful, I call it. Yes, some people can afford to go on strike. Elf and me can't afford to go on strike. If Elf went on strike he'd have one of these tempory lieutenants hopping into his uniform almost before he'd undone the top button."

John parted from Mr and Mrs Sayers affectionately.

"And if you ever find yourself in another war," said the porter, wiping his moustache, "you take my advice and join up with the Royal Navy again. You'll be safer there than in the Army."

"As if Mr Ogilvie was going to take advice from you, Elf!" his wife scoffed.

"If you'd have took advice from me you wouldn't have

voted for this pestering Government," the porter retorted. "Then we might have had a bit of peace by now."

"You don't know how I voted, Elf," she challenged, arms upon her drooping hips.

"Oh yers I do, because I found out where you'd been practising with a cross in the Guide To Women Voters in my Sunday paper."

"Fancy that!" Mrs Sayers gasped. "And he never let on until now. There's a cunning Isaacs for you!"

The porter laughed hoarsely. The personal triumph of the male over the female in the presence of another male was gratifying. He even nodded to one of the female inhabitants of Queensberry Mansions who passed him on her way out into Charing Cross Road.

"Elf!" his wife snapped.

"She's been a tenant for over six months," the porter explained apologetically.

"That don't make a decent woman of her. Scented Uzzy! I suppose you'll be telling me she's an angel next—jest because she lives three flights up."

"Yes, you behave yourself, Alfred," John advised him.

"He knows better than not to," Mrs Sayers commented severely.

But her countenance relaxed into a curious grimace which she believed was a smile when John pressed something into her hand as he shook it in farewell. Indeed, she did something she had never yet done since she came to Queensberry Mansions. She tossed her apron over her arm like a debutante's train and came out on the pavement to wave the parting tenant farewell.

"They'll be taking me for one of Elf's fly-by-nights," she put her head into the taxi window to tell John. "Pleasant journey, and send us a picture postcard from Italy. I'd like to see what Italy looks like."

John found David and Prudence waiting for him at Victoria.

"Oh, thank goodness you haven't missed the train," Prudence cried.

"Missed the train? Why, there's half an hour yet."

"Oh, I know, but you might have missed it," she babbled. "And I'm so frightfully excited. John, do look at my passport. Don't I look frightful in the photograph? I don't really look quite like that, do I?"

"I say, don't screech," David rebuked her. "The whole station's turning round to stare at you."

"But, David, I *am* so frightfully excited. It's the first time I've ever been abroad. And it's the first time you've ever been abroad."

"All right, all right," her brother protested. "There's no need to inform the whole station. Nobody would suppose you were going to be sixteen in a minute."

"Oh, I *will* be grown-up, David. I will really. Do you think we shall be sick crossing the Channel?"

"Shut up, you ass," he growled, lighting a cigarette and expelling the smoke through his nose as nonchalantly as a King's Messenger of a hundred Continental journeys.

"How beautifully you smoke, David! Doesn't David smoke beautifully, John? He looks like one of those bulls you see in pictures of bull-fights."

David regarded his sister with compassionate scorn.

They were to spend two nights in Paris so that the novices of travel could see the Venus of Milo and the Winged Victory and Monna Lisa and eat *belons* and *marennes* oysters at Prunier's and drive along the Bois de Boulogne and ascend the Eiffel Tower and stare at the camp-followers of the Peace Conference swarming self-importantly about the courtly pleasaunce of Versailles.

"I do wish we could see one of the Big Four," Prudence sighed. "Oh, look, I believe that really *is* Clemenceau over there."

"You ass, it's a gardener," David told her crushingly.

They went to the theatre to see Gabrielle Derozier give a glorious performance in some classic French tragedy and the two young people were so much interested when they heard that this was the actress who had played the heroine in John's play *Annette*, that he sent round a note to ask if he might bring them behind after the fall of the curtain to present them to her in her dressing-room.

My dear, I shall be enchanted. Gabrielle, came the reply.

"Oh, John, really, I think I shall faint with excitement," Prudence gasped when she was told what was in store for her.

"You've got very excitable of late," David observed critically; but John noticed that David himself pinched his tie and ran a lordly Etonian hand across his hair.

"Why, John, this is the most delicious surprise," Gabrielle exclaimed, kissing him on both cheeks. "And you are looking so much better than when we met . . ." She hesitated for a moment.

"In the September of 1917," he reminded her.

"And this is your little brother and sister! She is like you, John, but with such blue eyes which you have not."

John made a grimace of despair at Prudence.

"Well, everybody says that, John," she assured him. "So I suppose I must put up with it. Oh, mademoiselle, I did enjoy the play. We read it at school last term, and now I wish we were going to read it again next term because it's all alive since I saw you to-night."

"*Ah-ha! C'était bien dit*," Gabrielle nodded to John, a sparkle in her big grey-green eyes. "She already makes a very pretty compliment. *Merci, mademoiselle*."

David was looking round the dressing-room and taking in the details. A worldly knowledge of a famous French actress's dressing-room would win Waterloo over again on the playing-fields of Eton, and as a freshman's tale at Balliol next autumn it should not be ineffective.

"But what a pity, John, that you have not let me know you were coming to Paris, because to-night I have to go out to supper. And you pass on to Italy to-morrow. *Mais écoute*, you do not go from the Gare de Lyon till eight. You will come to my five-o'clock."

So that exciting finale was arranged for two days in Paris already packed with excitement.

Gabrielle was still in the apartment overlooking the Parc Monceau, and Victorine with the merry eyes was still her maid.

"And I shall have Aristide again when the Conférence is finished," Gabrielle told John. "He will have no more generals to drive then. Oh, how beautiful to have peace! But I think nobody quite understands what we have suffered in France. Even I who am half English become *agacée* by this fear to make the Boches suffer also. I find it extremely strange. And here is M. Tracilowski who will tell you that in Poland they feel terribly because Mr Lloyd George is so *entêté* about Poland. *M. Ogilvie aime beaucoup votre pays, M. Tracilowski.* Come now, my dears, and I will give you some tea."

This was said to David and Prudence, and John was left with the good-looking young Pole.

"You have been to Poland, monsieur?" he asked in French.

"Yes, indeed, and I have been longing for Poland to be restored ever since I read at school of the Partitions."

The young Pole's eyes brightened. Most of the Englishmen he had met in Paris so far had the haziest notions about the history or geography of his native land.

"Then you will appreciate, monsieur, how impossible it will be for us to rebuild our country unless we are given back that part of what they call West Prussia which was robbed from us, and unless we have Danzig as a port. Mr Lloyd George cannot understand that the Germans who are now perhaps a majority in what they call West Prussia were placed there deliberately to drive out the Poles."

"Mr Lloyd George is in an awkward position," John observed. "He has to justify the partition of Ireland on the ground that the English and Scottish planters who were deliberately put there to drive out the Irish cannot now be compelled to be loyal Irish."

"Yes, I understand that Ireland has been very barbarously treated," Tracilowski said. "You are perhaps Irish?"

"No, I am Scottish, but that doesn't prevent my sympathizing with the Irish point of view."

"It is very bad what Mr Lloyd George has done against all the other delegates," Tracilowski went on. "Many perceive that it is necessary to have an absolute barrier between Germany and Russia because otherwise Germany will either become Bolshevik or will try to exploit Russia and perhaps make another war with the West. Perhaps one day England will be sorry for the decision that was taken against the recommendation of the allied Commission in Poland. It will be the same thing with France. You will see that France will be denied the Rhine country which should be hers for the future securing of Europe against Germany. This talk of destroying Prussian militarism is foolish. It was destroyed before by Napoléon and with England's help it grew again. Now England has helped to destroy it, but again with England's help it will grow again. And do not think that the Germans will be grateful. There is only one way to make a German grateful and that is to hit him hard on the head with a hammer, and then perhaps he may be grateful you did not hit him with an axe. Whatever the Germans lose at Versailles they will feel themselves wronged because they believe that they were intended to have the whole world, and since that is the case the sooner that idea is taken from them the better, because although they will continue to believe that they ought to have the whole world, they will find it less easy to conquer it."

John and the young Pole discussed the future of Central Europe until John found the future of Central Europe was so insoluble that he was reduced to saying '*vous avez raison*' to every racial theory adduced by Tracilowski, which did nothing towards finding a solution but was less tiring than the effort to disentangle Ruthenia, Slovakia, Lithuania and the Ukraine.

"There was a good deal to be said for the Austrian Empire, wasn't there?" he suggested at last.

"The Poles in Austria were better treated than the Poles in Prussia or Russia; but the Austrian Empire was rotten before the war, and Germany made the war to annex it."

"Yes, I suppose that was the fundamental cause."

"Because otherwise Germany was afraid Russia would annex it first. But, *pardon*, *monsieur*, the English delegates were so stupid and so content to take the German colonies that they will save Germany at the expense of Austria."

"They're all too tired, of course," John said. "And that is equally true of the other delegates except President Wilson, and he isn't tired enough."

"Enough of politics!" Gabrielle came across to declare. "One hears of nothing except politics in Paris to-day."

The young Pole bowed apologetically.

"I must talk a little bit with you, John," she said, leading him over to the window-seat which looked across the budding trees of the park. "And so you are going to Citrano. How well I remember Citrano! We had our great quarrel the night after we had lunch with your American friends there. In April also! *Et il y a déjà six ans.* Six years ago we had *our* April, John. It was the sweetest April I have passed. *Tu crois ça? C'est vrai, mon ami.* I would like excessively to pass now such another April. But not with you, *cher ami.* So do not look so frightened. One does not repeat the Aprils of time past. And you are still faithful to the memory of your Greek love, John. That was terrible for you. You were so thin and worn and ill when you came to see me that September. Have you not found another love?"

John felt embarrassed. She was so frank and friendly. It seemed unfair not to tell her about Athene. But it would not do to admit to Gabrielle that the quarrel on that sirocco-laden day six years ago had since been so completely justified from her point of view.

"As you see, I am not yet married, Gabrielle."

"I think it is time you are getting married, *mon ami.* You must not be too old when you have a daughter."

"Why a daughter necessarily? Why not a son?"

"Because you are such a ladies' man, my dear John. That is right, is it not? I speak so little English that I begin to forget the little turns."

"Evidently I shall have to think seriously about marriage," he said.

"*Moi aussi,* John. Perhaps I shall marry Camille Varenne after all. I am quite glad that he is not here this afternoon. He would be so jealous. *C'est ridicule, n'est-ce pas?* He was always so jealous of you, and when he could no longer make wittinesses about my lovers because he had made them all, he could only ask me to marry him and make an end of my lovers like his wittinesses."

"Witticisms, if you want to talk correct English," John told her.

"*Merci, mon ami.* How different time makes things! Once I could not bear you to correct my English. Now

I am grateful. Could one express better the change of *l'amour* into *l'amitié*?"

"Could anybody effect such a transformation more gracefully than yourself, dearest Gabrielle? And by the way, my new play is a big success. Will you act in another play of mine in London if I write you a good part?"

"You must be quick then, John, because Varenne would be so jealous."

"Let's both wait until we are married. And I'll give you a good part for a wedding present. Well, this has been a delicious meeting, and David and Prudence have been enthralled."

"Prudence? It is a dangerous name to give a girl with your mouth, John. *Alors*, *mon ami*, *au revoir*, and not for quite so long a time again, please."

On the way to the Gare de Lyon Prudence asked John if he had ever been in love with Gabrielle Derozier.

"I'll tell you when you're older," he promised.

"But when I'm sixteen I'll be practically grown-up," she insisted.

David jeered at his sister.

"It's all very fine for you to snort at me, David; but don't forget that a girl is always considered two years older than a boy of the same age. So from a phys . . . physi . . . from a natural history point of view I'm four months older than you are now, and you consider yourself quite grown-up."

But there was a fall in store for her pride. John and David shared a wagon-lit, and Prudence had to share one with a strange woman. Her luggage had been put into it, and she had sat with her brothers in their wagon-lit until the attendant came round to put up the beds. When John and David were waiting outside in the corridor for the transformation to be effected, they saw Prudence open the door of her wagon-lit, stand for a moment in the entrance, shut it again, and come hurrying back along the corridor, her mouth agape, her eyes staring.

"What's the matter? Have you seen a ghost in your wagon-lit?" John asked.

"No, but something much worse! John, *do* you know who's in there standing in the most frightful knickers like riding-breeches? Miss Bracebridge!"

"Who on earth is Miss Bracebridge?"

"Our head-mistress! The head-mistress of St. James's School!"

David let out such a wild peal of schoolboy laughter that the attendant making the beds bobbed out of the wagon-lit under the impression that some maniac was perpetrating a *crime passionnel* in his sleeping-car.

"John, don't stand there grinning like a clown," implored Prudence. "What am I to do? Oh, do ask the attendant to put me in another wagon-lit."

"I'm not going to spend the night with Miss Bracebridge. And I don't suppose David will either."

David, still convulsed by the spasm of mirth he was trying to damp down, could only shake his head feebly.

"Yes, but there may be another wagon-lit. Do ask the attendant, please John. And I'm sure Miss Bracebridge won't want me in with her."

The attendant was full of regrets, but there was not a single vacant berth in the car.

"It's the most frightful thing that has ever happened to me," Prudence lamented. "Do you think she's going all the way to Rome?"

"*Oui, mademoiselle, jusqu'à Rome*," the attendant put in.

"I was afraid she would be. She's supposed to be frightfully High Church," Prudence groaned, and then her eyes brightened. "Oh, but to-morrow I'll introduce her to you, John, and to you, David. Ha-ha! I shall score in the long run. What a sell!"

This time Prudence knocked at the door of the wagon-lit, and after listening for a moment entered primly.

"What happened?" her brothers demanded next morning when she came along to them.

"Well, when I went back and knocked there was no answer because she'd gone into the washing-place. I could hear her humming and splashing."

"What was she humming?" John asked.

"Oh, I don't know—Bach or Wagner or something. I'm not frightfully good at music. But do listen. The door of the washing-place opened and she stalked back into the wagon-lit, and what do you think she was doing?"

"Brushing her false teeth?" David suggested.

"No."

"Swinging her false plaits?" John tried.

"No. Give it up? She was smoking! And when she saw me she grabbed the cigarette out of her mouth and threw it behind her into the washing-place."

"I think that's rather pre-war behaviour," John commented.

"But, John, you don't understand. There was a most stupendous row at school last term because two girls were caught smoking in the shed where we dug up the big lawn to plant potatoes for war work, and Miss Bracebridge addressed the whole school and said few things had disgusted her so much in the course of her whole scholastic career as the thought that two Jacobeans . . ."

"You don't mean to say you female imitations of the genuine article have the nerve to call yourselves Jacobeans," John interjected. "That shocks me as an Old Jacobean much more than anything Miss Bracebridge did."

"Two Jacobeans," Prudence continued firmly, "should degrade the school's good name by surreptitious dissipation which would be intolerable in their own homes but which on the school premises was nothing short of revolting. And now I've caught her out smoking!"

"Did she try to excuse herself?" John asked.

"No, she just said, 'dear me, Prudence Ogilvie,' and I said 'yes, ma'am'."

"Do you call your mistresses 'ma'am'?" David asked indignantly. "I thought only Eton Dames were called 'ma'am'. And the Royal Family of course."

"We only call Miss Bracebridge 'ma'am'."

"Pretty good cheek anyway," David muttered.

"And when you'd said 'yes, ma'am', what did Miss Bracebridge say then?" John asked.

"She asked if I was going to Italy and I told her I was going to stay with you, John, and she said 'is that the playwright?' and I said 'yes' and she said she'd seen a very interesting play of yours about cowardice or something produced by the Sunday Play Society and I looked a bit blank because I didn't know you'd written a play about cowardice, but I asked if she would mind if I introduced you to her and she said 'by all means, Prudence'. She was really quite human. Only she snored rather, and I thought the hot-water pipes had gone wrong. Pouff! It was frightfully hot in the wagon-lit, and Miss Bracebridge shook eau-de-Cologne all over it."

"She was probably swigging brandy under the bedclothes and didn't want you to smell it," John suggested.

"No, no, John. Really I don't think she was. And you won't try to make me laugh when I introduce you, will you?"

"It doesn't take much to make *you* giggle," David observed austerely.

However, when the introduction was made in the dining-saloon at lunch Prudence was not tempted to disgrace herself, for Miss Bracebridge was extremely agreeable and at once fell in with John's proposal that she should sit at their table, where they discussed the drama together, as it seemed to David and Prudence, somewhat too earnestly. There was a memorable moment when the coffee arrived and John offered the head-mistress a cigarette, which she declined, without adding, however, that she did not smoke.

"I think she's charming," John told his sister afterwards.

"I told you she was quite human really."

"Very human," he commented, "considering that owing to the loathsome tactlessness of one of her pupils the unfortunate woman will have been deprived of tobacco for thirty-six hours by the time we reach Rome."

"I got the cigarette she was smoking," Prudence announced. "It was rather soggy, because it fell where she'd been splashing. And I think I'll present it to the school museum when I leave."

. . . Turin, with twenty minutes wait which gave one time to drink vermouth in its perfection. . . . Genoa, massed in coloured tiers above the sparkling Mediterranean. . . . The countless tunnels of the Riviera di Levante, with silver strands between. . . . Dusk, and the Leaning Tower of Pisa like a shaft of moonlight. . . . Dawn over the Campagna, and the broken aqueducts, and the flowers, and the blue Alban hills, and the long slow fascinating circuit of Rome's back-gardens, and at last the city herself in the golden light of an April morning. . . .

"You lucky pair," John exclaimed, "to stand upon the Esquiline so young. I had to wait until I was thirty."

He was thinking of his own farewell to Gabrielle in that April six years ago, when she drove northward in her light-green Panhard out of their liaison.

They spent two nights in Rome at the Grand Hotel, which was mottled with the toadstool profiteers of war, and two days of classic sight-seeing.

Then Naples, and the first view of Vesuvius looming to left of the train against a cloudless sky, and the drive round the Bay, and the oranges and lemons of Sorrento, and the climb up to the ridge spanning the two gulfs, and down into Citrano about five o'clock, and the thronged piazza, and Fofo's, and the Torre Saracena steeped in the amber of an April afternoon, and Margarita and Caterina beaming under the creamy Banksia roses already in blossom round the door.

"*Ben arrivato, signore! Ben arrivata, signorina! Ben arrivato, signorino!*"

"Oh, I do adore being called 'signorina', John," Prudence bubbled. "It gives me a shiver down the spine. I feel like Carmen."

"You'd feel more like Carmen if she called you 'señorita'."

"You are so crushing, John. But I'm too excited to be crushed. I'm really almost delirious, John."

After dinner the two of them were standing on the roof of the tower when the moon came rolling like a great gourd along the fretted outline of the church on the opposite horn of the small bay.

"It reminds me of when we saw the moon across the river that week-end I stayed with you just after my tenth birthday. Oh, I did so love that week-end," she murmured as she took his arm in an access of affection. "I used to think about it just before I went to sleep as the nicest thing I could think about. Do you remember we saw the funeral procession of the suffragette who was killed at the Derby, and you told me to remember it because in a few years I would hardly believe there had been a time when the cowardice of politicians made such a procession necessary."

"Did I say that?"

"Yes, because I was so impressed that I repeated over and over again to myself what you'd said. And you were right, John, because now women have the vote. Miss Bracebridge gave a dinner to celebrate it."

"Yes, I was a feminist six years ago, but since the last Election I'm beginning to think the majority of women will use the vote to support the Conservative Party, and that means disaster for the country."

"Why?"

"Chiefly because the Conservative will always prefer what *is* bad to what *may be* good."

"I'll have to remember that when I become a woman voter."

"You're still fourteen years away from that," he said.

"And then, do you remember, John, you took me to a matinée of *Mr Wu* and to the White City in the evening and to Westminster Abbey on Sunday morning?"

"My god, I wonder I wasn't dead by the afternoon."

"But we went to the Zoo in the afternoon, and then I sat up for late dinner, and after dinner we watched the moon coming up behind Lambeth Palace and listened to the people walking along the Embankment, and after I'd gone to bed you came up and read me fairy scenes from *A Midsummer-Night's Dream*. And now you've brought me to Italy. Oh, John, I do love you. It's so delicious to be your sister. And now won't you tell me if you were ever in love with Gabrielle Derozier? I think you must have been, weren't you?"

"A long time ago perhaps I was."

"I liked her awfully. I wish I had greyish-green eyes like that. Everybody almost has blue eyes. And, John, as we're on the subject of love may I ask you about the girl you were engaged to in Greece? Mother told me you were engaged and then she told me that she was drowned. How terrible for you!"

"Well, we won't talk about that."

"John, you aren't annoyed with me, are you? I'd do anything rather than annoy you. It's only that I can't help being fascinated by the idea of a woman being in love with you."

"Avoid such morbid fancies," John commanded. "And now where's David? We'll walk up to the Piazza and see if they're dancing the tarantella to-night."

There was no tarantella, but Fofo's was full of people, and Fofo himself had recovered his pre-war look of bland hospitality. He took John aside for a moment to say what a blow to Citrano the death of Wacey Langridge had been.

"It spoilta too much, *quella maledetta guerra*. *Povera signora*, and now she has gone to America. *Peccato, peccato! Gente molto per bene*. Very good peoples. And when come your friends to the Allegra?"

John had not yet had a definite date from Julius. "But I'm putting my young brother there while he's staying with me. Margarita has arranged his room."

"*Benone*."

Geoffrey Noel looked round the door of Fofo's at that moment and at the sight of John came dancing in to greet him.

"I've just been to fetch the post—m-m—and there's a letter from my wife to say she proposes to come to Citrano some time in May and asking me to arrange for rooms at the hotel. I feel quite *sottosopra* at the news."

"Have a drink," John suggested.

"Thanks, I will. I haven't seen her now for over eight years . . . yes . . . m-m-m . . . Who's that charming fair-haired boy at the table in the recess?"

"That's my brother David."

"Is it? I'm going to have a drink with you, aren't I? Really I think I'll have a whisky to steady my nerves."

But poor Noel had hardly had time to establish conversation with David when Ostápof came into Fofo's and rushed to their table with a bellow of jubilation.

"I thought you'd been swallowed up by the peace conference."

Ostápof's noisy laughter was too much for Noel on top

of the news about his wife's coming visit, and he returned to his *villino* after engaging David to meet him in the Piazza next morning.

"Provided you have no particular plans, Ogilvie? Are you going to start bathing to-morrow?"

"No, I'm not," said John decidedly.

David thought he should rather like to bathe, and Geoffrey Noel could not resist pre-dating his usual bathing season by at least a month in order to have the pleasure of calling for him at the Allegra.

And thus the fortnight which was all that ruthless school allowed to David and Prudence rushed by in bathes, walks and expeditions, the myrtles in flower and the yellow genista in full bloom.

"You will ask me to stay with you again, John, won't you?" Prudence called from the window of the railway carriage. "And you will try to persuade mother to let me leave school as soon as possible?"

When he got back to Citrano after seeing off his guests John wrote to Athene:

> *I am so glad you were able to be ten days with your own people before you had to devote yourself to the Langridges, though of course I understand the responsibility you feel. All the same I do hope that you will be at home as much as you can. It* is *a strain to have somebody one loves in a background which one cannot visualize and moving among people one has not even seen. You had not quite six months of that and now I shall have not quite six months of it.*
>
> *I have enjoyed having my brother and sister here. They had a grand time. On the way through Paris I took them to see Gabrielle Derozier, who was charming. She is thinking of getting married herself to the dramatist Camille Varenne, an old flame of hers, and she was most anxious for me to get married as soon as possible. It*

was all I could do not to tell her about you, but I could not face the triumph of feminine instinct.

David slept at the Allegra, and now I have just had a letter from Daniel Rayner the novelist, who wants to hear of rooms in Citrano, and I have offered him the Allegra until Julius and Leonora Stern arrive. I don't know if you've read any of Rayner's books. I don't know him at all well, but he's a fascinating study of the species genius and I hope he'll come. His wife is a genial bouncing Hanoverian. They had rather a rotten time during the war, due in part to Rayner's own intransigence. I do hope they'll come. Another expected arrival is Vanessa Noel, the thought of which makes Geoffrey hop about Citrano instead of tripping. Not even Francesco's demobilization and the breaking off of his engagement to "that girl" avail to tranquillize Geoffrey, who however had the gratification of squiring my young brother about Citrano. Everybody speaks to me with sorrow of poor Wacey. I think Fofo misses him more than anybody. He does feel his loss profoundly.

At the moment your nation as a nation is not popular, owing to Wilson's objection to Italian claims in Northern Dalmatia and the row about Fiume. As you know, a street was named after him here when he first arrived in Europe and the Italians had great hopes of his support against British and French unkindness to Italian claims. Alas, the Via President Wilson lasted a very short time. Last week the sign was taken down and the Via President Wilson is now the Via Vittorio Veneto. The Italians are too much disgusted with their own representatives at Versailles to accord them the honour of a street. The peace conference drags on and on, and I fear that in the end nobody will be pleased with the result. Compromise is really understood and appreciated only by the British. The Greeks have got Smyrna and Mileto, which gives me pleasure, but whether they'll be able to hold them is another matter.

'All Or Nothing' continues to play to big business, but the play I wrote when I first got back from the war, 'What It Was Really Like', did not tempt any manager to give it a production at a West End theatre after the Play Society gave it a Sunday evening. A revulsion has set in against anything to do with the war. It's not surprising. I hope it will last long enough to keep the world out of war while you and I live.

People here talk gloomily of a Red Revolution in the North of Italy. A medaglia d' oro (gold cross for valour) told me that officers cannot go out in uniform in some northern cities without being jeered at in the streets. A revolution in Italy would probably be an unpleasant and bloodthirsty business while it lasted. The financial condition of the country is appalling. A young American who had failed to get over with the A.E.F. turned up in Citrano last week from across the Atlantic and when I asked him how he was enjoying Europe he said he was enjoying it all right but it was so shabby!

Daniel Rayner's enquiry to which John alluded in his letter to Athene had come on a postcard from a private hotel in Bloomsbury:

You told me just before the war that we ought to come to Italy. Can you find rooms for Hildegarde and me in Citrano? D.R.

The Rayners arrived two days after David and Prudence left. Hildegarde looked exactly the same as she had looked in August 1914, even to the floppy dress of some light material which she was wearing then and apparently was still wearing now. She was not fuller blown nor less buxom. Her teeth were as dazzlingly white, her smile as wide and genial, her guttural talkativeness as rollicking. Rayner himself had grown a reddish beard and the pallor of his face had taken on a kind of tralucency during the weary years of the war.

But weary was not the epithet for Rayner's time during the war. It had been for him a period of continuous mental torment. Even before the war he had been to a large extent at odds with circumstance. In the first place he had sprung from the people, preserving the Midland accent of his upbringing among the ribbon-and-lace makers of Warwickshire and his education at a council school. Neither should have been a handicap at the University of Birmingham, but that English respect even for the synthetic gentility that is painfully manufactured by third-rate public-schools pretending to the authentic tradition of the historical factories of the English gentleman implanted in him early a resentment against the reminders, sometimes real but often imaginary, of his humble origin. The natural result was that conscious of his own genius he became aggressive and self-assertive. During his time as a student at Birmingham he had met the German wife of a prominent doctor in the city, and the two of them fell in love, brought together by their discomfort in and hatred of English provincial life: she a foreigner of good family married to the wrong man, he a clever young man with a scholarship being educated, as was believed by the smug bourgeois, above his station. They had eloped, and in due course had been married. Rayner's poems and novels published before the war had brought his genius immediate recognition from most of what mattered in contemporary opinion, and the onset of war revived all the worst horrors of existence for the outraged egotism of genius. To him the war presented itself as an outrageous intrusion and interference. His wife, herself in the galling position of a German woman among the enemies of her race, fed Rayner's bitterness. There were one or two silly pieces of self-assertiveness which brought them into trouble with local authority. Blinds were left up in lighted windows. The roof of a cottage they had been lent on the Welsh coast was painted with black and red cubes, which alarmed the coastguards and led to the Rayners being expelled from South Wales. On top of that the Home Office had prosecuted a novel of his for obscenity, committing thereby one of those insufferable acts of bureaucratic oppression of which the wretched dullards of that institution have too often been guilty.

John wished that Rayner had taken it into his head to come to Citrano in the autumn of 1917, when he could have fed his own mood of disillusionment. In his present eupeptic mood made up of relief at the end of the war, of exhilaration at the prospect of being united again to Athene by next autumn, and of the reassurance about his own ability to entertain the post-war world, he feared he might exasperate Rayner's discontent.

However, greatly to his pleasure, Hildegarde told him that Rayner had let her know on the very night of their arrival that in John he believed he had found somebody with whom he could feel perfect sympathy and who seemed likely to feel an equal sympathy with him.

"I have never known R-r-rayner so happy as he is now since the war," she proclaimed enthusiastically.

In spite of his own eupeptic outlook at the moment, John was not feeling any undue confidence in the ability of western man to extricate himself from the morass in which he was already struggling before the war, itself a desperate and convulsive effort to do so.

"But there's not going to be another war," Rayner declared one day as he and John were walking back to the Allegra down a walled alley. And then snatching John's stick from him he struck the wall. "*I* won't have another war," he proclaimed shrilly.

John was not sure whether Rayner was displaying incipient messianic megalomania or whether he was by a violent figure of speech identifying himself with the common secret resolve in the heart of the average man. He decided at the time to accept the latter explanation, and agreed that, however deep western man was plunged in the morass, a convulsive effort like war was certainly not the right method to free himself.

"To what do you attribute the sickness of western man, Rayner? I incline more and more to say it is the gradual abandonment of the practical teaching of the Christian faith, which incidentally is leading me toward an inevitable belief in Christ as the only complete expression of God. And I think this abandonment has been rapidly accelerated by the development of machinery."

"Wait a minute," said Rayner, "let's begin with the first. I don't accept the practical teaching of the Christian faith, because the Christian faith has failed to sustain its practical teaching. I've exhausted the Christian faith. I've tried it. I was even a local preacher when I was young. It's an impotent faith. It saps. Why should I accept as God a man whose teaching I know to be wrong, and whose magic I know to be either his own trickery or the trickery of his disciples?"

"In the first place I don't accept your statement that the teaching is wrong. As for your accusation of trickery, argument can never settle that, and, anyway, once convinced that Christ was the complete expression of God's love I should not be worrying my head about miracles. You say you were a local preacher. That leaves me unimpressed. As a local preacher you merely voiced your own interpretation of the already inadequate interpretation of whatever Little Bethel or Ebenezer you followed. You observed that the professing Christians in your neighbourhood were miserable examples of a creed's influence, and you turned against the creed itself. You are like the people who claim to have lost their faith in God because He allowed the war, which is to accept determinism as the motive force of the universe. But let's put aside the discussion of the Christian faith and take my second point. Is machinery to man's advantage?"

"I have no grudge against machinery if it's used as man's slave instead of his master."

"Don't you think that the comparatively swifter evolution of the machine may have outstripped man's capacity to evolve within the same lapse of time a mind adapted to deal with the transformation of values which machinery has effected?"

"Man went off the track long before machinery was developed," Rayner replied contemptuously. "Man went off the track when he started to think here," he tapped his forehead, "instead of here," he pointed to the generative centre. "I want to find people who think here," he declared passionately, and somewhat to the surprise of passing country-folk stood still in the middle of the alley with his long white index finger directed like a signpost toward the fly of his trousers. "And I'm going to find them," he declared, as they walked on. "I may find them in the South Pacific. I may find them in Mexico. They're not to be found any longer in Europe. I believe they vanished with the old religion of Etruria. I believe those damned Romans destroyed them in Europe."

"Aren't you restating in your own terms the Genesis story of the fall of man?" John suggested. "And anyway your solution won't touch the problem created by machinery. The subtlest phallological process won't help that."

"If men go back to thinking as I intend they shall think, that will settle machinery," Rayner insisted.

"Yes, if man could go back on his own development much would be settled, but I don't believe he can," John argued. "The invention of steam may have been a disaster. For that matter so may the invention of printing. . . ."

"For that matter then the plough may have been a disaster," Rayner broke in.

"The Golden Age," said John meditatively. "Darwin made such a conception sound absurd, but orthodox Darwinianism has been so badly shaken during the last twenty-five years that perhaps there *was* once a Golden Age when man was in perfect harmony with the natural order. That Golden Age is a constant feature of all religious folk-lore. It responds to some atavistic memory in all of us. It was your mention of the plough which set me off on that. What I fear is that the evolution of man may be directed now toward the achievement, on an infinitely vaster and more elaborate scale, of what has been achieved by bees and ants and termites. Individual man may be doomed, and this rapid acceleration of mechanical progress may be the sign of that doom. That is why I dread this default from Christianity. By strictly following the teaching of Christ individuals can exist without detriment to the existence of other individuals. Christianity is mocked at by lunatic egoists like Nietzsche as a religion of slaves, and certainly it throve among the oppressed classes. Yet without Christianity what would have emerged from the collapse of the Roman Empire? Isn't it because Christianity has become to a large extent a convenience for the privileged to maintain their privilege that you distrust it?"

"What do *you* know about privilege?" Rayner asked scornfully. "You can know nothing about privilege so long as you are a part of it. If you had had my beginnings you could begin to talk about privilege."

"Do you regret your beginnings?"

"That's a damned silly question. Nobody can regret what he is. All I'm telling you is to shut your mouth about privilege because unless you are one of the unprivileged you can't know a damned thing about it."

"Imagination . . ." John began.

"Imagination rubbish! The kind of imagination an old man has when he sticks a paper cap on his crown and thinks he's a child again. It doesn't take in real children, does it?"

"No, but . . ."

"No, but my eye! Nor will your imagination take you far with the unprivileged," Rayner snapped.

"All right, have it your own way, but in that case think what an advantage you have as a creative artist over somebody like myself dragging round with him the impedimenta of a public-school and university education. You question my imagination. I shall question yours if you can't appreciate that. I am denied, if you like, the ability to project myself into the point of view of the unprivileged. You are denied the ability to project yourself in the other direction. Who loses more? You or I? I do, every time."

"You have an easier life, though."

"Do you want an easier life? I doubt it. You rejoice, and rightly, in the washing of your own shirts. It is an expression of the independence you cherish. The war interfered to an intolerable extent with that independence, but the war is over. You gained a great deal more by not taking an active part than I did by doing so. But we've come down to talking about ourselves, which was not what I intended when I asked you for your diagnosis of the sickness of western man."

Day and night for nearly a month John and Rayner talked, and then early on a June morning Rayner came to the tower when John was still in bed and announced that he and Hildegarde were leaving Citrano that morning.

"I'm choked here," he announced. "These small bright people get on my nerves. It's like watching a butterfly on the inside of a greenhouse fluttering up and down with the glass between him and the sun."

A week later John received a postcard from Monte Cassino: *This place is rotten with the past.* A year later came a postcard from Rarotonga: *If you are thinking of coming here, don't. These soft brown people are disappointing.*

So, like an angry red star, Rayner sank below the horizon. Was he a prophet of woe? Had he, rising from the myriads who by the trend of the time were doomed to be the first victims of man's own ingenuity, been sent to warn them against the mechanical progress which would destroy them? Was he a portent, a phenomenon, or merely a freak? Were the circumstances of modern life exasperating to egomania the consciousness of his own vital personality? These maddened egos were becoming more and more frequent. It was Nietzsche all over again. Byron's jealousy had stopped short at Shakespeare. The jealousy of Rayner and Nietzsche extended to Jesus Christ. Perhaps Rayner could not be called mad yet, but he seemed moving toward madness. Yet in this muddled world might not what was held madness be the only true sanity?

Yet what salvation was offered to the spirit of man by Rayner's gospel? It could not even save his own soul from the terror of the road along which humanity was hurrying. To fling away sterile cerebration and substitute for it the fecundity and warmth of feeling? Back to the land . . . back to the noble savage . . . back to simplicity . . . nudism . . . negro sculpture . . . primitive rhythms . . . atonal music . . . a mess made of the Divine order, and a revolt from it to human disorder in a vain attempt to escape from the results of mechanization. . . .

The departure of the Rayners was a blow to Geoffrey Noel, who had been using the presence of Rayner in Citrano as a last desperate bait to help his wife make up her mind. It seemed she was a fervid admirer of his work. Four times Mrs Noel had telegraphed that she was arriving in Naples, and four times had her husband made the journey to meet her only to find on returning to Citrano after meeting a series of trains that she had postponed her departure.

"Utter thoughtlessness—m-m-m—just utter thoughtlessness," he spluttered to John when for the fourth time his wife had failed to materialize. "In many ways I should like to be rich, but if being rich means sheer wanton consistent lack of consideration for other people—m-m-m—I really think I prefer to remain as I am, though I wish as she's not coming herself that Vanessa would send my allowance. I suppose she thought she would give it to me herself. She'd enjoy doing that," he added bitterly. "But what's the use of that if she never arrives?"

And Mrs Noel never did arrive that summer. She remained a legend of immense misspent wealth.

"I could have spared myself the worry over her disappointment in not meeting Rayner," said her husband when Vanessa's final decision to go to Biarritz instead of Citrano had been communicated to him. "I really won't wear myself out like this again." He blew savagely through his pipe to expel an obstinate bit of wet tobacco. "If she wants to come to Citrano she must make her own arrangements. Fortunately she did have the grace to send some of the back money that was owing to me, but all my relief at getting that was done away with by the news Francesco broke to me this morning."

"What was that?" John asked sympathetically.

"Why, that hussy he was keeping company with before he was demobilized has had a baby and the silly boy insists on marrying her. Well, there's nothing else for it.

They'll both have to live with me. Luckily I have my room at the back and shan't hear the infant squalling. But what a summer I shall have! The war years seem quite peaceful, looking back to them now."

And that, thought John, was one of the false Arcadias of the future. All over Europe the birth-pangs of the new world which statesmen had been promising as the reward for victory would become so difficult that within a short while people would be looking back with a regretful sigh to the financial irresponsibility of war-time in which so many of them, however humbly, had shared.

"Do you remember, Noel, how when war broke out everybody said it could not last more than six months because none of the nations could find the money?" John asked.

"Very well."

"Nevertheless, at Versailles it is proposed to exact an indemnity of eleven thousand million pounds from Germany. How can that conceivably be paid? The money to carry on the war was nearly all imaginary money created on paper by credit, and presumably we in Great Britain at any rate—the Irish may be luckier if they hold out—we in Great Britain shall be paying in interest on imaginary money more than the sum total of our pre-war budgets. I suppose, as we've won the war, we shall be able to do it, but how can Germany conceivably pay? If they pay in goods they will destroy the trade of the rest of Europe; if they pay in transport they will ruin the shipping; and they cannot pay in money because the money is imaginary. Now if credit can be created to arm the world for war, why cannot credit be created to arm the world for peace?"

"Really, I don't know, Ogilvie. I'm no economist. I know I find credit very difficult to maintain let alone to create."

"Did you read Brockdorff-Rantzau's reply to the delivery of the volume of peace terms handed to the

German plenipotentiaries?" John asked.

"I don't think I did," Noel replied somewhat irritably. "For the last fortnight I've been run off my feet between here and Naples."

John took out his pocket-book and read from a cutting of *The Times*:

"Gentlemen, we are deeply impressed with the sublime task which has brought us hither to give a durable peace to the world. We are under no illusions as to the extent of our defeat and the degree of our want of power. We know that the power of the German armies is broken. We know the power of the hatred which we encounter here, and we have heard the passionate demand that the victors shall make us pay as the vanquished and shall punish those who are worthy of being punished. It is demanded of us that we shall confess ourselves to be the only ones guilty of the war. Such a confession in my mouth would be a lie. We are far from declining any responsibility for this great world war having come to pass and for its having been made in the way in which it was made. The attitude of the former German Government at the Hague Conference, its activities and omissions in the tragic twelve days of July, 1914, certainly contributed to the disaster, but we energetically deny that Germany and its people, who were convinced that they were waging a war of defence, were alone guilty. Nobody will contend the disaster originated only in the calamitous moment when the heir to the throne of Austria-Hungary fell a victim to the hands of assassins. Imperialism had developed in all European countries during the previous fifty years, and this had reached its climax in the Great War. The Russian mobilization unfortunately took the dispute out of the hands of the statesmen and gave it into those of the soldiers.

"The world is now resounding with the crimes which Germany is said to have committed. A wrong was done to Belgium and that ought to be repaired. But the German crimes were not the only crimes. We in Germany cannot forget what has happened since the Armistice. It has taken the Allies six months to lay down the conditions of peace. Crimes committed in war may not be excusable, but at all events they are committed in the heat of the struggle. The hundreds and thousands of non-combatants who have perished since November 11 by reason of the blockade were killed with cold deliberation, after our adversaries had conquered and victory had been assured to them. Think of that when you speak of guilt and punishment. The measure of guilt of all those who have taken part can only be assessed after an impartial inquest by a neutral commission, before which all the principal persons in the tragedy are allowed to speak and to which all the archives are open. We have demanded such an inquest, and we repeat this demand again at this Conference, where we stand facing our adversaries alone and without any allies. Yet we have the protection of the principles which were accepted before the armistice by all the Associated Powers. Those principles, laid down by President Wilson, were binding upon both parties to the war; we realize that, and we are prepared to play our part, and in particular to right the wrong done to Belgium. We are prepared to assist in the reconstruction of the devastated part of France. We think, however, that it would be unjust and cruel to have this work carried out by enslaved German prisoners.

"The remedy for all these evils must be found in the League of Nations, which should be thrown open to all the nations who are really ready to assist in preserving the peace of the world. A peace which cannot be defended as just before the whole world will in the end cause resistance to the terms imposed. Nobody will be capable of subscribing to it with a good conscience, for it will not be possible of fulfilment. Nobody will be able to take upon himself the guarantee of its execution which ought to lie in its signature. We shall examine the document handed to us with good-will, and in the hope that the final result of our interviews may be subscribed to by all of us."

"Didn't he read his speech sitting down?" Noel asked when John had finished.

"Probably because the unhappy man was so much shaken by the position in which he found himself as the spokesman for a vanquished and humiliated people. I don't believe for a moment that he intended a braggart discourtesy. But I wish that public comment had paid more attention to what he said than to the attitude of body in which he said it. Noel, you know your Thucydides. Doesn't that speech strike a chill of foreboding in you like one of the speeches made before the Peloponnesian war?"

"I don't think we can trust the Germans," Noel demurred. "If they had won we should have had very short shrift."

"Oh, I'm not pretending the problem of their future is not overwhelmingly difficult to solve," John admitted. "Still, that speech fills me with foreboding for the future of Europe. However, I suppose we can feel fairly secure of escaping any war of revenge in our time, provided always that the debts to which we shall all be bondslaves do not drive Europe mad again. But that speech haunts me, and all you bothered to remember about it, Noel, was that it was delivered sitting down. Well, there are two courses of action for our men of state. Either we must see that the terms laid down are kept to the letter or we must revise the treaty in a year's time. I suppose we shall do neither."

Julius and Leonora reached Citrano in the middle of June.

"And you've not brought Sebastian," John reproached them.

"Why, no, John, we left him in Vermont with his nurse in the house of an adorable friend of ours, Marian Carpenter, who's sheltering him till we reach home again. Momma was a little peeved we didn't leave him with her, but we thought the Vermont air would be so good for him. He's the cunningest . . . but I'm not allowed to rave about him," she broke off, with a glance at Julius.

"No, my god, you're not," he said firmly.

"Ferocious fellow, isn't he?" John laughed. "I didn't think your eyebrows could grow any bushier, Julius, but they're hedges now!"

Julius had thickened considerably during the five years since 1914, and looked older than Emil now.

Leonora had hardly changed. The *petite*, fair, exquisitely dressed Leonora of five years ago was here again.

"John, it's just heavenly to be back here, and to see you once more," she trilled softly, as she slipped her arm in his. He divined that life with Julius, and motherhood, had taken the metal out of her voice, or rather had replaced the aluminium by silver. "It's perfect to have this delightful villa," she went on, "but I'm sad about the poor Langridges. I'm sure you miss them terribly."

John knew that he was not going to find it easy to keep from confiding in Leonora about Athene. The sound of that American voice on this terrace was too disturbing.

They dined that night in the Torre Saracena.

"This is pretty good, I'll say," Julius declared in a satisfied tone when they sat up on the roof after dinner face to face with the earthy summer moon.

"John, it's too adorable," Leonora echoed. "Julius and I used to talk about you such a lot away over in California and wonder when we'd be together again. And now here we are, and peace will soon be signed, and the poor old world can start floating along as comfortably as that fat yellow moon."

"Julius, I'm not going to let you off," John warned him. "There were two things I used to promise myself when the externals of existence were most foul—one was to sit in my room and listen to your mother playing the piano and the other was to sit up here in the moon's eye and listen to you playing the violin. So do your stuff, my lad. You can't refuse me what you did for the Red Cross."

"I didn't bring my fiddle," Julius objected.

"I know you didn't, but I did," John replied.

He noticed Leonora's quick glance, half apprehensive, it might be fancied, of how Julius would take such a liberty.

"The war hasn't cured you of impudence," Julius guffawed. And Leonora echoed his laughter gratefully. "I believe that's taught me more than anything what friends you two are," she said. "Julius hates anybody to touch his violin."

"He learned to put up with me about the same time as I learned to put up with him," John laughed.

When Julius went downstairs to fetch his violin, Leonora told John that never in the last five years had she known Julius so glad at the prospect of anything as this visit to Citrano.

"Of course, it was here that he was received into the Church. That has something to do with it. But he's so devoted to you, John, and—perhaps I oughtn't to say this—I think you're linked up rather specially with the time he first met me. And they've been such wonderful years for me, and you were always so sweet and encouraging when I used to fret whether I was the right woman for Julius to have married. I wish you'd come and stay with us in America. Julius wants to start his orchestra again next winter."

"I might accompany you on the voyage home."

"John, but how ravishing that would be! And then you'll see Sebastian."

Julius came back at this moment.

"Where did you get that Bechstein?" he asked.

And when John told him he said that it was very like a Bechstein he had given to Sister Franzeska who had stood godmother at his baptism.

"It's probably the very instrument," John said. "The Grey Sisters were all interned when Italy declared war on Germany, and their stuff was sequestrated. We'll ask Fofo to-morrow where he got the piano."

"Interning nursing sisters!" Julius growled. "That's the kind of thing that makes one despair of human sanity."

"I'm afraid the poor souls had a bad time," John said. "The superior was a Prussian."

"That was Sister Franzeska. She was my godmother. I must ask the *parroco* about it."

"He's just been made a bishop. His diocese is somewhere in Campania."

"I shall pay him a visit," Julius announced.

Then he took out his violin and played one after another of Brahms's Hungarian Dances.

John wrote to Athene:

> *Julius and Leonora Stern arrived a week ago and have succeeded the Rayners at the Allegra. Dearest, dearest, an American voice on that terrace!*
>
> *The three of us went with Geoffrey Noel and stayed for a couple of nights in that tumbledown old palazzo on the beach of Cantone where we were staying when we heard the news of the Archduke's assassination that June. It was the same weather as five years ago, and the fisherfolk in the palazzo seemed quite unchanged, and if some of their children had grown up there were others looking just like the children we saw that day five years ago. Then when we all sat after supper on the dark sand of the marina a young moon was setting behind Monte San Costanzo. This time after supper an old moon was rising over the olive-covered slopes east of Nerano. But that was all the change except that you and Wacey were not with us.*
>
> *We went for a picnic to the Punta and I tried to find another terra-cotta head of Minerva, but this time I was unsuccessful. And the following is true. If I look back now on the expedition we made in June 1914 and the one from which we returned yesterday the June days of five years ago are more vivid than those of this week. It would be a lover's privilege to claim that this was because his love was not there this week, but I'll have to*

be honest and find another reason in the blunting of one's impressions by the continuous hammering of them during the years of the war. I suppose it is the exhaustion of war which has made the peace so unworthy of the effort put forth and the suffering endured to attain it.

Julius and Leonora are returning to America from Southampton at the end of August. I am going to take Leonora into my confidence. Apart from the practical advantages of such a course in the way of meeting you I simply cannot resist telling her. I am going to suggest that she invites you to stay with them in New York. Then if I come out we can meet there and we can either get married in America or come back together and get married over here. Or would you prefer to come over here and I'll be waiting at Plymouth with a special licence from the Archbishop of Canterbury? I say Plymouth because I hope to secure a little house down in Cornwall where we might spend the winter if you liked it. I've set my heart anyway on going to Cornwall as soon as we are married, and you will guess why. Then in the spring after a little time in London we can come out to Citrano, or possibly we might go up to Scotland. But you *must settle whether to cross to America or not. I know you don't want to hurt the feelings of the Langridges, and for that reason you may not want to be married in America. I'm sorry to put on to you the decision about these movements, but you are better able than I to judge what is the kindest way for other people. And then there is Arthur. You may prefer to bring Arthur back with you alone. All this is full of 'ifs'. But three months of the six months since mid-March have gone by and we have to be practical now. That is another reason for confiding in Leonora. You will be able to discuss everything with her, and a cable will bring me across or bid me wait for you in England. For goodness' sake don't change your mind at the last minute.*

You were very emphatic on the subject of my freedom to say I'd thought better of marrying you. I'll be less proud and stoical and declare right away that if you do change your mind I shall be in despair. Do not expose me to what poor Geoffrey Noel has been enduring since half-way through May from an American wife who cannot make up her mind where she intends to spend the summer. And now to crown his woes Francesco is to marry 'that girl'! She has anticipated matters by producing the infant already, which at any rate will spare Noel the nervous strain of an accouchement in his villino for this year.

Citrano has emptied agreeably for the nonce, and our deep summer peace is already upon us, but I hear from Fofo that the Neapolitans will arrive from July onwards thrice as numerous as last year. A large new hotel is being built, and the cisterns have already been excavated. The sinister figures of business men who have done well out of the war haunt the piazza, bent on developing Citrano as a 'balnear' resort. I've a feeling we shall not spend many more summers or winters here. Bodisko and Olensky have turned up for a fortnight, and when Bodisko asked me if I had ever contemplated selling the Torre Saracena I felt the chill hand of impermanency upon my shoulder.

Any more Citrano news? Mrs Heighington is more prepotente than ever. Noel calls her the Peace Offensive which I think is good. The Bufalò has let the Villa Bufalò to one of the disgruntled Italian peace delegates. Your President grows more unpopular daily. He is supposed to have told Orlando on the strength of his three-day visit to Italy last December that he knows better what the Italian people feel about Fiume and Northern Dalmatia than Orlando! Am I right in thinking that the Italian vote in the U.S.A. is not considered as important as some other nationals by political leaders wallowing in the democracy for which they have secured a safe conduct to eternity?

John told Leonora about Athene when Julius went off to pay a visit to the late parish-priest of Citrano in his episcopal see. They were sitting on the terrace of the Villa Allegra under the thatch of genista boughs.

"Do you remember, Leonora, when we sat together over our morning coffee on the terrace of the Sirene and you told me to my boundless astonishment that Julius had gone to church?"

"I certainly do, John. That was the morning you decided Julius hadn't made a mistake in marrying me."

"I think a thatch of genista must encourage confidences, Leonora, for I must tell you now that I am going to marry Athene Langridge."

"John!"

"That announcement has caused *you* boundless astonishment, eh?"

"I wasn't exactly expecting it," she admitted.

"The only other person who knows my intention is Miriam."

"Well, I guess I'd sooner share a secret with her than with any woman. Athene Langridge! You know, John, it isn't so astonishing when I think about it. I didn't get to know her well. She wasn't very easy to know. But I believe if anybody were to have asked what was the kind of woman whom you'd have chosen to marry I might have picked on Athene Langridge. How strange that you and Julius should both marry American women!"

"Julius was quicker to discover his own mind than I was, though perhaps if Athene hadn't been married already I might have discovered my own mind more quickly."

Leonora looked at him.

"But, John, you must have discovered you did love her while she was still married."

"I did."

He told her briefly what had happened.

"I guess you must have known in your heart a long long time before that party at Ostápov's. You couldn't have gone off like that, prepared to go through with a divorce on the strength of a sudden impulse. And poor Wacey Langridge died! Well, I guess it was better like that for him and for everybody. You were facing up to a pretty difficult proposition, John. Athene couldn't have hoped to hide from him for long that she aimed to marry somebody else. I know the kind of man Wacey Langridge was. You thought I was hard when you first met me in the fall of 1912. Perhaps I was until the man I wanted happened along. I had half a dozen Wacey Langridges among my beaux, and there was one of them I nearly married just because he thought I was so hard. It's the kind of fool thing a girl of nineteen will do."

"Wacey was an awfully nice fellow."

"Don't I know it? That's the root of the trouble. The man I nearly married was just as nice as he could be. And it just wore me out saying 'no' to him. But once I had married him would he have let me go? I might have done anything, but he wouldn't have let me go. And if another man had complicated the future he would have clung closer than ever. No, John, either Athene and you would have had to run for it or you might have whistled for a divorce till you were both too tired to whistle any more, and that would have been the end of the story. It's a kinda tough thing to say, John, but if you and Athene counted on being happy together it's better the way Fortune has stepped in to help you. But, John, don't let's talk of the past, let's talk about the future. I'm so glad for you. There isn't anybody I'd sooner see happily married than you. You were terribly sweet to me, John."

He put before Leonora the problems of behaviour that had to be solved in the autumn.

"But you said you were coming back to America with us. And I'd had the notion to persuade Miriam to make the crossing too. And we could have had a wonderful winter."

"We'll come later, next year. I know Athene won't want to be much with people. She's so terrifically sensitive, and she'll be fretting about Wacey's people. I want you to discuss everything with Athene, but the more I think of it the more I think it would be better if I waited for Athene in England; only, mind I don't want you to persuade her into this. If you think she'd rather I came to America and married her there, you've only to send me a cable and I shall take the next ship. I'm going to leave it all to you, Leonora dear, confident that whatever you advise will be the best advice. But do persuade Miriam to go back with you. I think that's a grand idea. I do want you to know each other really well."

"I love her, John, but she still frightens me quite a lot. I can write to her and she sends me the loveliest letters. But when I see her I seem to have nothing sensible to say. I think she'll like Astrid better than me."

"Nonsense," John affirmed.

"She's fonder of Emil than of Julius," Leonora insisted.

"All the more reason for being fonder of you than of Astrid," John said. "But it won't be quite fair to poor Miriam to let her affection be watched and measured by two observant daughters-in-law. You can't expect a mother not to feel something for her first son that she cannot give to anybody else in the world. Besides, now that Julius has grown up into a stocky Hercules after being expected to die at any moment for two alarming years in his childhood, he rather frightens her. There was a time, dearest Leonora, when you were a little frightened of him yourself."

"John, I was perfectly terrified of him. What I went through the first year of our marriage! And even after Sebastian arrived I still used to worry whether I mightn't be interfering with his music. I still worry sometimes. Well, pretty often, if it comes to that. But I console myself by thinking that if he did find me a burden he'll just walk out of my young life without hesitation."

"I think he would. However, I shouldn't worry if I were you. I see no shadow of a sign of anything like that happening. I'd call you two perfectly matched for life."

"John, you are such a very very comforting person," she declared fondly. "You heard I became a Catholic? Honestly, I was afraid to do that for ever so long because I thought Julius might resent it as an intrusion on his private life. That's the frightening part of artists—the way they just retire into themselves and lock the door. I tell you, John, for months I looked at a Catholic church as if it was Bluebeard's forbidden room."

"But you're happy now that you have become a Catholic?" John asked.

"Why, surely. Think what a difference it makes to one's background. One belongs everywhere. You never thought of becoming a Catholic, John?"

"Oh, I've thought about it a lot, but the compelling moment has not yet arrived."

"It means so much to Julius. He seldom speaks about it, but . . . well, see the way he's taken himself off to visit the old priest who gave him instruction."

"And won't his lordship be glad to see him? Did Julius ever tell you about his house in Poland and the village priest who played the violin and the schoolmaster who played the piano?"

"Oh, yes, John, it's like a cunning fairy-story. He was lamenting on the voyage across that we had never been able to visit Poland owing to the war, but now we shall be able to come over every year, and next year I want to bring Sebastian. You'll have a stepson of eight?"

"Eight, yes."

"And Sebastian's only four. But, John, perhaps you'll have a son of your own, and a daughter," she trilled on that silver note. "You must have a daughter, and then one day perhaps Sebastian will marry her. Wouldn't that be too adorable for our old age? You and I would be grandfather and grandmother to the same children. Why, I think that would be the cutest thing to be. And oh, John, I've just realized something."

"What?"

"That you and Athene must have talked about your future on this very terrace," she murmured.

"We did, and sitting in the very chairs in which you and I are sitting now. And, as I said to her in my last letter, 'an American voice on that terrace!' "

"Did you, John dear. Why, I'm glad you said that. Did it give you just a tiny pang for somebody's voice you were missing?"

"It did."

"And then you took me into the secret. John, I'm so proud. Say, isn't it about cocktail-time?"

She jumped up to search for Assunta, who had been taken on as maid. In the entrance to the sitting-room she turned.

"Oh, help! what's the Italian for glasses and gin and all the rest of it?"

"I don't think you need worry. Just ring the bell. Assunta will guess what you want at about half-past six of a June evening."

She came back on the terrace and smiled at him affectionately.

"It *has* been a lovely afternoon, John, and you just

don't know quite how proud I am that you took me into your secret."

"And you don't know quite how glad I am that I did. So, now having tossed those bouquets at one another, let us drink to the years ahead."

The next day Julius returned from his visit to the Bishop.

"Well?" John asked.

"Wonderful! A small town on a hill at the foot of a mountain. Burnt out by the sun now, and in winter I should think icy. The old man was glad to see me. He gathered me up from my genuflexion and kissed me on both cheeks. The whole place stark. His own residence sizable, but furnished with the bare minimum. A table and chair or two of bleached chestnut wood. The only thing on the walls a crucifix and a picture of the Sacred Heart of Mary. When the South is ascetic how much more ascetic it is than the North! Stark, stark. Ravaged, by the sun. You know the smell of stale sunlight. Faintly acrid as if the goodness had been burnt out of everything. The town itself so empty in the sunlight. The very dogs had vanished. And the old man chattering away as he took me across to see the Duomo and blessing non-existent creatures of his flock automatically every other sentence. The flock were panting somewhere in the shade. If there *was* any shade anywhere. The heat crackled in one's ears. And then the dusty coolness inside the Duomo. The wax-faced images dressed up in dusty eighteenth-century brocades. The tawdry artificial flowers. The bloodstained Christs and weeping Madonnas. The crude little oblongs and squares of coloured glass round some of the windows. Superficially the whole building an insult to beauty and an outrage on piety. Yet as I walked round with the old man the life of the place began to grip me. It was a true sanctuary from the destruction and cruelty of the enemy sun. We northerners who regard the sun as a mild and beneficent deity forget his hatefulness to a hill town in the province of Benevento. He has scorched them for generation after generation. Frizzled their livers. Charred their kidneys. Drained the juices and exudations of their mummified bodies. The enemy! The demon that lurks in the glare of noon. And when his power declines, icy blasts succeed him so that the people long for the tyrant to return and torment them. You must have suffered that tyranny before you can understand why the peasant of southern Italy finds comfort and assurance from his tawdry churches. The rich blood upon their Christs, the luscious tears upon the cheeks of their Madonnas are as fountains to the fancy of the parched minds which pore upon them. Humility, John, humility! We must seek humility. How dare we criticize the tawdriness of a Neapolitan church when we have not festered in a Neapolitan slum? Ah, the assurance of eternal life in that Duomo! God in the tabernacle on the altar never revealed Himself so clearly to me. That small town on the hilltop at the foot of Mount Taburno. Sun-smitten, sun-seared, sun-exhausted. A picked bone, a dry snail-shell in the sand. That small town burnt out by the sun, cut by the winter's blasts, rocked from time to time by earthquakes. And nowhere have I received so positive a pledge of immortality. Samnites, Romans, Goths, Byzantines, Normans, Austrians, Spaniards have held that hillside in turn. Sun and ice, wind and dust, drought and plague and fever and earthquake. A place not fit for a lizard without a tail, and it's there I receive so tremendous a reassurance of eternal life."

Julius had clearly passed through one of those spiritual convulsions the experience of which John himself would have welcomed with such eagerness.

"We both had intimations of immortality when we were young," he reminded his friend. "I in that church in

Cracow, you at Fontainebleau sitting under an oak-tree. But it has been a unique experience in my life. For you it has been repeated. You are fortunate, Julius."

"Yes, except for the shattering effect such experiences have upon one's work," the other answered. "The insignificance of one's own creative efforts becomes too pitiably evident. I feel after what I learnt on that visit to the Bishop that unless I can convey in one of my musical compositions what was then conveyed to me it is idle to continue writing music."

"In surrendering to that despair, aren't you assuming that music is capable of expressing more than it is able to express? What I mean is," John went on hastily as he saw the bushy straight eyebrows meeting in a frown, "that even if you conveyed to the satisfaction of yourself the spiritual experience you have just undergone it would be no guarantee that you had conveyed it to anybody else. If I could set down an experience in words which satisfied me that they conveyed what I was trying to convey I should expect that at any rate a percentage of my readers would share it with me. If every reader failed I should have to assume that the failure was due to myself. *You* needn't assume that. The greatness of a Beethoven can be accepted without any of his listeners feeling the least security that they have understood a note of what he wrote, if by understanding music it is intended to suggest the possibility of the composer translating his own feelings to the listener. And surely the failure to satisfy yourself is a general phenomenon of creative work. The deeper the sense of gloom after achievement, the more probable the value of the achievement, because achievement demands fatigue and even exhaustion, and exhaustion begets despair. And anyway, who in words or music or paint or clay has ever uttered the unutterable or communicated the incommunicable? Even St Paul made a very poor show at telling what happened to him on the road to Damascus.

And if you read Willie James's *Varieties of Religious Experience* unless you have had a religious experience approximating to what is therein related I don't believe you would be any the wiser. As a matter of fact you complained to me in Cracow, being then fifteen, that you had been unable to convey in your playing the experience you had had under the oak-tree in Fontainebleau. You had been changed, you argued, but the critics and the public still treated you as a child virtuoso."

"Ah, well, in the end all discussion of the processes of creative art is sterile," Julius declared. "The wind bloweth where it listeth. And that's really the end of the matter."

"The effort you made giving those concerts for the American Red Cross may have tired you more than you thought," John suggested.

"I'm not worrying about my future," Julius said. "Besides, I shall have my orchestra going by next winter. Some orchestra, John! By the way, I found a letter from my mother when I got back from my ecclesiastical jaunt. She's decided to accompany Emil and Astrid when they visit us at the end of July."

"She'd better stay with me in the tower," John suggested.

He was thinking about the likelihood of the daughters-in-law measuring Miriam's affection for them.

At the end of July John received a letter from Athene:

I've thought and thought, and thought about everything, John, my dearest, and I've come to the decision that I would rather travel across to you than have you come here either at the end of August or the beginning of September. You say that the production of 'All Or

Nothing' on Broadway has fallen through, so that there is no obvious reason why you should be in New York. However, that wouldn't matter if there was no need for an atmosphere of pretence, but unless I profess surprise at your being in America and all the rest of it it will be clear to everybody that you have come over to see me. If on top of that I go back to Europe with you everybody will be sure of it. I don't want our life together to start in an atmosphere of pretence, even though it would be pretence for the sake of other people's feelings. In the end I decided to tell my mother just what had happened. I don't know why I didn't tell her right away as soon as I reached home. I suppose I'll have to be honest with myself and admit I did not tell her because I feared you might change your mind about wanting to marry me. Forgive such lack of faith, my beloved. I won't try to excuse myself.

My mother strongly urged me to cross over to England in the fall, meet you wherever you say, get married quietly, and leave her to break the news to both families over here. She also urged me to leave Arthur over here for a year. She agreed he would have to spend half the time with the old Langridges, but promised it should not be longer. I know that this is good advice, and indeed I shall be extremely glad to think of him with my father, who no doubt will spoil him but not in the kind of way that old Mrs Langridge will spoil him. I can't tell you what a weight is off my mind now that I have decided what to do. It rests now with you, darling, to say when I'm to present myself before you all ready to be married! Only, don't forget to give me time to get some clothes and book my passage. If you cabled me a date when you get this letter I could manage to sail from New York before the end of September. I'll cross in a ship that calls at Plymouth. I've told you already how I adore the thought of the little house in Cornwall. But oh, John,

John, I adore the thought of everything so much. If the Sterns make New York by the middle of September, you know how wonderful for me it would be to be seen off by people who knew why I was crossing the ocean. I'm glad you told Leonora about us and that she was sympathetic. I never got to know her well that summer before the war, but then I never got to know anybody well—not even you, my heart.

To this letter John cabled:

Plymouth earliest possible middle September I shall be thirty-seven in October

Two or three days after Athene's letter reached Citrano Emil and Astrid arrived with Miriam, who as John had suggested stayed with him at the Torre Saracena. He intended to do his best to persuade her to go back to America with Julius and Leonora, but he was doubtful of being successful.

John could have wished that Emil and Astrid had come to Citrano before it filled up with Neapolitans, who were noisier than ever this August and, as Fofo had prophesied, three times as numerous. It was difficult to know why they bothered to leave Naples at all, for there was nothing they could do at Citrano which could not be done much more easily at home. However, fashion had decreed a *villeggiatura* at Citrano, and there they were. Fortunately down by the Allegra and as far as the Torre Saracena there was comparative peace.

"I wonder what pleasure people get from making so much noise," Emil speculated.

"They are very primitive, I find," Astrid judged severely.

Emil was in a state of exasperation with the way that, after what he called the poisoned loving-cup of Versailles had been drunk, the dregs of it were now being scattered over Russia.

"One could have some respect for these various expeditions supposed to be supporting the Counter-Revolution if they were animated by any genuine desire in the rest of Europe to undo the work of the Revolution. But there is no such desire among the body of the peoples. And you will see presently that the British Government with an eye on the electorate will back out and leave the counter-revolutionaries in the cart."

"I wonder why you assume so easily that the other peoples of Europe are in sympathy with the Russian experiment?" Julius asked his brother somewhat aggressively. "Obviously an upheaval like that is bound to have repercussions all over the world, but so far as there is any extended sympathy for it such sympathy arises from lack of understanding what the principles of Bolshevism imply for the future of humanity."

"Your point of view is doubly distorted," Emil replied. "In the first place you have become a Roman Catholic. In the second place you have spent your life feeding on the patronage of the 'haves', and your instinct for self-preservation dictates your economic opinions."

"I find that true," Astrid commented.

John felt that Leonora was about to leap in to the support of Julius, and he laid a restraining hand upon her arm.

"Let Julius fight them both," he murmured. "He's well able to look after himself. You sit back and listen, my child, like me."

They were all up in John's library at the top of the tower. Julius and Miriam had been playing two violin sonatas which he was considering for his repertory. One was John Ireland's *A minor* which had had its first performance in 1917, the other was Gabriel Fauré's *E minor* which had just been published.

"Oh, the Fauré is incomparably better music," Julius had declared. "The other is a facile response to the emotion of the moment. But this Fauré is good. Astonishing vitality for the composition of a man of seventy-two. The finale is uninspired hack-work, but . . . oh, yes, I shall put this Fauré sonata into my repertory. I dislike the feeble spirit of wandering about and mooning that infects contemporary chamber-music. How it reflects the formlessness and dithering uncertainty of the time!"

It was then that a party of shrieking Neapolitans had passed along the sands within earshot of the Torre Saracena. It was then that Emil had speculated what pleasure it gave people to make so much noise, and perhaps impatient even of the music being played by his mother and brother had tossed his challenge to anti-Bolshevism.

"Ah, my point of view is doubly distorted, is it?" Julius asked, putting back the violin into its case. "Well, let me have a look through your clearer glasses. Through them you can pierce the blood-red cloud that enfolds Russia and perceive the Promised Land. All right, Moses, tell us all about it."

Julius had flung himself down in an armchair, a hint of truculence in his tone. His mother had left the piano and gone to sit by the window open to the starry west. The young moon had already set, and Venus was sinking into the sea like a spent firework.

"I have been nearer to the Revolution than you," Emil reminded his brother.

"That may not be an advantage," Julius retorted.

"Except that I have met some of the men who made it," Emil answered.

"So have I. So has John. Ostápov's villa was lousy with them before the war. Jews most of them, fired by that joy in destruction which you know is the radical passion of our race. It's the way we have preserved ourselves as a landless people through the centuries. Why do you suppose God was incarnate in a Jew? Because He designed the only perfect revolution, a revolution which involved the destruction of the result of man's free will, and sacrificed Himself to achieve His revolution. He chose the Jews as His people because He required for His purpose a people in whom wickedness and folly and rebellion against that purpose were most capable of development by reason of their excess of vitality over other races. The example of human perfection was to be demonstrated against the best example available of human imperfection. The Jews rejected Him and they remain to-day in the world the most conspicuous example of the results of that rejection. Yet Christianity requires them, and not until they become Christians can the complete expression of God's sacrifice become plain to all."

"You are not arguing as a renegade Jew with an orthodox Jew," Emil coldly reminded his brother. "I do not accept the fairy-tale of our origin. I do not believe in the existence of this muddle-headed old gentleman who made such a mess of his creation that he had to begin all over again by demonstrating in his own person the way he meant his ill-conceived and ill-executed creation to work."

"Then there is no first cause?" Julius asked. "Life is a causeless accident, eh? But I'm not going to be deflected from Russia. What I want to know is whether you defend Bolshevism because it is good for Russia and you do not recognize the right of other countries to interfere with the progress of what some particular country believes to be good for itself, or whether you look forward to the Bolshevization of all mankind."

"To both. But it imports odium into the argument to talk about the Bolshevization of all mankind. I prefer to use 'Communism'. A Bolshevik is merely the Russian word for the member of a majority party, and it is a trick of the opponents of communism to suggest that the extension of communism involves class-warfare on the scale of the class-warfare during the Russian Revolution."

"You deprecate that?" Julius pressed.

"I deprecate violence certainly," his brother admitted. "But the violence of Bolshevism was the result of the counter-revolutionary movement. It was the counter-revolutionaries encouraged by hostile elements outside Russia who were responsible for the violence."

"I see. But at what stage in a revolution does non-resistance become a moral law?"

"When I said I deprecated violence," Emil elaborated, "I did not intend to suggest I was not prepared to use it in the achievement of what I believed was right, true, expedient and just, and owing to the strength of the bourgeois a communist revolution without some violence is not imaginable in any country. But I really don't know why I argue about this. If as I believe communism is right, true, expedient and just, the deaths of millions who either actively oppose it or even passively resist it seem to me to lack importance."

"Do you mind if we take your epithets in turn?" Julius asked. "You maintain first that communism is right, and by using 'true' as a second epithet I assume you mean by that morally right. What is your standard of morality? You deny the existence of God. At what stage then in the evolution of Homo Sapiens do you grant him the concept of morality? Before you answer that question I will allow you to withdraw the epithet 'right' if you wish and include it in your final epithet 'just'. I do not want to score a mere debating point in this struggle between dialectical materialism and dialectical non-materialism."

"Very generous of you," Emil said. "But my logic is not in need of charity. I assert that during the struggle for existence Homo Sapiens has learnt to recognise a moral law by the aid of which he has averted the destruction of his species."

"But 'expedient' was another of your epithets. Aren't you now including 'right' in 'expedient'?"

"I do not think so, Julius. I do not agree with that," Astrid put in. "We must admit—oh, how do you say it in English?" She spoke rapidly in German to her husband. . . .

"Subjective idealism," he translated.

"So communism may be ideally right, but it may not be expedient at a certain stage in human development," Astrid continued.

"I'm afraid I think subjective idealism so much windy Germanic megalomania," said Julius. "The late war was the result of subjective idealism overriding objective morality. The Germans are the most subjective idealists in Europe. It's a disordered ego. The Devil was a subjective idealist. Luther was a subjective idealist. His justification by faith alone is a perfect example of Germanic idealism."

"Don't the English accept that doctrine?" John put in.

"They did," Julius replied. "But as I see them, they have been slowly moving back toward Catholic doctrine ever since they were jockeyed out of it. The Englishman's word of honour is the recognition of a moral command to which he submits his egotism. A German cannot conceive honour in the Englishman's sense. To the Germans the sinking of their fleet in Scapa Flow appeared an action of the highest honour. To the English it appeared a dirty trick inspired by vainglory. However, we mustn't turn aside. I see that I shall have to leave Emil his first epithet, or we shall spend the rest of the night trying to find a solid foothold among the cloudy wastes of subjective idealism. All right, Emil, you believe, by some mental process along which I cannot follow you, in a moral law evolved parthenogenetically by Homo Sapiens to preserve himself; and communism, you maintain, is enjoined by this moral law. Very well, I'll leave you your little superstitious sentimentality. Now then. You say that communism is true. Are you using the epithet as I might use it for doctrine? Or are you using it in the sense of natural?"

But Emil noticed his brother's trap.

"I am using it as the answer to the empiricism of Homo Sapiens. Communism adopted universally will show the falseness of previous economic experiments."

"And the application of it is now expedient because the growing confusion of a capitalistic society demands the remedy?" Julius asked.

Emil assented.

"I suppose your fourth epithet 'just' is an answer in advance to the criticism that the sudden application of communism must entail immense injustice."

"Less injustice to the bourgeois by its application than the withholding of it entails upon the workers," Emil replied.

"Well, I'll have to surrender to you over the economics," Julius said. "I admit that the world is in an economic mess and that unless a solution can be found for it we are likely to spend the greater part of this century in war. I suppose it's the development of machinery which has allowed capital to exploit labour beyond the limit of further toleration. And if communism were restricted to economic revolution I'm not sure I should be prepared to oppose it—as another experiment. But what I object to in Bolshevik communism is its doctrinaire atheism. The solemn abolition of God by a pack of uneducated, uncivilized, undeveloped manual workers and peasants at the bidding of seedy demagogues would be comic if it were not for the tragic persecution which attended the abolition. The Russian Orthodox Church may have been a rotten mass of superstition and venality, but the worst of it was good beside the bestiality of what was unleashed against it."

"If religion has suffered material damage in Russia," Emil argued, "religion has its own materialism to thank for it. Religion has been a narcotic in the hands of the people's enemies. Class-warfare had to recognize that. If a powerful organization is supporting a lie, sentiment cannot be allowed to interfere with counter-measures. Organized religion has encouraged the poverty, the slavery, the semi-starvation of the workers, lulling their discontent in this world by the promise of plenty in the Kingdom of Heaven. Those who do not believe in such a Utopia have the right to resent its being used as a bribe, and to take steps to provide that it shall no longer be used as a bribe. I have been tormented ever since I possessed the power of reflection by the thought that in a world richer than it ever has been, millions are condemned by the circumstance of their birth to pass through it in misery. Mechanical progress which should already have released millions from the slavery of the economic struggle has only enslaved the workers more severely. You have found happiness, Julius, in pursuing what I believe to be a delusion of the mind. I find happiness in pursuing what I know to be an attainable standard of economic security for all mankind. Let organized religion cease from encouraging those who desire to place obstacles in the path of economic progress and no form of organized religion will be interfered with. Marx has demonstrated conclusively that every aspect of human society reflects the economic conditions of its epoch. A world-wide revolution with communism as the economic basis of the future cannot produce a worse society than we know, and we believe that it will produce a much better one."

"It's this credulity about man," Julius expostulated. "You believe, I suppose, that he is perfectible? You certainly don't believe in original sin. In the end we come back to Genesis. As I tell you I'm not enough of an economist to argue with you about the ability of communism to solve the economic confusion, but this I do know, that whatever economic system he adopts, man himself will smash it sooner or later by his own character."

"You don't accept progress?"

"In certain directions, but always, as I see it, at the expense of something else. A man may have his leg amputated more comfortably to-day than a century ago but his nervous system has deteriorated meanwhile. Progress, as I see it, is a continuous attempt by man to ameliorate conditions created by his own greed and jealousy, and if by a new economic order you succeed in eradicating one lot of ills brought about by greed and jealousy, his greed and jealousy will produce another."

"If your religion results in pessimism like that, I do not understand how you can find happiness in it."

"Because I'm incredulous about the ability of Homo Sapiens to behave himself. I'm not incredulous about God's purpose. If life in this world were the beginning and the end of Homo Sapiens I might ally myself with you, Emil, and try to make the best of a bad job caused by a causeless accident; but I believe this life is a prelude and therefore I do not think it is to be judged solely by the standard of its material comfort in this temporary world. Go on, achieve your communist society by all means, but if in the process your communist society gains the whole world and loses its soul I shall not congratulate you on the achievement."

"But a soul, what is a soul?" Astrid broke in to ask in bewilderment at the notion of anybody's using such old-fashioned terminology. "It is just a poetical expression for the effect of a body. But it is not a scientific term. It is a—a phrase."

"I don't agree with you at all, Astrid," Leonora burst out, unable to keep silent any longer. "I have a soul and

I have a body, and my soul lives in my body."

Astrid shrugged her shoulders, and John was on the point of intervening with a remark that would draw the fire of both sides on himself, when through the windows floated the sound of a musical instrument being played presumably by some serenader at the edge of the sea.

"Somebody's soul has escaped from his body," John exclaimed. "What a god-forsaken noise! It's like a child left alone in the bath by its nurse, and crying because it has swallowed the soap. What on earth is it?"

"A tenor saxophone," Julius said.

John asked if that was a newly invented instrument.

"About eighty years old," Julius replied. "They use them a lot in French military bands. But where the saxophone has come into its own is for blues."

"Blues?" John echoed.

"It's a melancholy kind of chant the darkies have, and the dance bands over in America are beginning to use 'blues' as a contrast to jazz."

"Jazz?" John echoed again. "Oh yes, I remember now. They were talking about it in London this spring."

"It's a kind of more elaborate ragtime," Julius explained. "Queer thing, along the Mississippi the word used to mean sexual intercourse before it was used for a dance rhythm."

"Really?" John laughed. "What a pity I didn't know that when Rayner was here. I'd have recommended a pilgrimage there to find out a race of people he is searching for."

"I guess that must be an American boy playing," Leonora said.

It was decided to go and invite the minstrel in for a drink. John and Julius found him sitting on a rock tootling his complaint to the star-sheened sea. As Leonora had guessed, he was an American youth. Homer Bilderbeck was his name. He was about eighteen, loosely-knit, with fair fluffy curls, a Byronic collar, and a middle-west burr. He was accompanying an aunt on a tour of Europe, and they had had words that evening.

"She was sore because she lost a burg called Assisi somewhere between Milan and Florence or between Florence and Rome. Somewhere she lost it, and she blamed me. She was writing up her diary this evening and that's how she got wise to losing this burg. She suddenly called to me that the route mapped out marked two hours at Assisi on August 2nd. 'I can't remember anything at all about Assisi,' she hollered to me. 'Can you, Homer?' So I said I couldn't remember what we'd seen and what we hadn't seen by now. I said one burg in Italy looked pretty much like the next one. And that got her goat. She said I couldn't have arranged it right with the hotel porter in Perugia. She said she had her suspicions of that hotel porter in Perugia as soon as she saw him. 'And you just let him fool you out of Assisi, Homer,' she said to me. And she kept nagging at me all evening until I came down here on the beach."

"And are you enjoying your trip to Europe?" Leonora asked.

"Why, I wouldn't say I'm enjoying it exactly," Homer replied. "But it hasn't been so bad as I thought it might be."

"But you'll be glad to be home again?"

"I sure will," Homer declared, with a heartfelt sigh.

"Let's have a tune," Julius suggested.

The young man smiled and picking up his saxophone tootled his longing to be back in the heart of a continent.

"If you folks want to dance?" he suggested when the melancholy strain was finished.

"Come on, Leonora, we'll dance on the roof," John proposed. "Come on, Mr Bilderbeck."

"I'm not a great dancer, Astrid," Julius growled. "But shall we try?"

"Yes, I like very much to dance," she said. "You will not dance, Emil?" she asked him.

"No, no, no. But you dance. Don't mind about me," he replied, turning to talk to his mother.

John told Leonora how deliciously she danced.

"And so does Astrid," she said, indicating the slim figure in white and silver that slipped through the starshine on the tower's roof.

"We should shock Homer if we asked him to play so old-fashioned a waltz as *Gold and Silver*," John said. "But it would be an appropriate melody for the pair of you."

"You don't think Julius and Emil are angry with one another?" she asked anxiously.

"Not a bit."

"They said some pretty fierce things once or twice. . . . You know, I do like Astrid, John."

"So do I."

"I like her very very much," Leonora repeated firmly.

John laughed.

"But she *could* annoy you, eh?"

"Oh, John, she could make me so darned mad . . . but I guess that's because she's so much cleverer than I am. But I was at Vassar, John. I'm not such a moron as all that. Why, I even learned Greek."

Presently John and Julius changed partners. Leonora had been right. Astrid did dance deliciously. She was supple as a Damascus blade.

"I'm glad you can be frivolous sometimes," he told her.

"I do not find it frivolous to dance," she replied gravely.

"Well, as you take dancing so seriously I think you ought to teach Emil to dance."

"Quite impossible. He could dance very well if he would, but he will never choose to dance. He is so concentrated now on his work. We will open our bookshop in February. We have so charming a shop in New Oxford Street. It will be very very attractive. I think we will have many progressives coming there. It was so strange to hear Julius arguing with Emil to-night. For me it was like listening to somebody talking in a nineteenth-century book. To play so beautifully, so very very beautifully and to talk so foolishly. It is quite strange."

"I gather you were not impressed by Julius's arguments."

"It was like talking in sleep. You found that, I think?" she asked.

"To be candid, I was more inclined to agree with Julius than with Emil."

"Ah, but you like to write old-fashioned plays. It is good for you that you can keep these old ideas because you can speak to your audience which would not understand otherwise. But I liked very much your play about the war. It is a pity you do not always write plays to teach the world a little."

"I came back from the war with a certain amount of ambition in that direction, Astrid, but I'm afraid I'm lazy mentally."

"That is very bad. You must fight against that," she said seriously.

"I feel like dancing through the next ten years," he told her.

"You will dance for ten years?" she exclaimed in horror.

"Not all the time," he laughed.

"Indeed no, I hope you will not. For me to dance is a great pleasure, but I could not dance all the time."

"I've a notion people will dance more and more," John said. "I think the world has been so shaken about by this war that dancing will be the expression of the general restlessness. All through the war dancing has been growing more and more popular. Do you like this instrument?"

"It is modern in its feeling, I think, yes? For me that is always a pleasure."

And John would look back to this night of dancing to Homer's saxophone on the roof of his mediaeval watch-tower beside this classic shore as symbolical, for good or for ill, of American influence over the life of post-war Europe.

"You didn't much care for the saxophone," he said to Miriam, when the others had left the Torre Saracena.

"Rather a nasty slithery noise, I thought."

"Oh, it's a despicable noise," he agreed. "But I think it voices the spirit of man at this moment."

She made a wry face.

"We're in for an era of self-pity, I fancy," John speculated. "The majority of people are in the mood of futility I was in during the autumn of 1917. Action has left them tired out, and they're beginning to realize how little there is to show for such an expense of effort. Young people have become prematurely old, and middle-aged people, spared the rivalry of so much youth, have remained irritatingly young. Those who have managed to acquire a positive faith, whether it be in God or man, are inclined to be so impatient of this indecision and futility that they try to impose their definite outlook on others. Hence the Irish resistance to England. Hence militant communism. Hence even in our exhausted Italy these terrific threats by D'Annunzio of violent action over Fiume. Hence these blue-shirted *nazionalisti*, and I hear now of a new movement in the north by groups of ex-service men banded together in clubs to resist the arrogance of the factory-workers. *Fascismo* the association is called. And if things are bad in Western Europe, what can we say of the misery and horrors of Central and Eastern Europe?"

"And you think that rather disagreeable instrument

expresses the spirit of man at this moment?" Miriam asked. "If it does, then it seems to indicate a feeble collapse of European civilization. I don't think Julius and Leonora will persuade me to cross the Atlantic."

"I don't believe you ever had the faintest intention of going back with them," he challenged.

"I should loathe America, John. You forget what an old lady I'm becoming. I can't adapt myself to so sudden and profound a change of environment. I want to see my grandson, but they have promised to bring him over next year, and I've made up my mind to wait in patience."

"I'd rather hoped you'd bring back Athene with you."

"Oh, so you'd planned that I was to be her duenna, had you, John?"

"Not seriously," he replied. "But I wanted you to have a chance to get to know her. You'd find her so different to the woman she was last summer."

"I'm sure I shall."

The Ogilvie family were away in Worcestershire when John returned to London at the beginning of September. He went down almost at once to Cornwall to make the final arrangements about Nanphant. He received a cordial welcome at Pendarves House from his kinsfolk, who included this time the two boys, the elder of whom, Hugh, had just finished his first year at John's old college, Exeter.

"I've a young half-brother, David Ogilvie, going up to Balliol next October. You might look him up."

"Rather, of course. It's going to be somewhat odd at Oxford next term," Hugh said. "By what we hear the place will be full of demobilized officers who were either undergraduates before the war or would have been undergraduates during the war. Rather strange to have been a captain or something and come up as a fresher."

"Very strange."

Jennifer and Christabel drove their cousin in the jingle to Nanphant, but declined to come in with John and call on Edmund Corfe, his painter landlord, in case he might be drunk.

"Because we always giggle if we meet anybody drunk," Jennifer explained.

"And some drunk people don't like it," Christabel enlarged.

However, Edmund Corfe was not drunk when his tenant arrived. He was rather too much like the conventional Bohemian of late nineteenth-century novels not to rouse a certain amount of prejudice in John's mind at a first impression; but the queer gaunt shape of him and the stilted way in which he walked and his jerky movements like a monkey on a stick might have made him in a less Bohemian rig-out just as fantastic.

"Now the war's over I'm going to start to paint," he proclaimed, fixing John with the earnest gaze of the toper who revels in the consciousness that for once his eyes are not glazed. "I haven't begun to paint yet. I've been meditating for five years now on what I want to do, and by G——, I'm going to surprise 'em. 'Corfe's finished!' Go to St. Ives. Go to Newlyn. That's what you'll hear. 'Corfe's finished. Poor bloody old Corfe!' Is he? Not by any means. Oh no! Corfe isn't finished. I know now what I'm going to do. I didn't know before. You understand me? You're a man of imagination, Ogilvie. You *can* understand me. And you do, don't you?"

Again that earnest unglazed stare fixed his tenant.

"I think I do," said John, who decided that this was the most likely answer to induce the painter to relax.

"You think you do. But I know you do. Is that right?"

"Quite right."

"Exactly," the painter sighed. "And I knew that

you'd know you did." He tapped his forehead. "It's there. I see my way. You understand?"

"Yes, indeed," said John quickly, for he was determined to avoid any shadow of ambiguity this time. He made a tactical mistake.

"You do understand, eh? But what do you understand?" the painter demanded, with a piercing glance.

"Damn the fellow," John thought, "he's got me." And then aloud he added, "I think I understand what you understand."

The painter shook his head.

"Doubtful. Very doubtful," he muttered. "Still, I'm not going to deny you have imagination. No. But the point is that I see my way. I want you to realize that, Ogilvie. Poor bloody old Corfe sees his way. And I'll show them in St Ives! And I'll show them in Newlyn. Do you know my opinion of the Arts Club at St Ives?"

"I'm afraid I don't."

"But I do. I know my own opinion of the Arts Club at St Ives, from which I was asked to resign! Why? Because for two years I didn't pay my subscription. Is that art? Now perhaps you are beginning to have a glimmer of what I mean when I say that at last I see my way. On September 15th, 1919, Ogilvie, when I hand over Nanphant to you until March 15th, 1920, with right to occupy Nanphant for a further three months until June 15th, 1920, by giving me due notice on or before January 15th, 1920—I think that's all quite clear in our agreement—on September 15th I am going to begin painting."

"Where?" John asked, hoping to hear it would be a long way from Nanphant, for he thought this kind of conversation might become wearing.

"In Paris, which is where I thought I began twenty-five years ago. This time I really shall begin. And that's all I shall say now. Well, I hope you'll find everything comfortable here. I understand you will keep on the servants?"

"That will be the easiest way."

Corfe retired from the room in what seemed a series of hops and could be heard shouting down the passage for 'Janie'. Presently he came hopping back followed by a genial spherical woman, as she seemed, contrasted with the thinness of her employer.

"This is Janie Bolitho," he announced.

"Very glad to see you, sir, I'm sure."

"You will stay on with us, Janie?"

"I'll be only too pleased. I belong to do everything with just what little help my sister's little girl, Loveday Williams, can give me. And of course Harry Dunstan, that's the gardener."

Various details were agreeably settled, and John took his farewell.

"I shall be getting married as soon as my fiancée arrives from New York."

"I hadn't realized that Nanphant was to shelter a honeymoon," said the painter, "when Mrs Pendarves wrote to me about letting the place."

"Mrs Pendarves herself didn't realize it," said John. "In fact she won't realize it till I tell her this evening."

"Well, I hope you'll be happy here. I was married myself for a year or two a long time ago, oh, years and years before my aunt left me Nanphant. Janie was with my aunt. So she'll be used to women's ways in a house."

They parted with mutual good wishes, Corfe's for John's marriage, and John for Corfe's new start in painting.

"Was he frightfully drunk?" Jennifer asked when he joined the girls and the jingle at the end of the deep ferny lane that led down to the minute cove of Nanphant.

"He wasn't drunk at all," John replied. "But I thought he seemed a bit mad."

"Oh, yes, he is mad as well," Christabel admitted. "But I do wish you'd seen him when he's drunk. Jennifer and I saw him once, and he was lying on his back and he'd put a cap on one foot and a sou'wester on the other, and he was holding up his legs and pretending they were talking to one another. Only he heard us giggling and he got awfully angry and called us . . ." She stopped and looked a question at her elder sister.

"No, of course you can't, Christabel."

"Well, he called us two little what Jennifer won't let me tell you, though I don't see why. It's a word you can hear in any kennels."

"Christabel, you are *not* to," Jennifer said sternly.

"Puppies. Go on," said John.

This sally had a success with the two girls, who laughed uproariously.

"I wish I could have you both in the front row of the stalls at every performance of my plays," John told them. "But don't laugh at my next item of news, because it's serious. I'm going to be married at the end of the month."

"You aren't! Are you really?" the two girls gasped.

"Oh, glory," Christabel exclaimed, "then you'll have a honeymoon at Nanphant. And I've never seen a honeymoon yet. Oh, what is her name?"

"Athene."

"But that was your mother's name," Jennifer said. "And it's not at all a common name. What's her other name?"

"Athene Gilmer, she was. She's Athene Langridge now. She's a widow."

"I say, that's not awfully romantic, is it?" Christabel commented in a somewhat depressed voice.

"You might wait and see her before you decide that," John suggested.

"And you are rude, Christabel," her sister rebuked.

"But I didn't mean to be rude," Christabel insisted. "I meant exactly the opposite, if you know what I mean."

"You're becoming as Sibylline as Mr Corfe," John laughed.

And by using such an epithet he had become Sibylline himself. So he had to explain the allusion, and that led them to the descent of Aeneas into the Plutonian Kingdom.

"And altogether you've had an extremely instructive drive," he told his cousins.

The jingle was now crossing the wildest part of Goonhilly Down; but with the August sun the fierce rose had faded from the wandering Cornish heath and it now formed a rolling expanse of mingled madder pink and brown.

"I think I'll have to get a jingle to drive over to see you when we come to Nanphant," John said.

"Not a car?" both girls cried in dismay.

"We were positive you'd have a car," Jennifer lamented.

"And we were going to ask you to teach us to drive," Christabel added.

"But I can't drive myself."

"Good gracious!" Jennifer exclaimed.

"Good lord!" her sister gasped.

"I can't get near the earth in a car," John said, whereupon his young cousins exchanged glances. They seemed to fancy he had been caught up in the eccentricity of his painter landlord.

Henry Pendarves applauded John's refusal to get a car. "Very glad indeed. Don't want 'em. Beastly things. Well, John, it's a pleasure to think you're going to be here for a few months. You've not seen my daffodils yet. I have one for Truro next year. . . ."

Words failed him.

As soon as John returned from Cornwall he went down

to Worcestershire to let the family know of his approaching marriage. He was touched by his father's response to the news.

"So I shall have a daughter-in-law called Athene," he murmured to himself in astonishment. "And you are going to take her to the Meneage, John. These fantastic tricks that life plays upon one. May your happiness in your Athene, John, equal that which my Athene gave to me. I don't know, but somehow this news has made me realize that I am turning into an old man."

And later Elise told John that she had never known his father so profoundly moved throughout their married life.

"It made me feel an interloper for the first time," she said.

"Don't be so foolish, dear Elise. It was you who humanised my father. He may have loved my mother, but she never succeeded in humanising him."

"I don't think that's fair either to him or to your mother, John."

"Then don't call yourself an interloper. Remember that I shall be a second husband."

"I count her a lucky woman, John."

"Do you? And I count my father a very very lucky man . . . and myself a very very lucky stepson to find so rare an elder sister."

David was too much preoccupied with the adventure of going up to Balliol in October to be excited by the news of John's marriage. Moreover, every time that John answered one of his questions about the etiquette and procedure of a freshman he would observe gloomily that he did not know why he was asking such questions since obviously all John's information was very much pre-war.

"Anyway, I'm sure you won't find any difficulties to baffle your easy Etonian *civis Romanus sum* attitude," John assured him.

"Well, two people I rather like will be going up to

Balliol," David said hopefully. "Noll Erpingham and Tom Price-Harley."

"An invulnerable trio," John commented.

Prudence's welcome to John's approaching marriage was a little qualified by her disappointment at its upsetting a prospect of her own.

"I was going to suggest to mother that I should leave school at the end of next summer when I shall be seventeen, and come and live with you and keep house for you. Don't grin, John. I've been working at Domestic Economy, and I've started shorthand and typing in case it would be useful to you. You see, mother is revoltingly old-fashioned. I consider I've been brought up like Charlotte Yonge. Mother doesn't really grasp that the world is going to be quite different now. You haven't got a pre-war mind, John, so you don't realize what it means to be out of it."

"Out of what?"

"Out of what's going on to-day. Things have changed, and mother simply can't see it. Because she didn't do this or say that she can't grasp that it's quite different for me to do it or say it. At this rate when I come out I shall feel I smell of moth-balls like a dress that's lived for years at the bottom of a drawer. I do hope Athene will like me, so that I'll often get asked to stay with you. I'm hideously worried about my future. It is a bit grim, you know."

"I used to feel exactly the same at your age," John assured her. "And yet I've managed to stagger on into the present without being treated as something that's escaped from Madame Tussaud's. The Judge used to seem mediaeval to me. And it was your mother who knocked the armour off him."

"I know. That's the trouble, John. Because she brought darling father up to date she thinks she's in touch with me. And she isn't. I sometimes watch her at work on her tambour and wonder if she could even have been my age in the 'eighties. I mean to say, John, she's been tight-laced! It's ridiculous to complain of me showing my knees when she belonged to the age of bosom-worship. Knees! I ask you, John. You can't call knees voluptuous, can you?"

"What devastating strides you've taken toward young womanhood in the last four or five months," John exclaimed.

"Well, I shall be a young woman very soon now, and I wish you could manage to make mother understand it. But it's piggish of me to be belly-aching about myself when you're going to be married. I wonder when I shall be married. All the boys I know are so dull, John. I can't imagine myself married to any of them. Isn't it strange to think that somewhere the man I'm going to marry is walking about at this moment and I don't know him, and if I saw him in the tube or on a bus I probably wouldn't notice him?"

After spending a couple of nights with his family John returned to London, where presently he satisfied the Faculty Office in Knightrider Street, Doctors' Commons, that he was entitled to a Special Licence from His Grace the Archbishop of Canterbury at a cost of £25, which meant that he could be married at any place at any time without previous residential qualification. With this in his pocket he and Athene could be married in Southampton as soon as she arrived on October 1st. A cable had come to say that the ship in which she was sailing was not calling at Plymouth.

He spent most of the time quietly by himself in Hampstead, writing letters to various friends and sketching outlines of several plays he had in mind. He looked back to his childhood and youth in Hampstead when September had always been so hateful a month, overshadowed as it always had been by the return to school. He really would make a supreme effort to rescue Prudence after next summer. September was the last month in which twenty years ago he could have imagined himself looking forward with such joy to the future.

He heard from Leonora on the Saturday before Athene had sailed:

> *We had a perfect trip back, and found Sebastian enormously grown. It was blazing in New York, so Julius stayed up in Vermont. But I'd met Athene before we went north and I thought she'd like to have me see her off and generally help. I'm not going to take up a whole lot of time telling you what you know already. But we've had some fine talks about you and about marriage, and though she didn't tell me a great deal about her first marriage—you wouldn't expect Athene to do that—she let me understand pretty well how it was. She's a little anxious over leaving Arthur like this for so long, but she knows she's doing the wisest thing she could do. I understand just how she felt about Poppa and Momma Langridge because of course I have the same trouble not with in-laws but with my own father and mother, both of whom would turn Sebastian into one nasty mess of melted candy if they were left to it. Well, John, you won't be married by the time this reaches you, indeed Athene will hardly have sailed, but it's the last letter you'll get from me before you are married and you can guess just how much I wish you in the future. Love and blessings from*
>
> *Leonora*

So Leonora had torn herself away from Sebastian in Vermont and come back to the heat of New York in order to help Athene with her departure. The light of the mellow autumn morning was illuminating every corner of the long drawing-room, but it seemed to become brighter suddenly when John read Leonora's letter. This was his third day alone in the house. The family were coming back before dinner from the summer holidays.

By the next post he had a letter from Fitz:

TINORAN,
CARAGH LAKE
September 18, 1919.

Dear Judge,

Aren't you the lucky one to pull such a peach from the tree! Well, unless we're all wiped out by the British—Hell take the dirty spy who's reading this—we shall look to see both of you in Tinoran when Ireland is free.

Now the first thing I want to tell you is that these police who have been shot were all of them spies. Don't be misled by the British press which prints only what it's told to print by the British Government. We're dealing with a herd of spies, informers, and worst of all agents provocateurs. There isn't a house in the remotest part of the country which is safe from their dirty work. When you hear of a constable or an inspector being shot be sure it's because of the work he's doing against his own country. There are some beauties in the G Division of the Metropolitan Police in Dublin. They're all plain-clothes men. One of the brightest of them was shot in the street at the end of July. But the British mean business. On September 7th one of our brigades attacked a military patrol in Fermoy, and a Tommy was killed. Next day two hundred or so British Regulars sacked the town and did some thousands of pounds of damage. This seems to have encouraged the British Government, for ten days after that Dail Eireann was suppressed. Now remember Dail Eireann consists of lawfully elected members of parliament who made it clear when they stood what they stood for. They considered themselves elected by an overwhelming majority of the Irish people to constitute an Irish republic. Yet their lawfully elected representatives are marked down as dangerous conspirators.

Meanwhile Dev is doing grand work over in the States, in spite of what Britain is spending on propaganda to discredit the Irish case. I don't believe Britain can get away with it this time after all this talk about the League of Nations and self-determination for small nations and gallant little Belgium and plucky little Serbia and putting Poland back on the map of Europe and recognizing Finland and Esthonia and Latvia and this place with a name I can't spell, Czecho something or other.

Can't you get into the heads of your British friends that Ireland is no more a domestic matter for Britain than Poland was or is or will be for Germany or Russia or Austria? Can't you make them understand that Ireland has been held for over eight hundred years by force of arms, and force of arms alone? It's true that Anglicization had nearly been accomplished, and if the fools had granted Home Rule and not allowed the Tory party to use 'Ulster' as a dirty electioneering trick to get back into power the Anglicization might have been completed, and the boys that gave their lives in 1916 might not have had that opportunity to make the sacrifice of blood. I don't believe the British people would stand for the rotten game their Government is playing on them if they knew the truth. We heard a hell of a lot during the war about the way the poor innocent Germans were deceived by their rulers, but the British are just as much deceived. Only the British ruling classes do it better. I know well that at this moment people in England are shaking their heads about the cowardly way kind nice policemen are being shot from behind hedges. You can't get into their heads the principle of the thing.

Well, I hadn't meant to inflict all this on you, Judge, and it's a poor kind of a letter to be sending a man on the eve of his marriage. But I've a sort of a feeling that things are going to be very bad in Ireland, and I'll be wanted with our boys. A doctor will be wanted. So I may not have another chance to write to you for a long time. So forgive my politics and I'll drink your health in that grand green bottle you gave me in Citrano and which I smuggled back all the way here and swore I wouldn't tap till I drank to a free Ireland. But I love you, Judge, and I'm going to tap it to-night and drink to your happiness. Give my regards to the lady. Nora sends her love, and so does my mother and tells me to thank you again for the part you gave Ellen. I see your play is running strong. Padraig's still as mulish as a damned Orangeman over my Irish. God bless you. I pray for you always.

Your old friend
Fitz

Of John's other friends Miriam Stern was staying with some friends in the country. James Yarrow had resumed his walk to Pekin, which had been interrupted between Damascus and Baghdad in August 1914.

The railway strike threatened for September 26th had much alarmed the Government, and a variety of war measures were revived. Rationing began again. Volunteers were called for to help in the national transport, which turned out as usual to be the security of London's food supplies. There was no difficulty in persuading thousands of the lately demobilized middle-classes to come forward and protect the country from the Bolshevism that was suspected to be animating the leaders of the Trades Unions, inspired by the unpopularity among the working-classes of the half-hearted war against Soviet Russia. An immense milk depot was established in Hyde Park, and London felt it could face the railway strike with a stout heart and a full belly. The Prime Minister made an impassioned appeal at the City Temple for brotherhood between nations and brotherhood between classes. He looked forward to a new Britain freed from ignorance, insobriety, penury, poverty, squalor, and the tyranny of mankind over man. The spirit in which these tasks should be faced was the spirit of war, which some of his listeners, who were members of the International Brotherhood Congress, must have been astonished to hear consisted of comradeship of classes, a passionate desire to see justice done to all classes, deep sympathy with the wronged, and readiness among all ranks to make every necessary sacrifice to achieve right. In this spirit of war he called for co-operation in the making of a new world, and upheld the League of Nations as an organized attempt to substitute fair play for force. He appealed finally for a national brotherhood in the building of a new Britain which should be a monument to the heroism of the immortal dead.

On the same day as this speech was made the military and police raided the offices of the *Cork Examiner* and destroyed the machinery in revenge for the paper's having published an advertisement of the Irish National Loan to develop Irish industry and commerce, and generally for national purposes as directed by the elected representatives of the Irish people, two of whom, Sinn Fein M.P.s, were arrested. Meetings and assemblies were prohibited, and more papers which published the prospectus of the Irish National Loan were suppressed. Over 40,000 British troops were costing the new brotherhood of Britain nearly a million pounds a month. On the last day of September the Government admitted to 5588 raids on private houses in nine months. The soldiers who had sacked Fermoy were transferred to Cork, which they looted a few weeks later. The Trades Union Congress passed a resolution demanding justice, freedom, and the right of self-determination for Ireland, and this convinced the middle-classes that the ruling-classes were right in believing that Ireland's attempt to preserve the spirit of the West was being financed by red gold from Moscow.

John went to call on Emil and Astrid in their flat at the top of a big house in Brunswick Square.

"It amuses me," he told them, "that you should build your nest in one of those monuments to the solidity of English capitalism. How cosy you are up here!"

"But it is old-fashioned," Astrid complained. "It is so strange that it is quite impossible to find modern convenience in London except for a price which is beyond anybody except those who have been made rich by the war."

"You'll get to like it in time," John prophesied. "You must remember we don't have extremes of climate in this country. Well, Emil, what are the prospects of sovietizing England? If I were not so certain that communism would not end in a bureaucratic tyranny worse than anything we have experienced yet, I believe I should throw myself in with it; but I dread the result on the freedom of man."

"Freedom! What is freedom?" Emil asked. "Not even the artist is free. It is an illusion, and a dangerous illusion too, because it has been the inspiration of revolution until now. Hence the power of reaction which has always known how to exploit the disillusionment of the man who rose in the name of freedom against oppression only to discover that the freedom he thought he had achieved did not exist. Marx did not allow himself to be deluded by unattainable abstractions. He knew that man was the prisoner of himself. That is why the

Russian Revolution is so much more tremendous than the French Revolution. It recognizes no compelling motive for human action or thought beyond the economic struggle, and having faced up to that fact its influence cannot be destroyed."

"You think then that man shall live by bread alone, and that the advice in the Koran to the man with the two loaves to sell one and buy anemones was economically unsound?"

"He was not advised to sell both loaves," Emil pointed out. "But you must admit, John, that the fundamental inspiration of human thought and so of human behaviour is economic security. I believe indeed that the capitalist who apparently in full possession of economic security continues to amass wealth is actuated less by greed than by the instinct to provide a wide margin of economic security. Conceive an earth in which it was the birthright of everybody to claim adequate food and shelter throughout his life in return for the amount of labour necessary to do his share of the maintenance of a highly mechanized world. Wouldn't you welcome that, even if it did involve a great extension of bureaucracy?"

"I should welcome it if I were sure that such an administration of men and women in the mass would not prevent the advancement of mankind through the individuals on whom evolution has laid the burden of its process. You never had a play acted, Emil."

"I never wrote a play. What has that to do with it?"

"I find this interesting, John," Astrid put in.

"If you had watched a play of yours being acted, Emil, you would quickly realize that an audience is a lower intelligence than the average intelligence of the individuals who comprise it. In certain moods I would go so far as to argue that the intelligence of an audience is not higher than the lowest intelligence of any individual in it. The demagogue is well aware of this fact and plays upon it. Mob-oratory is a contemptuous phrase. I once attended a play of mine for six nights in succession in order to study its effect upon the audience, marking in the script the reaction. Those reactions to lines and situations varied with every audience, but the reaction was always far below in quality the personal reaction of individuals who I knew were in those audiences. Now, under communism once you have established a least common multiple . . ."—he turned to Astrid apologetically—"I hope my arithmetic is right . . . once you have established a standard well above the standard of living accepted under capitalism as adequate for the wage-slave, won't there be a risk of humanity's becoming static? Obviously that is what has happened in the rest of creation. Every organism developed what for it was the irreducible minimum necessary to secure its survival in the vital struggle, but no evidence exists of any development after that. As the association of the honey-bee or the termite or the umbrella-ant is to-day, so it was millions of years ago. The monsters of the past vanished because they developed brawn at the expense of brain. No doubt, just as individualists like them have vanished, innumerable imperfect associations of insects and badly arranged herds have vanished too, before man appeared on the scene. By what I can make out Marx claims a biological law from the development of man based on his economic environment, so that once the economic environment is perfected, so as to avoid the individual or the mass struggle for existence, man must become a static form of life. Art, already threatened by mechanical development, will vanish completely, and science, once the common purpose of economic security has been achieved, must vanish too because it will not have the spur of amelioration behind it; and a discontented scientist in a perfect Marxian world would be as much of a threat to it as Plato considered poets would be to his Republic. Birth-control will be so stringently directed that in the end the sexual impulse will be weakened and some synthetic breeding process will have to be devised unless Homo Sapiens is to expire of his own perfection of environment."

"You do not like birth-control?" Astrid asked in amazement. "You think it good that women should be kept in degradation of excessive child-bearing?"

"The amount of children women want to bear will have to depend on the ability of women to resist their greater pleasure in and greater capacity for the sexual act," John answered.

"But I think that is a so wrong argument," Astrid declared. "Women are much less promiscuous than men."

"Which is surely one proof in favour of what I maintain," John replied. "Man's instinct for variety is a testimony to the comparative feebleness of his sexual potency. Another proof is that on woman falls the burden of child-bearing, to provide for which nature has endowed her with the deeper urge. Mechanical birth-control is a concession to woman's weakness. Aristophanes recognized woman's weakness in the *Lysistrata* long ago. It astonishes me that woman, by countenancing and even advocating mechanical birth-control, should admit her readiness to be used as a machine herself."

"I think that is a very disgusting thing to say," Astrid retorted.

"Disgusting or not, it is a fact to which women had better face up. Did you read a remarkable book published last year by a female scientist called Marie Stopes? I will prophesy that *Married Love* will effect a revolution in female morals during the next decade much profounder than that effected in its day in male morals by Jean-Jacques Rousseau's *Confessions*."

"I have not read this book," Astrid said. "Emil, you will please obtain it for me, I think."

"It's just popular sexology," Emil told her.

John winced.

"Et tu, Brute! Are you going to encourage these Graeco-Latin hermaphrodites of words and talk English *au gratin*?" he asked reproachfully.

"This aesthetic timorousness is so tiresome," Emil scoffed, "this horror of the functional even in language."

"But you've not answered my contention that universal communism if successfully achieved will leave man static," John reminded him.

"Because I don't think your contention was sustained. In any case, that is a remote danger. We communists do not aim to achieve communism as an end in itself, but as a means towards an end. We recognize the muddle and misery of humanity and we believe that our experiment may cure the world of muddle and misery."

"So would the tenets of Christianity if every individual practised what he was supposed to believe," John claimed.

"But we are not handicapped by moral ideals which we do not accept as literal injunctions," Emil pointed out. "We have a practical remedy, compliance with which we shall enforce."

"Meanwhile, the first step in this country will be the railway strike?"

"A strike is merely evidence of a state of discontent with existing conditions," Emil replied. "No strike could be considered successful which did not end in nationalization. And until the Trades Unions discover that they will get no further. It is a dissipation of effort for the transport workers to strike in the spring, the railways in the autumn, and the miners in the summer. A general strike is essential, and a general strike not for wages but for nationalization of all the basic industries."

John thought of Emil in Icaros concentrated upon the

business of obtaining information about the enemy, and before that at Mileto in his white house with the squat cupolas looking down across roofs and minarets and almond-blossom to the harbour. He had been a devoted Marxist then, but somehow the practical side of his theories had seemed remote. That had been brought so much nearer now in this world shaken to pieces by the war, and all the time his emotional determination would be fed henceforth by Astrid. Where would it end? The ruling classes were nervous of the future, and the strength of them in England was the way they held together at the threat of danger. The attitude they had taken towards Ireland was significant. A strange sinister set, when one divined the cold force of egoism beneath that civilized exterior. And always at their service some Scotsman or Welshman or even renegade Irishman whom they could flatter or bribe to do the dirty work and then discard when the dirty work was done. Moreover, they were invulnerable to criticism because they were unaware of their own astuteness. They sincerely believed that they were good-natured, tolerant, lazy creatures without an *arrière pensée*. The English gentleman was incapable of an *arrière pensée*. The phrase itself had to be borrowed from a double-dealing nation like the French. And that *fausse bonhomie* which covered such depths of greed, that was not admitted in England. Once again the phrase had to be borrowed from the French who with their deadly perception of human motive could recognize the *faux bonhomme* in their midst. There was a fifth thing too wonderful for Agur after being baffled by the way of an eagle in the air, the way of a serpent upon the rock, the way of a ship in the midst of the sea, and the way of a man with a maid, and that was the way of an adulterous woman who ate and wiped her mouth, and said she had done no wickedness. Had he lived two or three thousand years later he would have found a sixth thing too wonderful for him, and that would have been the way of an Englishman with the rest of the world. Yes, Emil with all the wisdom of Solomon and with all his experience of British officialdom would find his task a good deal harder than Lenin's.

People had dropped in to the flat in Brunswick Square, and John who disliked finding himself launched upon arguments with people he did not know, decided to withdraw. As he walked downstairs through the great solid house he smiled to himself at the reflection what the bewhiskered merchant or banker in the secure heart of Queen Victoria's world would have thought of the queer collection of people who would one day frequent the top floor of his house. Even in 1919 they looked odd enough. It was natural for incipient revolutionaries to rebel against social conventions; but John wondered why so many of them enjoyed being simultaneously polychromatic and grubby. One or the other would have been an effective protest against the tyranny of ordinary life, but the combination gave them the appearance of a mouldering collection of butterflies whose pins had come unstuck from the cork-lined drawer of the cabinet. And why did communists who aimed at a happy mean take such pride in distinguishing themselves from their fellows by the extravagance of their attire?

On the afternoon of the Friday on which the railway strike was due to begin at midnight, John was walking down Piccadilly towards his club when just outside the Ritz he ran into Turner Rigden at the end of a long thick cigar.

"My god, it's Johnnie Ogilvie," the little man exclaimed. "Just the man I want. Say, do you know anything about lamp-shades?"

"Nothing at all," John replied, emphatically.

"Damn it, you'd know whether you thought a lamp-shade was a good one or not?" the member for South-East Kensington pressed.

"I'd know if I liked it," John admitted.

"Well, old man, that's all I want," Rigden said reproachfully. "Come on into the Ritz. I want your advice about a proposition that's been put up to me."

John could not resist Turner Rigden when he was in quest of financial adventure, and he followed him in through the Arlington Street entrance of the hotel, where Rigden stopped to ask the porter if the Marquis was up in his room.

"Not yet, Mr Rigden."

"Well, he's expecting me. I'll go right up to his room. Send the page up with the key."

In the lift Rigden explained to John that the Marquis had invented a new type of shade for electric-lighting, and had offered him the world's rights for manufacture and distribution.

"I think it's a proposition," he said, taking a gold-handled pair of scissors out of his pocket and snipping off the overchewed end of his cigar. "Prices are soaring. There's going to be a lot of money made in the next few years. And the more prices soar the more people are buying. You don't blame them, do you? They've been kept from buying by the war and now they want to enjoy themselves. Squandermania? Squandermania my aunt! Squandermania's going to put the country on its feet. That's what I told my constituents yesterday. 'If you want to see the old country rolling comfortably along again,' I told them, 'buy as much as you can. Some of you have come out of the war poorer than you went into it, but some of you have more money to spend than you ever had before the war. And it's the duty of people like that to spend as much as they can in the interests of those who can't spend now but will be able to spend if you do your bit at spending now and encouraging trade.' "

"Very lucid," John commented.

"My god, they nearly cheered the roof off. That's one thing about an English audience, John, give 'em common sense and they'll respond to it. Hullo, here's this guy's room."

The page boy unlocked the door, and left them in a large private sitting-room which at first glance looked like the cave of the Forty Thieves, for it was crowded with standard lampshades of various shiny metals. On the sideboard and tables stood other lamps, and two rows of them were suspended from a kind of scaffold in the middle of the room. The globes were made of some material that resembled glass, cut into every sort of shape and stained to every shade of colour.

"What do you think of 'em?" Rigden asked. "Luminole the stuff's called. It's unbreakable and can be coloured or shaped at a quarter the cost of glass and *I* reckon with the way prices are soaring one can sell it at four times the price of ordinary glass. It's a novelty. And that's what the post-war public's going to demand. Novelty! Wait a minute. I'll light 'em all up."

Rigden searched round the room for the master switch without success.

"Hadn't you better wait till the inventor comes in?" John suggested.

"Don't worry, I'll find the damned thing in a minute. I know it's somewhere over here."

At that moment the room was so abruptly lighted up by about a hundred lamps that John thought for a moment the Ritz had been struck by lightning.

"I must have trodden on the switch," said Rigden. "Never mind. I've lighted 'em. That's the main thing. Well, what do you think of it?"

Oranges, lemons, birds of paradise, palms, moons,

suns, scarlet octagons, golden pentagons, stars, tulips, roses, cherubs, orchids, flamingos, opals, fiery hearts, amethysts, aquamarines, topazes, dragons, and a predominance of naked nymphs, goddesses and gay ladies, blazed in luminole.

"Very tasty," John said.

"Gee, I take my hat off to the guy who invented this. I'm buying," Turner Rigden affirmed. "Say, I think I'll use his lavatory. I've been too busy to go all day."

"But who is the inventor?" John asked.

"He's a Spanish marquis. Name as long as your arm, and hardly speaks a word of English. I'll be back before he comes in." And the Member for South-East Kensington vanished into the inventor's bedroom.

John was wondering how he was going to account for his presence in this blaze of a hundred lamps when the Marquis himself came in.

John knew enough Spanish to ask a chambermaid for hot water, but he did not know enough to explain that he had come up to the Marquis's suite in the company of Turner Rigden, who after turning on his lamps had retired to the lavatory.

"Who is you, please?" the Marquis enquired. He was an olivine young man in a too beautifully cut black suit.

"Pardon, monsieur le marquis, vous parlez français?" John asked.

"No, I speak you to English. Who is you, please?"

"I'm a friend of Mr Turner Rigden."

"Reegden? I know him. Where he is?"

"He's in your lavatory."

"How? I am not understand you. You make these lamps?"

"No, Mr Rigden lighted them."

"Where he is?" the Marquis demanded again suspiciously.

Fortunately for John's embarrassment the Member for South-East Kensington reappeared from the Marquis's bedroom at this moment.

"Ah, Marquis, how are you? This is Mr John Ogilvie. He likes your lamps very much. We shall do business I think. My secretary will give you a ring early next week. Come on, John." He tapped a luminole Venus rising from a luminole sea. "Bong!" he declared. "Au revwore, Marquis. We've got to hurry along."

"You let me in for a nice embarrassing two minutes," John told Rigden presently. "He thought I was a burglar."

"That's all right. You want to be off-hand when you're doing business with these inventors. I'm going to make him an offer for luminole next Monday. I don't want him to think I'm too anxious. I think I've got the very showrooms I want in New Bond Street. A busted corset-shop. The war did a lot of damage to corsets. And now you're coming back with me to Wickets to-night."

"I'm not," said John.

"But first of all we'll go and crack a bottle at the R.A.C."

"And I won't drink champagne at five o'clock in the afternoon."

"My god, John, if you aren't the damnedest pig-headedest cuss I ever met. You've got to come down to Wickets. You haven't seen the place since I bought it. I've transformed it. There's nothing left except the walls. It'll do you good to have a night or two of Hind-head air. Get me a taxi!" This to the porter at the Arlington Street entrance, who for taking two paces to the edge of the kerb, opening and shutting the taxi door, and directing the driver to go to the R.A.C., was rewarded by the Member for South-East Kensington with half a crown.

"That's what I like about the Ritz," Rigden said. "You get good service."

"I'll come to the R.A.C. with you, but I won't drink champagne and I won't come to Wickets," John declared firmly.

"I'll let you off the champagne, but you're coming to Wickets for the week-end," Rigden replied.

"My clothes are up at Hampstead."

"Damn it, the car will be round at the club by half-past five. We can drive up there and fetch your blasted clothes. Anyway, you don't want clothes at Wickets. Dorothy's been on at me ever since we got the decorators out to bring you down."

Dorothy was Mrs Rigden, whom John liked.

"But I only got back from Italy three weeks ago."

"All the more reason to come down to Wickets. I want to talk to you about a play for next year. May Lavender's coming down after the show to-morrow night."

"But I'm going to Southampton on Monday."

"Hindhead's on the way."

"I've got luggage to collect. Luckily my father's lending me his big car. So I shall be independent of the strike."

"You're not going to America, are you?"

"No, but I'm meeting somebody coming from America."

"I'll bet you it's a woman," said Rigden, swinging round in the taxi at the end of his cigar.

"It is. I'm going to marry her as soon as she arrives."

In his surprise Rigden let go of his cigar, which dropped on the floor of the taxi with a dull thud. John stamped it out, which was rather like stamping the life out of a plump little animal.

"My god, John, if you don't beat the band! You mean to say you're going down to Southampton to marry a woman just like that? You writers!"

"So you now understand, Turner, why I can't come down to Wickets."

"I understand why you *must* come down. Dorothy would never forgive me if I told her you were going to be married and I let you get away without seeing Wickets first. She's a bit annoyed with me anyway because I refused a knighthood."

"You did, did you?"

"I certainly did. And my agent reckons it's done me a lot of good with my constituents. He told a few people in confidence, and that was good publicity. But Dorothy was mad. She liked the notion of being Lady Rigden. You know what women are, and if you don't you soon will. I told her I was taking nothing under a baronetcy, and I didn't intend to pay too much for that. She said that was all very nice for me, I got Bart after my name, but she didn't get Bartess, and we hadn't got a son. That's always fretted poor old Dorothy. But she still hopes. Queer creatures, women, as you'll soon find out. Well, fancy you getting married. That's broken your second resolution."

"How d'you mean?"

"You *are* going to crack a bottle with me. Here, where's this damned driver going?"

Rigden leaned out of the window and shouted 'R.A.C.'

"You go on into the smoking-room, John," he told him when they drove up. "I want to leave a message with the porter."

John knew by now that he would give way to Turner Rigden and go back with him to Wickets. The little man's zest for the moment was Epicurean and irresistible. Moreover, perhaps it would be as well to talk over the plans he had for one or two plays, and he did not want to be disturbed for the winter.

"All right, Turner, I'll come back with you to Wickets," he told his host, when the latter came along to the smoking-room.

"I know you will," Rigden replied.

"But I'm *not* going to drink champagne at ten minutes past five in the afternoon. I want some tea."

"That means I'll have to drink a whole bottle," Rigden said. "Sure you wouldn't like a bowl of gruel?" he asked John. "Well, here's your health and happiness, old man, and may your marriage have as good a run as *All Or Nothing*."

"Give it a little longer than that," John said.

"Figuratively, old man, figuratively. That's the right word, isn't it?" he asked quickly. "Damn it, I've got to watch my mouth the way a terrier watches a rabbit-hole when I run over three syllables with you writing chaps. What's the lady's name? Oh, a widow, eh? Well, there's a lot to be said for settling down quickly."

A magnate of transport passing the table at which they were sitting stopped to ask Rigden what he thought of the railway situation.

"I'm not worrying any, Jewster."

"You never do. It's my opinion the strike has been deliberately fomented as a test of the Government's ability to handle it. We shall see something like a revolutionary movement presently."

"You'd better read my article in the *Journal* on Sunday, Jewster. Everything is still costing twice as much. Give the railwaymen a fair deal. We want to keep up the spirit of industry by spending freely. That's the broad line I'm taking. And don't forget that heavy freight hits me as hard as anybody."

Sir Herbert Jewster passed on, with a grunt of disapproval for what as an old-fashioned and cautious financier he considered the recklessness of these spendthrifts who had emerged with the fortunes of war.

"A fossil, that's what Jewster is," Rigden declared. "Yes, when he bought the Ark from Noah he was a good man of business, but to-day he's a fossil. Keep up prices and keep up wages. That's my policy to get the old country rolling along comfortably again. Before we know where we are people like Jewster will have us back on the gold standard. Then they'll get the country into such a damned muddle that they'll want another war to get us out of it."

"I don't think we shall see another war in our time, Turner."

"No, perhaps not," said Rigden, with what sounded like a note of regret in his tone.

Presently John called his attention to the time.

"If I'm to go up to Hampstead and pack some clothes and you don't propose to keep Mrs Rigden waiting for dinner, oughtn't we to be going along soon?"

"I'm just waiting for something. Ah, here it comes, I think."

A page boy approached with a small parcel.

"Give it to Mr Ogilvie," said Rigden.

"For me?" John asked in surprise.

"Go on, open it," Rigden urged.

John did so and found a gold vanity-case and a gold cigarette-case.

"Little wedding presents for you and your merry widow," said Rigden, his blue eyes sparkling with enjoyment of John's astonishment. "I told the porter to send along to the Goldsmiths' shop in Regent Street. They know the kind of thing I like to give my friends. I hope Mrs Ogilvie that is to be won't take offence. They understand giving presents in America. Well, come on and we'll go and get these clothes if you must have clothes. But you won't want 'em at Wickets."

In spite of this Rigden himself was in tails when they

sat down that night to eat an elaborate dinner off gold plate.

"I hate it," Mrs Rigden told her guest, "but you know Turner is mad on gold and when he heard the Duke of Salop was selling his service nothing would satisfy him till he'd bought it. But I hate it. Your fork makes such a noise!"

Dorothy Rigden was about eight years younger than her husband, with hair dyed to the colour it was when she was in her early 'teens, and a complexion of the same period. The two daughters of the house were up in Scotland.

"Turner wants a deer forest," his wife explained. "So we sent Madge and Dolly up to have a look round. I don't know what he wants a deer forest for. It never stops raining in Scotland."

The only others at the table were Mr Pritchard the first secretary, Miss Weir the second secretary, and a middle-aged female cousin of Mrs Rigden's. All were thin. All wore glasses. All were silent.

"Does Janet Lundy get on my nerves!" Rigden exclaimed, when they were seated after dinner in his smoking-room, the walls of which were hung with the trophies of big game. "That woman has been staying with us since the middle of August, and the only topic on which she's chirpy is hot-water bottles. Never mind, May Lavender's coming down to-morrow night and bringing a girl friend to chaperon a boy friend. Why, she's bringing Ellen Fitzgerald."

This was welcome news to John, who looked forward to having in Ellen a companion with whom to enjoy the absurdities of this household.

"I didn't know that May went in for chaperons," he said.

"Chaperons?" Rigden exclaimed. "Why, she brings her mother down here most times. Well, I suppose she's right. After all, she's a great little actress, and she doesn't want people to say I put her into the Sheridan for anything except her talent. Then there's Bill Meeching and Charlie and Daisy Girdler and Tom Trollope and of course Lady Vawdry."

"I'm at sea," said John. "Why of course Lady Vawdry?"

"Tom's running her. Tom Trollope is a director of half a dozen big companies and a big noise in banking. Bill Meeching is the chairman of Meeching & Pick, the biscuit people, and Charlie Girdler made a packet during the war out of the Girdler torch. All business people. We'll be a very jolly party."

"Where did you shoot that hippo, Turner?" John asked pointing to a huge head bulging above the mantelpiece.

"Bought it," Rigden replied complacently. "I used to plan I'd be a big game hunter when I was a kid, but I didn't make enough money in time. It's a good collection." The heads of the lions and tigers and grizzlies and buffaloes glared at this owner innocent of their blood. "It's snug in here, isn't it? But Dorothy hates it. Still, a man wants a den of his own. Say, do you get the ozone in this room?"

John said he hadn't noticed it above the tobacco smoke and smell of fur.

"I'm not joking, John. I've had an ozone diffuser fitted. You regulate it with a handle in every room. A week-end at Wickets is as good as a week-end at Brighton. In fact it's better, because we have the pines as well here. You're breathing in as much ozone in this den of mine every minute as you'd get from a twenty-minute walk in a sou'west gale. Say, would you like a swim?"

"Not now."

"I've had a splendid swimming-bath fitted. I'd like to show it to you."

John would have preferred to sit quietly smoking, but Turner Rigden's relish of his toys was too naïve and childish not to be humoured. So they visited the swimming-bath which brooded in empty aqueousness. Above the greenish water hung a line of what are known in school gymnasiums as travelling-rings.

"Do you dare me to make the journey once up and down?" Rigden challenged, his little blue eyes flickering with aggressive fire.

"Don't fall in," John urged.

That was enough. The Member for South-East Kensington seized the nearest ring and leapt forward, his coat-tails flying. At any moment John expected him to plunge on his back into the water; but he reached the farther end, and with a whoop of exultation came swinging back towards his guest, by whom, crimson in the face but without a spot of water upon his patent leather shoes, he stood safe on the mosaic edge of the bath.

"I felt it a bit in a boiled shirt," Rigden confessed. "But by jiggs, I'll lay there isn't another M.P. fifty-three years old who could do that after dinner."

"I wouldn't care to back one of them," John declared emphatically.

"Well, let's go back to my den," Rigden said. "But don't tell Dorothy I did that. She says it's a waste of energy."

They discussed one or two of John's ideas for a play to succeed *All Or Nothing* when it was required, in the course of which he happened to mention the musical version of *Annette* produced in America before the war.

"Say, why don't *we* put on a big musical show?" Rigden demanded. "And a chorus. A real chorus. My god, if I can't find a real chorus in London I'll go to New York for them. Do you think that friend of yours would write the music? Say, I'm taken with this idea."

"But can May Lavender sing?" John asked.

"Never mind about May Lavender. We'll keep May quiet with a comedy. John, I'm going to put on a big musical show. I'll spend money on it. And by jiggs, I'll light one scene with luminole. John, it's a cinch! What's the time? Gee, it's one! You'd like some eggs and bacon?"

"You don't want to rouse the servants at this time of night for eggs and bacon," John protested.

"Servants nothing. I've got a room downstairs among the kitchens specially built for me to cook bacon and eggs at any hour of the night or day I want to cook 'em. That's my standing orders. If I went in there and didn't find three dozen fresh eggs waiting and the stove alight and the rashers cut there'd be hell raised in Wickets."

So Rigden led the way through the vast underworld of Wickets to the small white room that stood ever ready to gratify his desire for eggs and bacon. He certainly fried well. John asked him where he learned the accomplishment.

"I learnt to fry bacon in the lumber-woods when I was seventeen. Anybody can fry eggs."

"You *are* Canadian then?"

"Not at all. Because I bought up a big slice of forest for my paper mills that doesn't make me Canadian. No, I'm a Tiverton man. Tiverton's English enough, isn't it? I ran away from home to Canada when I was sixteen. That was early in '82."

"The year I was born," said John.

"Sir Turner Rigden, Bart! It doesn't sound bad, eh?"

"Most impressive."

"I bought that lot of ancestors very cheap," said Rigden dreamily, switching on the frame lights in a row of eighteenth-century portraits along the gallery down which they were passing on the way to bed. "If I get a baronetcy without being too heavily soaked by the

Central Office of the Party I'll call it a career. Well, here's your room. Your bathroom's through there. Ring for what you want in the morning."

Next day it was wet, which was a blow to the host, who had wanted to show John the outdoor wonders of Wickets.

"Never mind, we'll play billiards," he said.

The billiard room was a cross between the Parthenon, the entrance hall of the National Liberal Club, and the Whispering Gallery in the dome of St Paul's. When play was in progress purple velvet curtains excluded all light from the large and heavy french-windows between Doric columns of porphyry, leaving the light to fall from the dome.

"This room cost me a hell of a packet," said Rigden. "It's supposed to be very modern." He was about to pull the purple velvet cover trimmed with gold lace from the billiard-table when he thought better of it and rang a bell. "I've got such a goddam crowd of lazy loafers leaning up against one another in plush breeches that I must remember to give 'em something to do," he explained apologetically.

Two footmen appeared and ceremoniously removed the cover from the billiard-table.

"Will you be requiring the marker's presence, sir?" one of them enquired.

Rigden shook his head, and the footmen retired with stately languor.

"One day, John, I'll take a running kick at those plush bottoms," Rigden prophesied. "It'll just come over me to do it, and I'll do it. What are you staring at?"

"The cloth," John said. "I've never seen a mauve billiard-cloth before."

"That was the architect's notion," Rigden explained, a little sheepishly. "He didn't want to spoil his colour scheme. I told him it was a goddam silly notion, but you know what these architects are. They're more difficult than actresses."

"I'll give you a motto for this room, Turner. You like Latin mottoes. They're all over the house."

"That was that blasted architect again. I don't like mottoes. Hell, I crash every time I'm asked which means what. Tempus Fudgit, and all the rest of it."

"Well, I'm going to give you a Latin motto for your billiard-room," said John. "*Nudaque simplicitas purpureusque pudor.*"

Rigden groaned.

"What's that mean?"

"Bare simplicity and purple modesty."

"It's no damn use, John, I'll never remember. Still, I'll have it fixed up over the scoring-board. It may rile the architect," he said hopefully.

"And I think you ought to have this room lighted with amethysts in luminole. Come on, you've got to give me twenty-five in a hundred. You're used to playing on this mauve surface. I'm not."

In the course of the afternoon rich-looking cars with rich-looking chauffeurs and rich-looking luggage arrived, first with Mr and Mrs Girdler, then with Mr Meeching, and finally with Sir Thomas Trollope and Lady Vawdry. Every one as he or she alighted from Rolls-Royce or Sunbeam said what a disgraceful piece of bolshevism the railway strike was. Sir Thomas Trollope, known to his friends as T. T., was the most severe on the subject of working-class discontent.

"They've been spoilt during the war. That's what it is," he declared, toasting a square yard of tweed-clad rump at the fire in what was called the library, in which the only sign of literature apart from the illustrated weeklies were the backs of dummy books fixed to the doors.

"I don't agree with you, T. T.," Rigden challenged. "I'm for keeping prices up and paying wages accordingly."

"Rubbish," snorted Sir Thomas, his mulberry cheeks becoming suffused with blackberry juice. "The more they get the more they'll want. It's devils like you, Turner, with your confounded Sunday rags, which make the working-classes discontented. We can't afford to play with the situation. We've got a very nasty ten years in front of us. And I don't know that the Prime Minister is the man to handle it."

"I thought he was a friend of yours, T. T.?" Rigden said.

"So he is," Sir Thomas replied, "but that doesn't mean to say I'm going to follow him blindly if I believe he's leading the country along the wrong road."

"I think T. T.'s stuck to him too long as it is," Lady Vawdry drawled. She was a handsome woman of forty who had become thin instead of slim and whose roseleaf complexion was turning to pot-pourri. Sir Thomas Trollope kept her in luxury, but not so luxuriously as to leave her without that something the hope of attaining which reminded her to make a suitable response. Her husband Lord Vawdry amused himself with sport, which he could manage to do successfully as long as his wife Muriel was financially off his hands. Sir Thomas's wife preferred that her husband should maintain a peeress than a chorus-girl. She was of humble origin and did not feel that T. T.'s liaison with a fading aristocrat undermined her own position.

"I think Turner's right," put in Charles Girdler. "We can't cut the workers' wages so drastically when living is still 120 per cent above July 1914. It's all very well talking about bolshevism in England, T. T., but we're going the right way to get it by being too drastic." He was a large fair man under forty, with a handsome and most expensively dressed brunette for a wife.

"I'm with Turner every time," declared Mr William Meeching. "Keep up prices and wages."

"Yes, because you sell biscuits, Bill. It's the same with Charlie's torches. Both of you would feel it if wages came down with a bump."

The four men started an argument in which figures were flung about with an agility of ready reckoning that left John silent in amazement at the virtuosity of gain.

"Aren't they dreadful!" Daisy Girdler exclaimed in a shrill cockney voice, which, coming from such luxurious chic, was as unexpected as hearing a black leopard talking like a cockatoo. "Money, money, money! For god's sake, shut up, Charlie. Mr Ogilvie thinks he's fallen among thieves. Dorothy, do stop them."

"T. T.'s happy now," Muriel Vawdry drawled. "There are only two things which make T. T. happy. Talking about money and putting on his K.B.E., which is *the* most bloody awful decoration they've contrived yet. T. T., do wear your K.B.E. for dinner. It'll look grand in Turner's billiard room. And Turner shall tell his orchid-manager to give me a spray of cattleyas."

"Was T. T. being obstinate on the way down?" Mrs Rigden asked.

"Obstinate?" Muriel Vawdry echoed. "He was being mean, that's what T. T. was being."

"All right, Muriel," said Sir Thomas, emerging from percentages with an apprehensive look in the direction of Lady Vawdry, and offering her a cigarette as a sleek black spaniel comes fawning from the water with a stick in its mouth, to lay it at the feet of its mistress.

But Muriel Vawdry did not intend to let him off too easily from demurring on the way down to a silver-fox stole on which she had set her heart.

"Oh yes," she drawled, lighting up the cigarette. "There is something else which makes T. T. happy. That's when he can put on breeches. You love your nice silk breeches, don't you, T. T.? So long as you can get somebody else to button them below the knee? Of course, the trouble with T. T. is that he's a romantic snob. He adores court functions. He loves to read in a gossip column that . . ."

"Now, that's quite enough from you, Muriel," Sir Thomas muttered.

And instinct warned Lady Vawdry that if she did stop sneering at Sir Thomas Trollope now she would get her silver-fox stole.

"Dear T. T., you know I'm teasing you," she drawled soothingly, and put out an indulgent hand to pat Sir Thomas's beefsteak of a paw.

The weather remaining wet, a four for auction-bridge was made up in which Sir Thomas and Mrs Girdler were partners against Lady Vawdry and Charlie Girdler. The pigeon was Sir Thomas. If he lost he paid Muriel. If she lost she owed him. This was equally true of the Girdlers, but at least the money remained in the family. The host carried off Bill Meeching to billiards. John took the opportunity of talking to his hostess.

"But you're sure you don't want to cut in for the bridge?" she asked.

"Nothing would bore me more," he declared. "I want to have a talk with you."

"It was so nice that you were able to come down with Turner yesterday, and he tells me you're going to be married next week. I didn't say anything about it because I thought you mightn't want all these people to know."

"That was kind and tactful of you, Mrs Rigden."

"I do hope you and your wife will come and stay with us here sometimes. I'm longing to meet her. May Lavender's coming down to-night."

"Yes, with a friend of my boyhood, Ellen Fitzgerald."

"Oh, she's an exceptionally nice woman. And she always talks so enthusiastically about you. . . . May I call you John? And would you mind calling me Dorothy?

It pleases Turner so much. He's so anxious for us all to keep young. And he's such a boy himself. Sometimes I think, too much of a boy."

Dorothy Rigden with her head on one side like a sparrow regarded pessimistically the splendour that surrounded her. Then she sighed and turned to John.

"I sometimes wonder how long it will last. Turner is so reckless."

"But he's very shrewd with it all."

"Yes, but you have to be very shrewd to spend in the way Turner spends. I often think that if we'd had a son he might have been more careful. However, it wasn't to be, and I don't suppose it will happen now. Tell me, do you like May Lavender?"

"I shouldn't worry my head over her if I were you," said John answering the question in Dorothy Rigden's mind. "She's an extremely clever actress and both Turner and I owe her a lot for the success of *All Or Nothing*. But she *is* an actress. She's ambitious, and she has no need now to think about anything except her ambition. Besides, in justice to Turner, it was merely her talent which captivated him. Don't you worry about May Lavender."

"Oh, I haven't been worrying, John, but Turner *is* such a boy, and we have been married twenty-seven years now, and I wouldn't like to be in the position of Lady Trollope. I'd hate it. It's so undignified for a middle-aged man to be led round like that. Oh dear, I think one can have too much money," she sighed. "I'd rather Turner didn't make so much. It frightens me. Besides, I find it all wrong somehow to be talking as they were talking before tea when poor people don't know what they may have to face. I'm not surprised they do get bolshie ideas. I'd have bolshie ideas if I was a poor man's wife and heard them cutting five shillings a week off my necessities for them to spend it all on luxuries. It's no use. I can't really enjoy the way we live. I look back at this terrible war we've come through and the suffering all over the world, and it makes me feel ashamed. Turner says it's all good for trade, but I feel it's tempting Providence. Turner thinks I'm disappointed because he refused a K.B.E. He thought I wanted to be Lady Rigden. But that wasn't the reason. I thought a K.B.E. might steady him. Yet I don't know, T. T.'s a K.B.E. and look at him. Just a butt for a hard woman."

"I fancy Trollope can look after himself," John said. "She'll go too far one day—or spend too much."

"But what pleasure can it be to a man to know that he has bought a woman?" Dorothy Rigden asked, in a pucker of perplexity.

"I should guess that a man like Trollope got pleasure from that very fact. Most rich men are insensitive. They wouldn't have become rich otherwise. When you've put on one side a few with imagination and foresight who deserve their wealth, most of the rich men you see have made their money by a combination of being quick at ready reckoning with complete shamelessness, and shamelessness must imply insensitiveness."

"I don't think Turner is insensitive," said Dorothy Rigden, a little wistfully.

"Nor do I. But I don't count Turner a typical rich man."

"But you're quite right about shamelessness, and I have known Turner do several shameless deals in business."

"But I expect he knew it was shameless."

"Yes, he just boasts about it. So I suppose he is insensitive in one way. But he is generous, John. Even when he's being most greedy he's generous."

"Nobody knows that better than I do."

"And I don't think he's generous for effect. He's awfully bad about subscribing to public charities."

At dinner that night the conversation happened to

come round to the Prince of Wales's tour in Canada, and in an outburst of loyalty inspired by the advantage to big business of the services of one who looked like becoming the world's drum-major, his health was drunk.

"There was a big threat from bolshie movements in the west of Canada," said Rigden, "but I reckon the visit of that lad has given the K.O. to bolshevism in Canada."

"Do you really think that?" John asked incredulously. "That seems to me just sentimental nonsense. No doubt he has an attractive personality, but I don't believe the most attractive personality imaginable can have any influence over convinced bolshevists."

"He's a big asset to the Empire anyway," Rigden declared. "I don't pay any attention to you, John. You're a writing chap, and all you writing chaps are a bit bolshie yourselves. We expect it. And so far as I'm concerned you can be as bolshie as you like if you'll write another play for May Lavender as good as *All Or Nothing*. Two hundred and fifteenth performance next week, and it'll run well into the New Year."

The heroine of *All Or Nothing* arrived at about a quarter-past one with Ellen Fitzgerald and an extremely ladylike young man called Dennis Amberley.

"My *darling*," he cried in an ecstasy at supper. "We're eating off golden platters. How too amazing! My dear, I'm so excited I can hardly cut my chicken. I *never* thought I should eat off gold until I lost all my teeth and had a gold plate. This is too marvellous!"

"Good god," Turner muttered to John, "where in hell did May pick up this jellied eel? He's not on the salary list at the Sheridan, is he?"

By the time Sunday was over John was feeling that week-ends like this were an even greater mistake than he had been ready to believe them. However, in so far as he had been able to interest May Lavender in his outline of a new play for her which he was to write this winter, he could console himself that the experience was not a complete waste of time. Indeed, if she and Ellen Fitzgerald and the ridiculous young man Dennis Amberley, who turned out to have excellent ideas for dresses and decor, had been the only guests, it might have been positively enjoyable. But the senseless Midas luxury and display of the other guests was intolerable. Daisy Girdler, with an opportunity to put it across a star actress and a peeress, took the fullest advantage of it. In spite of the house being centrally heated in the latest style, she availed herself of a remark on the mistiness of the night to ring for her maid to fetch her a chinchilla wrap which she threw round her for a few minutes and then left lying over the back of one of the chairs, maddening with the sight of it May Lavender and Muriel Vawdry as effectively as a *torero* maddens a bull by fluttering his cloak. Both of her arms were strung with a dozen bracelets of rubies and diamonds.

"Like a couple of barber's poles in a back street," Lady Vawdry drawled to May Lavender; but no flash of bitter wit could dull the gems or get over the garish fact that Daisy Girdler was carrying at least £10,000 worth of gewgaws on each of her white arms. Moreover, both Muriel Vawdry and May Lavender knew that if anybody had commented on these bracelets Daisy Girdler would have pretended to be astonished that trinkets for a Bohemian week-end in a country-house should be noticed, with the implication that she was wearing none of what *she* called her jewellery.

"Well, John," Ellen Fitzgerald said to him when they found themselves secluded for a while from the rest of the party, "I suppose you'll call it sour grapes, but I don't believe I'd be a bit happy if I were wearing bangles like that."

"I shouldn't expect you to be," he said. "Any more than I should expect you to use £100 notes for curl-papers."

"John, will there be a part for me in your new play? It's rotten of me to ask you, but it has been so wonderful at the Sheridan."

"Of course there shall be a part for you," he promised.

"And May has been very sweet to me," she added. "Oh, I know my mid-thirty plumpness and contrasting complexion don't stand in her way. Still she has been very sweet. And you know she is one hell of a good actress."

John asked Ellen if she had heard anything of her brother lately.

"Mother wrote that things were getting worse and worse over in Ireland. It's no use, John, I can't feel this is worth while. It's too narrow. It's living too much in the past. However, I know you sympathize with Edward, though why I can't for the life of me understand."

"It would take a long philosophic talk to explain, Ellen, and Wickets is not the background for philosophy even if you had the patience to listen. But briefly I believe that a movement which cannot injure England and will certainly benefit Ireland depends on the willingness of people like Edward to sacrifice themselves as an example, and as there is every sign of that willingness I can only admire the fortitude that sustains them."

"But I can't see that it will benefit Ireland to all that extent. In the end we shall always be dependent on England. Look what I owe to England. My dear old father was a good nationalist, but he always recognized that he earned his living from England, and loved the English. I keep off politics, but I never find any enmity in England against us Irish, and I resent fanatics like Edward stirring up bitterness by their wild behaviour. You always did encourage him, John, when you were boys together. And I wish you hadn't. And I wish you wouldn't now."

"Edward didn't and doesn't need me to do that," John said.

"Well, he's much more devoted to you than to any man alive, and if you showed that you disapproved it might have some effect," Ellen urged.

"But I don't disapprove," John told her.

"There's been enough fighting and misery in the world for so long," she lamented. "Oh well, it's useless to argue with men. I only hope when you're married, John, that you'll appreciate the advantages of a quiet life. I hadn't meant to talk politics, anyway. I'd only meant to thank you again for the chance you gave me and to wish you so much happiness in your marriage. John, dear John, I can see you now at seventeen gazing at Connie Fenwick and looking so depressed when she told you that your line was humour and that you'd make a better Touchstone than Orlando. I'll be forty the year after next, and in February at that, bad cess to it. Still, I'm deducting the years of the war and so I shan't be forty till 1925. Och, I think Time, the dirty old tax-collector, owes us that rebate."

John chose a small church in the heart of the New Forest in which to exercise the authority conferred upon him by Randall Cantuar for £25 to be married where and when he liked. The Vicar of Hawthorn Lacey was rather excited. It was, he said, the first time he had ever seen a marriage licence from the Archbishop of Canterbury.

"Not bad pickings for the old boy," he observed to John.

The Reverend Stephen Donnet was a young parson

who had served as a chaplain out at Gallipoli, where he had been severely wounded.

"What a sanguinary muddle, eh?" he observed to John. "Forgive the ecclesiastical euphemism. I'm training on to be a rural dean one day."

"It was a bloody muddle," John agreed, "but . . ."

"Thanks. I like to hear it from a layman. It's a neater and more expressive word," Mr Donnet broke in.

"But the muddle was made at home."

"I agree with you, old chap. Now, of course, you don't know when you'll arrive on Wednesday to be tied up. But it doesn't matter, we have no rush for weddings in Hawthorn Lacey. Most of my parishioners are trees. You'll stay in Southampton to-morrow, I suppose?"

"And to-night," said John.

"I can give you a bed here if you like," the parson suggested.

John hesitated. It would be much pleasanter to stay in this small thatched house than in some fidgety Southampton hotel.

"It will be a kindness to me," the parson urged. "And I've got some fairly decent claret. The only thing is I can't put up your palatial car. You ought to be able to find pyjamas and a toothbrush among all that luggage."

"It's terrific, isn't it?" John said ruefully. "I'll have to leave most of it in Southampton because I'll have my wife's luggage to pack in. This railway strike is the deuce. I expect my man can find a room in the local pub."

"He could go into Lyndhurst and park the car there. We don't even run to a pub in Hawthorn Lacey."

Thus it was settled, and John could have wished for no better lodging than he found with the parson. The housekeeper produced a capital meal in which a jugged hare figured prominently. The claret—a Haut Brion—was more than fairly decent: it was good.

"I suppose you think a parson of my age ought to be doing a job of work in a city instead of burying himself like this in a parish of trees?" asked the host when they had pulled a couple of grandfather chairs up to the log fire and were sipping some '93 brandy, which glowed with the sun of that supreme summer.

"I criticize no man for keeping out of a city," John said.

"This brandy's a little young, perhaps," the parson decided. "But it's not bad. Well, after I came out of hospital I did try to work down at Haggerston. And I don't know, weakness, I suppose, but I jolly nearly had a breakdown. You get to feel in a slum parish that the war was a bigger crime than you thought it was. I'll be frank. I just couldn't stand the sight of so much wretchedness. I kept thinking of all that was being poured out on destruction and saying to myself that what was spent in a day on the war would do so much for Haggerston. Well, we've got peace now, and I can't see that we've gained much even materially."

"We've gained nothing," John affirmed, "except perhaps the knowledge that war is in no circumstances worth while. The problem is how long that bitter and costly experience will be remembered."

And then they drifted into reminiscences of Gallipoli until hours had passed like an hour.

"By Jove, it's midnight!" the parson exclaimed.

"And already," said John, "the war which we consider such a crime against humanity and so monstrous a sin against God is an engrossing topic for fireside tales. We play it over and over again like a game of golf."

"Or the escapades of our schooldays," the parson added. "Even my wound now seems no more serious than a nasty hack in the scrum."

The nutty sweetness of October was pungent in John's room at the parsonage, and from his bed he could see through the open lattice the stars of a clear night above the high trees. His last thought before sleep was that it would probably be calm for the next thirty-six hours.

"Well, I shall expect you when I see you to-morrow," the parson said when John was leaving for Southampton that afternoon.

"I'm hoping we shall get to Hawthorn Lacey by noon," John told him.

"Don't forget the wedding ring."

"Great Scott!"

"You haven't lost it?" the parson asked, grinning.

"No, I forgot all about getting a wedding ring. I *am* glad you reminded me. Oh, well, I'll find one in Southampton, I expect."

"I expect so. They do have weddings even in Southampton," Mr Donnet laughed.

The first thing John did on reaching Southampton was to visit a jeweller's, and he felt rather an ass when he was asked for the size of the finger the ring was to fit.

"I'm afraid I'll have to let you know to-morrow," he told the man in the shop.

"That will be quite all right, sir."

John sincerely hoped it would be.

The *Ruritania* was announced to berth shortly before ten o'clock on that October morning, an adverb which John translated somewhat lavishly by arriving at the quay a long while before the liner had entered Southampton Water.

"She won't be alongside for a good hour and a half yet, sir," he was informed by a porter.

So John wandered through the sheds to notify Crafford of this fact.

"Yes, I thought we were a bit on the early side," the

chauffeur said. "Perhaps you'd like to have a look at my *Daily Mail*, sir."

John got into the car and glanced through the paper. The French Chamber had ratified the Treaty of Peace by 372 votes to 52, with 73 abstentions. The prospect of a settlement of the railway strike was more hopeful. Conferences were taking place in Downing Street. Several members of Dail Eireann had been sentenced to two years' imprisonment for making seditious speeches. Three more republican papers had been suppressed. It was expected that there would be 50,000 British troops in Ireland by the end of the autumn. It was also expected that the weekly sugar ration would be raised from 6 oz. to 8 oz. presently and that the price of butcher's meat would rise sharply.

John returned the *Daily Mail* to its owner and went back to the quay.

At last the *Ruritania* towering toward her berth! The passengers and crew looked like ants swarming about a honeycomb. And then he caught sight of Athene gazing down over the rail. The quayside had become crowded and noisy; but it seemed more empty and more quiet than when he arrived two hours ago. There seemed nothing except Athene, and the serenity of the October sky, and himself. She was in brown. She had not seen him yet. She was in brown. She had not seen him yet. She was . . . she had seen him! And as he raised his arm to wave he abruptly became aware that he was standing in the middle of a bustle of people.

"Athene!"

"Oh, darling, my darling!"

Two travelled American spinsters, with that sugar-dusted look they so often have, turned to note the embrace. It explained why throughout the voyage so good-looking a woman travelling by herself had provided them with no gossip.

The problem of the heavy luggage was solved by leaving most of it in the charge of a carrier who guaranteed delivery in Cornwall within a week. The rest of it filled up the Judge's car.

"But there's still one problem to be solved, Athene—the size of your finger. Give me a third-finger ring."

She took a ring from a jewel-box in her dressing-case, and when he came out of the Southampton jeweller's he noticed that her left hand was bare.

"I've found the most perfect little church in which to be married," he told her. "Hidden away in the Forest like something in Malory's *Morte d'Arthur*."

"What a lovely way to be married," she murmured, and when she looked round at him, all life in her deep brown eyes, it seemed as if the car left the road like a rising plane and flew toward Hawthorn Lacey.

"Half-past one," said the young parson. "I kept lunch back till two on the chance we could turn it into a wedding breakfast. And I've got hold of a couple of bottles of fizz from Lyndhurst. It's probably gooseberry, but it won't hurt us. Now, if your man will be one witness, my housekeeper can be the other."

And so they were married in the little church of St Swithun, Hawthorn Lacey, among the oaks of the New Forest. And from a red-berried thorn-bush beside the open door to the west the cadence of a robin's song rose and fell to the cadences of the nuptial vows.

I, Athene, take thee, John, to my wedded husband, to have and to hold from this day forward, for better for worse, for richer for poorer, in sickness and in health, to love and to cherish, till death us do part, according to God's holy ordinance, and thereto I give thee my troth.

And again the robin's song rose and fell.

With this ring I thee wed, with my body I thee worship,

and with all my worldly goods I thee endow; in the Name of the Father, and of the Son, and of the Holy Ghost. Amen.

They drove along as far as Bournemouth that night instead of to Exeter as John had planned; but that was all the better because they stayed in Plymouth the following night and could travel west in time to arrive at Nanphant by midday.

"What shall we send our delightful parson as a memory of yesterday?" John asked before they left Bournemouth. "I think a cigarette-case, don't you, as a permanent memorial and a box of cigars as a fleeting one?"

So they wrote to be engraved on the inside of the lid:

From John and Athene Ogilvie

Hawthorn Lacey,
October 2nd 1919

And then westward to Blandford and Dorchester, and westward again to Exeter and Plymouth, and, with the west wind blowing now, on through Launceston and across the Bodmin moors where the mist was curling round Brown Willy, and westward still to Helston, the mist vanquished and the great white October clouds sailing across the rich blue sky of the west, of the life-giving west from which love and music shall come until the day of the seven whirlwinds and the crack of doom. . . .

At the end of the deep lane whose grassy banks were starred with the white flowers of the stitchwort called adder's eyes by the Cornish children, Nanphant dreamed by the unwrinkled surface of the lily-pool; for here the wind broken by the cliff westward did not reach below the top of the ilex grove that barred the north and east. The tree which John had noticed when he first saw the little house in May was now hung with crimson strawberries larger than fat Royal Sovereigns, and the pink ivy-leaved geranium climbing over the ivy roof carried still many heads of bloom.

Beyond the garden a dark boulder of serpentine, the shape and size of an elephant, thrust itself from the bastion of the cliff to break the south wind rushing up through the narrow gap from the minute sandy cove.

"John, it's the cutest place I ever saw," Athene declared.

"I was determined to have you to myself once I did get you," he told her.

"And how much I have wanted you to have me to yourself," she answered low.

The luggage was taken upstairs, where from the windows of the bedrooms a dancing blue and white sea was visible above the elephant rock in the gap of the cliffs. Crafford prepared to depart.

"I was to give you this, m'm, before I left. Sir Alexander gave it to me with special directions."

He handed Athene a parcel.

"Good-bye, Crafford, and thanks for all your help," said John.

"Oh, it's been a pleasure. There's nothing more you'll be wanting, sir?"

"No, thanks, Crafford. Tell her ladyship that we arrived safely and will write in a day or two."

"I will sir. I'm putting up at Plymouth to-night. Nothing more, sir?"

"Nothing more, Crafford."

"Shall I leave you my *Daily Mail*?"

"No, I've read it, thanks."

"Well then, good-bye sir, and I hope you'll both be very happy in your new life."

In the embarrassment of delivering these good wishes, Crafford accidentally sounded the horn, and he drove off up the lane in confusion.

"I wonder what this special parcel from my father is," said John when they reached the sitting-room where one or two other parcels were standing on the table.

Athene undid the paper.

"A travelling-clock," she said. "How sweet of him!"

"It's his own travelling-clock," John exclaimed. "It was one of my great treats in childhood to unveil it at the end of a journey." He pressed the catch of the lid and pulled up the leather-covered shutter. At that moment the elfin chimes struck two. John slipped the shutter back into its slot and closed the lid lined with faded violet velvet. A note had fallen upon the table.

"For you," he said.

Athene read it, and looked up, her eyes brimming.

"He could have thought of nothing so kind and sweet," she murmured, and gave the letter to John:

My dear Athene,

Elise and I have sent you a more conventional present, but I am anxious to give you something which I have treasured for thirty-eight years. It is the travelling-clock which my first wife—another Athene Ogilvie—gave me on our wedding-day in June 1881. You will be spending your honeymoon within a few miles of her father's house, in the garden of which in April of that year I asked her to marry me. The clock has stood upon my desk ever since, and I cannot recall that it has stopped since she wound it for me first. I am parting with it now because I know my dead wife would be glad to think that it was in the keeping of another Athene whom her son has chosen to be his wife. I believe that you will understand from this gift how much John's father desires your happiness as his son's wife. God bless you, my dear Athene. I did not think I should ever write that name again to one who is alive. I shall give myself the pleasure of intruding upon your honeymoon in the next vacation.

Your affectionate father-in-law,
Alexander Ogilvie

"John, I just can't tell you in words how deeply that has touched me," Athene said in a husky voice.

And while he held her to his heart, above the rustling of the west wind in the tops of the holm-oaks, the travelling-clock ticked that rapid sibilant tick to which in childhood he had listened when his mother used to lift the clock from the case of dark crimson morocco-leather so that he might see in its enclosed crystal the wheels with their tiny ruby and diamond pins, and the fine spring of blue steel quivering as if the clock breathed and was alive.

The more conventional wedding present to which the Judge alluded in his letter was a cheque for £250.

There were also letters and presents from Elise Ogilvie and Miriam Stern, cables from Athene's people and from Julius and Leonora who had been sent cables from Bournemouth the day before yesterday. Prudence wrote to Athene:

Dear Athene,

I am longing to meet you. I do hope you will like me very much because I adore John. If he makes half as nice a husband as he has been a brother you will be very happy. And he understands women very well as no doubt you have discovered without me telling you. I was somewhat disappointed at first when he told me he was going to be married because I had planned to live with him and keep house for him. That being now crushed as a notion I must seriously consider the prospect of matrimony for myself. I haven't got you a wedding present yet because I cannot find what I want but for-

tunately you didn't have a society wedding and I can have time to choose. David will do the same, but he will not write because he says he would feel such an ass writing to somebody he did not know. Besides he can think about nothing except what he will want at Oxford. I hope you will ask me to come and stay with you during the Christmas holidays by myself if possible because I wouldn't be so shy then and when I am shy I am inclined to talk too loud which distresses my mother.

Your loving sister-in-law (very grand!)

Prudence

P.S. A girl at school told me rather a good jape to play on John. A friend of her brother played it on a friend. I was going to send him a postcard, 'Not knowing her cannot congratulate you. Knowing you cannot congratulate her.' But I thought it might strike a low note as you didn't know me and might have thought I really meant it.

P.P.S. I was wondering if you would like me to bind John's next play for you as a wedding present. I shall be pretty hot at book binding by the winter after studying under Miss Holland as a voluntary handicraft. She is a wizened female but as strong as the village blacksmith.

"Poor Prudence," Athene commented.

"Why?"

"I was thinking how disappointed she must be not to keep house for you."

Janie Bolitho came in to say that lunch was ready, and that she'd thought as she didn't know just what they would be wanting she would make them a Cornish pasty.

About four o'clock the sound of wheels was heard, and John peeping cautiously from a window saw Jennifer and Christabel handing an enormous bunch of flowers to Loveday Williams, Janie's youthful niece.

The two girls were turning back toward their jingle, but John ran out and bade them come in.

"Oh, but John, are you sure you want us to come in?" Jennifer asked.

"Because we were longing to come in," Christabel added. "But mother said we should be *de trop*."

"Of course you must come in."

"Oh, cheers," Christabel exclaimed. "Did you see us from the window?"

"We told Loveday she wasn't to tell you we were here till we'd gone," Jennifer said.

"I didn't tell, Miss Jennifer. I kept my mouth shut so tight as wax," Loveday protested.

Loveday was absolved, and the two girls came in with the flowers.

"Two cousins for you, Athene."

"Mother thought you would like some flowers, and she hopes you will come over to lunch on Sunday," said Jennifer.

"That's in the note, Jennifer," Christabel pointed out severely.

"My, what perfectly lovely flowers."

Athene put up a bunch of biscuit-coloured clusters to smell.

"John, what does that smell of?" she asked.

"Honeycomb," he said at once.

"Honeycomb for a honeymoon couple," Athene laughed.

"It's Buddleia auriculata," Christabel told her.

"What a mouthful! And what are these?" She picked up a bunch of deep cherry-coloured flowers.

"Schizostylis coccinea," Christabel told her.

"My, that's an even bigger mouthful!"

"You can call them Kaffir Lilies if you like," said Christabel. "They're early this year. Usually we don't get them till it's nearly November."

"And what are these?" Athene asked. "They look to me like gladioli, but I never saw gladioli of that sunset colour."

"They *are* gladioli," said Jennifer.

"They're father's latest primulinus hybrids," Christabel added. "Are you frightfully fond of flowers?"

"I love them," said Athene, "in a very ignorant way."

"You'll get on with my father then," said Christabel. "He's absolutely dotty on flowers."

"I think we ought to be going now," Jennifer put in.

"Not at all," John contradicted. "Surely you can stay and have tea with us?"

"Mother told us if by chance you did ask us to tea that we were on no account to accept," Christabel said gloomily.

"I'll take the blame," John promised his cousins. "You can tell your mother that I wanted to consult you about getting a pony and jingle. Or rather a pony. Harry Dunstan tells me he knows of a jingle for sale at Cadgwith."

Christabel glanced eagerly to see how Athene was taking this news of her husband's transport plans.

"It's no use, Jennifer," she sighed. "She likes a jingle too."

"We were hoping you might insist on John's having a car," Jennifer explained, and turning to her sister she added, "And don't say 'she', Christabel. It's frightfully rude."

"I don't know what we ought to call her."

"I should hope you'd call me by my own name," said Athene.

"Oh, thank you so much," Christabel said, in a voice of profound relief. "We did hope you'd suggest that as soon as possible after we met you. And we *did* hope you'd insist on a car. Can you drive a car, Athene?"

Athene shook her head.

"Oh, then it is hopeless," Christabel decided in the voice of one for whom life can bring no added bitterness. "You see, Jennifer thought you might be able to teach us to drive."

"My poor children, isn't that too bad?" Athene condoled. "Well, I'm going to suggest right away to a very fond and very kind and very sympathetic husband that later in the fall he should let me have lessons in driving an auto, and then perhaps we could all three of us take lessons."

"Oh!" the two girls gasped. "Jennifer! Christabel!"

"It might happen, Jennifer!"

"Oh, it must, it must!" the younger girl cried.

"It shall," Athene promised.

And when after tea John escorted his two cousins to their jingle, both declared that Athene was far nicer than anything they had believed likely.

"So you don't think now that it's unromantic to marry a widow?" he asked Christabel.

"I think she's adorable and lovely," Christabel assured him.

"And I love the way she talks. I thought all Americans talked through their noses, but she doesn't talk a bit through her nose. It's a deep way of talking."

"It's the way they talk in the South," he told her.

"I'm not surprised everybody wants the poor South to win in the American Civil War," said Christabel.

"And you won't squash the idea of her learning to drive a car, will you?" Jennifer begged.

"Certainly not. When you both have honeymoons of your own remember to make hay with your husbands while the moon shines," John advised.

"I don't think I'm going to get married," said Christabel.

"Oh, aren't you?" her cousin asked gravely.

"No, I think I'll hunt instead, because I love horses. I don't *only* like motor-cars," she explained.

Jennifer asked if Prudence could drive a car, and was informed that it was generally admitted except by her brother David that she could.

"She's sixteen, isn't she?" Jennifer asked.

"Seventeen next May."

"I expect she'll think we're rather kids," Christabel decided dolefully from the sundering flood of twenty-six months that surged between herself and Prudence.

"Speak for yourself," Jennifer advised. "I'll be sixteen in April."

"Come on, Summer Time stopped last Sunday," Christabel urged, "and if it's dark when we get back mother will be in some frizz. Good-bye, John. On Sunday. Oh, but how will you come?"

"I'll get hold of the local dog-cart. And look out for that pony."

The jingle went crackling up the deep lane, and John turned back indoors.

"Shall we go down to the cove?" he suggested to Athene. "You won't be blown about."

"John, I don't mind when I'm dressed for it."

They wandered down by the edge of the small stream which ran down over a loose bed of blood-streaked serpentine to break in silver tresses over the sand. The wind was now still. The sun had dropped behind the cliffs of the Lizard, and the dying afternoon seemed touched already by the first faint bloom of dusk. A liner moved like a ghost along the horizon.

"But not the *Ruritania*," said John. "She doesn't sail until to-morrow. And you passed by on your way up Channel last Tuesday evening coming to me. Athene, is it true? Is it real? Are you here, or are you a mermaid who has landed on this beach from a dream?"

"I wish I'd known I should pass so close to this house

which is my dream," she said. "Wouldn't Arthur love this cunning little beach?"

"You're wishing you hadn't left him in America," John said quickly.

"No, no, John, it was the only possible thing I could do. Now please don't think that I'm sighing for Arthur, my dear. I've had a long long time to make up my mind what I was going to do. And no woman ever came to a decision with a more complete conviction that it was the right decision. I don't repine."

"I know you don't, but you'll have to forgive me for wondering sometimes. I vow it's not touched by jealousy. I shall only wonder because I don't want there ever to be the most minute flaw in the perfection of your happiness. And I'm still in the condition of hardly being able to believe that you are mine at last, that we are married, and that one voyage has ended in this harbour."

"One voyage? Why, John, I think that's a very discouraging remark to a bride of just about fifty hours."

"Oh, no more voyages for women," he said, laughing. "But I won't stop voyaging on various other quests. I'll have to voyage after a play presently."

"I know you will, dearest boy. And I'm so thrilled . . . well, I'm too thrilled by that really, and perhaps I'll end by being a darned nuisance the way I was when my mother started an incubator and I used to go in and shake the eggs to see if the chickens weren't beginning to hatch out. You'll be stern with me, won't you, about that?"

"I wish I'd met your people. It's rather dreary for them having an unknown son-in-law."

"Father was so amusing, John, about my marriage. You know what he looks like from my photographs. A fierce Southern gentleman, old school. You meet them in best-sellers. 'Well, Athene, you married a Yankee against my advice, and if I advise you not to marry a Britisher you'll do it. So I pass. If you have a flush

I'll be a happy parent. If you have a broken straight I won't have ante'd you up beforehand and egged you on out of cussedness.' However, father was too much annoyed by the prospect of prohibition to worry very much about me. We're all laying in huge cellars against the fatal day, and hope they'll last till the Amendment is repealed. Oh dear, I'll have to write to old Mrs Langridge to-morrow," she sighed to herself. "John, John, nothing's going to make her believe that this wasn't why I wanted to break with Wacey."

"I don't suppose it will," he agreed. "Still, she won't be able to say that anybody else knew anything. I wonder what Arthur will think of a stepfather."

"Arthur's so wrapped up with a baseball outfit Grandpa Langridge gave him that he can't think about anything else just at present. And Grandpa Gilmer who thinks a ball game is . . . well, there just aren't any words for what he thinks of ball games . . . anyway he has a pony waiting for Arthur and by the time we go across to America to fetch him he'll probably refuse to desert his pony."

"You're not cold, Athene?"

"No. Why do you ask?"

"I thought you shivered," John said.

"Did I? I didn't think I did."

But John thought it was better to go back indoors.

"And I *must* unpack," she said. "And I *must* have a consultation with Janie about domestic matters. After all, John, you've not married a school girl bride. And the young matron must display her experience."

"What a delicious evening!" John exclaimed, when the elfin chimes of the clock struck eleven.

"Was it, honey?" she asked softly. "Just you and me talking?"

"Which is what I've been longing for since I said good-bye to you under the stars a year and a month ago next Tuesday," he told her.

Athene took the clock with her when she went upstairs and put it on the mantelpiece of their room.

"I think I'd better wind it," she said. "I wouldn't like it to stop."

"The key lives here," John told her, pulling it from the velvet pocket into which he had loved so much to dip his four-year-old fingers. "My dear, you don't know how doing that brings back my mother. I wish I could believe with complete certainty that she knows I am here with a beloved Athene in the country of her girlhood. She probably knew old Miss Corfe who owned Nanphant then, and perhaps came to tea with her like those two young cousins of mine this afternoon. Forgive these sentimental speculations, but when a mother one loves dies when one is eight years old she lives for so long in dreams afterwards."

"Eight years old. Arthur's age now," Athene murmured.

"Dearest," he urged, "you *are* worrying about Arthur."

"No, no, John, I'm not. I'm not. Besides, I'm not going away from him for ever."

"Oh, don't even breathe such a thought," he said sharply.

"You were remembering poor Zoe, weren't you, John?"

"I was remembering that there is a happiness which makes the heart afraid, and you, my dear, have given me much happiness."

She was winding the clock.

"Time, be kind to us two," she murmured.

Suddenly he caught sight on her dressing-table of the terra-cotta head of Minerva he had given her that June day when the Archduke was killed in Sarajevo.

"You have it still!" he marvelled.

"Why, yes, John, I told you I had."

Soon she was lying in his arms. Through the open

window a humpbacked moon was seen on her slow southing. The room was filled with the aromatic sweetness of ripe geranium leaves. The Atlantic murmur was constant as in a shell upon the quiet of the October night. A curlew whistled from the tide's edge.

"And do you love this little house?" he whispered.

"I love it. But oh, my heart, how much much more, how infinitely much more I love you."

And lifting himself upon his elbow he watched for a moment or two in the moonlight her mouth dark as a carnation, and on the pillow her prodigal brown hair.

On the morning of his thirty-seventh birthday John scribbled with a diamond pencil on the pane, this verse from the first book of the Odes of Horace:

Felices ter et amplius
Quos irrupta tenet copula, nec malis
Divulsus querimoniis,
Suprema citius solvet amor die.

"And what does that mean?" Athene asked.

"To paraphrase impromptu:

"Thrice happy they and more than thrice
Whom an unbroken bond holds fast
And whom unvexed by arguments
Love will not loose until the last.

"But the Latin says with emotion what cannot be said in English without sententiousness. The poignant awareness of the present's immediacy which affected all the classical writers *we* get only from music. Yet Herrick could convey it. Odd that, considering he was a Church of England parson who ought not to have been so sharply distressed by fugacity.

"So when or you or I are made
A fable, song, or fleeting shade,
All love, all liking, all delight
Lies drowned with us in endless night.
Then while time serves, and we are but decaying,
Come, my Corinna, come, let's go a-Maying.

"That peculiar poignancy seems to fade from poetry after Catullus and Horace and Propertius, is heard again in Herrick, and for us to-day is most perfectly expressed by the adagios of Mozart sonatas and quartets. I don't know why I am in such an elegiac mood this morning. Perhaps it's because I shall be forty in three years. With you here in Nanphant I may feel I am not yet twenty, *sed fugit interea, fugit irreparabile tempus*, and when irreparable time rules that our honeymoon has waned we shall ask ourselves how time fled so fast when we did so little, for the annals of happiness are as short and simple as the annals of the poor."

"John, this is a sermon," Athene protested.

"I know. Stop this flow of platitudes," he laughed. "We'll drive over to Gunwalloe Church Cove and search for silver Portuguese dollars in the sand. It will be the low spring of the new moon at midday."

But indeed there was justification for John's platitudes, so swiftly did that autumn and that winter pass. In south Cornwall the very seasons conspire with time, so late does autumn linger, so rathe comes spring, that winter can seldom assert himself; for blow he never so hard, the wanton blue days that succeed mock his fiercest efforts to make the hours seem long and weary. Athene and John would no sooner have paid one visit to Pendarves House than a week would have fled by and another visit was due. In the jingle which Harry Dunstan found for them in Cadgwith, driven by the pony which Jennifer and Christabel secured for them in Manaccan, they explored the whole of the peninsula from Coverack to Kynance, from the Looe Pool to the Lizard. They heard the wind sing in the tall aerials of the Poldhu wireless station and watched the tide churning round Mullion's black islet. They sat in the parlour of the Helzephron Inn listening to the roar of the sea just across the road. This was nearer than any inn to Robert Louis Stevenson's *Admiral Benbow*, John declared. In January they watched the ravens at their nesting on Helzephron's high cliff and gathered at the foot of it the first primroses of the year. They explored the Helford's wooded creeks, and reached as far as Roseland. Praa Sands saw them, and Landewednack and the lonely Ruans. There was not a cove to which they did not scramble down, nor a winding cliff-path by which they did not wander above the ocean. The magic of the west that haunts the air from Biscay to the Hebrides is nowhere more potent than in the Meneage, where, as in the north-west the basalt, the serpentine breaks into the granite, dark and strange as the Phoenician traffickers of long ago.

"I believe more firmly than ever in the lost Atlantis," John averred, when they were sitting in a green fold of cliff on a December day that smelt as sweet as April. "Some atavistic memory assures me that the Cornish half of me came ultimately neither from the heart of Asia nor from the Mediterranean, but from Atlantis, and that perhaps what we call now Celtic now Pictish now Iberian now Silurian is neither one nor the other but Atlantean—the survival of a blood-stream from a submerged continent. I can't account otherwise for the profundity of the difference between what is usually called the Celt and the Saxon. I see no reason for it as between Celt and Saxon, for they are both Germanic. If we read about the Gauls in Caesar they seem very much the same as the Germans we read of in Tacitus. The Germans remained outside the Roman civilization and therefore affect the rest of western Europe with an impression of barbarian wrong-headedness, but the fundamental temperament must be the same."

"Well, John dearest, you may have come many thousands of years ago from Atlantis, but I most certainly come from Atlanta," Athene reminded him, with a smile.

"Yes, by Jove, I'd forgotten that, when I was burbling reflections on the lost Atlantis. I think Spain must contain the highest proportion of that Atlantean blood. What a pity the Spanish Armada was defeated! What a different culture in the German sense ours would have been! Bristol would have become the capital of England, and England would have been dominated by Wales and Scotland. Knox and his savage Calvinistic mob would have vanished like a bad dream. Galway would have been the capital of Ireland. Belfast would have been the commercial metropolis of the Isles. Glasgow would have been the cultural centre of Scottish life. Brittany would have been separated from France, and probably Aquitaine as well. Eastern France would have formed a nation with western Germany, Prussia would have been kept in the Baltic. The ruinous wars between France and Austria and Spain would have been avoided. There would have been no French Revolution, no Napoleon, no Pitt, no Victorian Age, no industrial defilement, no joint-stock banks, no Disraeli—oh, the golden prospect stretches infinitely wide and fair."

"There might have been no United States," Athene suggested.

"Oh yes, but they would have been spared New England, and Maryland might have remained what it was when it was founded by Calvert—a new ideal for human nature."

"Well, I don't know, John. You and I might never have met if the Spanish Armada hadn't been defeated, and everything had gone along on different lines," she said doubtfully. "And now, you terrible old reactionary, when are you going to let me drive you to Land's End by auto?"

The lessons in driving had been carried out as promised, but John, with the warm support of Henry Pendarves, had obstinately refused to be taken on any drives.

"The thought of you rushing madly about the Duchy gives me just the impulse I need to sit down and swot away at this new play," he told his two cousins. "You shall drive my father from Helston to Nanphant."

The Judge came in January and brought Prudence with him, leaving her at Nanphant after a stay of three or four days. He and his daughter-in-law made friends immediately, and on the night before he went away he expressed to John with an ease which testified to the affection she had kindled in him his delight at the marriage.

"You waited longer than I did, but I'm bound to say I think it was indeed worth waiting so long. You are a lucky fellow, John. You have had success early in a profession which allows you the maximum of personal liberty. You have had the remarkable experience of the war. Yes, I know you discount that, but nevertheless I fancy you'll be grateful for it when you reach my age. And now you have done something better than either. You have found the right woman. By the way, forgive me if this strikes you as an impertinence, but I hope you will make it very easy for Athene to have her young son with her."

"Why, surely Athene didn't suggest . . ."

Sir Alexander held up a judicial hand.

"Certainly not, certainly not," he said with a touch of impatience. "I was thinking of myself and of how much I owed to Elise in my relations with you. You will probably make a much better father to a stepson than I made to my own son. You have a kind of natural gift for understanding and getting on well with youth. I have always lacked that. I'm not saying that David and Prudence are not very fond of me. I think they are. But I realize that they regard me as a conventional father. They humour me and make allowances, but I am never under the faintest illusion that they regard me as anything but a being from another and rather ridiculous world. Perhaps as I grow older I grow more sensitive to that because as I've told you before, John, a judge is a lonely man. But I did not mean to talk about myself. I was merely anxious to explain why I ventured to make that suggestion about your stepson. If I had been taken and your mother left, I do not believe that on my deathbed I would have wanted your mother to marry again. I believe that even at that moment so thick was the egotism in which I had been encrusted by my pursuit of worldly success my vanity would have craved an assurance from her that she would never care for any other man. I think . . . I hope I have cut away some of that crust now. I have tried to. You take after your mother in character much more than after me, but you must have something of my character in you, and it is for that reason I have permitted myself the impertinence of expressing a hope that you will make it very easy for Athene to have her son always with her."

"I had no intention of doing anything else," John declared emphatically.

"Then forgive me, my dear boy, for the intrusive suggestion, and forget it was ever made. It is a tribute in one way to your wife that I made it, because I could easily sympathize with the desire to keep her all to oneself. But there again I am judging you by myself, which is what I have no right to do."

Nevertheless when John thought over what his father had said he could not help recognizing that there was not in fact any urgent desire in his mind for the time when

Arthur would require his mother. His first impulse on facing up to this fact was to suggest to Athene that they should go to America early in the spring and fetch Arthur back to England. Yet such a proposal might disquiet her with the notion that he believed her to be fretting for her son, and he knew that this would upset her because she would fancy that the strength of her decision was being suspected. She would, he was sure, prefer that the original plan should be strictly followed. He felt she would be grateful for his confidence in her own ability to decide for herself. All the same, he was glad that his father had spoken like that. It was necessary to watch oneself all the time and deal ruthlessly with the indulgent egotism of self-deceit.

"Phew!" Prudence exhaled when the Judge had gone back to London. "I simply adore Sir Alexander, but he is getting almost too judicial. When we took the wrong turning yesterday afternoon he talked to the fisherman from whom we asked the way as if he was a witness in a murder case. Can a father try his own daughter?"

"My dear, what for?" Athene asked.

"Oh, for taking drugs or something. Wouldn't it read well in the headlines? Drug-taking daughter of judge throws herself on father's mercy. Sensation at the Old Bailey. Famous counsel invokes unwritten law and quotes Hall Caine."

"Why on earth should any counsel famous or infamous quote Hall Caine?" her brother asked.

"The Deemster, of course. Surely you remember when the Deemster sentenced his son to banishment? You *are* badly read, John. And you haven't answered my question whether a modern judge can try his own daughter?"

"He obviously wouldn't, even if there was nothing against it in the Constitution," John told her.

"Have you ever taken drugs, Athene?"

"I certainly haven't, child."

"What's all this curiosity about drugs?" John asked. "Surely Miss Bracebridge hasn't caught any of your young friends taking drugs?"

"No, but a girl called . . . well, perhaps I'd better not mention her name as it's a criminal offence . . . well, this girl found some cocaine her mother had, and she brought it to school and some of us sniffed it. And nothing happened at all. We just sneezed. I thought you had marvellous dreams if you took cocaine. It was a frightful frost."

"You mean snow," John corrected. "It probably wasn't cocaine at all."

"Well, this girl's mother does take drugs," Prudence insisted.

"Anyway you're a set of young asses to play around even with talcum powder," he said.

"Why, I think so too, Prudence," said Athene. "And who wants marvellous dreams anyway? You wake up from dreams."

"It's all very well for you to talk, Athene. You've married John, and you're lovely to look at, and you've got exquisite clothes, and if you wanted to bob your hair you could, and you're not still at school and . . . well, you haven't got any need to dream."

"You have life to dream about," Athene said. "You'll be seventeen next spring. I'll be thirty-one."

"How old were you when you married first?" Prudence asked.

"Twenty."

"Do you think you'll have your hair bobbed?"

"Will I have my hair bobbed, John?" Athene asked, turning to him.

"Not if I can dissuade you," he declared fervidly.

"I can't think why men are always so old-fashioned," said his sister. "Even John, who's much less old-fashioned than most, has forty fits at the idea of a new fashion. Why shouldn't she bob her hair if she wants to, John?"

"Because it's lovely hair," John replied. "If she had hair like yours I'd buy her a new pair of scissors."

"Oh, very funny," said Prudence. "But unfortunately for the sting of that personal remark everybody says that my hair is exactly the same colour as yours when you were young."

"I'm sure it is," Athene said. "And don't listen to him. Your hair's a lovely colour and texture. Such waves of chestnut brown!" she said, brushing it back from a lilyrosed forehead.

"You're very consoling, Athene."

And John knew that fondling thus Prudence's hair Athene was thinking of him once upon a time and picturing themselves together when she was sixteen and he but twenty-two.

However, if Prudence felt the disgrace of her youth beside her sister-in-law she had the compensation of being adored for her age and wisdom by Jennifer and Christabel.

"We think Prudence is much much the nicest older girl we've ever met," Christabel confided to John.

"Much the nicest girl older or younger," Jennifer amplified. "She doesn't put on any side."

"And we think Richard's rather keen on her," Christabel added.

"But Richard's so frightfully susceptible," Jennifer said. "He was keen on Agnes Vivian in the summer hols."

"And on Dorothy Trevilian in the Easter hols," Christabel reminded her sister. "Yes, Jennifer's right. He's too susceptible really. All the same I think he's keener on Prudence than he was either on Agnes or Dorothy."

"But is Prudence keen on him?" John asked.

"I don't think so," Jennifer replied.

"I'm sure she isn't," Christabel added, "because she

said to me 'what a nice kid your brother Richard is,' and he's older than her. She wouldn't call him a kid if she was keen on him, would she?"

"It's a term of endearment in America among adults. If you'd seen more films you'd know that."

"Prudence is going to drive us into Penzance to see a film," Jennifer said.

"And she said I might drive a good deal of the way," Christabel added. "Richard's awfully keen to come too. And I told him I'd try and manage it if he swore he wouldn't touch the wheel once, and not give me any advice when I was driving."

"Did he accept those terms?" John asked.

"Yes."

"I'm beginning to see him as a serious suitor. Ask him not to elope with her till they've both left school. I don't want to interrupt my honeymoon chasing theirs," John said.

Just before Prudence returned to London in the third week of January she and John went for a walk together without Athene, who was staying at home to deal with her American mail. They chose for their goal a part of the coast where the cliffs gave place for about a mile to a level tract of green sedgy land, the pasturage of cattle in spring and summer, but too moist in winter, when it was deserted by men and beasts. This tract was fringed on the sea side by the coarse coltsfoot leaves of the winter heliotrope, whose small tufted spikes of pinkish mauve bloom bewitched the still air with a fragrance that not even the salty sea scents could contend against; and beyond it at low tide an expanse of firm gleaming sand ran the whole length. It was at low tide that John and Prudence came here on that January day tranquil as a turquoise; and leaving behind the sweetness of the winter heliotrope they walked by the edge of the ocean, which on such a day expired upon this level beach as delicately as a lake. As they walked on, a small flock of dunlins rose and alighted again before their progress, to resume their researches along the lacy opalescence of the tide's edge, running hither and thither with such inquisitiveness that the sand was meshed by the pattern of their tiny tridents in an endless intagliation.

However brief the flight these birds never broke their trim formation, and however busily they were individually occupied on the sand they never failed to rise as one and alight as one again a few yards ahead of the human beings who were intruding upon this solitude.

The ocean itself was empty on that turquoise morning except where beyond the glittering horizon the tenuous plumes of two or three steamers, hull down, breathed upon the southern sky that was faded by the low wintry sun. The gannets were not striking that placid expanse like shells. The dark sheeny cormorants were resting snakily upon those white-capped rocks. The gulls and guillemots were basking bemused upon the silver water. So quiet was the noontide hour that if John and Prudence stopped to listen they could hear after the trill of the dunlins' flight the whisper of their footprints' pattern upon the sand until it was muted by a sigh from the sleeping ocean.

"I feel I ought to walk on tiptoe," Prudence told her brother. "I feel we've no business to be disturbing this place. Oh, I wish I weren't going back to London to-morrow. I have so loved being here."

"We've loved having you," he replied. And then he stopped to marvel to himself once again at the pleasure of uttering that first person plural.

"You've given me quite a new idea about marriage," she said presently.

"Really?"

"Yes, when one sees two people like you and Athene as much at their ease with one another as . . . well, as I am with you, I begin to think there really is something in marriage after all."

"You've made a discovery which bears out what the human race has been thinking for quite a long time," John said, twinkling.

"No, don't tease me, John. I want to talk about this seriously. You see, one gets into the habit of thinking about marriage as something for middle-aged people, because when one is small one thinks one's parents are frightfully old and when one begins to get older oneself they *are* old. The consequence is one always thinks of marriage as something rather stuffy."

"You must remember that your father was a good deal older than your mother, and also that she was his second wife."

"Oh, I know, John. But all marriages have had the same effect on me. That's why I planned to live with you. We wouldn't have had children and so we wouldn't have had to build up a pretence of ourselves for children, because that's what all the married people I know do with their children. And that's why you and Athene have given me a different idea of marriage. If you have children you won't do that. At least I don't think you'll do that. And now if I'm going to be married I must begin to think seriously of the kind of man I want to marry."

"There's still plenty of time to consider that question," John suggested.

"But is there so much time, John? I'll go on being educated for another year and a half, not at St James's School perhaps, because I must leave there at the end of next summer term. I don't want to go to Oxford or Cambridge. I'd rather go to France till it's time for me to come out. Well, then I'll be finished in France, and then with a rather muddled set of ideas in my head about Magna Carta and some polite French conversation I'll be a deb. And mother with many groans will trail me round a set of dances at which I and a lot of other debs will be on show rather like Circassian slaves waiting to be bought. And if by the end of my second season I've managed to attract the eldest son of a war-profiteer called Lord Putney Heath or Lord Wimbledon Common I'll be considered to have been the most dashing deb of my year. But I wouldn't be a bit excited to be the Honourable Mrs Archibald Jimjams, with the prospect of being Lady Wimbledon Common when I'm fat, fair, and forty. Of course, I *may* meet a young man I like, and fall in love with him, but I don't care for young men. They're particularly unpleasant just now, because they're rather scarce and that makes them very conceited. And then there's this business of sleeping with a man."

"Yes, of course there's that," said John, slowly.

Behind them stretched the long line of their footprints beside the ocean. In front stretched the virgin sand, like his young sister's mind. He must step cautiously through this turquoise stillness.

"I'm not going to ask you any embarrassing questions, John," she assured him. "I know the theory of the business, which sounds pretty grim when one looks round at men, whatever age they are."

"So it should," said John, quickly. "It's when you disentangle somebody from the crowd and it doesn't sound so grim that you begin to think seriously about marriage. However, you are perfectly right to consider that grimness, even if it does make you seem over-fastidious."

"You're a perpetual relief to me, John. I tried to go into this question with mother, only to be told that at my age she had never thought about such things. Now, that's what I object to, this pretence that one jumped out of one's cradle into bed with a man and became a mother in the same way as one was given a doll at Christmas. Mother was twenty-seven or twenty-eight when she married father, and can she seriously expect me to believe that she never thought about this problem until then?"

"Well, in fairness to your mother, she might argue that there's a gap between sixteen and twenty-seven."

"Seventeen in May," she reminded him. "And if I've grasped the theory of this business correctly, and I think I have, I've got just as much right to be considering my future in that way at sixteen as I should have at twenty-seven."

"Yes, I think that's a reasonable contention," John assented. "But what an older woman fears is that if a girl lets her mind become too much preoccupied with the mysterious problem that presents itself to every girl, she may allow her curiosity to master her, and be indiscreet—I suppose you follow what I mean by indiscretion in that sense?"

"You mean I'll start letting young men make love to me to find out whether I like it?" Prudence asked. "Well, of course I know that some girls do awful things, but those aren't the girls who would be likely to ask their mothers any questions."

"You told me you weren't going to ask me any embarrassing questions," John said. "But there's evidently a question you do want to ask me. You'd better ask it. Unanswered questions of this kind are apt to go bad if left lying around too long."

"Well, what I do want to know, John, is whether if a man asks you to marry him you ought to know beforehand that you will want to sleep with him, or whether you will find that out after you have married him. There," she sighed her deep relief, "that's what's worrying me."

"The general answer is that it depends on the girl and that a rule cannot be laid down; but that's as good as no answer at all, and I'll risk the amount of disposition we must share in common as children of the same father, and by the fact that Gabrielle Derozier observed the likeness between your mouth and mine, to advise you most strongly not to marry any man unless you are sure that you look forward to all that marriage means. Otherwise I shall expect to be called in to advise you how to extricate yourself from a matrimonial tangle."

"Why should my mouth being like yours help you to answer, John?"

"Because the mouth is the indication of that side of one's disposition," he replied. "And I, knowing how much depends on physical intimacy, can feel fairly sure that an equal amount of your happiness will depend on it. At the same time, for heaven's sake remember that if you should meet a young man with whom that side of marriage does not sound grim it is not by itself enough. If it had been, I should have had as many wives as Solomon by now. You are likely to be extremely attractive to young men, and older men too for that matter, and when one is young and curious that gives one a dangerously powerful key to satisfy one's curiosity. You have been good enough to congratulate me on having given you a different idea of marriage. Would you mind remembering in the future that on a January morning in the year 1920, the sea being dead calm and the tide at a low ebb, your brother twenty years older than yourself with a long and varied experience behind him, warned you, and that the rooms which that dangerous key unlocks almost all turn out to be exactly alike when they are entered? In other words, will you promise me not to experiment with your attraction? I can tell you, so utterly and degradingly easy are most men, that you will not find it worth while and that if you do experiment you will bitterly regret it if and when the right man comes into your life."

"You mean I mustn't flirt, John?"

"Oh, you can flirt as much as you like, provided you know it is flirting." He put his arm into hers. "But you asked me a serious question and in answering it I haven't treated you as a schoolgirl. So do remember what I've told you, if ever a moment should come for remembering it, and don't let the memory of this walk be obliterated as easily as that long double line of footprints will very soon be obliterated by the flowing tide."

"I will remember, John darling," she promised.

John's new play reached Turner Rigden as a valentine; but *All Or Nothing* was still running and with the way business was booming it looked as if it might run through the autumn. However, as Gosnell insisted, there was no point in offering it to anybody else. May Lavender liked it, and it would be better business to let Rigden have it for the Sheridan. On the other hand, John Gould was looking for a play. What about it? So John wrote another play during March, which John Gould accepted for production at the Muses' Theatre in May.

"So I think London in April," he told Athene. "Though I hate to leave Nanphant."

"I can't bear to leave it, but it's no use my pretending I'm not terribly thrilled at the prospect of a first night, sweetheart."

It had been discovered that the birthday of Athene and Jennifer Pendarves fell on the same day—the fourteenth of April, and before the departure from Nanphant fulfilment of a promise made in the winter that John and Athene would spend a couple of nights at Pendarves House for the celebration was claimed and honoured.

Hugh Pendarves was home for his first Easter vacation from Oxford. Richard was home for his last Easter holidays from Sherborne. It was a jolly family gathering, youth unshadowed by the threat of war and dancing forward to the bright new world which the ordeal of older people had made them so much more ready to let youth enjoy. Not that Henry Pendarves was particularly aware of any bright new world. He regarded the result of the war as a disastrous speeding up of all the tendencies he most deplored. However, the excitement of daffodil-time while it lasted always banished his pessimism, and Christabel herself could not have put more eagerness into the proposal of a plan than he put into an invitation to John to be with him in the garden by seven o'clock on the morning of the fourteenth of April, when he fancied that he should be able to effect a piece of cross-pollination which he had not yet achieved. John promised to be up.

With the appointment with Henry Pendarves on his mind John woke much too early, and going to the window he saw a flawless cold blue sky waiting for the lances of the sun to prick it into warm azure. He pulled the chintz curtains together again and stood listening to the birdsong, trying to distinguish the various notes, and in the end, as usually happens, listening to one thrush as one listens to the solo instrument in a concerto.

"Honey, are you up already?"

He turned to the bed.

"Darling, I woke you."

"No, I just woke. You didn't wake me."

"Well, I'm two hours too soon for our host. And so many happy returns of the day."

The travelling-clock chimed five strokes as he held her in his arms.

"This may have been my mother's room once," he said. "But what is certain is that this is the first birthday you have begun in my arms."

"Such a lovely way to begin a birthday," she murmured.

Athene had fallen asleep again and did not wake when John rose and dressed for his appointment with Henry Pendarves. He found him on the undulating lawn in a coat of many pockets.

"Ah, here you are," he said. "I was wondering if you'd overslept yourself. It's a splendid morning. I like to get my pollination done before nine o'clock. Some people make a rule not to begin till after ten. Well, everybody to his taste. Now then come along, and we'll get down to the beds." The dark lanky man was in a state of high excitement and as he kept thrusting his neck backward and forward nervously he hummed to himself what he must have thought was a tune, though it was not recognizable as such to anybody else.

They reached the daffodil beds in a small walled garden trellised to break the force of the gales, and John followed his host past the white and yellow companies until he stopped before a group of long golden trumpets of the Ajax class in which half the flowers were tied up with veils of fine muslin. He gazed at John with the eyes of a retriever bitch whose puppies are under inspection.

"Isn't that *Saffron Maid*?" John asked. That was the daffodil of his cousin's own raising whose rich colour the painter of his portrait had in his opinion failed to express in oils.

"By Jove, John, you've got the root of the matter in you!" Henry Pendarves shouted in glee. "I never thought you'd recognize it, but I hoped you might."

John had not the heart to tell his cousin that he was extremely long-sighted and had spotted the name on a label half hidden by the leaves. He felt a fraud, but on account of the pleasure he was giving, a justified fraud.

"Now the point is, usually *Saffron Maid* is much too early for the Triandrus pollen, but this year I have managed to retard her flowering. I deanthered her yesterday and the stigma should be ripe this morning."

"What is deanthering?"

"Cutting off the anthers to prevent self-fertilization. Now the worst of *Saffron Maid* is that though the pollen is extremely potent she is a very shy seeder. That's the Maximus blood. She was by *King Alfred* from a yellow Ajax of my own called *Golden Girl*, and *King*

Alfred of course was from Maximus pollen on either *Emperor* or *Golden Spur*. Now I want to get a Johnstoni—that's a cross between an Ajax and a Triandrus—with the constitution and colour of my *Saffron Maid*. But as I say, owing to the Maximus blood *Saffron Maid* is a shy seeder, though her pollen is as potent as any Triandrus. Now let's see if the lady's ready." He stooped down, and after untying the bridal veils of muslin, eyed the stigmas. "Beautiful!" he declared. "I'd a feeling you'd bring me luck, John. I believe she's going to take this time. You look at those pistils and tell me if you don't think the stigmas are in perfect condition."

"I shouldn't know whether they were or not," said John.

"You'll notice that they're just at the right stage of viscousness for the pollen to adhere."

John looked at the pistils which with their stigmas looked like minute champagne-whisks.

"They seem pretty sticky."

By this time Henry Pendarves had taken from one of his pockets a pill-box, the bottom of which was covered with pale greenish-yellow dust. From another pocket he took a camel's-hair brush. This he moistened slightly from his lip and then, catching up the pollen from the pill-box, he dusted the stigma of *Saffron Maid*. When all the blooms had been fertilized he tied round each one the bright scarlet thread that told the world of a virgin the less.

"I should like to see the husband of *Saffron Maid* if it's possible," John suggested.

"Triandrus? Oh, they're over here. But this pollen comes from Geoffrey Vivian's Triandrus. Pollen is more potent from a distance. His own *Saffron Maids* were not retarded. So I shall make the contrary cross on my Triandrus from my own *Saffron Maids*." He showed John a pill-box with golden dust. "The general rule is that the pollen-parent gives colour and the seed-parent form."

"I like this mutual business," John said. "It's symbolical of the perfect marriage."

They walked to another part of the walled garden, where John saw the most elegant daffodils like tiny cream and white fuchsias with their reflected perianths and unfrilled trumpets.

"He looks very small compared with his wife," John declared.

"Angel's Tears the growers call them. Catchpenny name, but not so bad as some. That bigger fellow is Calathinus. It's found only in some islets off the coast of Brittany."

"Another survivor from the lost Atlantis," John observed.

"Very likely. Very likely. I say what do you know about Atlantis?" Henry Pendarves asked eagerly.

"No more than any of us," John replied. "But I play with the notion that we dwellers by the seaboard from the Hebrides to Biscay have in our veins the blood of survivors from that legendary cataclysm."

"By G——, that's what I think!" Henry Pendarves shouted. "Here, don't let me get so excited, or I shall smash my pollen-boxes." He had just thumped his thigh vigorously. "Well, I am glad to hear you hold that theory too. And you know it's an extraordinary thing the potency of all these little fellows. There are a whole lot of others of these Atlantean daffodils, but I won't bore you with a long string of Latin names, and they're all potent. It's a dominant strain. It shows why we Cornish and Britons and Irish and Welsh and Galicians and Gaels still hold to our own way against the world. We are the ultimately invincible West—men or daffodils! But look here, we mustn't start this fascinating topic now. I have a lot of other deanthered patients to console from my pill-boxes."

So for another hour with camel's-hair brushes Henry

Pendarves moved around his garden, tying up the fertilized brides with scarlet thread and entering his marriages in the notebook that was his register.

"I do hope *Saffron Maid* will seed this time," he said when they took a last look at her.

"When will you know?"

"Oh, I shall know pretty soon, but I shan't be quite sure till I have a packet of hard shiny ebony seeds early in June."

"You must drop me a line," John told him. "I shall be interested to hear of my efforts as best man."

"I will, I will," the gardener promised.

The family were at breakfast when they reached the house.

"Many happy returns of the day, Cousin Jennifer," John said.

Athene came into the dining-room at that moment, and there was a chorus of birthday greetings to her.

"What a pity you're going to London in such lovely weather," Christabel sighed.

"I don't think somehow we shall be very long away from Cornwall," Athene answered.

John thought he had never seen her eyes so bright as upon this April morning.

It was originally intended that this Series should consist of four volumes only—The Four Winds of Love. It has now been decided to insert an extra volume, to be called *West to North*, between this present volume and *The North Wind of Love*. It is hoped that *West to North* will appear in July 1940.

PRINTED IN GREAT BRITAIN
BY R. & R. CLARK, LIMITED
EDINBURGH